*Becoming
Bella*

Becoming Bella

SARAH HEGGER

ZEBRA BOOKS
KENSINGTON PUBLISHING CORP.
http://www.kensingtonbooks.com

ZEBRA BOOKS are published by

Kensington Publishing Corp.
119 West 40th Street
New York, NY 10018

All Kensington titles, imprints, and distributed lines are available at special quantity discounts for bulk purchases for sales promotion, premiums, fund-raising, educational, or institutional use.

Special book excerpts or customized printings can also be created to fit specific needs. For details, write or phone the office of the Kensington Sales Manager: Attn.: Sales Department. Kensington Publishing Corp., 119 West 40th Street, New York, NY 10018. Phone: 1-800-221-2647.

Zebra and the Z logo Reg. U.S. Pat. & TM Off.

First Printing: October 2017
ISBN-13: 978-1-4201-4245-7
ISBN-10: 1-4201-4245-3

eISBN-13: 978-1-4201-4246-4
eISBN-10: 1-4201-4246-1

10 9 8 7 6 5 4 3 2 1

Printed in the United States of America

To Renita Bradley Friese,
and all the other women who
courageously shared their stories with me.
And to the thousands of others
whose stories are still untold.
Bella is plagued by a stalker,
but abuse takes so many different forms.
It thrives in the dark and festers in silence.
Know that you are not alone.

#bebrave
#speakup
#tilithappenstoyou

Chapter One

*B*ella cranked the volume on Bing Crosby crooning Christmas carols until it carried into her yard. Let all of Ghost Falls hear that Bella Erikson was busting out of her mold and coming out. Not out-out, but out as in letting her freak flag fly. Besides which, Christmas wasn't Christmas without the Binger.

She wanted—no, invited—her neighbors to peep out their windows to see Bella, the new and improved version, taking charge of her life. Timer and lighting cord—ready. Rechecking the length, she made sure she'd bought the right one. Normally, Dad did this, but Bella had taken control, starting with Christmas, and these suckers were going up with her putting them there.

Ladder propped up against the side of the house, extension cord curled up like a forest-green snake beside it, she got down to item one of her "Spending Christmas Alone" checklist: decorate.

"You've got this." The ladder loomed above her. "There is nothing to fear but fear itself." And heights. Heights made her knees shaky. No, heights used to make her knees shaky. This Christmas Bella laughed at heights. She climbed ladders in stiletto heels if she wanted to. Bing hit the chorus and Bella joined in.

"Pick a focal point." She consulted the pamphlet she'd picked up from Lowe's when she bought her string of warm white Christmas lights. Reading it out loud to the tune of "Silver Bells" made it less daunting.

With a telltale squeak, her neighbor's door opened, and Liz Gunn stepped onto her matching porch. Bella waved and, this being the holidays, gave her voice a dollop of goodwill to mankind. "Hi, Liz."

Liz, known as Headlights Gunn throughout Ghost Falls because of her propensity for pointing her surgically enhanced chest at anything with a penis, tugged her cardigan over her painted-on sweater and nodded. "Whatcha doing?"

"Hanging Christmas lights." While Bella didn't like the nickname, Liz did always have her perfect double Ds rounded up and pointing.

Liz stepped off the porch onto the dried winter grass of her lawn. "On the house?"

"Yup." Waving her pamphlet, Bella tried to sound more competent than she felt. "It's easier than you would think."

Apparently, you still had to test the lights even if they were new.

"You're going to hang lights on the outside of your house?" Liz crossed the small strip of driveway separating their lawns.

"Yup!" She tossed Liz a chipper little smile. "It's Christmas."

"So I can hear." Toeing the dark green box of new lights, Liz stopped next to her and stared at her house. "You didn't hang lights last year."

"No, I didn't." Because last year she had spent most of Christmas, like so many Christmases before, wallowing in the bitter knowledge she would spend another Christmas single and stuck in her rut. This year there would be no more wallowing, no more pining, and definitely no more bemoaning her single state. As for her rut, today she'd hauled herself out and it all started with Christmas lights. "I'm getting into the holiday spirit."

"Aren't you spending Christmas with your family?" Liz peered over Bella's shoulder at the pamphlet. Those breasts stuck straight out and Bella moved her arm out of the way.

"No." She stomped on the residual all-alone pang and forced another smile. Being alone for Christmas didn't mean being miserable. "My family went to Florida and I stayed behind to look after the store."

Liz looked vaguely skeptical. "They left you here."

"I'm fine with it." Actually, she was more than fine. Not that she'd admit this to Liz, or anyone, but escaping Nana's gruesome turkey dinner didn't hurt in the least. Her plan for Christmas started with these lights and ended in a glorious new epoch in the life of Bella Erikson.

Liz eased the pamphlet out of her hand. "It says here you have to check the lights, even if they're new."

"I'm about to do that." Bella took her pamphlet back.

"You need to plug them in."

"I know that." Plug in hand, Bella marched over to the outside power outlet. Three years she and Liz had lived side by side, barely speaking a word to each other after the incident with the tree—which Bella still didn't quite believe hadn't been deliberate—and now Liz wanted to chat. Still, it was Christmas, which meant goodwill, peace on earth, and all that. She shoved the plug into the outlet. Her lawn lit up in a magical sprinkling of warm white. Bing provided the soundtrack and she loved it. "Did you need something, Liz?"

Liz bent down and connected another string to the lit

string. More warm white sprang to life. "Looks like these are fine, too." She flicked her Christmas-themed nails at the ladder. "Why don't you get up there and I'll connect the lights?"

"Really?" Liz wanted to help? Maybe the magic of Christmas had gotten to Liz too.

"Why not?" Liz shrugged. "I've got nothing better to do."

Bella's guilt monitor crackled. "You staying here for the holidays?"

"Like I have anywhere to go." Liz waggled her head and jammed her fist on her teeny-weeny hips. "Are we going to hang these lights or what?"

"We're going to hang these lights." Bella put her foot on the first rung. She needed a little mantra reinforcement first. *Thinking will not overcome fear, but action will.* Gripping the higher rungs with both hands, she climbed. First one rung, then two, and away she went. This really wasn't that bad, and before she knew it, the gutter came within easy reach. "Hand me those lights."

"Aye aye, Cap'n." Liz grinned up at her.

When she smiled like that, and not the coy lip smirk she did whenever a man wandered into view, Liz looked really pretty. An opportunity to bridge the gap with Liz opened and Bella took it. "Maybe when we get done here, we can hang lights over at your place," she said.

Liz pulled a face. "I don't do Christmas."

"Why not?" Everybody did the holidays in some way or other.

"Doesn't seem much point." Liz fed her the string of lights. "With just me on my own."

Bella clipped until she ran out of reach, then came down the ladder again. She'd never thought of Liz as lonely. With her flashy clothes and brassy attitude, Liz didn't strike her as the sort to have vulnerabilities. But then, everybody had a soft underbelly somewhere. Even if they kept it buried beneath a titanium exterior. "I'm on my own."

"It says here you need to make sure they're all either pointing up or down." Liz squinted at the gutters.

"Are they?"

"Yup. Pointing down."

"Okay, then." Bella moved the ladder across. "Let's keep at it."

Talk about weird. Her and Liz hanging Christmas lights like they didn't spend most days giving each other tight-lipped how-are-yous from safe sides of their yards.

They fell into a rhythm that took them all along one side of the house and into the front. When they reached the porch, the focal point, Bella stepped back and eyed the sloping gutter line. "We need to do something different here."

"Like what?" Liz stood shoulder to shoulder with her.

"A focal point."

"Huh."

"We could wrap the lights around the poles holding the roof up."

Liz scrunched up her face. "Nah! They're too skinny. A wreath would be nice."

"A wreath?"

"Yeah, hanging in the center there. Do you have one?"

A wreath would be great. "No."

"I do." Liz nodded. "I'll run next door and fetch it."

"I thought you didn't do Christmas." Bella raised her voice as Liz dashed across the lawn.

"I don't." Liz turned and trotted backward. "But I used to be married and we did Christmas. I got the Christmas decorations. He got a twenty-three-year-old blonde who looks like she should be decorating the top."

Ouch. She'd known Liz was divorced, but the younger-woman thing must bite.

"And these." Liz pointed to her chest. "Can you say alimony?"

Bella laughed. Turns out spending time with Liz didn't suck. See, this was what came of opening yourself up to new experiences.

Liz reappeared with her wreath. "If you wrap lights around it, you can hang it in the center there," she said.

"Are you sure?" Bella took the wreath. "We could always hang it over at your house."

"I'm sure." Liz pursed her lips. "Are we gonna stand here all night or get this shit finished? It's so cold out here my nipples are gonna break through any second."

Bella blushed. She couldn't help it. Nobody in her world spoke about nipples or boobs, or—God spare them—down there. Even in her head the phrase came with Nana's wide-eyed, furtive glance southward.

Daring to go where she never had before, Bella said, "Mine too."

Perched on top of the porch overhang, leaning forward to hang the wreath, Bella made the mistake of looking down. The ground rushed up at her, dipped and heaved to the side, taking Bella's stomach with it.

"What are you doing?" Liz peered up at her.

"Umm . . ."

"Hang the wreath and then we can get a glass of wine."

Wine would be lovely. "Err . . ."

"Bella?"

"I'm stuck."

"No, you're not." Liz moved to right beneath her.

"Am too."

Liz's eyes widened. "Are you scared of heights?"

"Yup."

She crossed her arms. "Then why didn't you let me go up the ladder?"

Because she hadn't exactly planned on freezing and sticking to her roof like a demented icicle.

"Edge back." As if directing traffic Liz waved her hands. "Move away from the edge and you'll be fine."

"I can't." Was the ground getting closer? Or was she leaning even farther over? A whimper escaped her and she shut her eyes. Dear God, that was worse. She popped them open to find Liz frowning up at her.

A smile suddenly spread over Liz's face. "You're really stuck?"

"Yup."

"As in can't move?"

"Yup."

"You know what this means?" With glee, Liz whipped out her phone. "I'm going to have to call the sheriff."

"Don't." It came out in a breathy hiss. The idea of Nate Evans having to rescue her off her roof burned through her. Ghost Falls would have a field day if that happened. She could hear them all now.

"Did you hear Nate Evans rescued Bella Erikson from her roof?"

"What was she doing up there?"

"Waiting for him to rescue her." Snicker, snicker. *"Is that girl ever going to wise up and realize she'll never catch Nate Evans?"*

She had wised up—mostly—and she could do this. All she had to do was edge back the tiniest bit to where she couldn't see the ground anymore.

"Hi, Sheriff Evans." Liz purred into her phone. "This is

Liz. Liz Gunn." She growled. "Liz Gunn from Grizzly Drive. I have a problem."

One, two, three . . . edge back. Nope. Bella's hands refused to let go of the roof lip. Years of limiting contact with Nate and now this.

"No, it's not like that time." As she spoke, Liz paced beneath her. "Actually, it's not me. It's my neighbor."

From up here, Bella could see the darker roots of Liz's platinum do. Nowhere in her grand visions of conquering Christmas had she needed a rescue.

Liz nodded. "That's right, Bella."

Oone . . . twooo . . . and three. Oh God, she was going to fall. She knew it.

"She's stuck on her roof."

All she had to do was release the edge of the roof and scooch back. This time, her butt scooched, but her fingers stayed stuck.

"Hanging Christmas lights." Liz hummed and glanced up at Bella. "Right now, she looks a bit like she's twerking on her roof."

Bella lifted her left index finger. Then her middle finger. The index finger snapped back around the ledge. Darn! Bella did not get beaten by a roof. Bella, for certain, did not get caught twerking on her roof by Nate Evans.

"Right you are." Liz keyed off her phone. "They're on their way. Do you need anything?"

"A frontal lobotomy."

Liz grinned at her. "Nate said to keep talking to you." She stopped right under Bella. "So? How you doing?"

"Not so good."

"I can see that. Let's take your mind off the fact that you're about twenty feet from the ground."

"Erp." Twenty feet? Her head went woolly.

"I know." Liz cocked her head. "Let's talk about our yummy sheriff."

"Um . . . no."

"Um . . . yes." Liz tucked her hands into the pockets of her bright pink cardigan. "Just how long have you been in love with him?"

"I'm not . . ." Everyone in town knew anyway. "I did have a crush on him. For most of high school." And a little bit after, but she wasn't confessing that. "Well . . . it started in first grade, but it ended when he joined the police academy in Salt Lake."

"Wow." Liz winced. "That's not what they say."

Oh, Bella knew that, only too well. And Liz had no room to talk, calling Nate out at least twice a week and answering the door in her negligee. "And you?"

"Oh, I'm in lust, not love." She waved a breezy hand. "I was married, remember. I don't want anything more to do with love, but lust . . ." She chuckled like a bordello madam. "Now that I've got time for."

Nipples and down there and sex—definitely sex—weren't things Bella had been raised to talk about. Ever.

"You all right, Bella?" Mr. Powell from across the road stepped out onto his porch.

Her situation plummeted from bad to hideous as Ghost Falls's biggest gossip followed her husband onto the porch. Bella was supposed to be launching her new epoch, darn it.

Bella put as much chipper into her voice as she could manage. She did not need the Powells coming over and getting a front-row seat of the action. "I'm fine, Mr. Powell."

"She's stuck on the roof," Liz called out. "We were hanging Christmas lights, but Bella didn't tell me she was scared of heights."

"Oh, dear." Mrs. Powell came across the road toward them. "I had a cousin who was afraid of spiders."

"Vertigo," announced Mr. Powell as he led the charge. "Irrational fear of heights."

That was acrophobia, but Bella was too busy having it to argue the point.

"Isn't that a movie?" Mrs. Powell tucked her hands into her pockets.

"Hitchcock." Liz scrunched her shoulders up around her ears. "Man, it's cold. How you doing, Bella? Hang in there."

Yes, dear." Mrs. Powell's face crinkled with concern as she gazed up at Bella. "I'm sure help is on the way."

"Did you call Sheriff Evans?" Mr. Powell stared up at her.

"Sheriff Evans?" Giggling, Mrs. Powell smirked at her. "Are you sure you're scared of heights, Bella?"

"Oh, she's scared all right." Bless Liz for coming to her rescue.

Mr. Powell took hold of the ladder and gave it a shake. "Just hop on the ladder, Bella. Seems sturdy enough."

"Mike." Mrs. Powell stood on her tiptoes and whispered in his ear.

Bella dug her fingers into the roof. She didn't need to be clairvoyant to guess what was being said. Would Ghost Falls, for the love of everything, just let this go? She was not wasting away for Nate.

"Oh." Mr. Powell scrutinized her. "Are you sure that's a good idea, young lady?"

Maybe she should end it now and throw herself off the roof. Then again, they'd only whisper over her coffin how she'd killed herself for unrequited love.

"Sometimes a girl has to take matters into her own hands." Mrs. Powell tossed her a conspiratorial wink. "It's not like you have all the time in the world, dear. You can't keep waiting for that man forever."

"I'm not—"

"It's a dreadful waste of taxpayers' money." Puffing out his chest, Mr. Powell stalked to the ladder and gave it another good rattle. "Now, buck up, Bella. You can't call the sheriff out unless it's a genuine emergency."

"Really?" Liz examined her fingernails. "It's one of the perks of living in this town."

"Disgraceful." Mr. Powell flushed. "The man is the representative of law and order in this town, not . . ." He sputtered and huffed for a bit.

"Man candy?" Liz looked smug.

Turning his back on Liz, Mr. Powell harrumphed and put his foot on the ladder. "I'm coming up."

Dear God, save her that.

"Oh no, Mike, your back." Mrs. Powell fluttered over to her husband. Small and compact, the top of her head barely reached his armpit.

"Perhaps you're right." Mr. Powell made a manful show of regret. "I would hate to risk her by dropping her."

Mrs. Powell patted her husband on the chest. "That's so like you, Mike, always thinking of someone else first."

Liz looked up at her and rolled her eyes.

Bella stifled a giggle and then choked on it as blue and red flashing lights turned into her street.

Oh boy. Nate couldn't be subtle about this, now could he? He'd delighted in tormenting her since first grade, when he'd dipped her waist-length braid in purple paint.

Chapter Two

Bella had a perfect view of the siren song to the ovaries that was Nate Evans as he climbed out of his SUV and sauntered across her front lawn. Her little audience parted like the Red Sea for him.

Liz swooned, Mrs. Powell looked wobbly at the knees, and Mr. Powell preened.

She might have gotten over her Nate thing faster if he didn't look so fine. All. The. Time. Couldn't he have developed a paunch, or maybe a tiny bald spot? She didn't ask for much; maybe the wrinkles around his eyes when he smiled could have made him look saggy instead of grabbable.

Nate reached the ladder and looked up at her. Lion eyes, so deep a girl could drown in them. "Hey, Bella."

"Hi, Nate." Her only excuse for the squeak that had taken over her vocal chords was the whole clinging-to-the-roof thing.

"You seem to be in a bit of trouble." He flashed his rogue grin at her.

Nate owned an arsenal of smiles, smirks, mouth tweaks, and grins. This one got her in the knees every time. So sure of himself, but with a hint of little boy to soften the arrogance.

"I'm fine," she said.

"Really?" Up went one eyebrow, a dark slash across his tanned face that matched the deep sable of his hair. Who looked tan in the middle of winter? Nate Evans, that's who.

"She's not fine." Liz pranced up next to him. "She's stuck up there."

"Oh, now." Mrs. Powell flanked him. "She must be frozen to death."

On cue, Bing launched into "White Christmas."

Nate climbed the ladder in about half the time it had taken her. His face appeared over the gutters. "Should I ask what you're doing up here?"

"Hanging Christmas lights."

He frowned, leaned back a bit and surveyed her work. "Why?"

"Because it's Christmas." It came out a bit growly. She always got this way when Nate appeared in her day. Some kind of leftover reflex from middle school aimed at convincing everyone, him included, she was so over her crush on him. It hadn't worked yet.

"Why didn't you ask your dad to help you?" He rested his forearms on the roof.

"My dad is in Florida." Someday she'd have a conversation with Nate Evans that didn't feel like nails on a chalkboard. One day when she and Nate could laugh about her and her alleged twentysomething-year crush.

He cocked his head. "They left you alone for Christmas?"

She would die, right here, before she let him feel sorry for her. "It's fine. I have a plan for the holidays."

He looked doubtful.

"I do." She put a decisive nod into it. "It's going to be fun."

"All right, then." He shrugged. "How about we get you off the roof so you can put that plan into action?"

Huh! Funny thing. She'd almost forgotten she sat perched way, way, way off the ground. "I don't know why Liz called you," she said. "I can get down on my own."

"Need any help there, Sheriff?" Mr. Powell stuck out his chest and strutted to the base of the ladder.

"I'm good, Mr. Powell." Amusement flashed in Nate's glance her way.

Mr. Powell tucked his thumbs into his belt loops and rocked from heel to toe. "Right you are, then. Just holler if you need me."

"Actually," Nate glanced down, "you might want to take Mrs. Powell back to the house. We don't want to spook Bella."

"We'll be very quiet," Mrs. Powell whispered, not keen to give up her information-gathering opportunity.

"Still." Nate gave her his reassuring smile, the one that promised to rescue people from burning vats of lava. "Witnesses often increase the victim's anxiety."

Great; the victim in this scenario being her.

"Right you are, Sheriff." Mr. Powell strode over to his wife. "Let's give the man space to do what he does best."

"I knew I could rely on you, Mr. Powell. A good man in a crisis," Nate said.

Nate's flattery was obnoxiously obvious, but it got the Powells out of her front yard and back into their house.

"Don't even think about it." Liz crossed her arms and cocked her hip. "I'm not going anywhere."

"Didn't you say something about wine?" Bella planned to head straight for a bottle as soon as she got off this roof.

Liz hesitated, then nodded. "Wine is my specialty."

"We'll be right down," Nate said.

Liz shut her front door behind her.

"Don't see you around much." Nate turned back to Bella.

He wanted to chat? Now? "I'm stuck on a roof."

"Yeah, I noticed." He stroked the side of his cheek. "The thing is, I got a problem here, Bella," he said in his deep, rumbly voice. "We have a couple of options and I'm not sure which to go with."

"Options?" She tucked her frozen fingers into her armpits to warm them up.

"I could climb up there and do the fireman lift down." He eyed the roof and then her. "But I really don't know how much you weigh and we might fall."

"I don't weigh that much," she said. She shivered as a cold wind stroked the back of her neck.

"No, I can see that." He smirked. "But the roof could be slippery and I don't like my chances of hoisting you over my shoulder. Given the terrain."

Neither did she. "What's option two?"

"I can call the fire department and ask them to bring a cherry picker and we can pluck you off the roof."

Nate, cherry, and plucked: three words her teen heart would have died to hear in the same sentence. "That means more people. What else have you got?"

"You could slide over a couple of inches and take my hand." His large palm stretched over the roof toward her. His face grew serious and his gaze remained steady on hers. "Just a couple of inches, Bella. Then you grab my hand and we climb down together."

Big, capable, and slightly callused, his hand lay on the shingles.

Bella slid a couple of inches over.

"That's it, sweetheart. I'm not gonna let you fall. I'm right here."

Bella kept their eye-lock as she managed a few more inches.

He clasped her ankle. "I've got you now. A bit farther."

Up her calf he slid his hand, then to her knee, and, finally, grabbed her hand and held.

His grip fastened about her hand, strong and sure. He kept talking in that soft purr that would have her stretching like a cat if she weren't so terrified.

"A little closer," he said.

She stopped in front of him, knees to her chest.

"Now comes the easy part." Not forcing her to move, he squeezed her hand. "You reach your feet out and I put them on the ladder for you."

"I'm not sure I can."

"Sure you can," he said. "I'm gonna be right here the whole way down to the ground."

"Promise?"

"Promise." He gave a tiny tug. "Come on, Bella. I've seen you take your lunch money back from Skyler Falks, and he was two feet taller than you. You've got this."

"It wasn't my lunch money." Bella pushed one leg out.

He gripped her ankle and put her foot on the top rung.

Her ass slid down the roof and she froze.

"No?" He moved his hands to her hips. "Flip onto your belly. What was the money for?"

Bella flattened her chest to the roof. "For my cheerleading uniform."

"You weren't a cheerleader." Guiding her down, his hands cradled her hips.

"I so was." She glanced over her shoulder.

He guided her second foot onto the ladder. Her knees shook and she gripped the shingles. The ladder would never hold her.

"No, you weren't." His arms pressed into her sides, sandwiching her between them. "Step down with your right foot."

"I was a cheerleader. You didn't notice because you were too busy boning Blythe Barrows," she said as her left foot joined her right.

"Boning?" He snorted right beside her ear. Warm breath tingled over her nape. "That's a very rude word for you, sweetheart."

"I know lots of rude words." Okay, a few, but she didn't like using them.

"You do?" Heat radiated from his chest at her back. "Let's take the next step together. I'm right behind you."

"Just because I don't say those words doesn't mean I don't know them." To spite him, she took two rungs.

He chuckled, a low, dirty, ovary-tingling sound that made her take another step. "Tell me another one."

"Nate Evans." They took another rung and then another together. "I'm not going to turn into a potty mouth so you can sweet-talk me off a roof."

"It's working, though," he said. "We're halfway there."

"We are?"

"Don't look down." He pressed her sides with his arms. "I've never heard you swear; it might be fun."

"Isn't there a law against swearing at a sheriff?"

"I hope not," he murmured. "Or half the folks in this town are going to end up in jail."

"Only the ones you stop for speeding." Her right foot hit the ground and then her left. Bella's head spun. "You did it."

"Nah." He turned her to face him. "You did it."

It had been years since she'd been this close to Nate Evans.

Thankfully, he stepped back before she gave in to the insane urge to fling herself against his broad, manly chest and stay there. "Thank you," she said.

"You are most welcome, sweetheart." He smiled at her. A nice smile, without any hidden meaning. "And stay off that ladder."

"What about my lights?" She couldn't leave the job half-done. She had a Christmas plan on the go, followed by a big life change. Big. Life. Change.

"I'll hang them after I get off work."

"I can't ask you to do that." She'd fueled the gossip engine enough for one day.

"You didn't ask." He turned and strode back to his SUV. "See ya, Bella."

Wine bottle clutched to her chest, Liz trotted out of her house in time to intercept Nate before he climbed into his car. "Won't you join us?"

It wasn't fair. Liz hit on Nate all the time and Ghost Falls hadn't turned that into their local soap opera.

Nate ducked around Liz. "Thanks, but I can't."

As Nate's SUV cruised down the street, Liz stood next to her and sighed. "He's so hot." She hefted her wine bottle. "Let's have a drink."

Bella entered her house, Liz on her heels.

Stopping inside the door, Liz looked around her. "This is nice."

Bella was proud of her home. She'd put it all together herself. Painted the walls throughout in a warm biscuit color and carefully selected each piece of furniture. She liked earth tones around her, with bright splashes of reds and oranges to give it life. Here, at least, she didn't have to consult Nana about what she chose.

"Thank you." She led the way into her cheerful kitchen.

"I expected more pink," Liz said as she took the bottle opener from Bella.

"Yeah." Bella pulled a face. "The colors in my store are not my choice."

She couldn't remember seeing Liz in her clothing store more than once. Pity, because now that she really looked at Liz, she would love to add a touch of elegance to her.

Liz shrugged out of her coat and draped it over the table.

Yup, all that skintight could do with a little toning down. Liz's jeans looked like she'd spray-painted them on this morning. Across her breasts, emblazoned in sparkles, scrolled "Flirt."

"So." Bella handed her the wineglasses, not sure what to say now that they stood in her kitchen. Hard to believe this was the first time they'd voluntarily spent time in the same room. "That was humiliating."

Liz snorted and poured the wine. "Please, that was nothing. Although Mr. Powell could have done the entire thing on his own."

Bella snorted a laugh. She risked letting her bitch show. "He's a giver. Except for his bad back."

"Except for that." Liz seated herself at the kitchen table. "It's funny how his back never stops him from standing on a ladder pretending to trim his hedges so he can look in my bathroom."

"Eww." With a shudder, Bella joined her at the table. "He does that?"

"All the time." Liz sipped her wine. "It's about the only action I get these days."

That made two of them. Bella took the seat opposite Liz. "Maybe he didn't mean to see into your bathroom."

"Honey," Liz rolled her eyes, "nobody's hedges need trimming that much."

All she'd really seen of Liz in the past was the mass of platinum hair and too much makeup. It tended to obscure the inherent sweetness of her face. In her youth, Liz must have been one of those girl-next-door types. "Well, so much for Christmas lights."

"Why were you so determined to hang lights?"

Not wanting Liz getting all judgy with her, Bella hesitated over her answer. "It's part of my Christmas plan."

"You have a Christmas plan?" Liz chuckled.

"It's not my plan." It came out sounding very defensive. "It's this thing I found on the internet about what to do if you're alone at Christmas."

"Really?" Liz looked genuinely interested, not wearing that what-the-hell expression.

"Yeah." Bella went over to her fridge and took her list from under her *If opportunity doesn't knock, build a door* fridge magnet. She put the list in front of Liz. "See, it's a list of ten things to do if you're alone over Christmas. Number one is decorate. So, I was decorating."

"You did the inside already." Liz took a long, slow look around her. "It looks nice. Very festive."

"Number two is volunteering." Bella read over her shoulder. "I'm not sure where yet, but there have to be plenty of places that need volunteers."

"Number three says to go out and do things you wouldn't normally do." Liz tapped her red and green nail on the article. "We could do that."

"Together?" Bella wasn't sure she and Liz liked the same things. Hanging lights and sharing a glass of wine in her kitchen seemed a long way from actually hitting the town together. "Like where?"

Liz shrugged. "I dunno, but I tell you what: You find somewhere for us to volunteer and I'll take care of number three."

Talk about bungeeing right outside your comfort zone. "Okay."

Chapter Three

Two pints of chocolate ice cream, her download of *Dr. Childers's Guide to a More Authentic You*, and her laptop, and Bella was ready for the next phase in her plan. Things had gotten off to a rocky start, what with the need for a rescue and all, but that didn't mean she had to quit.

Patti from Nebraska poured her story out over the speakers on Bella's laptop.

"I looked at my life, I looked at my three kids and my empty bank account, and I thought it couldn't get any worse." Bella agreed wholeheartedly. "Then I heard about Dr. Childers and at first I didn't believe it, didn't want to believe it. How could I own the pain caused by my cheating, lying dirtbag of a husband?"

Understandable. The man had walked away without a thought for his family.

"That ain't right, I thought," Patti said. "He left me and his children and a pile of debts higher than the roof of our mortgaged home. But I guess when a body's gone about as low as they can go, there's only one way and that's up." Patti's shrill chuckle filled Bella's dining room. "I took my pain and I hugged it tight to me, and I said *this is my pain, my hurt. I own this.*"

Ping went the light-bulb sound they played every time someone reached that point in their story.

"Own your life." Dr. Childers's raspy voice washed over Bella. "Say it with me. *This is my life. Nobody has the power to steer my destiny but me.*"

"This is my life," Bella said. "Nobody has the power to steer my destiny but me."

Except maybe for Nana and her constant interfering in the store. Well, Nana was sweating through endless mah-jongg games in Florida, and by the time she got back, there would be nothing she could do about it. Even the thought made Bella a little breathless.

Bella opened her web browser and found her site. Her brand-new, beautiful site where she planned to yank Bella's Boutique into the age of online shopping. She'd dropped *boutique* from the name, and it felt right. More like hers, despite the fact that it had been named after Nana, the original Bella. Of course, if life had gone the way it should have, it would be the twins, Bella and Gina, working side by side in the store. Bella liked to believe Gina would have wanted to freshen and update as well.

Regardless, tonight she took her baby online.

Wheeler Barrows had designed the site for her and saved her a ton doing it. Unlike the rest of his family, Wheeler had determination and ambition.

Bella traced the large white orchid on the right top corner of her screen. Simple, elegant, and tasteful, and so right for where she wanted to take her store—out of the eighties and straight into the now.

Patti's story murmured on in the background, but she'd heard most of it before, so Bella tuned it out.

Her finger poised above the Enter key, mouse arrow hovering over the Publish icon.

Click.

The room spun, then righted itself. The earth didn't open under her feet and a lightning bolt straight from Nana didn't strike.

She'd done it.

The empty kitchen nearly popped her bubble of excitement. No, she couldn't allow that. Tonight, she'd taken a huge step forward and she should celebrate hitting what Dr. Childers called a *keystone moment*.

Light shone from Liz's kitchen window. She could go over and invite Liz to share her triumph, but their acquaintanceship felt too new for that. Her good mood hovered on the edge of an anticlimax. What would Dr. Childers do? She would open her own bottle of wine and toast her own success.

The doorbell rang as she pulled the bottle of wine out of the fridge.

Maybe Liz had decided to come over and say hi.

Levering herself onto her toes, Bella spied through the clear glass diamond in the center of her front door. Her heart thudded and she jerked back. Nate Evans stood on her doorstep.

"Hey, Bella," he called. "You gonna let me in?"

God, how her sixteen-year-old self would have died to hear that. She checked her smile in the entranceway mirror. She managed friendly, welcoming, and not idiotic before she opened the door. "Hey, Nate."

He stepped back and jerked his head upward. "Just wanted to tell you I'm going to finish hanging your lights."

"Oh." One summer she'd spent most of it imagining Nate arriving on her doorstep, laden with gifts. Sometimes he brought flowers, other times chocolate or a book she liked, and on one doozy of a fantasy day, he'd brought a puppy. The words were always the same, though: *Hey, Bella. I've just realized that you really are the love of my life and rushed right over to tell you.* She couldn't totally blame the town for the legend when she'd done her fair share to build it. But that was over, starting tonight. "You don't have to do that," she said to the real Nate, standing at her front door and looking a bit wary at her long silence. "I'm sure I can get someone else to do it."

He frowned at her. "I said I would."

"Right." He had, when he'd talked her off the roof.

"It's mostly done." He stepped back and surveyed the roof. "Just this one more string on the other side of the door and then around the other side."

"Okay. Thanks."

"No worries." He winked at her. And how he could wink and make it not creepy she had no idea.

She stood in the doorway.

He stood on the lawn.

Somebody had to break the silence, so Bella said, "Um . . . maybe you'll let me thank you when you're done."

He glanced at her.

God, that sounded like a proposition. "I meant with a beer." Her voice came out all shrill and stupid. "I meant a beer, not anything else."

"Like what?" He raised his brow.

"Well, you know, like . . . I meant . . ." She caught the naughty gleam in his eye. "You're messing with me."

"Yeah." He nodded. "And a beer would be great."

"Great." God, she sounded like he'd solved world hunger. She tried to tone it down a light-year. "I meant, if you have time. I'm not doing much anyway." Now she sounded plain sad and desperate. Best she shut up. "I'll see you after."

Bella slammed the door and leaned her back against it. Sweat coated her palms and she rubbed them on her jeans. Clearly, she and Dr. Childers needed some more quality time together.

"He's just a man," she said. A smoking-hot, make-your-knees-melt, good-looking man, but he put his pants on over that fine ass one leg at a time like everyone else. Her imagination had built him into something he couldn't possibly be.

The ladder scraped against the gutters, followed by dull thuds from the roof.

Her heartbeat sped up. As puberty had set in, some of her Nate fantasies had gotten a bit naughtier. She was fairly sure one had started with a ladder outside her bedroom window. However, she hadn't been wearing her oldest jeans and a tatty old sweatshirt in any of them.

Too late; he'd already seen what she was wearing. Changing now would look desperate, or more desperate than usual.

Bella dashed to her bedroom. A little subtle makeup couldn't hurt. Everyone said men didn't notice specifics.

No. She stopped herself, mascara wand in hand. Getting hold of her life meant moving on. Not prettying herself up in case Nate had a sudden attack of Bella lust over his beer.

Everyone wore mascara. It didn't mean anything. And look at that? It was already on her lashes, so too late.

Gloss?

This stopped now. She forced her reluctant feet back into the kitchen and sat down in front of her laptop. Wiping her sweaty hands on her jeans, she opened her browser. Her new site was so pretty. Browsing it almost kept her mind from the thumps on the roof and what they meant. Should she bake something? Except she couldn't bake worth spit.

"This is my life," she said to the computer screen. "Nobody has the power to steer my destiny but me."

By the time he tapped on the kitchen door, for the most part she had it together.

Nate stepped into her kitchen. Forget together; please God, let her not make a fool of herself over jeans that clung to his butt and muscular thighs. He carried his coat in one hand and his long-sleeved Henley had a love affair going on with the sculpted planes of his chest and abdomen.

Could life do her a solid here and just once, could he not look like he was on his way out of or into someone's bed?

"All done." He smiled. "You should come and see."

"Really?" Kill her now for that squawk alone.

Nate followed her outside and stood next to her as they stared at the house.

Bella looked and looked at the neat row of twinkly white lights marching across her eaves and pushing back the early dark of winter. A bit more snow and she'd have Christmas in her yard. "It's beautiful. Thank you."

"No worries." He slung an arm over her shoulder.

The lights must be made of fairy dust. Bella tensed all her muscles to stop them from melting into Nate.

"Now." He gave her a small shake. "How about that beer before I freeze my balls off?"

Bella nodded and ducked away to hide her flushed cheeks. Nate could always make her blush, and from the chuckle that followed her into the kitchen, he knew it too.

She buried her head in the fridge for a second or two longer than it took to locate the longnecks on the bottom shelf.

"What's this?" Nate's voice came from behind her.

Bella brought his beer to the table, not even bothering to ask if he needed a glass. They'd grown up in a small town together, so she knew how he drank his beer, that he liked coffee with lots of cream and sugar, that he hated brussels sprouts and considered chicken a vegetable. All stuff her mind had hoarded away in case she might need it.

Nate stood by the table, his gaze on her laptop.

She handed him his beer and picked up her wineglass. Earlier, she'd been looking for someone to celebrate with; why not Nate? They'd been friends, of a sort, before he went away. "Actually, I'm celebrating." The website felt like a big step in the right direction. "I started a website for Bella's."

"You did?" He glanced at her over his bottle. "You did this?"

"Well, not all of it." Bella joined him at the table. On the screen her new baby sent a thrill through her all over again. "Wheeler Barrows did all the technical stuff, but I chose all the images and the stuff on it."

"Huh." He clicked the link to formal dresses and went quiet for so long Bella ended up drinking half her wine. He thought the site was lame. That must be why he wasn't saying anything. "You sell these?"

"Yup."

"Huh!"

"I changed some of the inventory when I took over. Actually, I've slowly been changing most of the stuff we sell." His silence unsettled her. "Nana had lost touch with what today's women want. So I started replacing a few of her items with others, and . . ." It was time to shut up.

"And your grandmother let you?"

"Not quite." Bella pulled a face. Not at all, in fact, and if Nana even suspected the extent of the changes she'd made, there would be war right here in this kitchen. "But it's my store now, and I need to do things my way."

He looked up and smiled at her. He clinked his bottle against her glass. "Well done, Bella."

"Thanks." Darn, there went her cheeks again.

"I don't know much about women's clothes." He jabbed a thumb at her laptop. "But that stuff looks nice."

"You think so?" He liked it, and that made her want to dance around the kitchen.

"Yeah, I think so."

"Thanks." It took a moment for awkward to creep back into the room, and when it did, Bella took another sip of her wine. "And thanks, again, for hanging the lights and talking me off the roof."

"No worries."

"Thanks."

"You said that already."

"Yup." She wanted to crawl under the kitchen table. For a split second there, things had felt normal between them.

"Actually, I'm glad this came up." Nate surprised the hell out of her by pulling out a kitchen chair and sitting down. "It's been a while since we spoke."

"Really?"

"Uh-huh." His face dared her to lie her way out of it. "Most of the time, when I see you, you're running in the opposite direction these days."

"Well . . ." Bella took a seat before she fell down. Dr. Childers's little *ping* sound went off in her head. A keystone moment. *Recognize the moment, own the moment, engage the moment.* Honest dialogue, Dr. Childers believed, opened the way to honest relationships. Bella scraped up her courage. "That's probably because I've been avoiding you."

Nate blinked at her. "You don't say. Care to tell me why?"

"Not really." Bella chugged the remainder of her wine. She didn't have the backbone for a keystone moment.

Nate chuckled and topped up her glass. "Tell me anyway."

"It's embarrassing." As if he couldn't tell by how hot her face was.

"As embarrassing as the time I got caught without my pants outside the locker room?" His gold eyes gleamed, lazy and full of confidence, like a lion.

As she recalled the pantless incident, Nate had carried it off with a laugh and a shrug. Smashing her teen heart to bits when she found out his current girlfriend had stolen his pants in mid-tryst. She'd had enough of pining. It gave her the behind kicking she needed. "I'mtryingtoburythecrushthing."

"Say what?" He raised a brow at her.

"Don't make me say it again." He needn't think she wasn't an expert on every one of his facial expressions. He'd heard her all right. Probably wanted to make her squirm saying it all over again.

"You had a crush on me?" He did his best to look surprised.

"Nate . . ." He needn't pretend, especially as neither of them was convinced.

"Okay, then." He pulled a face. "But you got over that. Right?"

"Yes." It came out way too loud. "Years ago. Ages ago. Not since high school. It's people in this town." All the times she'd said this speech in her head, wasted. "People gossip and they still think . . . Well, you know what they still think."

He nodded. "Is that why you avoid me?"

"Yup." She pressed her lips together to keep them shut.

"Right." Nate sipped his beer. "Yeah, that's probably for the best."

"It really is." She slapped a bright smile on her face. "And for the record, I did have a thing for you, but it was more of a low-grade thing, not an all-consuming one like everybody said it was. I mean, I had boyfriends. I had a life."

"Hey." He caught her flapping hand. "I get it."

It would be awesome if she shut her mouth now. "It's not

like I spent the last twentysomething years pining away for you or anything. That would make me pathetic and weird and—"

"Bella." He squeezed her hand. "We live in a small town. People decide who and what you are and stick to it."

Nate would know all about that too. From town bad boy to sheriff took a lot of attitude adjusting. The irony of Nate comforting her didn't escape her, and Bella laughed. "You're trying to make me feel better about this?"

"Hey." He let go of her hand. "It was flattering, in a strange way."

"Hmm." She didn't believe that, but this ease between them felt good.

"So, does this mean we can be friends again? No more running away from me?"

Was there a woman alive who could resist that smile? Not in this kitchen, at any rate. "We can be friends again."

Nate shifted and cleared his throat. "In the spirit of honesty and friendship, can I ask you something?"

Knowing she might regret it, she still nodded and said, "Sure."

"Why me? And why so long?"

"That's two things," she said, mainly to give herself time because she didn't really have the answer. She'd asked herself those two questions enough times that she should know the answer, but she really didn't.

Nate watched her and sipped his beer.

"Well, there's the obvious." Her face must be radioactive by now with all the blushing. "Your . . . looks . . . and all that." God, how could it be so hard to tell him what they both knew? The man had a mirror, for the love of God. "But it was more than that. Like the time you punched Grady because he stole my pencil. Or the way we both loved the same movies and music." She sounded lamer by the second. "I don't know really. I guess I liked you as well. No matter how cocky you got, underneath I always saw how kind you were, and how hurt you were after your dad passed. You always had so much more about you than the obvious."

Nate stared at her, his face blank. Then he took her limp hand in his. "You know, Bella. That guy, the one you had a crush on, that's not me."

"I'm pretty sure it is . . . was."

He chuckled, gave her fingers a quick squeeze, and let go. "No, I mean, I'm not the man you think I am. I wish I was." He stood. "But I'm really not worth a crush like that." His smile seemed a little sad. "Not from a girl as sweet as you anyway."

Chapter Four

$\mathscr{N}$ate waved good-bye to Bella and climbed into his cruiser. That had worked out well. Confused and a little pissed by her constant duck and weave, he'd been waiting for the chance to tackle her about it.

The drapes twitched across the road.

"Good night, Mrs. Powell," he called, and then, because he knew she would be watching as well, "'Night, Liz."

When they were kids, he'd known about Bella's crush. Who the hell hadn't? The way she'd looked at him, it was impossible to miss. As she was the closest thing to a positive influence in his life, some part of his teenage self had recognized that and wanted to hold on to it. And he'd liked Bella, really liked her. Liked her enough to recognize she was just about the sweetest thing in Ghost Falls and he had no business messing with that.

She still smelled awesome. Like honey and flowers and a touch of spice that the horndog in him had always appreciated.

Through the wild years, the one thing he'd prided himself on was not taking her up on that silent, tempting offer.

Bella's honey ran all the way to the bone, and he'd crushed more than his share of hearts. You didn't put a spun-sugar fairy into a pair of Neanderthal hands and expect it to survive.

With Bella, he hadn't pushed the friendship thing too hard either. He didn't do friendships with women anyway because it got too complicated. Marriage was not in the cards for him; he didn't do that sort of love. The sort of love that left his mom a wreck after his dad died. The sort of love that had tied his dad in knots when he was still alive. Nate had told her the truth tonight. He couldn't be the guy she saw because he didn't have it in him.

God, the people in this county must have been desperate to elect him. He thanked God they were, though. He liked his job, loved it. It beat the crap out of working in the city. When this gig had come up, he couldn't get out of the Special Victims Task Force fast enough. Women and kids, the kind of breathing victims that tore your heart out and stamped on it.

He started the cruiser and eased into the street. Light shone from the houses on either side. He caught glimpses of life inside those houses. Pat and Karen Kenny and their three kids, sitting around the dinner table. He remembered rushing Pat to the hospital in time for Karen to deliver their first.

Old Man Sharp, nursing his one whiskey from the porch, raised his hand as Nate passed.

Ghost Falls was special. One of a handful of disappearing towns across the country. Stuff like morals, family, and integrity still meant something here. If you fell on the sidewalk, somebody would help you up. People still had block parties and knew the names of all their neighbors. It was more than a town, it was a community, and it was his job to keep it that way.

Two kids loitered at the stop sign between Wolverine and Elkhart. Nate rolled down his window. "Hey, Maddie, Whitney. Shouldn't you girls be heading home?"

"Yes, Sheriff." Whitney gave him a killer smile that would take knees out in about fifteen years.

Fifteen years from now, he'd be into his late forties. Jesus, what a depressing thought. Because he might be almost exactly where he was now, except older.

Giggling and whispering to each other, the girls ran across the street.

Life moved on all around him. Even Bella was moving on. He'd like to see that. Inside the good girl Bella had always been, he sensed a little something wild lurking. His phone ringing provided a welcome distraction. "Yup."

"Nate?" The voice sounded vaguely familiar and he checked caller ID. An unknown number.

"Yup."

"Hey! So this is Daniel. Daniel Carver."

Holy shit. He pulled the cruiser over to the side before he crashed into something. "Daniel Carver? Last I heard you were doing five to ten."

"Yeah." Daniel chuckled. "Well, I've done them and now I'm out."

Shit, Daniel Carver. His near miss. His wake-up call. He and Daniel had run crazy through Ghost Falls until old Sheriff Wheeler gave them both a way out. Nate took the hand offered. Daniel went his own way. A rush of old anger and teenage need to kick out at something clenched in his gut. He took a deep breath. He didn't have to be that kid anymore, but Daniel Carver . . .

"So, your brother gave me your number," Daniel said.

Had to be Matt, who never saw the bad side of anyone. "What can I do for you?"

"First off, I'm checking in with the sheriff." Daniel

chuckled. "Sheriff? What the hell, bud, didn't see that one coming."

"People change." The pissy in his voice made him even madder.

"Yeah, they do." Daniel sighed down the line. "You've done well, Nate. You made a smart move."

"Thanks." He breathed deep. This past blast unsettled him. "So, you're back in Ghost Falls."

"Yeah. My folks died while I was inside. They left me their apartment."

"I know. I've been keeping an eye on it. Not me; the department."

"Thanks," Daniel said. "So, any chance we could meet up? Have a drink? A cup of coffee? I'd really like to connect with you again."

What the hell for? Meeting Daniel Carver was not something he wanted to do. "Why?"

"I'm not the same man either, Nate," he said. "I'd like the chance to prove it to you."

"Okay." Who the hell was he to say no if the man was really changed and reaching out? If Sheriff Wheeler hadn't reached out to him as a kid, he would have headed straight behind bars with Daniel. "Sure, let's meet."

Chapter Five

$\mathscr{B}$ella fitted the key in the glass front door to her store and shoved it open. Stale, weekend air rushed up to greet her as she flipped on the lights.

God! This place! This tired, old eighties throwback with its shag carpet and lipstick-pink furniture. Now, Bella liked pink as much as the next girl—more, in fact—but the store needed a serious update. Starting with the carpet, which trapped twenty years of odors in it and sent them into the air.

If the outraged call from Nana this morning was any sort of indication, the update might have to wait. How Nana and her chronic technophobia had found the site, she still didn't know. But found it Nana had, and made Bella forty minutes late with her lecture on change, which she followed up with a guilt whammy straight to the knees about how much Bella owed her for handing over her business to her favorite granddaughter. Her only granddaughter. Nobody said it anymore, but as the surviving twin, Bella sometimes felt like she owed it to Nana and her parents to make sure they never missed her sister. Sure, she didn't need Dr. Childers to break that down for her, but still she played second favorite to a sister who'd died before they had reached six months.

She put her bag in the back room, took a bracing sip of her nonfat caramel latte, and went back into the main store. The register hummed into life. It had taken three weeks of fighting Nana to get a computerized inventory system installed. Nana had liked having Bella and the books around every Sunday night for a report session. It had made Bella the world's biggest wuss that she didn't say no and point out that she owned the store, had bought it from Nana. The store was Nana's life and Bella couldn't snatch it away from her. Fortunately, the new inventory system confounded Nana, and the Sunday night interrogations had ended.

The bell over the door tinkled and Pippa walked in, giving Bella that killer smile that made her one of America's favorite reality-show hosts. "Hey, Tinker Bell!"

Tall, red-haired, and stacked, along with charming and successful, a girl could grow to hate someone like Pippa. Unless Pippa was your closest friend, and then any day that brought Pippa was a good one. "Hey yourself. When did you get back?"

"Last night." As always, Pippa looked great. Her hectic traveling lifestyle didn't seem to touch her; Pippa always had a sort of glow about her. It helped that she was married to the second-sexiest man in Ghost Falls, Matt Evans. Darn Evans brothers. Maybe if she'd moved away she might have gotten to the crush recovery stage a bit sooner.

Bella returned her hug.

"Oh dear." Pippa leaned back. "That's not a happy face."

"Nana found out about the website." Pippa's uncanny knack of winkling the truth out of a person made her TV show riveting to watch, but it also made it difficult for her friends to pretend everything was okay.

"You launched it?" Pippa smiled.

Bella let her happy grin free. She was proud of the website, and herself for doing it. "This weekend."

"Go you!" Pippa pumped her fist in the air. "So what did Nana have to say?"

"What do you think?" Bella pulled a face. The forty minutes had gotten ugly. "She went nuts."

Pippa strolled over to the pink velour chairs in the center of the salon. Chairs so pink they made Bella's teeth ache. "So, I guess you didn't get a chance to talk to her about the renovation."

"Gosh no." Bella got her duster out and went to work. Looking at Pippa would confirm what the other woman thought. She thought it herself often enough. Bella needed to stop being such a pushover.

"You know, Bella, you don't need her permission to do this, or even her approval."

"It's not that easy." Bella got behind the display of earrings with her duster. A lifetime of *stand up for yourself, Bella*, followed quickly by a *do it because I said so, Bella* didn't give her any hints.

"Yes, actually, it is." Pippa stood in an elegant sweep.

Bella dreamed of moving like that. Every motion Pippa made seemed choreographed. It helped that Pippa topped her by nearly a foot. Unfortunately, Bella's girlish dreams of being willowy and tall had stopped at five foot nothing.

"This is your store. It's your time that keeps it open; it's your money you spend on it." Pippa waved her hand to the snow-covered mountain outside the storefront. "Up there, those developments are getting bigger and bigger and bringing more money into this area. That's your market, right there. And you need to position yourself to take advantage of it." Pippa whipped the duster out of her hand. "The time for change is now, Bella."

Yeah, yeah, yeah; tell that to Nana. "Actually, speaking of change," Bella switched subjects before Pippa could really get going, "I've been making a few."

Cocking her head, Pippa studied her. "To the store, or what?"

"Nope." Bella grabbed her duster back. She couldn't talk if her hands weren't busy. "To me. Changes to me."

Pippa reared back a bit. "There's nothing wrong with you. If you were on my show I wouldn't have a clue how to make you over."

"Not the outside." Bella peered over the edge of a sale items rack, all horrible stuff left over from when Nana did the ordering that she could barely give away, let alone sell. "I've been listening to *Dr. Childers's Guide to a More Authentic You.*"

Throwing back her head, Pippa gave her husky, naughty laugh. "Dr. Rhonda Childers? The same Dr. Childers who ran out on her husband and four kids and is now living in Rio with the pool boy?"

Well, Bella hadn't known about that. "You're making that up."

"I swear I'm not. It was all over the gossip sites. You didn't catch it?"

"Nope." Bella rallied. "Still, just because she did that doesn't mean everything she says is a lie. And you know better than anyone not to believe in what people say."

"Ain't that the truth?" Pippa widened her eyes. "So, tell me what changes Runaway Rhonda has inspired in you."

Did Pippa have to call her that? Bella supposed she did, if the wicked grin Pippa gave her was any indication. "I'm taking charge," Bella said. "Of my life. The store and the good-girl, people-pleasing thing. And the Nate thing."

"You told me you were over the Nate thing years ago." Rolling her eyes, Pippa heaved a sigh. "Please don't tell me you really are still hung up on Nate because he's a manwhore."

"I'm not and I do know that he's a . . . what you said." The term *manwhore* sent her into a frenzied dust bunny pursuit behind a line of cardigans. Pippa would only tease her for blushing. And what did it say about her if the town manwhore hadn't hit on her? "I know I don't still have a thing for Nate. You know I don't still have a thing for Nate. But the town is still locked on this idea of who I am. It's more than Nate, though. It's how people perceive me."

Pippa popped up right in front of her. "Do we need wine for this conversation?"

"You know me and wine." Bella had to giggle. Her last girl's night with Pippa had ended with Pippa making her sign an agreement never to get drunk with her again. People wouldn't keep calling her a good girl if they saw her after a few drinks. Make that two drinks.

Pippa grinned back. "You're probably right. Now, start again, and stop trying to fudge over the details."

"Okay." Bella went after the dust that always gathered at the top of the display cabinets. "Dr. Childers has this thing about taking control of your life."

Up went Pippa's sculpted eyebrow.

"No, she's right," Bella said. "I do need to take control of my life. I've let Nana define the store, I've let my parents define me as the survivor child, and I've let this town define me as the girl pining away for the town manwhore." It came easier the more times she said it. "But I'm not those things, and it's time I proved it. It's the holidays, and Nana and my parents are in Florida. It's a great time to get started."

"You've really thought about this." Pippa studied her.

Bella nodded because she had thought long and hard about where her life was heading. "I found this list on the internet, and instead of spending Christmas like I usually do, I'm going to go out. Have fun. Experience new things."

"New men?" Pippa jammed her fists on her hips.

"Possibly." Definitely. "I made a new friend."

"Who?"

"Liz from next door."

Pippa gaped at her. "You made friends with Headlights?"

Bella expected as much; she'd certainly downloaded about Liz enough on Pippa's shoulder. "She's actually really nice."

"Even if she does call Nate every two days and answer the door in her underwear." Pippa plopped onto the sofa.

"But you see, that would only bug me if I was still hung up on Nate." Bella tucked away her duster and arranged the hangers. People always put things back in the wrong place. "And I haven't had a crush on Nate in years, so Liz and I can be friends. She even offered to come along on some of the things on my Christmas list."

"Huh!" Pippa folded her arms over her chest. "Well, be careful. That woman is on the hunt and she's not too fussy about what she catches."

Bella moved a size two back to its place near the front of the rack. "I think she's lonely."

"Or horny."

"That too." Bella couldn't stop her grin. "But maybe I am too."

"Bella!" Whirling around, Pippa grinned at her. "Did you just say that?"

Heat flooded Bella's face. "It's part of experiencing new things. I might develop a potty mouth."

"I'm not sure you could." Pippa's smile took any sting out of the words. "But you're making sense. Put yourself out there, see what comes back."

"I need to live my life on my terms."

Pippa nodded. "And you deserve it."

"Yes." Bella let that percolate. "I do, don't I?"

The bell over the door tinkled and Liz strutted in. She spotted Pippa, paused, and then sashayed over to the sofa and draped herself over the farthest end away from her. "Hello."

"Liz." Pippa nodded.

"This store." Liz waved a hand around. "Looks like the inside of a vagina."

Bella inhaled latte and came up coughing.

"It kind of does." Wide-eyed, Pippa took a long, slow look around her. "Bella, you have got to let me send Matt around."

Maybe one day she might be able not to blush when Liz said things like that. Perhaps even say them. "Did you need something?"

"A dress." Liz got to her feet. "A dress to inspire lust." She pinned Bella with a look. "Because you and I are going out."

"Oh?" Dear God, Liz worked fast. Bella hadn't even started on the charity thing. "Where?"

"Yes, where?" Pippa stared at Liz. "And I hope it's not next Saturday night, because Bella is mine that night."

"Oh?" Bella hoped it would be at Pippa's grandmother's house.

"A family celebration." Pippa gave a secretive little smirk. "I'll text you the details. Why don't you come along, Liz?"

Liz blushed and ducked her head, but Bella caught the pleased gleam in her eye. "I wouldn't want to intrude."

"You won't." Pippa waved her hand. "It's not a formal

thing." She settled herself into the sofa. "Now, tell me about ladies' night. When is it?"

"Whispering Pines is having a singles' night. Tonight." Liz announced it as if she'd pulled a rabbit out of a hat. "And as we're both single, we're going to march our asses up there and check it out."

"Tonight?" Bella looked at Pippa for support. "I don't know. Singles' nights can be kind of shady. All those desperate people prowling around."

"That's us." Liz motioned to herself and Bella. "I haven't gotten laid in months, and you . . ." She snorted. "I live right next door, and let me tell you, the lack of activity is a snoozefest."

"Maybe I don't bring my men home." Bella hated to admit Liz was right. She was, but that wasn't the point.

Liz rolled her eyes. "Honey, you live like a nun."

"I think it's a great idea." Sitting up, Pippa grinned. "It might be a huge time suck, but you'll never know until you actually go."

"You think I should go?" Bella could count on one hand the number of times she'd been to a bar. Going to a bar on the hunt? Never.

"I do." Pippa rubbed her hands together. "Ghost Falls is dead most of the time, and let's face it, the dating pool is rather shallow."

"Exactly." Getting to her feet, Liz examined the store. "Now, do you have anything in here that will do?" The doubtful look on her face was a bit insulting.

"She sure does." Pippa leaped to her feet. "Don't let the vagina-pink decor fool you; Bella's is loaded with good stuff."

"Let's get to it!"

"And luckily for you," Pippa said, "I've got nothing better to do right now than make sure you both look hot."

Liz sneered. "I don't want to end up looking like an old lady."

Pippa's professional face slid into place. "You won't, but you also won't go out looking like you're wearing your daughter's clothing."

Chapter Six

$\mathscr{V}$ ery few things had the therapeutic value of a red dress and a great pair of heels. Bella couldn't believe she hadn't done this years ago. All this time wasted being too shy to go to bars. This was fun. She took another sip of her appletini. Was it her third or fourth? She couldn't be sure and especially not with the two men vying to buy her the next one.

Who knew Ghost Falls could round up this many singles? Most of them came from the resort, but the crowd filled the bar and warmed the air enough for her to sit there comfortably in a sleeveless dress.

"Liz?" A short, balding man sidled up next to them.

Liz froze, then picked up her drink and took a slow sip. She looked gorgeous tonight. Pippa had tamed her down to a tight-fitting black dress that showed off all her curves but kept her skin decently covered. "Noel."

Noel stared Liz up and down and huffed out a breath. "I thought it was you."

"And you were right." Liz puckered up her red mouth.

She wouldn't be Liz without a little drama. "Did you want something?"

"Um." Noel dug a hankie out of his pocket and swiped it across his beaded top lip. "Just to say hi."

"Really?" Swinging around on her barstool, Liz's knees forced Noel to take a quick step back, into the large man behind him.

"Sorry," he muttered to the man before turning back to Liz. "Just thought I'd be friendly."

"Hi, I'm Bella." She stuck out her hand. The guy clearly felt uncomfortable.

"Noel." His took hers in a clammy grip.

"My ex-husband." Eyes glittering over the edge of her glass, Liz sipped her drink. "Of course, it's hard to recognize him without his bimbo in tow."

"Nice to meet you." Because what else could she say?

"Likewise." Noel nodded and mopped his top lip again. "You look good, Liz. And you, Bella."

"Thank you." She turned to her hovering drink buyers. "This is Adam, and that's . . ."

"Parker," said Parker.

The men exchanged greetings. Everyone was being so nice and friendly.

"Can I talk to you, Liz?" Noel blushed and jerked his head. "Maybe alone?"

Liz turned her back on him. "I'm with my friend."

Bella knew Noel had left Liz for a younger woman, but he looked so defenseless and nervous, she felt sorry for him. "It's okay. You can go and talk," she said to Liz.

"We'll take care of her for you," said Adam, the blond on her left and the more talkative of the two. He'd already stolen her cell phone and put his number into it and then called himself so he had hers. So determined to see her again. See, when you spent your time squished into a mold, you missed out on what was standing right in front of you.

"I have nothing to say to Noel." Liz motioned the bartender for another round.

"Please." Seeming to grow taller and more present, Noel locked his stare on Liz.

Pursing her lips, Liz tossed her hair. "Fine!" She pressed Bella's hand. "I'll be right back."

"No need to hurry." Adam leaned one elbow on the bar, sent her a killer smile, and got closer. "So, Bella. That's Italian for beautiful."

Bella laughed and sipped her appletini. "But I'm not Italian." She should really count how many she'd drunk because she had a bit of a drinking problem. As in, no filters when she drank. The line was corny, but Adam was trying.

"You sure don't look Italian," Parker said.

"Nope." Bella flipped her hair back. "But that didn't stop my parents from calling me Bella."

Of the two, Adam was the better-looking. Tall, broad, and blond with chiseled, even features and melty brown eyes. Parker was taller and built bigger, and he had a frat-boy thing about him. Frat boys generally ignored her. Not tonight, apparently. She giggled at her own train of thought.

"There's a story behind that smile." Breath brushing her shoulder, Adam leaned in. He smelled of Armani.

Bella peered through her lashes at him, the way she'd read a heroine in a book do. She rather enjoyed the peering. It gave her an air of mystery.

Jo took her glass and wiped the bar in front of her. Nate's sister worked here now, in one of the new bars that had opened as the area grew more developed. Prior to the opening of Whispering Pines, the only other choice for a drink out had been Ed's, a dingy dive at the far end of town that even the rats approached with caution.

"Another?" Adam indicated her glass.

"Bella?" Jo stared at her meaningfully. The problem with Ghost Falls was that everybody was up and in your business. Like now; Jo was trying to warn her not to drink anymore. That was because Jo had her pinned as a good girl.

"Please." Bella smiled at Adam. *Cosmo* said a girl should get him talking about himself. "So, what do you do?"

"Import and export." Adam shrugged. "Right now, I'm here to enjoy the snow over Christmas."

"No family?"

"No." He grimaced. "I'm an only child and my folks passed on a few years back."

"Lucky you." Bella sipped her drink. Oops; that had come out a bit harsh, and her cheeks heated. Maybe Jo and her look had something. "What I meant was, sometimes family can be a bit stifling. Not that yours were, only that . . ." She needed a quick recovery. "I'm sorry about your parents."

Over the edge of his scotch glass, Adam grinned. "I knew what you meant."

He had the most dreamy, melty chocolate eyes she'd ever seen. Like Colin Firth, or better yet, Theo James. Pity Adam didn't have a British accent; those were supersexy.

"So, tell me about your family," Adam said.

"I'd rather not." Bella wrinkled her nose. "I'm feeling way too happy right now to get into my family."

With a bigger scowl at Adam, Jo put another drink in front of her.

Bella didn't care. Tonight was for her, all hers. Bella of the ball.

Nate checked the address with dispatch. "Are you sure they didn't say Ed's?"

"Not unless your sister started working at Ed's," Gabby

snarled back. What was it with the woman? Nate couldn't remember the last time she hadn't sounded pissy.

"Okay." Sighing, Nate pulled onto the main road going up the hill to the new resorts. He'd spent his day on the road between county headquarters and a few satellite offices like the one in Ghost Falls. Everywhere the same story: not enough money, not enough officers to cover the ground. Fifteen minutes to the end of his shift and Jo called in. Damn! Tonight, he had a date with the splash back in his kitchen. Renovating his house calmed him, gave him a sense of peace.

Twinkly lights dotted the crown of the mountain. Matt and his other brother, Eric, were printing money with those new resorts they had going up. They'd done well to integrate them into the town without screwing up the nice parts of Ghost Falls, but still, extra bodies meant extra work for the sheriff. Like now, a call from Jo asking him to stop into the bar at Whispering Pines when he had the chance.

High-end SUVs choked the parking lot to overflowing, forcing him to stop the cruiser in the emergency bay and leave the engine running. Cold winter air hit him as he left the warm cocoon of the car. The tourists came here for the winter wonderland and Ghost Falls threw everything it had at them. A heavy dusting of powder coated the ground and trees in a postcard landscape. White icicle lights lit up the façade of the bar like one of those New York City restaurants. He couldn't think what Jo meant by calling him here. Did two drunken brokers get into a Twitter battle or something?

Voices hit him in a dull roar as he pushed open the door. Two huge stone hearths at either end of the room shoved out enough heat to have him shrugging out of his heavy winter coat. Fresh pine scent underscored a hundred different expensive colognes and perfumes. Hung with more white lights and crystal ornaments, a huge real tree decorated the entrance hall. It was a far cry from the fiber-optic midget they had propping up the front desk at the station.

"Hey, Sheriff." A drunken party girl in a tiny black dress batted her lashes at him. He made a note to send Gabby up here to card people. That would teach Gabby to get salty with him.

As he made his way to the bar, the crowd parted. Officially, he was already off the clock, and he'd seen the crowd at Blissful Meadows Retirement Community get more rowdy than this. He caught Jo's eye and jerked his head at her. "What the hell, Jo?"

"Hey, Sheriff." Another buzzed blonde with her cleavage spilling over the top of her dress got in front of him. "Did you bring the handcuffs?"

Yeah, like he'd never heard that one before. Nate gave her a polite smile and stepped around her and back up to the bar.

"God, you could cause a riot in here." Jo gave him her wicked grin.

"I'm tired and I'm hungry, Jo-Jo."

His sister rolled her eyes at him. "I thought you should know this."

"Uh-huh." He glimpsed a pack of thirtysomething women sidling over.

"Check it out." Jo jerked her thumb to the other side of the horseshoe-shaped bar.

Nate recognized a fellow male on the hunt. "The blond guy is working his mojo."

"Yes, he is, Sheriff Evans." Jo dragged out the syllables of his name. "Look closer."

"Some overdressed douche from the city and his . . ." He took a closer look at the blonde. "Shit!"

"Uh-huh." Jo folded her arms over her chest and waggled her head. "Now I think he's getting it."

"Is that Bella?"

"Sure is." Jo raised her brows. "Only Bella as I've never seen her before."

City douchebag had Bella crowded against the bar as he whispered in her ear. He made his move with all the subtlety of an eighteen-wheeler pulling a three-point turn. Douchebag laid his arm on Bella's shoulder in a proprietary move that set Nate's teeth on edge. "You called me to see Bella dressed up like a slut?"

"You're a dick." Jo glared at him.

"Sorry." Nate managed a tight nod. She was right; he was being a dick. Bella didn't look slutty; she looked fucking smoking, and why the hell did that guy have to keep stroking her arm like she was his family pet? "Do you know him?"

Jo shrugged. "He comes in here every now and again. Doesn't drink too much, tips well, and up until tonight, I've never seen him put the moves on anyone."

He knew for a fact Bella was over twenty-one. "It's a free country, Jo. Bella can date who the hell she wants."

"She's been drinking," Jo said.

In the middle of turning toward the door, Nate stopped. "How much?"

"A lot." Raising her brow, Jo flipped her bar towel over her shoulder. "Way, way past what she usually drinks, and Captain Smooth there keeps ordering her another."

The guy had broken no law Nate knew of, but suddenly it made all the difference. Bella didn't drink. Okay, maybe one or two glasses of wine every now and again. "How bad is she?"

"I called you, didn't I?" Jo moved off to serve a customer.

Buying a girl a drink was perfectly legal. Buying her a

few drinks to get her slightly buzzed? It happened all the time. He didn't like it, but there you had it. Douchebag wouldn't be the first guy to try to talk his way around a woman's inhibitions.

Damn it! That wasn't just any woman. Douchebag was moving in on Bella Erikson, Ghost Falls's sweetheart and, as of yesterday, his friend again.

Nate threaded his way through the crowd toward them.

A couple of young guys caught sight of him, started, and then ducked out of his way. Oh yeah, Deputy Gabby definitely needed to get her grumpy ass up here to start carding.

Bella caught sight of him about halfway there, grinned, and waved.

She was toasted all right. The big, sappy grin all over her face told him as much.

"Nate." Squealing, she threw herself off the barstool in his direction.

Nate caught her before she connected nose first with his chest. She had one helluva dress on tonight. Short enough to show off several above-the-knee inches and low enough to give him the sweetest view between her pert breasts.

"Hey, Bella." He peeled her off him and put her on her feet.

"Are you here for a drink?" She tottered back to her stool and hoisted her ass back onto it.

Douchebag had turned and eyed him as if he recognized another rooster in his henhouse. *Don't bother, buddy. This girl ain't for me, but then, she ain't for you either.*

"Come on, Bella." He grabbed her arm and tugged her off her barstool. "Let's get you home."

"No." Bella frowned at him and tried to pull her arm free. "I'm not going home. I'm having fun."

She wrinkled her nose at him in a way that was seriously damn cute. "You'll thank me in the morning."

"No." Bella shook her head slowly from side to side. "Because I won't see you in the morning." She spun about so suddenly he nearly lost his grip on her. "Have you met . . . Adam?"

"How you doing?" Nate gave a chin jerk in Douchebag's general direction.

"And . . . ?" Bella frowned up at her other circling dog.

"Parker." A second shark smiled down at her before turning to Nate. "How are you, Sheriff?"

"I'm good." Nate had pulled him over four nights ago for thinking his Porsche Cayenne operated on a different speed limit than the rest of the world. No way that guy got to put his moves on a drunken Bella. "Have you been buying her drinks?"

"Not me." With a smirk, Parker raised his own glass. "I'm driving tonight. Strictly diet soda this side."

"Is there a problem here, Sheriff?" Douchebag's money-boy, city-slicker voice oozed condescension. "The lady and I are having a good time."

"Were having a good time." Nate stared him down. "The lady is going home now."

"No, I'm not," Bella said.

Heads turned in their direction, and Nate hit his limit for stupid for one night. "Yes, you are. Now, you can walk out of here or I can carry you. That's your choice, Bella."

For a second he thought he might have to pull a caveman and upend her over his shoulder. Bella seemed to give it long and slow consideration. Then she rolled her eyes and huffed. "Fine. But you're driving because I took a cab here."

She slammed on the brakes with the door in sight. "Liz." She turned her flushed face up to him. "I came here with Liz. I can't leave without her."

"Headlights?"

"Uh, uh, uh." Bella waggled a pink-tipped finger under his nose. "You shouldn't call her that. She's very nice."

Sure, if you weren't packing a penis. "I'll text her and let her know I'm taking you home."

"No." Bella's head whipped this way and that as she scanned the bar. "No man gets left behind."

God help him. Liz sat at a table close to the hearth. Was that her ex with her? Nate towed Bella in their direction.

Liz looked up. For once she kept her lashes from batting.

"Bella's drunk, I'm taking her home."

Getting to her feet, Liz gathered her things. "I'll come with you."

"No." Noel caught her arm. "I'll take you home later. Please. Stay for a bit longer."

As Liz made up her mind, Nate counted the seconds. Then she nodded and sat down again. "I'll see you tomorrow, Bella."

"See ya." Bella waggled her fingers.

Nate loaded her into the back of the cruiser. Bella thought it was funny as hell, apparently, because she giggled and chattered on about handcuffs and being frisked. Then she took up singing, treating him to her "whip" and her "nae-nae" in the rearview mirror.

Damn, Bella was funny as hell when she was drunk. Funnier now that he had her out of the bar and safely on her way home. "What were you doing there tonight?"

"Hmm?" Bella stuck her fingers through the cage and sat forward. "Where?"

"At the bar?"

"Oh." She pressed her face into the cage. "Do you have any music in here?"

"No. What were you doing at the bar?"

"I can see a radio," she said.

"The radio is for official—"

"And I was getting laid."

"What!" He took the corner into Buckhorn too fast.

"Oopsie!" In a flurry of legs and stripper heels, Bella tumbled against the rear left door. Using the cage, she clawed her way back up. "You needn't sound so surprised, you know. I do like getting laid. Actually, I love sex. I miss sex."

She launched into an off-key version of "Oops (Oh My)."

He raised his voice as she got to the shirt-coming-over-her-head part. "What the hell, Bella? Since when are you the kind of girl who goes to bars for a hookup?"

"Since now." She shook her index finger at him. "You know, Nate Evans, just because you don't want to do me doesn't mean nobody else will."

In that dress, pretty much any man alive, Nate would bet. This conversation had veered way off track. "You should know better," he said, wincing as he sounded like a Sunday school teacher. "You don't know those men. They could have been anyone."

"I would have known them a lot better if you hadn't interrupted."

"And I'm not interested because I'm not good relationship material." He felt the need to get that straight because Bella was cute and pretty and, tonight—fuckable.

"I never said I wanted a relationship." Bella pressed her face against the cage. "Have you ever had sex back here?"

"No!" Her light floral perfume filled the cruiser. "And of course you're a relationship girl."

"Maybe I've changed." She peered down the front of her dress. "I should get the girls out more often."

"No, you should not." There he went again, sounding like a tight-assed dick.

"Did you notice my girls, Nate? Adam noticed my girls. He couldn't keep his eyes off them."

Thank God, he'd turned into her street. Nate sighed softly as he made the right turn. "Adam looks like a creep."

"No, he doesn't. How come you never noticed my girls?"

He parked in her driveway and climbed out. Jerking open the back door, he motioned her out. "This is your stop."

Bella shook her head. Her dress had ridden up, giving him a view of inches and inches of toned, smooth thigh. For a small girl, Bella packed some dangerous curves. "Not until you answer my question."

Nate gritted his teeth. This was why Bella should stay away from the sauce. "I noticed your girls."

"Really?" She perked up with a smile. "Did you think they were pretty?"

"Out!" He leaned in and got hold of her arm.

She came in a flash of pink silky panties, giggling so hard he had to hold onto her to keep her upright. Knowing it was probably a waste of breath, he still had to try. "Bella, you need to be more careful with men you don't know. And you shouldn't drink."

She blew a raspberry at him. "I'm a changed woman, Nate Evans."

"Funny," he said, "because you look like the same old Bella to me."

"Is that so?" Her eyes glittered up at him in a way that had him bracing for trouble. She pulled the tie on her side and wriggled. Her dress dropped to the ground and left him staring at Bella's girls, all pretty and spilling over pink lace. "Then perhaps you're not looking close enough."

Her ass sashayed away from him, round and inviting as a ripe peach in a pair of matching pink peek-a-boo cheeky panties.

Jesus! Nate snapped his mouth shut. How had he not known what Bella looked like beneath her clothes? His cock recognized a missed opportunity and woke right up. She had the sort of pert, rounded shape that made his hands itch to hold on and ride her hard.

With a glance over her shoulder, she opened her front door and stepped through.

She didn't lock her front door? He snapped out of his horndog trance. "You need to lock your door," he yelled.

"Okay." She tossed him a naughty grin and shut the door.

Nate charged toward the door. Someone needed to shake some sense into Bella. He grabbed the handle.

Click.

Motherfucker! She'd locked the door. Right in his face.

Chapter Seven

Bella choked down another mouthful of ketchup with a side of Nana's cottage pie. If anything tasted worse than Nana's lasagna, it had to be her cottage pie. The oozing gray mess on her plate turned her stomach and she swallowed hard.

Nana had stocked her freezer before she left for Florida because everyone knew Bella couldn't cook. Apparently she came by that honestly, but right now food was food. She'd woken late, hangover jangling, and felt too bad to make it to the store.

Her phone chimed from the table, telling her a new text message waited.

Nana couldn't text, so no chance of it being her, but she would bet it was one of her family, checking in to be sure nobody had murdered her since this time yesterday. Not that her family would talk to her right now. The telephone dustup with Nana earlier today pretty much had taken care of that. Still smarting from the internet site, Nana had ripped into her when she'd refused to pop over to the family house to pick up the store's Christmas decorations. Bella had her own ideas for Christmas in the store this year, and Nana's throwback plastic reindeer and foldout paper bells did not form part of it.

Bella dragged the phone closer. It could be Liz with another great idea for tonight. God help her. She still hadn't recovered from last night, but she did want to dig a bit about Noel.

The display read *My Adam*. Huh? A very flattering five texts, all of which she had missed because of her need for an afternoon nap.

The latest one read: "When can I see you again?"

The other four were variations on the same theme.

She needed to fill in the blanks around last night. In the meantime, Adam needed a reply. Five texts earned him that much. What would a smart girl say, one in control of her destiny?

Let me check my schedule. She hit Send and then immediately regretted it. What if he took that as a brush-off? Or she came across as a total bitch?

Her phone vibrated in her hand. I'll be waiting.

She got the sweet flutters in her belly. He'd be waiting to find out when she could fit him into her schedule.

A light tapping on her kitchen door dragged her scratchy eyeballs away from the phone.

Nate Evans lounged on the other side of her kitchen door as if *GQ* had posed him there.

It took a minute to register that she hadn't conjured him up in a wave of last night's alcohol fumes. He was actually leaning against her doorjamb.

She climbed to her feet. Black waves of dizzy hit her and she breathed deep until they cleared.

Nate waved from the other side of the glass and straightened. Damn the man for undulating into standing in a ridiculous ripple of muscled beauty. She opened the door to a blast of frigid air.

"Hey." He jerked his chin at her.

"Hey." Okay, she couldn't stand there and ogle him for the rest of the night. Besides, she had given the ogling a break. "What brings you around?"

"This." Nate held up a dress in his hand. Her dress. The one she had been wearing last night.

"Where did you find it?" Bella took the dress from him and hugged it to her chest. When she'd woken up that morning and found it gone, she'd been gutted.

Smirking, Nate cocked his head. "You don't remember?"

"Remember what?" Bella pushed open her door.

"Goddamn it, Bella!" Nate's yell stopped her. "I told you to lock your doors."

"Pfft." She flapped her hand at him. "The sheriff in this town is a quick draw."

"Don't make light of this." He tracked her across her small kitchen. "Not locking your door is asking for trouble."

"I know." Her day caught up with her and she didn't care to argue. "I forgot. I'll make a point to remember."

"Good." He shrugged out of his coat, pulled out a chair, and sat.

Bella blinked at him.

He rested his elbows on the table as if he had every intention of staying a while. Dressed in worn jeans and a tight T-shirt, he looked to be off-duty. Biceps bulged out of his sleeves and took her thought processes with them.

"Can I get you anything?" Bella laid her dress over a chairback.

"A beer would be great," he said.

Bella turned and opened her fridge. She took a moment to stare at the contents. What the hell was Nate Evans doing in her kitchen? Again.

"What is this?" He pushed her plate of half-eaten, ketchup-drenched cottage pie across the table.

"Dinner."

"That's just horrible."

Bella shrugged. "It beats cooking for myself."

He shuddered. "I should cook for you sometime."

Nate had no idea why that had come out of his mouth. Even more pertinent, what the hell was he doing in her kitchen? Staring at her ass, that's what. The same ass he hadn't gotten out of his head all day. Her ass even had him jacking off in the shower that morning.

Some things you couldn't unsee, and it turned out Bella's ass was one of those things. Even now, neatly covered in jeans, he could see it.

What color were her panties today? She struck him as a matching bra and panties type of girl.

She turned with his beer. Her breasts jiggled a little beneath her silky shirt. They were proving hard to forget as well. So, like the dog he was, here he sat waiting to catch another glimpse of that Bella. Why? No clue; he was running on pure instinct.

"So last night?" He took a pull of his beer. "You don't remember?"

She collapsed into a chair opposite him "I take it there's a story to why you have my dress."

"Nah." He shrugged. The idea of teasing her had lost its appeal and she looked tired. Dark shadows stained the skin beneath her eyes. She also looked sad. "You okay?"

"Not really." Her long, slim throat worked as she swallowed. "I woke up with a hangover, and that was the high point of my day."

"Wanna talk about it?" Did that come out of his mouth? Mr. Detached and Cool?

"It's Nana." She grimaced. "I made her really mad today."

Not too hard to do, Old Lady Erikson was hell on wheels. "What happened?"

She blinked her big blues at him. "You don't really want to hear this."

"No, I do," he said. Bella looking sad was like a kick in the balls. Ghost Falls's sweetheart should never get that droopy turn to her mouth. "Tell me."

"Christmas decorations." She winced and got up and went back to the fridge.

Nate waited.

"We had a fight about the Christmas decorations for the store."

"And you lost?" He waved away her offer of another beer.

"Nope." She collapsed into her chair and propped her chin on her palm. "I won. And that's the problem."

She looked like her dog had died. "If you won, why the face?"

"I never win," she said. Then she grimaced. "Nobody ever wins an argument with Nana. It's like family folklore or something."

Now that he could believe. Old Lady Erikson was tougher than boot leather and as fast as the speed of light to let rip with her opinions. "Ah." He nodded. "My mother does the same thing. Except she cries."

"Well, I made Nana cry today."

Nate tried to picture it and failed. Instead he got a visual of Old Lady Erikson storming into the homecoming dance and giving Bella's date hell. He couldn't remember who Bella had taken to senior year homecoming. Bella had left the dance with her chin up and her eyes glittering with unshed tears. "She cried? About Christmas decorations?"

"It's more complicated than that." Bella picked at the label on his empty beer bottle. "It's also about Gina."

"Gina?" Nate tried to place the name.

Bella grimaced. "My sister. My twin, actually. She died."

Now he remembered. Bella's mom had given birth to twins, one of whom hadn't made it. He gentled his tone. "What about her?"

"They miss her." She peeled the beer label in one go. "I always feel like I need to make up for her not being around." Before he could tell her how wrong that was, she shrugged and said, "The fight with Nana has been building for a while, and today it exploded."

He made a noncommittal noise because already he'd allowed himself to get more involved than he should.

"It's about me taking control at the store." Bella shrugged. "Nana doesn't want to let go and I have plans for the store."

"But it's your store, isn't it?"

"Yup." Bella tore the loose label into bits. "I own it fair and square, but she always thinks of it as her business. She built it, you know?"

"Yeah, but that doesn't mean she can keep hold of it."

"I know." Bella sighed, and it ripped a tiny strip off him. "But she doesn't see it that way. Neither do my mom and dad."

"Bella." He gripped her fingers across the table. "The store is yours. You have to do what you think is right with it."

"Yes, but Nana built it from nothing. That store raised all of us. After Dad lost his job, Nana and the store kept food on the table. She didn't have to sell it to me."

"It's yours, babe."

She blinked at him, long and slow, like one of those Disney princesses. "Okay."

And suddenly he wanted to grab her up and hug her until the sadness disappeared from her eyes. He got to his feet, sending the chair scraping across the kitchen. "I gotta go."

"Okay." She stood with him. "You never did tell me how you ended up with my dress."

"Another day." He had to get out of there before he gave in and did something stupid. "Actually, I lied, it was outside."

"But—"

"See you around." He almost ran for the door. One more look at that cute frown on her face and he would blow this.

He slammed the door behind him, stopped, and waited. "Lock the door!"

Chapter Eight

The next day, Bella dressed in a great tailored pencil skirt and paired it with a top that gave a peek-a-boo shadow of cleavage. Not enough to make Pippa raise an eyebrow about too much boobage in the morning but still give a hint at what lay beneath. She hopped into her car and listened to Dr. Childers tell her to "Go forth and be your power" all the way to work.

She popped into Mugged and bought her caramel, fat-free latte but changed up her banana-nut muffin for a crois-sant. Last night had marked an epoch in the evolution of Bella. She'd sat at her kitchen table and chatted—yes, chatted—to Nate Evans like they were old friends. Progress!

Juggling her breakfast, she answered her phone. "Hi, Dad."

"Hi, sweetheart. I thought I'd ask Pete from next door to bring around the Christmas decorations." Dad sounded sheepish. "In case, you know, you changed your mind."

"That would be a waste of Pete's time." Bella flipped on the lights. "I haven't changed my mind."

Dad took a long, deep breath. "Sweetheart, your nana

never slept a wink last night. This thing has got her all upset."

Guilt gave a hard yank as Bella put her coffee and croissant on the counter. "I'm not trying to upset her. I'm sorry this is hard for her."

"You have to understand Nana, sweetheart. Everything she does is for the good of the family."

And that made everything Nana did above reproach. Bella's hand clenched around the phone. "I know she means well, but the store is stuck in a time warp, and it's not going to survive if I don't bring it into this century."

Nana's voice sounded in the background. "Yes, I'm talking to Bella," Dad said. "Progress is good." His voice grew stronger again. "We all believe that, but rushing into things is dangerous."

Nana's voice again, words garbled but tone as strident as ever.

"I'm not rushing into anything." Bella sipped her latte and waited as Nana had her say in the background. "I need to run the store my way."

"I know that, sweetheart, but isn't there some middle ground? Somewhere you and Nana can meet?"

"That girl is too stubborn to meet anyone anywhere," Nana yelled.

Dr. Childers never said how difficult this owning-your-power thing really was. "I don't see how, Dad, when it's Nana's way or the highway."

"I can see why you would say that. It's just that we're a family, Bella. Families stick together." He sighed. "We always stick together. It's what gets us through hard times."

The double one-two, head-and-heart strike almost had her buckling under. Nobody ever spoke outright about Gina, especially not if Mom could hear. Instead, they fudged over that part of their history and called it hard times. "If Nana would give a bit, I could do that. But you know what she's like."

"All right, sweetheart." Her father's voice drooped. "I guess we'll see you when we get back. Think about what I've said."

"Sure, Dad." Like she hadn't run circles around her own head trying not to upset her family.

"You're still a member of this family, sweetheart. We love you."

"Love you too." Bella hung up and picked at the pointy crescent edge of her croissant. No matter what Dr. Childers said, it sucked to be the family bad guy. She'd towed the line her whole life. Nana picked out her wardrobe in elementary school and dictated what sports a girl should play. She had accepted Nana's approved date for prom and worn the dress Nana picked out from the store.

Dad had no idea how long this had been building. If you smiled like you were happy, it was enough for him. This feeling of drifting like a passenger in her own life had grown steadily, getting worse as she took over the store. Then Pippa had come back to town two years ago and Bella had had to face the truth. She had been absent in her own life up to this point, floating along on a Nana-sanctioned cloud of happy.

It was pathetic. At thirty-four she still lived another woman's life. Tried to compensate her family for having only one child when there should have been two of them. Even her crush on Nate seemed like another way of avoiding actually living her life.

Bella finished her latte and went about getting the store ready for the day. Hurting Nana or Dad was never the plan. She loved them, but the cost of that love had become too expensive.

The door opened and Debbie Palmer walked in with a

beaming smile behind a massive arrangement of red roses. "Look what I have."

"For me?" Only Dad had ever sent her flowers. Bella's heart gave a little skip. "Who are they from?"

"Read the card." Debbie placed the vase beside the cash register and stepped back. She tilted her head and then moved the arrangement slightly over and gave it a turn. "There."

Bella plucked the card from its plastic holder amid the flowers.

"I'm counting the days. Adam."

Wow! Stuff like this didn't happen to her. This was straight from a romcom. Bella's cheeks heated as she tucked the card under the register. Her day suddenly got a whole lot brighter.

"Who are they from?" Pale blue eyes alight, Debbie rocked on her toes.

Bella tried for nonchalant. "A guy I met."

"Some guy." Snorting, Debbie rolled her eyes. "That's some guy to send you roses like this after you just met him."

A little quiver of warm and nice slid down Bella's spine. She'd never been the woman other women envied. It felt a bit selfish but also really nice. "Yup."

Debbie stared at her, waiting for more.

A known gossip, Debbie would share this with everyone who would listen and this Adam thing didn't really exist yet. With a casual shrug, Bella slid behind the desk and moved the flowers an inch over to the left.

"Well, see you around." Debbie threw her one more look before she left with a sniff.

Bella waited for the door to tinkle shut, then buried her nose in the velvet crimson roses. Maybe this was some sort of sign that she was on the right track. From her bag, she dug out her phone and found Adam's texts from yesterday.

I got the flowers. They're lovely. Thank you.

She stroked one petal with her forefinger.

Her phone buzzed. Beautiful roses for a beautiful lady.

It sounded a little trite and practiced, but hey, he'd sent her flowers.

A new text popped onto her screen. Can I see you tonight?

Cosmo had led her right so far. No need to sound too eager. Sorry. Busy tonight.

Tomorrow?

Sorry, I have plans. She found an emoji sad face and sent it. Then she waited, heart pounding. Had she pushed too far?

Friday?

Taking a deep breath, Bella counted the recommended two minutes the article spoke about. Okay, they also said not to use smiley faces or emojis, but she was new to this coy thing. Friday is good for me.

See you then. Her phone buzzed. I'm looking forward to it.

She stamped on the urge to type back *me too* and settled for another smiley face.

She had a date. With a man who liked her. And he'd sent her flowers. Bella had to sit down to take it all in. Dr. Childers was right: Action equaled positivity and positivity had momentum. Time for a little more action. She picked up her phone and dialed a number she'd been putting off.

"Hey, Matt," she said when he answered. "Pippa said I should give you a call. I have a renovation project I want to talk to you about."

* * *

Liz popped by on Wednesday but remained tight-lipped about the talk with her ex. They ended up ordering pizza and watching chick flicks.

Friday rolled around faster than Bella would have expected.

Matt came by the store that morning and she went over her plans for the renovation.

"No problem." He smiled his great country-boy grin, which hadn't changed despite the big business he did with his brother Eric. "I'll send some guys around to take measurements. We'll work up a plan and then we can talk final numbers."

"Well, hello, Matt." Liz breezed into the store, whipping off her sunglasses as she came. Poured into a pair of red jeans, flashing a little midriff, she sashayed over to him.

Bella bit back her irritation as she recognized vintage Liz from before their fledgling friendship had started.

"Liz." Matt nodded and gathered up his papers. "I'll call you," he said to Bella. "And Pippa told me to remind you about Saturday."

"I'll be there," Liz purred.

Matt went a little pale but rallied. "Great." His voice boomed off the walls. A hasty exit set the bell above the door jangling.

"God." Liz threw herself on the sofa and dropped her bag beside her. "All those Evans men are seriously hot. I mean *haaawt*. I would so like to bounce one of them around my bedroom."

A hot surge of irritation shot through Bella and her mouth puckered up in a way she guessed must look a lot like Nana.

"What?" Liz narrowed her eyes at her. "You've got that look on your face."

"I don't." Bella fussed with some flyers on her desk. "What look?"

"Yeah, you do." Rising to her feet, Liz jabbed a sparkly blue nail at her. "It's the same one you wore every other time we ran into each other."

"No, I didn't."

"Did too." With a smirk, Liz crossed her arms over her chest. "I know it well."

Stumped for a comeback, Bella went with airy. "Did you come in for anything specific or just to say hi?"

Liz shrugged. "Just to say hi."

"Great." It sounded a little overenthusiastic, so Bella toned it down. "Hi."

"Tell me what's with the face."

Bella went hot and then cold. Her hands shook as she moved a pot of pens over to the right and back again. She didn't fight because it made her want to throw up, but Liz looked determined with her jaw sticking out like that. She reached deep and hauled out a stronger version of Bella. "You flirted with Matt."

"And?" *Tap, tap, tap* went Liz's dominatrix-type boot on the carpet.

"He's married." Why did she even have to explain this? "So?"

Bella snapped her jaw shut before she caught flies. "You can't go around flirting with married men."

"I flirted with him, Tight-butt Bella, I didn't fuck him."

The world skewed a little to the left before righting itself. Her hands flew away from her and knocked over her pen holder. "What did you call me?"

"Tight-butt Bella." Liz stuck out her hip. "Just like you've been calling me Headlights."

"Wh . . . well . . ." Nothing. Not a coherent thought in her brain. "Tight-butt?"

"Yeah." Liz tossed her head. "Because you always look like you have a stick up your ass. At least that's how you look when I'm around."

"I do—"

"You know what?" Liz snatched her bag and tossed it over her shoulder. "This isn't going to work. You think I'm the town whore and I think you're the town nun. We don't like each other." She adjusted the strap on her shoulder. "We had a bit of fun. No hard feelings. See ya."

On that, she stormed out the door, setting the bell jangling, but not before Bella caught the hurt hidden behind all that glittering anger.

"Damn." Legs shaking, she tottered over to the sofa and sat. The heavy musk of Liz's perfume hung in the air. She did have a look when Liz appeared. At least she used to, until the hanging of the Christmas lights. Nana had that same look when she disapproved of something someone did. In Nana's case, the look made it onto her face all the time.

Was she that bad?

Bella got up and stood before one of the floor-length mirrors. Her eyes looked too big in her pale face, but it didn't really echo Nana's pursed-up face. Dredging up Liz flirting with Matt, she tried again.

Her squeak sounded loud in the empty store. Nana stared back at her. "No."

Light shone from Liz's windows and spilled golden onto her snowy yard as Bella arrived home that night. She'd thought about it all day, and she didn't want to lose her friendship with Liz. Okay, too soon to call it a friendship, but she liked Liz.

Before she chickened out, she strode up Liz's walk and rang the doorbell.

Liz yanked open the door and glared at her. "Yes?"

"You left today."

"Yeah." Liz sneered. "That's what I do when I know someone doesn't want me there."

"The thing about Tight-butt hurt."

"Oh, and Headlights is so much better." Liz crossed her arms, hunching her shoulders up around her ears.

Bella gathered her courage. "You're right. It's not a nice thing to call you, but I don't call you that anymore. Not since I got to know you a bit better."

"Huh?" Liz looked like she might stay mad for a long time.

"Anyway." Bella motioned toward her house. "I have to go, but I wanted to say sorry about Headlights."

She turned and walked back to her house.

Liz's voice stopped her before she hit her porch. "Going anywhere special?"

"I have a date." Her nerves started up, saying it aloud.

"With that guy from the bar?"

"Uh . . . yes." Liz had seemed far too busy with Noel to notice much at the bar.

"He the one who sent you flowers?"

Debbie had a big mouth and must have been exercising it. "Yes."

Liz took a couple of steps onto her porch. "I don't call you Tight-butt anymore either."

Warmth flickered into life inside Bella's chest. "Good. I'm glad."

"I still think you're a bit uptight." Liz rubbed her arms against the cold. "But you have potential."

"Thanks; I think."

Liz grinned. "And I totally overreacted today." She trotted across the lawn separating their houses. "I just get so mad when I think people are judging me."

Maybe if Liz toned down the vamp routine people might not judge her so harshly. Then again, maybe if people took the time to get to know Liz, they wouldn't be so quick to judge. Of course, Bella chickened out of saying any of that and nodded.

"So." Liz stopped at the bottom of the porch. "What are you wearing tonight?"

A tiny, wavering olive branch but held out to her nonetheless. "I don't know. Want to help me decide?"

For a woman who dressed herself like a pole dancer, Liz surprised Bella with her taste. They agreed on a slightly retro slim-fit dress that curved in all the right places but didn't scream desperate. They went understated on the makeup and the hair loose and wavy.

Bella checked herself out. Somehow, they'd achieved the right balance between looking like you took the date seriously and not as if you hadn't had a date in three years. Not that Bella intended to admit that to anyone. Ever.

Shallow Ghost Falls dating pool aside, Bella took some of the blame for her dating dearth. When you spent your teens fixated on one man to the exclusion of all others—and a man who didn't share your fixation—you got in the habit of having no man.

On Liz's advice, she called Wheeler Barrows for a lift.

"If the date goes well, Adam will be driving you home," Liz said. "But don't, whatever you do, sleep with him on the first date."

Bella snorted. "Is that your dating philosophy?"

"Ah, hell no." Liz scrunched up her face. "But I date to get laid. I'm thinking it's different for you, so hold on to the poontang."

Who but Liz said poontang? Still, Bella had no intention of handing over the . . . er . . . poontang.

"And if the date's a total bust." Eating her leftover Halloween candy, Liz lounged on her bed. "You get Wheeler to take you home and you don't have to do the awkward failed-date car ride."

Wheeler pulled up outside her door in time to stop her joining Liz at the Halloween candy. Nerves hiked up her need for chocolate.

"Wow, Bella." Wheeler got out and opened the door for her. His cheeks went a little pink. "You look really nice."

The only Barrows kid who amounted to much, he was saving for college by running the one and only Ghost Falls taxi. Rumor had it that Pippa's grandmother, the former opera diva Philomene St. Amor, had helped him buy the car. Then again, Philomene had her bejeweled fingers in all sorts of Ghost Falls pies.

Still, he deserved a good tip, and his compliment had given her a little bit of desperately needed confidence.

Adam waited in a small reception area in front of the restaurant. A broad smile on his handsome face, he stood as she came in. "Bella." He took her hand and kissed it. "You're well worth the wait."

The hand-kissing she could have skipped, but the sincere warmth in his brown eyes fizzled through her like moon rock candy on her tongue. "You look nice yourself."

She meant it. In a dark, beautifully cut suit with a crisp white shirt and understated tie, Adam looked great.

As he guided her through the bar, several women gave him a quick eye strip. "I thought we'd have a drink first and then get some dinner." He pulled out her barstool for her. "Unless you're hungry."

"I'm good with that." A drink would settle those remaining butterflies.

"Perfect." He beamed at her. "Shall I order for you?"

"Umm . . ."

"Appletini?"

Not again. She still had that vague notion that something had happened with her dress and Nate that she really needed to remember. "I'll have a glass of white wine."

"I was sure you were drinking appletinis when we met." He looked even more handsome when he frowned.

"I was." She smiled and decided to skip the explanation. "But I feel like something else tonight."

"Great." He smiled, but the crease between his brows lingered. When he turned back from placing their order, Clark Kent was back in place. "So, tell me all about Bella."

"There's not much to tell really. Raised in Ghost Falls. Still in Ghost Falls. I took over the family business."

He raised his eyebrows, which she took as a sign to tell him more.

"It's a high-end women's clothing store. Called Bella's." Her face heated. She would love to change the name, but that fight she didn't have the stomach for. One thing for certain: If she ever had a daughter, she wouldn't be naming her any permutation of Bella. In fact, she wouldn't be naming her anything vaguely Italian-sounding. With a last name like Erikson, it only led to confusion. "At least I'm making it into a high-end clothing store."

"What is it now?"

Jo appeared on the other side of the bar with their drinks. "Hey, Bella."

"Jo." Bella liked the one Evans sister. It had to have been

tough growing up with all those brothers. "You working here now?"

"Yeah." Jo scrunched up her nose. "Trying to make up shifts to pay for college." She arranged a coaster beneath Bella's wine. "I mean, Matt or Eric would totally pay for it, but I want to do this myself."

Bella knew exactly what she meant. "I think it's great that you are."

Jo laughed, a beautiful flash of white teeth and sparkling eyes. "Yeah, just a lot tougher."

Adam cleared his throat.

"Ah." Heat crept back over her face. She smiled an apology at Adam. "I'm sorry. Adam, this is Jo Evans. An old friend. Jo, this is Adam . . ."

"Smith." Adam held his hand out to Jo. "Adam Smith."

"Seriously?" As she took his hand, Jo grinned.

Adam flushed and rolled his eyes. "Seriously. It's only one step away from John Smith. Nice to meet you, Jo."

Adam lifted his scotch and toasted Bella. "To the most beautiful woman in the room."

"Anyway." Jo swiped her cloth over the bar. "I don't want to interrupt. I'd better get back." She made a vague waving motion toward the other end of the bar.

"Bye, Jo." Bella fanned her face. Admittedly, she was a blusher, but this beat her all-time record, set at the time she'd had to act as Nate's wife in drama class.

"Why don't we move into the restaurant?" Adam cupped her elbow and boosted her off the barstool. "Then I can have you all to myself."

Chapter Nine

The rest of the evening went so smoothly, Bella had to keep reminding herself they were on a first date.

Adam stayed attentive throughout. He didn't even peek at Blythe Barrows's on-display cleavage as she served their meal.

Bella accepted a lift home from him happily.

The ride down the mountain stayed light and fun. Adam drove a brand-new Lexus, as clean inside as the gleaming exterior. Only when he stopped in front of her house did tension ooze into the car. Here it came, the awkward moment. The how-well-did-this-date-really-go moment.

"Thank you for a lovely evening." Bella squeezed the words out a little breathily. And, seriously, could she have picked anything lamer to say than that? She needed a crash course with Liz on dating repartee. On second thought, she shuddered to think what Liz would blurt out in this situation. All of which kept her from having to think about this moment.

Adam watched her with a slight smile. "You seem uncomfortable."

"I am." Bella let out her held breath. "This is always the worst moment."

"It doesn't have to be." Adam turned off the ignition and shifted to face her. "I had a great time tonight, Bella. I'd like to do it again soon."

"Me too." Anytime now, the universe could step in with a good line or two.

Leaning closer, Adam cupped her cheek. "I'd really like to kiss you."

"Okay."

His lips against hers were firm, nice. He smelled great, woodsy and fresh all at the same time. Adam pulled away slightly. "Relax, Bella, this is as far as my move goes."

Officially, the most ridiculous woman anyone had dated ever. "It's not that. I haven't done this in a while."

"Dated?"

"Yes."

"Kissed?"

"Yes." She needed to stop this before they stumbled over her three-year dry period. A time and place for letting that out of the bag would crop up, but the first date wasn't it. Bella pressed her mouth to Adam's.

Adam tasted nice, nice enough to start a small flutter in her belly, nice enough to raise her body temperature. Okay, the earth didn't move, bells didn't ring, and her knees stayed firmly where they should. But nice was good. A good start anyway.

Adam drew back and stroked her cheek. "Good night, my Bella."

"Good night."

He came around the car and opened the door for her. His

handsome face wore a gentle expression as he kissed her cheek. "I'll see you soon?"

"Sure." Bella made it up the walkway and into her house without tripping over her feet. She closed the door behind her and leaned against it. She'd done it. Her first date that didn't feel like she'd used a stand-in for Nate.

Bella floated into Mugged the next morning and went all out on a double mochaccino with whipped cream. She hesitated over the chocolate croissant and then went for it. Tinker Bell had curves and she rocked them. This being Saturday, she opened a little later than the weekdays.

A bouquet of flowers took up most of the space in front of the door. A seriously large bunch of flowers that she had to hop over to get into the store. Leaving her coffee and croissant on the store counter, she went back to pick them up.

Red roses, rich and velvety, with dark blue irises poking out between them. She pulled the card of the plastic holder.

"I can't wait to see you again. Adam."

Lord, Debbie must have had a field day with that over at the florist's.

Nate met Daniel at one of the fancy bars where the new rash of tourists hung out. Daniel must have changed one helluva lot to be hanging out in a place like this now.

Jo looked up from behind the bar as he walked in and nodded. She moved down the bar to put two glasses of wine in front of another customer. She'd lost weight in the last couple of months and her jeans now hung low on her hips.

"Hey, Jo-Jo. Didn't you work last night?" He eased onto a barstool.

Her smile didn't quite hide the dark smudges under her

eyes. "Yup. They're busier than expected, so I got to pick up a couple of extra shifts."

"You coming to Pippa and Matt's thing later?"

She shrugged. "Depends what time I get off shift. I'll try to show my face later."

"Do that." Jo had her fair share of pride. Stiff-necked like the rest of the Evans kids, so Nate chose his next words carefully. "Doesn't all this work mess with your studying?"

Out came her stubborn chin and he cursed himself. "I know what I'm doing."

"I know that." He grabbed her hand from across the bar and gave it a squeeze. "You look tired is all."

"I'm okay." Her face softened and she returned his squeeze before dropping his hand.

"You let me know if that changes." He held her stare. "I'm not rolling in it like Eric and Matt, but I've got enough set aside to help my little sister out."

Shit! Jo must be tired because she dropped her head, but not before he caught the glimmer of tears in her eyes. "I'm okay."

"I know that, but you don't have to fly solo on this."

"Yes." She sniffed. "I do." Her gaze met his, hers full of resolve. "I have to do this on my own. You get that, don't you?"

He did get it, and Nate nodded. Jo, Isaac, and he owed their big brother Matt everything. When Dad died, Matt had stepped in like some kind of modern-day superhero and taken over as man of the house. He'd turned down a full-ride scholarship to run their dad's failing business. Matt did everything. Put food on the table, propped up their mother, and even kicked their asses to get their homework done.

Isaac had disappeared, having some sort of late-life rebellion. But he and Jo, they'd had their rebellion on Matt's watch, and they both would die before they made their adult problems Matt's.

Happily married to kick-ass Pippa and in business with Eric, Matt had found his bit of magic now. He'd sacrificed everything for them, and Nate would be damned before he asked Matt for one more thing. He nodded to Jo. "Yeah, I know."

Down the bar, a blond guy signaled Jo for his check and she moved away.

The guy from the other night, the night that had started an ongoing series of filthy morning shower sessions with Bella playing the starring role in his imagination. The guy looked up, caught him watching, and nodded a greeting.

Jo came back and ran the guy's credit card.

"You know that guy?" He kept his voice low enough not to reach the other patrons.

Jo glanced at the card. "Adam," she read. "Adam Smith. Yeah, I think he's staying at the resort."

The guy gave Nate a bad feeling. "Stay away from him."

"Huh?" Jo eyed him askance. "I serve him drinks. What's your problem with him anyway?"

"I dunno." Because he really didn't, and some part of him got that he was being a dick for no reason. "Just a feeling I get."

"Uh-huh." Jo cocked her head and grinned.

"What?"

She smirked. "This have anything to do with the fact that he was in here last night with Bella?"

"No! What?"

"Last night." Jo leaned her elbows on the counter, her eyes laughing at him. "He and Bella looked pretty cozy."

"Did Bella drink?" He didn't want to think about the bolt of unadulterated possessiveness that shot through him.

"A little." Jo moved back and grabbed Adam the Dickhead's credit card and the slip.

"Well, next time she comes in with him, you cut her off at one."

Jo scrunched her face at him. "Are you serious right now?"

"As a death threat." And he ought to know what happened to Bella when she went over her limit.

"Sure, Nate." Jo rolled her eyes. "I'll start cutting off my paying customers at one drink. Or do you think I should substitute with soda?"

Smart-ass. Nate tried to hide his grin and failed. He was being a jerk. If Bella wanted to get hammered and strip in front of Adam the Dickhead, it really was none of his business. "Just keep your eye on her, if you can."

"Will do." With a perky salute, Jo went back down the bar.

Adam signed his slip, nodded to Nate, and left. He almost collided with Daniel on his way in. Both men nodded to each other and moved away.

Daniel Carver hadn't changed much. He looked older, but then, they all did. His face was leaner and he'd bulked up some, but Nate would still have picked him out in a crowd.

"Hey." Daniel took the stool next to him. "Sorry I'm late. I got caught up in a thing."

Nate's hackles came up. Daniel's *things* did no good for anybody. "What thing?"

In the midst of taking off his jacket, Daniel stopped. He stared at Nate for a moment before he shrugged out of it and laid it over the back of the stool. "A volunteer thing. For charity." He settled his ass on the stool. "And before you ask, I'm not the charity."

It dragged a smile out of him, and Nate said, "Sorry. Old habits die hard."

"No worries. I earned my share of suspicion." Daniel signaled Jo for a drink.

Jo hesitated, a motion so tiny, Nate nearly didn't catch it before moving over. "Hey, Daniel. What can I get you?"

"Coke." Daniel showed his teeth in a tight smile.

"Coming right up." Jo sounded a little too jaunty.

What the hell? Nate turned from his sister and looked at Daniel. "Something going on I should know about?"

"Like what?" Daniel lied like a man born to it, which was exactly what he was. Daniel came from one of those families that made social workers tear their hair out. Alcoholic mother, flyby father who bounced in and out of the hospitality of the state. You didn't have to look far to find the reason why Daniel had ended up like he had.

"Like stay away from my sister."

Daniel opened his mouth and shut it again. He nodded. "No problem, man."

"I mean it." Nate kept his eye on Jo as she slid the soda in front of Daniel.

"Got it." Daniel sipped his drink. He turned to face Nate. "Thanks for meeting me."

A platitude almost made its way out of his mouth before Nate stopped it. He had to be at Pippa and Matt's thing in an hour, and he and Daniel had gone way past this. "Why did you want to meet?"

Daniel took a deep breath, turning his glass around on the cardboard coaster. "Yeah, this isn't so easy."

Nate's nape prickled. He didn't want to hear about another of Daniel's fast-track-to-riches schemes.

"So, you know I've just gotten out of prison," Daniel said.

Nate nodded.

"And I got into a program while I was inside. AA actually."

No shit! Nate had to snap his mouth shut. Daniel had always liked his beer, but AA? "You did?"

"Yup. Turns out I take after my mother." Daniel twisted his glass until the one edge matched with the edge of the coaster. "After you took old Sheriff Wheeler up on his offer, things got a bit more out of hand for me. Actually, they got way, way out of hand."

"No shit." This time he did say it out loud.

"Anyway . . . Cut a long story short, I ended up a guest of Uncle Sam, ended up in my first meeting just because I heard they had better coffee than the shit they served the rest of us, and stayed to hear what they had to say."

Nate knew the program. He'd guided a couple of people into it over the years. "Is this like an eighth-step thing?"

"Ninth step." Daniel cleared his throat. "This is a ninth-step thing, and if you give me a minute to find my balls, I'll get right on it."

"Fuck me." Nate had trouble getting his head around this. When Daniel said he'd changed, he'd meant changed-changed, like really changed. "I never thought we would be having this conversation."

Daniel laughed and took a sip of his soda. "Yeah, me neither."

And when Daniel did a ninth step, he went all out. Spared himself no detail, cut himself no slack. Some of this stuff Nate really didn't like to think about anymore. It reminded him how close he'd come to slipping off the knife edge. He and Daniel, with a small group of others, had run wild for a few years there. Blurring the line of legal on more than one occasion. Jesus, he'd gotten lucky.

"And that's it." Daniel's hand shook as he reached for his soda and took a swig. "Other than the part where I ask for your forgiveness."

"You got it." Nate didn't even have to think about it.

Daniel had paid his debt and, knowing what it was like for ex-cons, would continue to pay it for a while longer. An uneasy silence fell between them. "Do we hug or something now?"

Daniel jerked. "Do you want to?"

"Hell no!"

Chapter Ten

The call came in as he left the bar, on his way to Dame Philomene's place. Nate would like to call it a house, but Phi's Folly defied any attempt to put a name on it.

"Two-thirty to four-fifteen."

He answered the radio. "What's up, Gabby?"

He did it to mess with her. Deputy Gabby had a thing about proper radio protocol. "Four-fifteen, we have a possible—"

"Cut the crap, Gabby. What's going on?"

"Headlights." She nearly spat the word. "Seems she's had her regular prowler around again tonight. Want me to send someone else?"

Shit! Gabby must be having a horrible day not to get on him about procedure. "Nah." Nate didn't have the heart to do that to Jeff. "I'm going right by there on my way. I'll look in."

"Ten-four." Gabby's voice crackled.

The street looked quiet as he pulled up, but no big surprise there. Liz was a couple of days late on her call-in.

Liz opened the door, bright red underwear, which answered the question loud and clear as to how she'd earned her nickname, escaping her bathrobe.

"Sheriff." She purred and did this rubbing thing against the doorjamb. "If I'd known you would come, I would have worn something more appropriate."

Ah, hell no. Nate dug his hands into his utility belt. He didn't even want to think what Headlights considered appropriate. "Gabby says you have a prowler. Again."

She glared at him. "I do."

"Uh-huh" He had a schedule to keep here. "Liz, my family is waiting for me. Can we get to the problem?"

"I'm invited too, you know." She straightened and twitched the collar of her bathrobe into a more modest position. "And I really did see something. At least, I think it's a prowler."

They were breaking new ground here. Normally, Liz invited him into the house to show him from which window she'd seen the prowler. Depending on how feisty she felt that night, it could be any room in the house. Nate paid better attention. "What do you mean, you think you have a prowler?"

"Not me." She grabbed a coat from the rack next to the door and slid it on. "I thought I saw someone over at Bella's."

"Bella's?"

"I'll show you."

"That's okay." Nate blocked her exit. After all, the boy who cried wolf had seen that wolf eventually. "Why don't you tell me where you thought you saw this prowler and I'll take a look?"

"Round back." Hunching her shoulders, Liz shivered. She had to be cold in those red bits of nothing. "Near the kitchen window." She frowned. "I'm not sure, though. It was a shadow really, there and then gone."

"I'll check it out." Nate leaned in and shut her front door.

Shit! He really didn't like the sound of this. And he'd put his balls on a block that Bella hadn't learned to lock her door yet.

Bella was running late, what with this being the festive season and a few last-minute shoppers looking for that perfect dress to wear to ring in the New Year. One of the best parts of owning your own clothing store was never being short of a quick change when you needed it. Slipping into a return she rather fancied, Bella freshened her makeup and locked up the store behind her. Her new Christmas wreath twinkled at her through the window, simple, elegant, and classic. Nana would hate it.

The car parked beside her own looked a lot like Adam's Lexus. In a town like Ghost Falls, coincidence didn't really factor into things, and she peered through the window.

Smiling, Adam waved back and motioned to the phone at his ear.

She waggled her fingers good-bye and drove to the diva's house.

Where else would Pippa have a get-together but at Phi's Folly?

Bella pointed her car down the sweeping, tree-lined driveway. With the house set barely a hundred feet from the road, the serpentine drive had always mystified Bella. But then, after you'd met Phi a time or two, nothing much surprised you anymore.

She'd grown up with the infamous Diva Philomene St. Amor as Ghost Falls's most illustrious resident. The diva had been born and raised in Ghost Falls and had retired here several years ago now. Bella hadn't really gotten to know Philomene—or Phi, as everyone called her—before she'd grown close to Pippa when she'd returned home under the cloud of being America's most hated celebrity.

The drive wound its way onto a wide, turning circle in front of a part Gothic mansion, part gingerbread house. People milled about in the light spilling through the windows. Phi threw a great party and, by the looks of things, nobody had turned down Pippa's invitation.

Bella parked behind a compact CUV and did one more hair and makeup check because there was a good chance Nate would be there. She might be over her crush on him, but a girl still liked to put her best foot forward.

"*Ma petite Belle!*" As she crossed the threshold, Phi descended on her. Swathed in gold spandex and glittering to rival the massive Christmas tree in the entrance hall, Phi tugged her into a patchouli-scented hug. "So small and sweet, like a special Christmas bonbon." Phi beamed at her. "We need to find some big, strong man to gobble you up."

Bella's cheeks heated. She never knew quite how to take Phi. The diva winked at her, eyelids encrusted with sparkling gold shadow, and chuckled.

"Dear God, Phi." Pippa emerged from the crowd with a rescuing arm. "Bella hasn't even stepped in the door and you've got her blushing."

"I simply cannot resist." Phi conducted the air in a clash of bracelets. "She wears that glow of radiant innocence."

Did she? Bella tripped after Pippa as the other woman led her into the throng.

"I'm going to need you," Pippa whispered. "Cressy is here and she's in fine form tonight."

Matt's mother had moods: a lot of them, all the time. After her husband's death, she'd clung to her oldest son. The arrival of Pippa, and Matt and Pippa's subsequent relationship, had exacerbated Cressy's moods.

As she and Pippa reached the midpoint in Phi's cavernous salon, Bella spotted the problem. Cressy had taken up a position by the bar. Dressed tonight in head-to-toe black, she peered into the throng with a palpable air of martyrdom.

"I'll go talk to her," Bella said. She and Cressy had a weird bond. They'd both been struck in the past by the death of a family member.

"I owe you." Pippa gave her a fierce hug. "Get yourself a strong drink while you're there."

"I'm fine." Bella had to smile at how grateful Pippa looked. She couldn't help it; she felt sorry for Cressy. Yes, she knew how toxic she could be, and she totally saw how difficult she could make life for Pippa, but Bella's heart went out to her. She couldn't help but think how unhappy Cressy must be to make life so difficult for herself and her five grown children.

"Bella." Eric Evans stepped into her path with his signature bad-boy smirk. In a beautifully tailored pair of black pants and a button-down, the second-oldest Evans brother had a definite edge to him that had most of the Ghost Falls female residents catfighting each other to get closer.

"Eric." He still managed to pull a flirtatious smile from her. Just by being Eric. He could make a nun bat her lashes.

Taking her hands, he held her away from him. His hot dark eyes wandered her from top to toe with a gleam that made her blush. "Damn, girl. You are looking fine tonight."

It was like a shot of adrenaline straight to the ego and she'd have to be long dead not to appreciate it. "You say that to all the girls."

"You're right." Eric grinned. "But I only mean it when I say it to you."

God help the woman who ever fell for that line. Bella chatted to Eric for a bit longer before threading her way over to Cressy. She knew a lot of the people here and she always enjoyed catching up.

In response to her greeting, Cressy gave her a sad smile. An attractive woman in her late fifties, all the Evans brood had inherited her dark hair and impeccable bone structure. Bella didn't remember Mr. Evans well, but he'd been a big man with a great smile and an easy laugh.

"Pippa tells me you're all alone for Christmas," Cressy said as Bella accepted a glass of wine from the barman. Typical; Phi had hired a barman who looked like you could bounce a coin off his abs.

"Yes, Nana and my parents went down to Florida. Nana says the cold makes her arthritis worse." Bella tried to inject a little enthusiasm into her voice, but the topic didn't lend itself to bubbly.

Cressy's eyes went huge. "What will you do? All on your own?"

She made *all on your own* sound like a chronic condition. "Oh, I have a plan," Bella said, feeling a bit like a chirping canary. Whenever she got around Cressy, her natural instinct to jolly the older woman along kicked in.

Cressy dug into the dip with a chip and crunched. "What sort of plan?"

"I got it off the internet." She made it sound like a miracle cure, but Bella couldn't seem to get a grip on her tone. Cressy and her glass-half-empty approach pinged her need to make happy. "It's a series of ten things to do if you find yourself alone on the holidays."

Cressy went for another chip and chewed like it was the Last Supper.

Jolly Bella went in for another try. Part of her brain—the part not twittering like a demented sparrow—wished Liz would get there and slap her. "First, I decorated the house. I put up a tree, decorated. I even managed to get some lights on the outside." All on its own, Bella's head bobbed up and down. "Well, actually, there's a funny story about my outside lights."

"Oh?" Cressy's mouth turned down at the corners. "I love funny stories."

"Well . . ." Dear God, could someone please stop her? "There I was on top of my roof, and you'll never guess what happened." Now she sounded like she was entertaining the first-grade class at Ghost Falls Elementary. "I got stuck."

"No." Cressy paused with her chip midway through the dip. How the woman managed to still fit into a size two with the way she shoveled up Tostitos and spinach-and-artichoke dip baffled Bella.

"I'm scared of heights." An honest-to-God titter escaped her. She had no backbone. Even Dr. Childers would be itching to kick her butt right now. "My neighbor had to call Nate."

Cressy's eyes sharpened. "Nate came?"

Uh-oh! One thing you never did was bring up any of her sons to Cressy. Every girl who'd grown up with the Evans brothers, especially those who aspired to date one, knew that. Stupid, stupid, stupid.

"It's his job." As fast as her four-inch heels allowed, Bella backtracked. "I'm sure the last thing he wanted to do was rescue stupid me from my roof."

"You should be more careful." Apparently pacified for now, Cressy went back to the dip. "Nate doesn't have time to rescue people who do silly things. He's the sheriff. The youngest sheriff in county history."

They stood in silence for a while. Bella finished her glass of wine. "So, how have you been?"

"Fine." The corners of Cressy's mouth headed south. "As good as I can be under the circumstances."

"Is something wrong?" Across the room, Pippa caught Bella's eye and grimaced.

Cressy took a deep breath. "I don't like to air my troubles in public. Especially not at a party."

Appeasing Bella had wrestled control once more and said, "It's not good to bottle these things up."

"You're right." Cressy sighed and accepted a glass of wine from the bartender hottie. "But it's what I do."

"Oh, well, if you don't want to talk about it." Liz had arrived and was being greeted by Phi. A fairly typical Phi greeting, if the bemused expression on Liz's face was any indication.

"It's just that he still hasn't called," Cressy said.

"Sorry?" Bella hid her grin as even Liz went beet red. The diva could make anyone blush and had a wicked knack for finding the right trigger. Dark and dirty, Phi's laugh rolled over the room. In her fantasies, Bella had a laugh like that, and she spoke like Phi, not giving a darn who heard or what they thought.

"He's my youngest, you know, and a mother never loses the desire to protect them from life."

"Absolutely." Now Phi peered down the front of Liz's dress, as she motioned toward her impressive rack. Phi looked enthralled.

"I suppose many would say it's because I coddled him too much. I only tried to protect him from the harsh realities of life."

Slipping into the Appeasing Bella personality was a godsend sometimes because she managed to say, "Who could blame you?"

"Eric does." Cressy's wrathful tone penetrated and dragged Bella's attention away from what looked like a great conversation happening between Phi and Liz. "He's always telling me to let go. He says I'm smothering all the children." Cressy grabbed a handful of chips and dipped. "It's so easy for him to speak. He doesn't have children; he doesn't understand. He doesn't even have a dog."

"Isn't he allergic—"

"I knew something was wrong, and I tried to tell all of them that. Do they listen?"

Phi motioned Pippa over with an imperious wave.

"Does who listen?"

"Everyone." Cressy sniffed. "Something is very wrong with Isaac and nobody will listen." Jabbing herself in the chest, Cressy blinked away tears. "I'm his mother and I can feel it."

So, that's what they were talking about. Isaac had left town about the time Pippa came home. "Surely if something bad had happened—"

"Matt is too busy with his married life now. I love Pippa; I really do." Cressy paused for effect. Not even Appeasing Bella could respond in the affirmative to that one. Cressy would toss Pippa off Lover's Leap if she thought she could get away with it. "Now they're having this party and they won't even tell me what it's about. You would think I would be the first person they'd tell if they had something to share. Not just fling me an invite along with everybody else."

Pippa stared at Phi, openmouthed.

Phi motioned to Liz's breasts and then her own.

Half-laughing, Pippa shook her head.

Bella so wanted to hear what they were talking about.

Nate walked through the door.

Cressy carried on talking, but Bella didn't hear a word.

Even beating Liz to the punch, Phi descended on Nate.

Still in uniform, cheeks wind flushed and hair tousled, he sent a quiver of lust through her that made her thank God for the drink in her hand.

"Nate's here." Bella cut across Cressy's soliloquy. "Maybe he's heard from Isaac." Look at her multitasking. Some of what Cressy had said must have penetrated. Then again, Cressy did tend to pick at the same scab over and over again.

"He might have." Cressy motioned to Nate. "But then, why would he tell me?"

Nate caught sight of his mother and stiffened slightly, but he still made his way over. Then his eyes met hers and he crossed the room with a lot more purpose. No, he didn't. Old habits were making her think he hurried a bit to reach her.

"Bella." He rose from kissing the cheek Cressy presented to him. "I've been looking for you," he said in that slightly raspy voice that made anything sound naughty and delicious.

Cressy locked eyes on them.

Nate's hand fastened around her arm, and the heat of it shot through every nerve ending Bella had. Every. Single. One. More Dr. Childers loomed in her future. Like tonight, as soon as she got home.

Nate's gaze bored a hole into her. "Are you listening to me?"

"Yup." It was all she had.

"I checked your door again tonight and it wasn't locked." Nate had his angry face on. Bella finally recognized it through the cloud of unfortunate lust surrounding her.

"What were you doing at Bella's house?" Suddenly all ears, Cressy's sharp glance darted between them.

"Liz called in a prowler," Nate said.

Well, there was nothing new in that.

"And I think, this time, she might have actually seen something." Nate cut off the dismissive reply Bella had all ready to launch. "You really need to be more careful."

"I'm fine. I've lived in this town my whole life and been fine."

Nate's brow clouded over in a ferocious frown. Wow, he even looked hot when he glared at her.

Her phone chimed a perfect rescue. "Excuse me."

Adam: You looked beautiful in that blue dress.

See, someone appreciated the dress. She shot a look at Nate.

He blinked at her. "What?"

"Nothing."

Adam lit up the screen again: Let's set another date.

When? she typed back.

Now :) The sooner the better.

Could he be any sweeter? She smiled down at her phone.

"Are you texting while I'm talking to you?" Nate looked more pissed off, hence even hotter.

Bella tucked her phone behind her back. "Someone texted me. I had to reply."

"Is that him?"

Bella shoved her phone in her purse. "What? Who? Him?"

"The guy from the bar." Raising one dark brow, Nate crowded her. "The one Jo saw you with."

"Bella has a man?" Cressy sounded as if such a thing lay beyond the bounds of possibility.

Combined with Nate's bossiness, it lit enough of a fuse within for Bella to say, "Yes, I have a man."

"A hot one too." Liz sidled up, eating the little air between her and Nate. She eye-stripped Nate and pursed her bright pink lips. "Seems like he has money too."

"You know this guy?" Nate switched his grumpy face to Liz.

"I've met him." Liz shrugged. "If Bella hadn't gotten in there so fast, I might have tapped that."

Cressy gasped, her hand stopping midway between the dip and her mouth. She sniffed at Liz. "That's a bit vulgar, Liz. Especially at our age."

Bella braced for a gale.

Liz cocked her hip and jammed her hand onto it. "Cressy, you're about ten years older than me and we both know it."

Say what you would about Liz, she looked incredible for her age. Especially tonight, when she'd gone for a figure-flattering black dress that had Pippa screaming from every refined seam.

Liz stuck out her chest. "Got rid of the old and now I'm going to get me some." She eyed Nate like an ice cream cone. "Might as well make it young and tasty while I'm doing it."

"Don't you dare." Cressy dropped a gooey, dip-laden chip onto Phi's lurid, floral rug. "Elizabeth Harper, you go near my son and I'll . . . I'll . . ." She opened and shut her mouth. "It'll be very bad."

She stalked off, grinding chip and dip into the carpet.

Hitching up her boobs, Liz grinned at Bella. "Worth every penny." Turning away, she gave Nate a ringing slap on the ass. "For the record, pretty boy, you're too young for me. Helluva fun to drool over, but I like a man with more tire tread on him."

Bella snapped her mouth shut as Liz sashayed away. One thing you could say about Phi, she never threw a dull party.

Nate took her arm and steered her a little ways away from the bar and into a quieter corner. "Tell me about this guy you're seeing."

What the hell? Nate never showed any interest in the men she dated. Not that there had been that many, but there had been some. A few. Okay, a very few. Three. She didn't so much date as get into tepid relationships that dribbled a long way past their sell-by date.

"I like him." She pulled her arm free. The lingering warmth from Nate's fingers still tingled on her bare arm.

"But what do you know about him?" Nate got right into her personal space bubble.

How many times had she wanted him right here, but now that he was, Bella had to suppress the urge to shove him away. Especially when he wore that carrot-up-his-bum lawman face. "That's why we're dating."

"My friends." Phi's voice cut through the chatter. For a woman who could bring Covent Garden to its knees, a Ghost Falls party, however loud, presented no problem. She clinked a fingernail against her glass. "I suppose you're wondering why I called you all here tonight."

"I called them, Phi." Pippa stepped up beside her grandmother.

Matt got between the two women and slid his arm around Pippa. "Why don't we get to our news?"

Bella got an inkling as Matt and Pippa exchanged a sweet look. The sort of look a girl went to bed every night dreaming about. "She's pregnant," Bella murmured.

"Eh?" Nate glanced down at her.

"I'm going to be stepping down from the show for a while." Pippa beamed.

A low grumble of protest greeted her words. Pippa had soared from America's most-hated celebrity to one of its best loved, her show ringing rating bells season after season.

"Because I'm going to be taking on a new role." She cuddled into Matt. "Matt and I are having a baby."

"Darling!" Cressy plowed through the crowd and flung herself at Matt. "I'm so pleased for you. You'll make a marvelous father." She glanced at Pippa with a tight smile. "Well done."

Nate groaned. "Mom just can't help herself sometimes. It's bigger than she is."

"I propose a toast." Phi raised her glass. "To the parents-to-be. And to me." A naughty grin slid over her face. "It took me years to get them to this point."

Bella lost Nate in the hugging and kissing fest that ensued. She made her way closer to Pippa. She waited patiently for others to hug Pippa. Finally, Pippa turned to her and her face softened. "Can you believe it?"

"Yes." Bella swayed her from side to side as they hugged. "You're going to be a great mother."

"And I'll be there every step of the way to see that she does," Cressy announced, raising her glass.

"Oh God," Pippa whimpered against her shoulder. "Both of us aren't going to make it through this pregnancy."

"Of course, women today think they can have their career and raise children," Cressy said to the group at large. "We didn't have those options."

"Oh yes we bloody did." Phi looked angry for the first time since Bella had known her. Face haughty, she was every inch the diva who had terrified conductors throughout the world. "There are always choices, if you're prepared to live with the consequences."

Cressy paled and slid back into the crowd.

"Now," Phi threw her arms wide, "we drink. All except Pippa, who won't be drinking for months."

"You were right about Liz," Pippa said under the congratulatory hiatus of people heading for the bar. "She's nice when you get to know her."

"Nice?" Bella tried that word on for size with Liz. "No,

she's not nice. Nice is your Sunday school teacher. But she is very genuine and she has a big heart."

"Speaking of," Pippa rolled her eyes, "Phi is now convinced she wants her boobs done. She was asking Liz about her surgeon."

Bella giggled. Look out, Liz's plastic surgeon.

Pippa's smile disappeared. "Did you know Liz had breast cancer?"

"No. I always thought she had them done after her divorce." Bella found Liz in the crowd, making eyes at Eric.

Eric seemed to be giving as good as he got. He had his face very close to Liz's neck, whispering something that made her giggle.

"You don't think she'll sleep with Eric, do you?" Pippa worried her bottom lip.

"She might." Bella shrugged. "Who could blame her?"

"Bella!" Pippa choked on her soda and came up laughing. "I've never heard you say anything like that."

"It's the new me." Bella grinned.

"I like it." Pippa gave her a hug. "And Eric looks like he can handle himself just fine."

"Eric looks fine. Period." Bella surprised herself at her own daring.

"Stay away from Eric." Nate appeared at her elbow, still glaring, only it seemed to have gotten worse now. "He's a manwhore."

Bella shook her head, not sure she'd heard that right. "So are you."

Nate clenched his jaw. "That's not the point."

"Then what is the point?"

"Yes, Nate." Pippa cocked her head and grinned. "What is the point?"

"The point is," he dragged in a deep breath, "Bella needs to be careful of the men she chooses. She has terrible taste in men."

"I had a crush on you forever." Bella couldn't believe her own balls, but she rather liked having them.

"Exactly." Nate peered down his nose at her. "Find me when you're ready to go home. I'm coming with you."

He stalked off into the crowd.

"Somehow I don't think he means what you want him to mean." Pippa frowned after him.

"Wanted." Bella tested the new sense of freedom inside her. "What I wanted it to mean. Not anymore."

Pippa eyed her skeptically. "Really?"

"Okay, maybe not quite yet. But I'm almost there."

Chapter Eleven

For their second date, Adam surprised her with a picnic at Lover's Leap. The famous make-out spot from high school, and one she'd only been invited to once—when Trent Winters took a bet from Declan Myers that he could hit a home run with the town good girl. The night of one of her biggest humiliations, because who had rescued her? Nate Evans. Of course.

Adam unveiled his surprise with so much delighted anticipation Bella didn't have the heart to tell him the history. He'd brought along a soft plaid blanket, which he spread on the ground. A second blanket he draped over her shoulders. A dark, star-speckled night twinkled around them. Cold and bracing, the air carried the hint of coming snow.

"I had the resort pack me a picnic basket," he said as he unloaded a large wicker hamper from the back of his Lexus. He put it next to her on the blanket and opened the top. "Now, let's see what we have here. Whole-wheat baguette." He held it up. "Because my lady likes it better than white. With fresh tomatoes and romaine, not iceberg lettuce. Also turkey breast because she prefers that to the deli slices. No stinky cheeses, no matter how good people say they taste."

Bella melted. He'd remembered all the things she'd told him.

"White wine." He produced the bottle. "Because red gives my lady a headache."

Bella knee-walked over to the hamper. "Oh my God, you even remembered the brownies."

The cork left the bottle with a pop. "But of course." Adam dug out two glasses. "Real glass, not plastic, because it changes the taste of the wine."

How did he remember all of that? Some men couldn't even remember their wife's birthday after years of marriage and Adam had gleaned all of this from one date.

"Wow," she said, not really sure what she could say to express how special he made her feel. Also, her butt was getting a little numb from the cold ground, but he'd gone to so much effort, she couldn't complain. "You thought of everything."

"You deserve everything." He touched his wineglass to hers. "To you."

Her face heated and she managed what could be the lamest smile ever. "It's too much."

He smiled and sipped his wine. "So, tell me all about Bella."

She'd never been the focus of so much intense attention and her mind blanked. "There really isn't that much to tell."

"Tell me about your plans for your store, then."

Something she could talk about for hours. It seemed like she did as Adam kept passing her good things to eat. She told him about her intention to renovate, how her website was getting more and more hits every day. Finally, her long-term vision for the store. "I want to create a place women can come and find themselves," she said. "Not just buy a dress but learn the best way to dress themselves."

Adam made a great listener. He even suggested a thing or two. "I get it," he said with one of his white smiles. "A place where a woman can rediscover her inner beauty."

Bella waved off his offer to refill her wineglass, wanting to stay clearheaded throughout this date. More advice from Liz, along with her rattiest pair of panties. Because, according to Liz, the sort of panties no woman would want any man to see her in made the best form of willpower. Beige grannies with sagging elastic would do the trick. "So, how come you know so much about this?"

Adam blushed and darn, it looked sweet on him. A flush of color high on his cheekbones, his gaze not meeting hers. "Google," he mumbled.

"Say what?"

"I Googled it." Adam laughed and filled his wineglass. "When I found out what you did, I Googled it so I wouldn't make an idiot of myself in front of you."

Did that not beat all!

"I like you, Bella." He took the wineglass from her hand and set it aside. "Much more than I should. You're everything I've ever wanted."

An alarm tinkled in the back of her mind. This was only their second date, but his big brown eyes stared right into hers, softening as he studied her face.

"I know it's too soon," he whispered, cupping her face. "And I know we've just met." He gave a self-deprecating chuckle. "It's crazy. I know it's crazy, but when I'm with you . . ." He feathered her lips with his. "When I'm with you, I can't seem to keep my head straight."

Bella responded to his tentative kiss and brought her arms around his neck. What girl didn't want to hear what he'd just said? Her unease disappeared under the onslaught of feel-good. Nobody had ever even hinted that they'd lost their head over her. Adam could have any woman he wanted. He had the looks, the charm, seemed to make a good living, and he'd chosen to say these things to her.

Adam slid his tongue into her mouth on a groan, deepening the kiss, taking over her mouth.

It was all a bit overwhelming. Bella tried to keep up, but Adam seemed to be totally into the kiss. Not that she wasn't. Just not as much.

He pressed his weight into her.

Bella braced. If he kept coming, he would have her on her back, and the part of her not engaged in the kiss resisted.

He broke off the kiss and slid his mouth to her neck. "You're so goddamn beautiful."

She jumped as he lightly nipped her skin.

His hands slid over her ribs, heading north.

He leaned into her.

Bella pulled back.

Adam's breathing sounded sharp and jagged, color flagging his cheekbones.

They were out here alone, and a shiver went down her spine. Not a jump-his-bones shiver but something else. This time she paid attention. "I think we should slow down."

"Slow down?" Adam reared back a little. "Are you kidding me? All I did was kiss you."

True, but the pressing back, the hands on her rib cage, the fingers very close to her breasts spoke of intention. Inside, her people-pleaser jumped up and down. This was so awkward. Bella wriggled a couple of inches between them. "Like you said, we've only just met. I'm not the sort who jumps into these things."

"These things." Adam sneered. The expression morphed

into a smile. "I want you, Bella. More than I should. Don't you want me?"

She did. Sort of. She liked him. She even liked his kisses. "Y . . . yes."

"Well, then." Adam tugged her across the blanket toward him. "I'm an adult. You're an adult. Let's see where this thing takes us."

Bella ducked his descending mouth.

His hands tightened around her hips. "No?"

"I just want to—"

"Take things slow." He pushed himself away and stood. "Any slower and we'd be going backward."

His erection pushed against his zipper. Running impatient fingers through his hair, he turned his back on her.

"I'm sorry." The words came out of her mouth before she could stop them. Even as she said them, another part of her brain jumped in and argued with her. She had nothing to be sorry for. Things had gotten a little heated for her and she'd pulled back.

"You know, Bella," he loomed over her, "I didn't have you pinned as a cocktease."

That was too much and Bella stood up. "That's a disgusting word and don't you call me that."

"What else would you call it?" He waved his arm over the blanket. "I went to all this trouble. You came out here with me. That sends a man a signal. A signal that a grown woman takes responsibility for."

Words clustered up in angry groups in her brain but jammed trying to make it out of her mouth. "I want to go home."

He dropped his head, hands balled into fists. When he looked up again, his expression was apologetic. He stepped toward her. "No, I'm sorry."

Bella backed up.

"I'm an asshole." He stopped and shoved his hands into his pants pockets. "A total dick. You just make me so hot and I lost my temper."

Yeah, she might buy that from a high-school kid, but even then, it would be a stretch. She hadn't made it out of high school with her virginity intact by giving it up to the first guy to throw a tantrum when she wouldn't put out. "I'd like you to take me home."

"Come on, sweetheart." Expression pleading, he held out his hands. "I know I screwed up, but we could still have a nice evening."

She rather thought not. The picnic was nice, he'd been very thoughtful, but that didn't give him a free pass to behave like that. "It's getting cold. Please take me home."

Adam's jaw clenched, his eyes flashing pure rage at her.

For a nasty moment, Bella expected him to refuse. And then the contrite expression returned and he shrugged. "I only have myself to blame. I'll take you home."

They packed up the picnic in a tense silence. Well, she stayed silent. Adam filled it with cheerful chatter. He even tried a joke or two, and Bella managed to force out a chuckle.

She didn't relax until he drew up outside her house. Before he could open her door, Bella hopped onto the curb. The urge to get away from him rode her hard, but she still managed to thank him for the picnic.

Adam nodded, pulling away from the house with the slightest squeal of tires.

"You're back early." Liz popped out of her front door. Again, she hadn't brought her coat with her and stood with her shoulders hunched over. "I felt sure you would be much longer and not be coming home alone."

Suddenly, Bella didn't want to tell Liz some half-truth

and pretend everything was fine. "Have you got time for a glass of wine?"

"Always." Liz peered closer at her face. "What happened?"

"Wine?"

"You know me." Liz followed her into the house.

With atypical forbearance, Liz waited until Bella had their glasses filled and they were sitting at her kitchen table before she demanded the story.

Bella took a slug of her wine and told her.

"What a dickhead." Liz slapped her palm against the table. "He called you a cocktease?"

"Uh-huh."

"On the second date?"

That brought Bella up short. "What does the second date part have to do with it?"

"Well, everyone knows you have to wait until at least the third date for a girl to put out." Liz rolled her eyes.

"You put out on the third date?"

Liz gaped at her. "You don't?"

"No." Bella's cheeks grew hot. Third date? Why was she only hearing about this now? "I wait until the time is right."

Liz hooted with laughter. "And when is that?"

"I don't know." This entire conversation made her feel stupid and naïve. "Are you sure about this third-date thing?"

"It's not like it's written down anywhere." Liz grinned at her, taking some of the sting out of the words. "But if you like a guy and he likes you, sometimes you don't even make it to the third date."

Bella sat back in her chair and went over her shallow dating history. It didn't take long. "I've never done that."

"Maybe you should try it next time."

"Maybe I will." She matched Liz's taunting tone. Then her bravado crumpled. "But probably not. I would never get the sound of my nana's voice out of my head."

"That would certainly put a damper on things." Liz smiled into her wineglass and sipped. "But this thing with Adam, that's screwed up, girl."

"Tell me about it." Her night crashed down on her again. "And it started out so well."

Liz nodded. She made slow circles on the table with the base of her wineglass.

"What?" Bella had never known her to be this quiet. "What are you not saying?"

When Liz looked up, her face had grown serious. "I dunno." She shrugged and failed to lighten it up. "Something is a bit off here."

"With Adam?" Bella refilled their glasses. Maybe her warning voices weren't crazy after all. "In what way?"

Liz blew out a long breath. "Look, I've managed to date just about every asshole to cross my path, so I'm probably not the best person to talk about this. You might want to try Pippa." She cleared her throat. "But the flowers, the texts, tonight, it's all kind of . . . intense."

The word clanged home with a clear, pure tone. "Yes. That's it. It *is* intense. I mean, I don't want to sound ungrateful or anything, but the flowers were a bit much."

"See." Liz looked smug. "I mean, who sends an arrangement that size to someone they just met?"

"Two," Bella said.

Liz clacked her glass down on the table. "He sent you flowers twice?"

"Yeah." Bella went for a light shrug, but her skin still crawled. "Both huge. And lots of texts. Kind of all the time." She didn't like the way this stacked up. There went her dating prospects. "You think I should stop seeing him?"

"Yup." Liz grabbed the bottle and refilled their glasses. Funny; Bella hadn't counted her intake now, just when she was out with Adam. "I'm getting a weird vibe."

Her too. Bella stood and fetched her list from the fridge door. "You know what?"

"What?" Liz cocked her head.

"People told me to stop pining over Nate, and did I listen?"

"I'm gonna go out on a limb here and say no." Liz grinned.

"Give the lady a gold star." Bella slapped the list on the table between them. "I knew I should get over him. I knew they were telling me the truth, but I went for it anyway. And where did it get me?"

"Drinking cheap wine with a middle-aged divorcée on a Saturday night?"

Something about Liz's tone made her sad, and Bella said, "It's the best Saturday night I've spent in a long time."

For a moment, Liz's expression softened, and then she snorted. "I don't know which one of us that makes the sadder one. I'm voting for you."

"Of course you are." Bella let her get away with the diversion. She'd seen that little spark of pleased Liz hadn't been quick enough to hide. "We have a plan to get us through Christmas. We've decorated." Bella tapped her nail on item one. "We've gone out there and mingled. That's item three. Two is some sort of volunteering, but I really haven't gotten around to looking into it."

Liz perked up and rustled in her seat like a roosting hen. "I have an idea and you're gonna love it. It's a multitasker."

Chapter Twelve

Monday morning brought a steady stream of internet orders. Bella hadn't heard anything more from her family, but the good business might go a ways to appeasing Nana. In fact, if things got busier, she might have to work out a better system for filling and packaging all the orders. Maybe she'd even be in a position to employ someone. The thought trickled through her on a thrill of anticipation.

Mondays tended to be quiet and she got busy with her Christmas decorating. Not a plastic reindeer in sight. Hate the pink as she did, she was stuck with it until Matt could work his magic, so she went for a Christmas bling theme, adding touches of sparkle and glitter.

The bell over the door tinkled as she finished positioning a banner of glittery snowflakes over the front of her service counter. Speak of the devil. "Matt!"

"Hey, Bella." He responded to her smile with one of his. "And before you ask, Pippa is doing great. Jo is working too hard but seems to be enjoying it. I haven't heard from Isaac, Eric is still a dog, and Nate is Nate."

"I wasn't going to ask." She tried to get a bit huffy, but he had her there.

"Yeah, you were." He pulled a tube out from under his arm. "Because you always ask and you genuinely care what the answer is. Now come and see what I have for you."

"My plans?" The words came out in a breathy whisper. The plans for her new store. The world went blurry for a second. She wanted to do this so much, but there would be so much grief when she did.

Did she dare? How could she not? "Show me."

Matt strode over to her, snapping the elastic band off the tube of drawings. "You sure you want to see this?"

Bella couldn't seem to keep her feet still, shifting back and forth. "Yes."

"Sure-sure?"

"Matt!" He was killing her here.

"Okay." Matt laughed and spread the plans out on the counter. "But just so you know, I had Pippa give me a hand with these."

There, spread on her service counter, lay one of her biggest dreams. Suddenly, Bella didn't want to look. What if she didn't like them? Or worse, what if she loved them?

"Okay, first things first." Matt stabbed the plans with his big forefinger. "We need to move this counter toward the back of the store." He pointed to her wall of shelving. "Which means that has to go."

Finally, Bella dragged her gaze onto the plans. Her breath hitched. Tears formed and dropped onto the paper.

"Bella?" Matt's handsome face creased into a frown. "If you don't like them, I can change them."

"No." Bella tried her best not to cry, but too late, she was already blubbering. "They're great. Better than great. They're perfect."

"Damn, girl." Matt pulled her into a rough side hug. "You had me worried there for a moment."

Scrounging up a Kleenex, Bella mopped herself up. "Show me."

"Okay, so over here," Matt jabbed at the plan and then pointed to the back corner, "Pippa thinks we should put in some decent fitting rooms." He pulled a face. "And I'm under strict instructions to make sure the lighting is good. I guess that's a thing or something."

"It totally is." Bella gave one more sniffle. "Unless you've been swimsuit shopping under bad lighting, you can't know the torture."

"All right, then." Matt nodded. "Good lighting you'll get."

"Is this the size?" Bella leaned closer to the drawing.

"Yeah. Pippa, again, insisted on me making them a little bigger than standard."

The bell tinkled over the door. A massive bouquet of roses, above a pair of polka-dotted red and pink leggings, trotted through.

"Where do you want them?" Debbie's voice emerged from behind the blooms. "Only tell me quick because these are heavy."

Being the world's original nice guy, Matt leaped forward and wrestled them away from Debbie.

Round cheeks glowing, Debbie bounced around him. "More flowers for Bella." She poked her finger in the previous arrangement and tutted. "You need to water these or they'll die."

She bustled into the back and the faucet turned on.

"Where shall I put them?" Matt craned his head around the side of the arrangement.

On the sidewalk. Bella resisted the impulse and pointed him to a low coffee table in front of the divan. Hurrying in front of him, she cleared away a couple of magazines to make space.

"You're keeping me in business." Debbie emerged with a coffee mug and watered the dry arrangement. She gave Matt a severe glance and then beamed at Bella. "That man of yours could teach the men around here a thing or two."

Grinning, Matt crossed his arms. "Some men don't need flowers to keep their woman happy."

"Oh, you." Debbie went bright pink. "Now, remember to water the new ones too." As she stared at Bella, she rocked from her toes to her heels. "There's a card."

"Is there?" Bella tried to look at least a little interested, but she'd recognized Adam's handiwork.

Debbie shoved her hands in her back pockets. "Aren't you gonna read it?"

It didn't look like she had much option with both Matt and Debbie staring at her. "Okay."

She plucked a white card from its holder.

"Forgive me. Give me a chance to show you what a great guy I can be. Adam"

Pretty much as she'd expected.

"Well?" The word exploded from Debbie. "I don't know how you can just stand there. If it was me, I'd be jumping for joy. The guy sure does know how to apologize."

Debbie had written all the cards. Of course she knew what they said.

"Uh-oh." Matt raised an eyebrow and peered at her. "He must really have screwed up."

"He did." Bella crumpled the card and tossed it in the trash.

Debbie's mouth drooped as she stared at the crumpled little card. "Are you sure you don't want to keep it?"

"I'm sure." Managing a smile in Debbie's direction,

Bella straightened her skirt. "Thanks for bringing them around. They're beautiful."

"No problem." Debbie trailed out the door, casting a couple of forlorn glances over her shoulder.

"These are from the same guy." Matt pointed to all three bouquets.

Bella nodded. She really didn't want to talk about Adam.

"Wow." Matt shook his head. "He must screw up a lot."

It dragged a laugh out of her. Matt was always good for that. "The first ones weren't for screwing up."

"Yeah?" Matt studied the flowers as if they were alien invaders. "What did he send those for?"

"A looking-forward-to-seeing-me kind of thing." Bella marched over to her lovely new plans. "So, we were talking about the fitting rooms."

"Before the first date?" Matt scowled.

"Lots of men do that."

"None that I know." He sauntered over to the plans. "What did he do that made him send those?"

"I don't want to talk about it." Bella used her best repressive tone. The one she saved for kids with sticky fingers all over her clothes.

Matt rubbed the back of his neck. "See, that's not going to cut it, Bella."

"Huh?"

"Well, it goes like this." Mischief danced in his topaz eyes. "Debbie will tell her mother, who will tell Pippa's mother. She'll tell Laura and Laura will tell Pippa." He shrugged and held up his palms. "Pippa knows I'm here this morning and she'll want to know. Don't make me go home without the details."

Bella did her best to glare at him. "Stop twisting my arm."

"Honest to God, that's how it will go." Then he ruined his sincere expression with a wink. "And if you don't tell me, Pippa will come right on down here and make you tell her."

She didn't want to talk about it. After a bottle of wine with Liz, she'd made her decision. A couple of chick flicks watched together only strengthened their resolve. But maybe Matt could give her the guy's perspective on this.

"How would you define a cocktease?"

Matt's jaw dropped. "Say what, now?"

"When would you call a woman a cocktease?"

"I wouldn't." He huffed. "And I gotta say I'm not used to stuff like that coming out of your mouth and I don't like it."

Bella waved her hand at him to shut him up. People would have to get used to a whole lot of new stuff from her. "I want to know what makes a woman a co—"

"Nothing." Matt almost yelled at her. "A woman always has the right to say no."

"I know that." She tried to hush him with her hand. Everybody on the street would hear their conversation. "What I want to know is, when do you think a woman is leading you on?"

"Never." Matt clearly didn't have any concerns about the street. His outburst startled a mom and daughter on their way in.

"Hi there." Bella gave them her most reassuring smile. "What can I do for you?"

"Is this a bad time?" The mother glanced at Matt and sidled back a step.

"Not at all." Bella hurried over to them. From the looks of this pair, they came from the resorts, and she needed as many customers as she could from up there. "My contractor gets passionate about paint colors."

The mother eyed her doubtfully. "Actually, we were just browsing."

"Take your time." Arms wide, Bella stepped back. "I'll

just be over here with the contractor." She forced a strangled giggle. "Keeping him calm. About the paint."

"Okay." They slid into the store and moved to the racks farthest away from Matt.

"Did flower guy call you a cocktease?" Matt had lowered his voice, but his face grew stern. "Is that what the flowers are for, to say sorry?"

"Maybe." Under Matt's scrutiny, she wanted to turn and run. Matt's nice-guy overlaid a will of steel and an inflexible integrity. Bella sometimes forgot that when he played the charming, easygoing boy next door.

"Did he hurt you?" Matt went scary still.

"No." Bella squeezed his arm. "He didn't hurt me. He made me angry."

"Good." Blowing out a long breath, Matt straightened away from her. "Because you should be angry. Taking a woman out doesn't mean you're going to get some action. If he doesn't understand that, he doesn't deserve to take you out."

More for herself than anything else, Bella gave his muscular forearm one more squeeze. Matt had the sort of arms you wanted to gnaw on. Pippa said so all the time. "I shut him down. He got pushy and mean. End of story. End of Adam."

"Promise me." Matt's hard stare bored into her. "Because you're not so good at walking away from men who are bad for you."

Heat climbed her cheeks as she got his not-at-all-subtle reference to Nate. "I know that, but that's over now."

"It is?"

"Sure is." She gave him a perky nod for emphasis. "Adam and the . . . er . . . other one."

"Good." Matt stared for a moment more before turning back to the plans. "Now, let me show you the rest of these."

The store kept her occupied for the rest of the afternoon. The mother and daughter browsed long enough to try a couple of things on and eventually went away with two dresses. A couple of local women came in for something special to wear over Christmas, and a group of young girls from the resorts also kept her bustling.

Busy enough to stop her from checking her phone constantly. Every time she looked at the damn thing, Adam had sent another text. When he apologized, he went all out, it seemed. She ruthlessly deleted all of them.

Later, when she got home, she would call him and calmly tell him she couldn't see him again. Perhaps she should get Liz over for a bit of moral support. This time Liz could bring the wine because that woman could drink.

She turned into her street later that evening and swore.

A silver Lexus sat outside her house.

As she parked in her driveway and got out, Adam climbed out of the car.

"You're ignoring me." He strolled toward her, a small smile playing around the corners of his mouth.

Bella grabbed her house keys out of her bag. "I was busy at the store. I was going to call you tonight."

"Here I am." He opened his arms wide. "And I brought wine." He held up his offering. "Let's go inside and talk."

She prayed Liz would make one of her porch appearances. "We can talk out here."

Adam tilted his head and studied her. "Come on, Bella. You've made your point. I was an ass. I get it. Can we move on?"

"It's not that." He stood between her and her front door. "Not only that."

He raised an eyebrow, waiting.

God, she hated this. Her mouth dried and her heart

hammered away in her chest. Going through this with Liz in the kitchen last night had made it seem supereasy. Confronted with the real man, her courage wavered. "The thing is . . ." She cleared her throat. "I like you, Adam. You're a nice guy, but . . ."

"But?" His eyes went cold.

"I'm not really ready to date."

He shoved his hands into his pockets. "Is that so?"

"I'm just getting out of a thing." Nate could be described as a thing. Only a her thing, but still a thing. "And I'm not ready." God, so lame. She stood there with her pulse pounding away. A growing part of her wanted to make a run for the door and safety.

"I see." Adam nodded. "So, this is a brush-off?"

"No." She bet Pippa would have handled this with much more poise. "Maybe." Liz would have given it to him straight. Bella, on the other hand, vacillated, part of her wanting to take it all back and not hurt him and another part wanting to hide under the bed and avoid the confrontation. "I don't think we should see each other anymore."

"I don't agree." Adam shrugged. "I think we have a good thing here, Bella. I'll see you around." He strolled back to his car and activated the fob to unlock the door. "I'll give you some time to think about it."

Wait! What? She didn't need time. Bella opened her mouth, but the words didn't make it out.

A car turned into her street and hope surged. Maybe it was Liz on her way home. As the sheriff's SUV slid up to her house and parked, hope crashed into the ground. Nate unfolded from the driver's seat and stood there for a moment. The winter sunset caught the light on his dark hair and played happily over his perfect bone structure. He wore sunglasses so she couldn't see his expression as he turned toward Adam. But an expert in the body language of Nate Evans like her could read that his screamed angry.

He kept his attention on Adam. "Everything okay, Bella?"

Mr. Responsible Matt must have called Nate as soon as he left her store. "Everything's fine."

"Ah, the good sheriff." Adam rested one hand on his car roof. "Imagine seeing you here." He opened the car door before turning to her. "Is he your thing?"

God, open the earth and take her now. "Umm . . . no . . . not really."

"Yes," said Nate.

Bella heard the whistle of pig wings soar past her ear.

"You all done here?" Still looking at Adam, Nate strolled over to her.

Adam chuckled, a nasty sound that made her shiver. "For now."

"I'd say you're done." Nate stood beside her, not touching her but throwing her under the shadow of his protection. He couldn't have gotten more territorial if he'd lifted his leg and peed on her.

Adam returned his look before he climbed into his car and drove away.

Nate watched him drive down the street and turn at the end. He glanced at her. "You all right?"

"I'm fine." Or at least she would be if life gave her a break for a second. Taking charge of her life was about being strong, standing up for herself. Every time she tried that, she ended up needing a rescue. "Whatever Matt said, he was overreacting."

Hoping to get away from men for the day, she quick-stepped it to the door.

As she opened her front door, Nate caught up with her.

"Damn it, Bella." He shoved the door open. "Has that been unlocked all day?"

And what was with his door obsession? "Get over it."

Nate went deathly still.

Bella scurried into her house. She got the door halfway closed before he came after her.

With a gentle shove, he pushed her back inside and slammed the door behind him.

"What is it with you and locking the goddamned door?"

She yelled right back. "What is it with you and my door!"

She'd known Nate for far too long for him to think he could stand there and loom over her and bully her. Much.

"I'm trying to keep you safe." He kept coming, tall, broad, and intimidating the hell out of her.

Bella had seen him do this over the years she'd known him. She'd never had it directed at her before. It wasn't an experience she cared for much. "From what?" She forced her feet to stop retreating. Any sudden movements from her and God alone knew what he'd do. "This is Ghost Falls. Nothing ever happens here."

"I think I'm in a much better position to judge that than you." Nate had obviously never watched *Nat Geo WILD* because the whole predator/prey thing meant nothing to him. Even though she'd stopped running, he kept coming until his boot toes nudged up against hers. "Liz saw someone sneaking around your house."

"Liz sees people sneaking around her house all the time." Bella tilted her head up to maintain eye contact. Nate gave off enough heat to have sweat sliding down her sides. "Why are you so worried about it this time?"

"Because I saw the footprints." Nate pointed to her kitchen. "Outside the window."

"Oh." She didn't like the sound of that. Her heart gave

an erratic beat. Whether it did so because of Nate or the footprints, she couldn't be sure. Please God, she hoped it was the footprints. "They could have been mine."

He gave her the look of derision her feeble attempt deserved. "Be careful, Bella."

"Okay." She. Had. No. Backbone. Just call her marshmallow girl, and squish her between two graham crackers. "Thanks for being concerned."

His eye twitched. "Tell me about this Adam jerk?"

"There's nothing to tell." Had Nate gotten closer? The wall pressed cold into her back. Damn, but it had gotten hot in here. She needed to turn the central air down. "Matt is making too big of a deal."

"Matt has a good gut and he doesn't like what it's telling him."

"This is about Matt's gut?" Bella tried to get her head around that one. "You're here acting like a total caveman over your brother's gut?"

"Caveman?" His voice came out in a low growl.

Bella's hackles rose in response. Finally, her backbone snapped straight and she raised her chin. "Caveman." She poked his wide chest. Her knuckle bent on impact. "Barging into my house, yelling at me about the door, looming over me. What would you call it?"

"Tell me about the dickhead." Nate stood so still, like granite. His gaze fixed on her with an intent that made her fidget.

"Okay." She made a business of rolling her eyes. "He got a bit pushy on our date. I said no. He got pissy. End of date. End of Adam. End of story."

Nate shifted, bringing one hand to the wall near her shoulder. "And the flowers?"

"He sent me flowers." His wrist poked out from his

jacket. Dark, wiry hair covered it. A strong wrist, at the end of a large, blunt-fingered hand. A hand currently holding her captive. She moved to the side. His other hand came up. Bella glared at it. "Really?"

"How often does he call you?"

"Not often." She hunched her shoulders to make herself small. She didn't much like the pinning-up-against-the-wall thing. *Liar.* Nate Evans had her pinned up against her hallway wall and her girl parts were singing the "Hallelujah Chorus." "He texts."

"How often?"

"A few times." Her voice came out on a breathy rush. Her tummy clenched as he leaned even closer. His breath hit her face in a hot wash of mint and musk. Dear God, her knees had joined the all-out mutiny and refused to stay locked. "Maybe five, six times a day."

He ducked his chin. "Five or six times?"

"Maybe more."

"Bella." He rumbled her name on a bass warning. "Don't make me fetch your phone to check."

"Okay, more like ten, fifteen times a day."

"Fuck." Nate breathed deep, bringing his chest close to her breasts. Thank God her sweater hid her nipples, currently standing up and pleading with his chest to come a little closer. "And you didn't think that was odd? You still went on a date with him? What the hell, Bella?"

Okay, unfortunate lust aside, that was rude. "I thought he really liked me."

"I'm sure he does." Nate sneered. "What's not to like?"

"Sorry?" It came out in a humiliating squeak. Her tongue stuck to the roof of her mouth. She swallowed to ease the dryness in her throat.

"I've seen what you've got to offer." Nate's lids lowered over his eyes. "What man wouldn't want that?"

If she didn't know a whole, helluva lot better, she would think Nate was giving her hot eyes. The sort of look that said he wanted to do her up against the wall. Her knees buckled and she pressed her back into the wall. How many fantasies had she had with that particular scenario? "You haven't seen anything of mine. Ever."

"Have too." He leaned forward, his breath rasping against her ear. "You never did ask how I ended up with your dress."

She shook her head because . . . no words. No breath. Just a steady *dum-da-dum-da-dum-dum-dum* that started in the traitorous girl bits and headed north.

"You took it off." He skimmed her cheekbone with his mouth.

Da-da-dum.

"You slipped out of your dress and walked away from me."

She had? Bella's lust haze burned away under the scorch of embarrassment. "I did not."

"Did too." He reached the corner of her mouth and stopped. "I saw your pert little ass walking away from me."

"No." Nate Evans had his mouth within kissing distance. If she moved a quarter inch to her left, she could suck on that full bottom lip she'd been dreaming about ever since her hormones first had kicked in. Instead, she prayed the floor would open up and swallow her because she had the nasty suspicion he'd just told the God's honest truth here.

"Yes," Nate whispered. "Such an incredible fucking ass, I can't get it out of my head."

"No."

"Yes." His soft laughter brushed her lips. "I always knew

you'd be gorgeous, Bella. But that night . . ." He groaned, more breath than sound. "That ass."

"You should have looked away." Really? *Really?* That's what came out of her mouth?

"Not a fucking chance." He pressed closer to her, pinning her hips with his.

Nate was hard, impressively hard, and for her. Apparently. "What are you doing, Nate?"

"Damned if I know." He touched his lips to hers. "Did he kiss you?"

"Who?" She had no room in her mind for any man right now but the one with his mouth against hers.

"Dickhead." He ground his erection against her. "Did he get a taste of what keeps me hard at night?"

"Shut up, Nate." Since first grade she'd waited. Time for him to fish or cut bait. "Kiss me or get the hell out of my house."

He kissed her. Pinning her to the wall with his body, he thrust his tongue into her mouth.

Wanting, waiting, needing, dreaming, dying a little inside year after year. It all ripped through her in a wave and Bella lost her shit. Lost. Her. Shit.

Gripping his hair, she tilted her head and plunged her tongue into his mouth. There might only be this one time and it had better count. It had better be good enough to take her through the next twenty years. He tasted of spice and heat and he kissed her like he'd been the one with the crush all these years.

She wrapped her leg around his waist, straining onto her toes to get closer.

Nate growled; he tugged her hands from his hair and slammed them into the wall above her head.

It lit a fire in her, running beneath her skin like a fever, pooling between her thighs. Bella pressed her aching beasts against his chest. Not enough; she undulated against him.

He groaned, his kiss getting more demanding, consuming her with each thrust of his tongue.

None of her fantasies had come close to the reality. Nate kissed with his entire being. Hard body creating friction against her. Hip to hip, breast to chest.

Bella wanted to touch and she strained to get her hands free.

Nate tightened his grip. He kissed her as if he wanted to inhale her.

Bella met each stroke of his tongue, each grind of his hips. She wanted. Every part of her wanted and needed.

Nate tore his mouth from hers, breathing fast. He pressed his forehead to hers. "Shit."

Bella dragged herself back into her hallway. Her body responded slowly, still hot and achy. She closed her eyes, desperately clinging to the last few moments of utter insanity. Her heart twisted. What the hell was she supposed to do now? She'd patted herself on the back for how far she'd moved on from Nate, and in one devastating kiss he'd blown her theory to hell and back.

Nate raised his head. "Look at me, Bella."

She shook her head. If she looked at him now, he would see straight into the heart of her, and she couldn't be that raw. "You need to go."

"Bella—"

"Go." She dug her nails into her palms. She had about five seconds left before she came apart. Tears already welled behind her closed lids. "Please, just go."

His body heat left her and she slumped against the wall.

Her front door opened. "Lock this behind me," he said. "We're not done here."

The door slammed shut and his footsteps receded.

"We are done." Bella's legs gave out and she slid to the floor. "We have to be done."

Nate stopped halfway down her walkway and glanced back. His libido demanded he go back in there and finish what they'd started. He took a deep breath of the cold night air. The bite of snow rode the night and he pulled the chill deep into his body.

Damn! Shit! Fuck!

He'd done the one thing he'd promised himself he would never do. He'd kissed Bella. Sugar-sweet, big blue eyes, tempting little body, Bella. That Bella. The one decent thing he'd done all these years was never take her up on the offer she'd held out to him constantly. He sucked at making women happy. Instead, he broke hearts. He always had and everybody knew it. Somehow that had been enough to keep him away from Bella and inflicting his special kind of screwed-up on her.

Then she'd taken off her dress, and in his head, she'd moved from off-limits to pure temptation. The call from Matt had lit a fire in him. He should never have come around here tonight. Never have let the urge to rip that dickhead from her head overpower him.

Then he'd seen the prick on her front lawn, and Bella backing up.

His veneer of civilization had torn away, disappeared under the need to pound his chest and bellow *mine*. Then he'd gone and kissed her and crossed the forbidden line. Who the hell knew where that left him now? In a new kind of hell.

He crossed the lawn to his SUV.

A car started up the street. Habit had him checking it out. The car tore down the road in a flash of silver.

Caveman Nate balled his hands into fists. He was halfway into his car, determined to chase the bastard down before his head kicked back in. There was no crime in driving down a public street. No crime even in parking outside someone's house.

He hoped to God dickhead had seen that kiss.

Chapter Thirteen

*B*ella arrived at Mugged earlier than usual. Around five that morning, she'd given up on sleeping and decided she may as well start her day early. A check on the internet cheered her up. She had a couple more orders than yesterday, all of it on the new stock Nana had fought so hard against.

One thing about her grandmother she knew for sure: Nana might be a control freak, but first and foremost she knew the value of a dollar.

Even this early, the coffee shop buzzed with people getting their morning fix.

"Bella." She jumped as Adam appeared at her elbow. "I've been waiting for you."

Standing there, she managed nothing more intelligent than, "Oh?"

Pippa would say something concise and cutting and shake Adam off. Liz would probably let fly with profanity. All Bella managed was a sidle away from him, hoping and praying the four-deep line would disappear.

Adam smiled at her. "Let me buy you a cup of coffee."

"No, really, that's very nice of you, but I can get my own." Bordering on a personal-space violation, Bella edged as close as she dared to the woman in front of her.

"It's just coffee." Adam lifted his brow.

The woman turned around and Bella wanted to shrivel into her new heels as Blythe Barrows smirked at her. "Hey, Bella."

Why did Blythe always smirk at her? They'd known each other since first grade. Blythe had smirked then, too. "Hi, Blythe."

"And hello to you." Blythe turned all the way around and beamed at Adam. "I'm Blythe."

"Nice to meet you, Blythe." Shaking her offered hand, Adam amped up the charm. "I'm trying to buy my best girl a cup of coffee."

"Aren't you a sweetheart?" Blythe winked at him. "If she says no, I'll put you out of your misery."

"Or me." Next to Blythe, another woman turned, wearing nearly as much makeup as Blythe. Her jeans, however, seemed infinitesimally looser than Blythe's, as in allowing for normal respiration.

Suddenly, Bella felt like she was twelve again and Blythe and her friends were standing in the school locker room laughing at her training bra. Her head throbbed. Meanwhile, Adam, Blythe, and friend loomed over her and stared. This being short really sucked. Fighting for space in her head, Nana popped up and yelled at her not to be rude.

"Okay." The lump in her throat strangled her voice. "I'll have a vanilla latte."

"Vanilla?" Blythe snickered. "I could have guessed that."

Behind the counter, Kate came to her rescue as she asked Blythe and friend for their order.

"You're still mad." His breath brushing her ear, Adam leaned closer.

"I'm not mad." Out of her depth, feeling gauche, wishing he would go away and make this easier on her for sure, but not mad. Definitely creeped out by him breathing down her neck.

Adam quirked his brow at her.

"No, really I'm not." She moved to the side to wait for their coffees. "I just don't think we should date."

"Can you tell me why?" Adam stuck his hands in his pockets. "I thought we got on fine."

"We did." Reorganizing the sugar packets by ascending size, Bella avoided his gaze. "But you're . . . a bit . . . intense for me."

Adam hummed. Their coffees arrived on the counter and he fetched them.

"Thanks for the coffee." Bella did that lame toast thing with her cup. "I need to get to work."

"I'll walk you there."

"Really, it's just three doors down."

"Then I'll walk you three doors." Adam's smile looked a bit glued on his mouth.

Her options looked pretty crappy right now, most of them involving a mad dash for three doors and locking herself in. So she shrugged and left the coffee shop with Adam in tow.

While she unlocked the door, the perfect gentleman, he held her coffee cup for her. It didn't look like she could avoid letting him into the store. Clear glass window fronts should keep him in check, for the most part. If he asked her out again, she would have to grow a pair and say no.

"Thanks for the coffee." She turned on the register and logged in. "I really do have to get my day started."

"You kept my flowers." Adam stroked the petal of a red rose.

Oh-kay. "They're beautiful flowers. It was very kind of you to send them."

Adam wandered over to the flowers on her counter. "So, did you do anything last night?"

He didn't need to know about the scorching kiss with Nate in her entrance hall. She didn't want to see Adam again, but that would rub salt in the wound. "Nothing special. Watched a little TV."

"Really?" Adam stilled.

Duster in hand, Bella stopped. Something about Adam's lack of movement made her nervous.

"You mean after the sheriff left?"

"Yes." Her heartbeat sped up. The street outside the windows remained empty. She was alone with Adam and he'd been spying on her last night. "After Nate left."

The flowers hit the back wall in an explosion of glass fragments, petals, and water. It took her a moment to realize Adam had thrown them. "Adam!"

"You lie." His face appeared as calm as ever, but the violence crackled about him like electricity. His gaze seethed as he raked her from head to toe. "I saw you. With him."

In shock, she stared at the mess on the wall. A clinging rose slithered down and plopped into the puddle on the floor. "What did you do?"

"You're not listening to me, Bella."

Water speckled the cashmere sweaters folded on their shelves and spotted the silk blouses hanging nearby. He'd probably ruined them. "You have no right."

No right to do any of it. Bella charged over to the sweaters.

"I have every right."

Bella got a very, very bad feeling about this. Never mind the silk blouses. She wanted him out of her store. "Adam."

Holding her hands out in a placating gesture, she managed to keep her voice steady. "You need to go."

"You don't get it, Bella." He shook his head. "You don't get any of this."

"No, I don't, but you're scaring me right now."

He stalked over to the other arrangement. "Really?"

"Don't!"

Too late. He sent them flying across the store. The vase hit the racks of accessories and shattered.

"I gave you flowers." Adam stalked her. "I took you to dinner. I made you a picnic with all your favorite things."

Bella backed up.

He loomed over her. "And who did you fuck?"

"What?" She edged closer to the door. "I didn't have sex with anyone, Adam."

"I saw you with him." He closed in on her. "I saw you crawling all over him like the hot little bitch you are."

"You don't have the right to speak to me like that." He kept coming and Bella put the divan between them. "Get out."

"I'm sick of your games." Adam kicked the divan and sent it lurching toward her. "You can't play games with me."

"I'm not playing games." Bella ran for the door and held it open. "And I want you out of my store. Right now."

"You're a whore."

Enough! The name-calling lit her fuse and Bella saw red. "Get the hell out of my store!"

On the street, an older woman stopped, looked, and then hurried on.

Bella was way beyond caring. "Get out or I'll call the sheriff. And you're paying for any damages."

Adam stalked past her.

Bella shrunk away from making any contact with him. While he threw himself into his car and backed out into the street, she stayed frozen. As he narrowly missed clipping her front bumper, Bets Schumaker honked.

"You okay, Bella?" From the hardware store next door, Hank Baker came out onto the sidewalk. He narrowed his eyes and watched Adam's Lexus fishtail around the corner. "Who was that?"

"Nobody." Bella spat the word. "That was nobody."

She went back into the store. Pulse pounding hard, she pressed her hand to her heart. Damn, she was shaking. Shaking so bad, it hit her belly and then crept into her knees until she had to perch on the edge of the divan. Adam had made deep gouge marks on the carpet when he kicked the divan.

Pippa slid into the store. "Shit!"

Bella jumped and then let out a shaky breath.

"What the hell happened here?" Pippa stared at the mess of glass and flowers.

"Adam." Bella's mouth had gone paper dry. "He came in and got mad."

"About what?" Glancing at her, Pippa toed a rose out of her way.

"I told him that I wouldn't see him anymore. He saw me kissing Nate." Forcing her knees to hold her weight, Bella stood. "I'd better clean this mess up."

"No." Pippa had her phone out. "Let me take some pictures first."

She felt like she was looking at her store through a rainy glass pane. Her brain refused to work. "Why?"

"Because this isn't funny, Bella." Pippa clicked away. "This guy has a problem and you need to make sure you document it." She looked up suddenly. "Did he hurt you?"

"No." Bella waved a limp hand at the debris. "He just threw the flowers he gave me around the store."

"You need to file a report." Taking pictures, Pippa went

over to the second shattered arrangement. "He came into your store and damaged your property."

Her store clock confirmed it wasn't even nine a.m. yet. Suddenly, her day seemed way, way too long. "I don't want to press charges. I just want him gone."

Pippa got a set look on her face. "Bella—"

"Don't." Bella went into the back and fetched the broom. "Finish taking your pictures so I can clean this up."

"Bel—"

"Please?" Legs still iffy, she tripped and righted herself as she made her way over to the first piece of glass. "I think I might be in shock. Do you think I'm in shock? What does that feel like anyway?"

"At least tell Nate." Pippa bent and helped her pick up glass shards. "At least get it on record somewhere that he did this."

"Okay." That she could manage, but she wouldn't tell Nate; she'd tell Deputy Gabby. She couldn't face any of Nate's I-told-you-sos right now.

They worked in silence, cleaning up the mess and checking the damage. Two of the silk shirts would need to be looked at when they dried. The store smelled of wet vegetation, but other than that, the damage appeared minimal.

Pippa helped her drag the garbage bags out to the trash cans in the alley beside the store.

"There." Pippa banged the lid on the trash bin. "All done."

Bella nodded and went back into the store.

"I'll get us another coffee." Pippa snatched up the one Adam had bought her and tossed it into the trash can. "And then you can tell me what you meant about kissing Nate."

Chapter Fourteen

$\mathcal{N}$ate stayed away from Bella for the next four days, not that anyone was counting. The main sheriff's office piled enough shit on his plate for a valid excuse. The paperwork would kill him long before some rampaging criminal. He bet Wyatt Earp didn't have to do performance appraisals.

When he finally got clear enough to work his way back to Ghost Falls, his day started bad and kept sucking more and more. Most of the last three hours he'd spent outside of Ghost Falls in a tiny berg that also fell within his county, trying to explain that the legalization of marijuana in Colorado didn't mean a free pass for anybody with a plot of land to start growing and distributing.

Hauling some dealer into jail would have made his day, but this had been a family. Times were hard; people tried to do what they could to get by. Considering he'd probably spent his day destroying their only source of income, the elderly couple whose operation he'd had to shut down had taken it remarkably well.

On the way back, he'd gotten a call about a vicious dog

and had to take some kid's beloved pet to the pound. He'd get back out there in a day or two to see if he could calm everyone down. The dog hadn't done any damage, and Nate had spent a little time at the pound. Basically, the dog needed some training, but it didn't look like a dangerous animal. In the meantime, the little guy who'd lost his dog would probably cry himself to sleep tonight.

Big city police work this was not. On days like today, he found he actually missed the city. Not the adrenaline of it, but the anonymity. In cities, faces blurred one into the other and made it easy to keep your distance, not get involved. With the county budget stretched to the seams, it meant everyone knew his face, and most of them knew his name and enough about him to pass the time of day.

Deputy Gabby's voice crackled over the radio.

He didn't have the patience for it and snatched up his cell phone. "What is it?" he said when she answered.

"Sheriff?" Gabby sounded disapproving. "I was trying to raise you on the radio."

"I heard." Low blood sugar always made him bitchy and he'd missed lunch as well. "Lucky for you we have these neat little gadgets called cell phones."

A deliberate pause down the line almost made him apologize. Screw it! Gabby needed to fix her attitude anyway. She was a good cop, had great instincts and did her job thoroughly, but she could do with a bit of workplace etiquette.

"Liz Gunn called. She lives at—"

"Gabby, I'm there almost every second week. I know exactly where the woman lives. What does she want?"

"Just following procedure, Sheriff. Making sure you're aware of all the particulars." Gabby sniffed.

"What does she want?" Either he got some food in his belly or he'd rip her a new one.

"Seems there's a problem at her neighbor's."

That got his immediate attention. "Which neighbor?"

"Number—"

"Give me a name, Gabby, or I swear I'll have you handing out loitering tickets outside Walmart for the rest of your career."

Her sigh traveled down the line. "Bella's house. If you're still a ways out, I can run over and check it out."

After four days of not seeing Bella, Gabby had handed him the excuse he needed. "I'm on it."

"Sheriff?" It wasn't like Gabby to sound unsure of herself.

"What?"

She cleared her throat. "Before you go over there, you should know Bella filed a report a couple of days ago."

Frost crept up his spine. "What kind of report?"

"Some guy she knows made a mess of her store."

Spiking blood pressure did nothing for his mood. "And you're only telling me about this now?"

"She wanted to keep it quiet," Gabby said, sounding surer of her ground.

"And you agreed to that?"

"I said if anything else happened, I would have to tell you," Gabby said, her usual shitty 'tude back in control. "Something else happened and I'm telling you. Bella didn't want you to know."

He slammed the radio down. They would fucking see about that.

Bella stood on her front lawn, afraid to go near her front porch, barely recognizable under the mound of flowers, soft toys, boxes of candy, and balloons. "I take it Adam's been round."

Liz nodded. She'd joined Bella shortly after she'd gotten out of her car. "The deliveries kept coming all afternoon."

Four days and not a word and now this. "Damn."

"I think this might even qualify as a *shit* moment, or perhaps we could even go with *fuck*," Liz said. "I started taking photographs after the third truck." She nudged Bella and showed her phone. "I even got one of psycho boy himself dropping off a box." Liz tilted her head and stared at the image. "It's too small to be a boiled rabbit."

"Huh?" Bella took a hesitant step forward. Adam had desecrated her home, her safe place.

"Don't you know anything?" Liz rolled her eyes. "It's from a movie. *Fatal Attraction*? No?"

"Why?" She wanted it all gone.

"I think that's your best clue." Liz pointed to a row of balloons fastened on the balustrade and spelling out "Forgive Me."

Offerings covering her entire front porch and must have cost a fortune. "Why is he doing this?"

"Now, don't panic or cry or lose it or anything, but I think you might have a bit of a stalker." Liz rubbed her back.

"A bit?" A huge, lurid orange elephant stared at her with its dead beaded eyes. "This is crazy."

"I called the sheriff's office," Liz said. "I spoke to Gabby. What a bitch! But she made a note of it on the file. Apparently, this isn't the first time he's done something weird to you."

Bella told her about the other day and the flowers. The small box Adam had delivered personally sat on her doormat with a card attached. She didn't want to know what that card said. In fact, all of this had to go. Like poison,

Adam spread into more and more areas of her life. First her, then her store, and now her home.

"Why didn't you tell me?" Liz gaped at her. "If I'd known, I would have nut punched him when I saw him this afternoon."

Liz would do it too. Bella snorted a laugh. "You were busy."

"Yeah." Liz went redder than the big, stuffy heart blocking her door. "I've been doing . . . stuff."

Liz's front door opened and Noel appeared.

"Is that the stuff you've been doing?" Bella tittered at her own daring. Nothing she said would stand a chance of shocking Liz anyway. It was so freeing not to feel like the person you were with judged you, or waited to pounce on any transgression.

"Damn it, Noel!" Liz crossed her arms. "I told you to stay in the house."

"You sure did." Beaming at her, Noel trotted over. "But I wanted to remind you to take some more pictures."

"I know that." Liz snarled. "I'm not like that stupid bimbo you were screwing. While you were still married to me."

Noel pursed his lips. Then he gave a short nod. "Why don't I load all this stuff up and take it to the old folks' home? They'll get a kick out of all these flowers, and at their age, the only vice some of them still have is candy."

"You could take the stuffies to the rec center." Bella for sure wasn't keeping them, and they might make the kids there very happy.

"Good idea," Noel had a nice smile. It lit up his plain features and made his face interesting. The sort of interesting that clever people wore. "Did you get photos of all of it?"

Liz growled.

Noel hopped over to the porch and grabbed up a large

bunny, the big heart, and a basket of peonies. "My truck's over there."

Bella worked hard not to stare. Somehow, she couldn't picture Noel driving something like that. Huge chrome fender, oversized tires, and flame detailing down the side, not to mention the rack of horns planted on the hood.

"I know, right?" As Noel headed for his monster, Liz pulled a face. "You had him driving a Prius."

Bella laughed. She had indeed. "Shall we give him a hand? The sooner this stuff is out of here, the sooner I'm going to feel better."

"Sure." Liz shrugged and raised her voice as Noel headed back their way. "But I'm doing it for you, not him. If it wasn't for you, I'd make the little shit do it all himself."

"No stature jokes, honey." Noel stopped and gave Liz a reproachful stare. "Those are too easy for you."

It took a bit of determined cramming, but they managed to get everything into Noel's truck.

"I'll get the wine." Liz nodded toward Bella's house. "Meet you in five?"

"I'll be there." She opened her front door. Noel had left the small box on her *Ho Ho Ho* doormat. The name of a local jeweler scrolled across the top. Bella toed it to the side. She didn't care what that box housed, she wasn't going to wear it.

Liz arrived as she finished her quick kitchen tidy-up. Under her arm, she had two bottles and the jeweler's box in her hand. "I'm not even going to talk about that doormat."

"It's festive."

"It's . . . never mind." Liz put the jewelry box on the table. "Don't you want to see how much you're worth?"

"Nope." Bella took the wine from her. "I'm not keeping it anyway."

"Huh." Liz dropped into a chair, picked up the box, and

shook it. "You're a woman of principles. I would have kept the bling."

Trying not to dwell too hard on the fact that the first time a man had given her jewelry he turned out to be a whack job, Bella poured the wine. "Speaking of keeping things . . . Noel?"

"That's not even a decent segue." Liz, the big faker, hid behind her glass.

Bella needed the distraction of dissecting someone else's life for a bit. "Are you seeing him again?"

"Define seeing." Liz fiddled with the box. "If by that you mean am I sleeping with him again, that would have to be a yes."

Last month she would have turned up her nose at Liz's comment. Now, she enjoyed her honesty, envied it even. Bella took the seat opposite her. "Doesn't that get confusing?"

"Hell yeah." Liz sipped her wine. "Got anything to eat?"

"You don't want to eat anything I cook." Bella wrinkled her nose. "I tend to put pink marshmallows on everything."

"Everything?"

"Most things." She pushed away from the table and opened the cupboard. "But we can eat the marshmallows on their own."

"This vintage goes especially well with marshmallows." Liz tapped her zebra-print nail on the bottle. "It's the sex," she said. "With Noel, I mean. The sex is un-freaking-believable. I've never had it so good."

"Really?" Trying to picture that, Bella failed.

"Oh, I get you, sister." Liz raised her eyebrows. "He's nothing to look at, but that man is hung like a donkey. Even better, he can leave you boneless in the morning and then get up and make you breakfast."

"Boneless?"

"Like out of it." Nodding, Liz sighed. "He always says

if you're nothing to look at, you'd better be able to rock a girl's world."

This time, Bella sighed. "I've never had sex like that."

"Never?" Putting her glass back on the table with a clink, Liz frowned at her. "Not even with our yummy sheriff? I could have sworn he had that look about him. The one that says he knows what to do with a woman. Oh well. The hot ones are often the worst lays. It's because they don't have to try too hard."

Most of that went right over her head, so Bella said, "I've never had sex with Nate."

Liz snorted. "You kissed him like that and then kicked him out the door?"

Face burning, Bella got to her feet and went to rummage around for something else edible. "Did everyone in Ghost Falls see that kiss?"

"Nah." Liz gave a gutter chuckle. "Just me and Mr. Powell."

"Oh God." She thunked her head against the cupboard. "It was the best kiss I've ever had and now I wish it hadn't happened."

"Hmm." Propping her chin on her palm, Liz studied her. "You know, babe, if you were one of those women who could hit that and run, I'd be shaking your hand right now. But you're strictly picket fence."

"I am not." But her objection lacked heart because she kind of was. She wanted it all. The gorgeous husband, the family home, the children. Problem being, she wanted those things from a man who'd rather chew his arm off than give them to her. "I think I'm right back where I started. No progress in the getting-over-Nate department."

"I hate to tell you this," Liz winked at her, "but you never were making any progress. I only let you think so because I was kind of hoping you'd be able to fake it till you made it."

"Thanks." Bella snatched up her wine. "So, what are you going to do? About Noel?"

"Nothing." Despite Liz's shrug, Bella caught the flash of uncertainty. "He says he's sorry. That he wants to give it another chance, but that's not going to happen."

"Why not?"

"He screwed around on me." Liz's eyes flashed wrathfully. "That's bad enough, but he did it when I was undergoing my chemo."

"Ouch." Yeah, Bella didn't see a lot of wiggle room in that one. "What does he say about that?"

"That he's sorry." Liz drained her glass. "That he was scared and he did a stupid thing. He's never stopped loving me . . . yadda, yadda, yadda."

"Do you think he—"

Her front door crashed open. She and Liz jumped and looked around.

"Bella!" Nate's voice came from the entrance. "I told you to lock your damn door."

Looking windswept, pissed off, and so gorgeous Bella's knees gave way and she had to grab the edge of the counter, he appeared in her kitchen doorway.

"Hi, Nate." Liz saluted him with her wineglass.

"Liz." Barely pausing in striding across the kitchen, he gave Liz a curt nod but scowled at Bella. "How many times must I tell you to lock that door? Jesus, Bella. There's some psycho out there trashing your store and leaving shit all over your front porch and you're sitting here drinking with the door wide open."

"I know tae kwon do." With a smirk, Liz got to her feet. "Anyhoo, I'm gonna let you two crazy kids fight it out. I think I heard Noel head back a little while ago and I'm about ready for another round of his magic dick."

Nate flinched and looked a little ill.

Heat burning up her cheeks, Bella had to hide a grin. Liz needed a whole spoonful of sugar to make her palatable. It was one of the things she'd grown to like about her.

Liz's heels clipped down the hallway. The front door squeaked open and shut again. More footsteps made their way down the porch stairs and grew softer.

Nate's face stayed grim, but his tone had softened. "Are you all right?"

With those intense eyes burning into her, she couldn't lie. "I'm fine. A bit freaked-out but fine." She took a tentative step closer. The need to touch burned through her and she placed her hand on his chest. "I did lock the door when I went to work. I just forgot with Liz coming over."

Dropping his head, he stared at her hand, pale against the khaki of his shirt. "I was worried about you."

"I know." That hit her even harder in the knees than his overwhelming physical presence.

His chest muscle tensed beneath her fingers. "That's maybe not a good idea."

"Why?" Beneath her hand, he burned hot, his heart beating strong and sure.

"Because I don't think so clearly when you touch me." He took her hand, pressed a kiss into the palm, and released it. "We need to deal with this Adam asshole, Bella. Before he gets worse."

Chapter Fifteen

$\mathcal{N}$ate's words cut straight through Bella's heat haze. "Deal with him?"

"You have a stalker here, Bella." Nate stepped away from her and shrugged out of his winter jacket.

Surely not. Okay, Adam was a bit intense, and he showed up wherever she was, but a stalker?

"You need to face this." Nate shoved his hands into his pockets. "He follows you, he makes unwanted contact with you. What he did in your store could even constitute a credible threat."

"Wow." Bella slumped into a kitchen chair. "What do I do?"

Nate pulled a face. "It's not so cut-and-dried. Different stalkers pose different threats. But let's start with the basics. Have you made it absolutely clear that you want nothing to do with him?"

"I think so."

He took the seat opposite her and leaned his elbows on the table. "That's not good enough, sweetheart. You need to let him know in no uncertain terms that you don't want anything more to do with him and that any contact on his part is unwelcome."

"I told him I don't want to see him anymore."

"You mean *the thing* you told him about when I was here?"

Bella nodded.

"These guys don't think like you or I. If you say you don't want to see him because of someone else or a *thing*, what he hears is that he has a chance if that person or thing doesn't exist."

"Wow." Sooner or later she would manage something a little less inane, but for now it was all she had.

"You call him and you arrange to meet with him," Nate said.

"No." Bella might not be an expert on stalkers, but she sure didn't want to face Adam again.

"It's better face-to-face." Nate tapped the table. "And I'll be right there next to you."

"Can't I call?"

Shaking his head, he took her hand. "You have to take all room for doubt away. You need to look him in the eye and tell him you don't want to see him and he isn't to contact you again."

"That can't be right." She scrabbled for some kind of out. "From what I've heard, you should stay away from a stalker, never make contact."

"You heard right." Nate sat back in his seat. "With some stalkers, hearing it in person will be enough to get them to leave you the hell alone. And that's what we want here, sweetheart. We want this dickhead out of your life."

"And if he doesn't?" Her mouth had gone dry and she took a slug of her wine.

"To be safe, we assume he won't." Nate grimaced. "Now

comes the pain-in-the-ass part. You need to change your phone numbers—cell, home, and business."

"I can't do that. The store is my business." She needed more wine, but they'd already gone through Liz's first bottle and she'd taken the second home with her.

"It's another way for him to get hold of you," Nate said. "And if he knows where the store is, you can bet your ass he has the number."

"I hate this." No wine around, she dropped her head onto the table.

"We also need to change the locks on both your store and the house." He rapped the table. "Pay attention, sweetheart."

"I am." Bella sat up. Suddenly, people had their sticky hands in her life and she hated it. "This is a lot to take in."

"I know." His face softened. "But you need to make sure you're safe, and that means getting paranoid until we can make him go away."

"You're going to help me with this."

"Sweetheart." The way he said it made her insides all mushy. "Now." He went back to all business. "We change the locks, and I'll send a security company around to install alarms."

Bella pulled a face. She had a knack for tripping alarms, which was why she'd had the one in the store removed. "I hate those things." Even she had to concede she sounded petulant.

"Have you eaten?" Nate glanced around the kitchen.

"No."

"Damn, me neither. I'm starving." The chair scraped as he stood.

Bella stood with him. "I could make us something."

"Um . . . Bella." He cleared his throat. "Let me do the cooking."

She would take offense, but then, she'd foisted enough mac and cheese with pink marshmallows on him to know better. Waving her hand to indicate he should take over, she sat back down again.

He rummaged around in her fridge and came out with some bacon, cream, eggs, and a tub of Parmesan. "You got any pasta?"

Bella pointed to a cupboard to his left. "What are you making?"

"A version of carbonara. I haven't eaten since breakfast. I'm starving."

"You can afford the calories," Bella said as he got to work.

Nate flashed her his signature wicked grin. "So can you. I've seen the evidence."

Her face heated, but the incident had lost its sting. It was kind of funny when she let it be.

Bacon sizzled in the pan, filling the kitchen with its mouthwatering smell.

"Let's finish this so we can enjoy dinner." Nate put a pot of water on to boil for the pasta. He worked efficiently in the kitchen, like he'd had a lot of practice. Did the hotness of this man ever quit?

Bella nodded. She rather thought they had finished.

"You need to be aware." Nate leaned his fists on her chopping board. "Know who's around you at all times. Who's in the car behind you; that sort of thing. And if he pops his head up, you let me know." He gave the bacon pan a twist. "You have my cell number, right?"

Be still her beating heart. How many times had she almost gone into orbit at the idea of Nate Evans giving her his number? Of course, none of those scenarios had a stalker in them. Bella bit back a sigh. "No."

"You don't?" He cocked his head. "What sort of half-assed crush was it when you didn't even have my cell number?"

"I was waiting for you to give it to me." She appreciated his effort to lighten the mood. "Maybe I should have grabbed it ages ago."

"You're not that kind of girl."

Which brought up an interesting question. "What kind of girl do you think I am?"

"The nice kind." He didn't even hesitate. Pouring the pasta into the boiling water, he said, "The kind you get serious about and plan a future with."

"The boring kind." Bella really wished she could summon up the spirit of Liz at will and be that confident.

"No." Nate tipped up her chin. His gaze warmed her from within. "The sweet kind. The one a man needs to be worthy of having."

Snorting, Bella pushed away from the table. She'd better have some beer in that fridge. Yup; she silently blessed her creature-of-habit self who always stocked up. "Beer?"

"Sure." He shrugged. "I'm now officially off-duty."

She popped the cap on two beers and handed him one.

He raised it in a silent salute to her. "To good company."

Well hell, wasn't that every girl's dream right there, and just what she wanted to be: good company? She had trouble remembering this was the same man who'd pushed her up against the wall and kissed the sweet girl out of her. What if she suddenly pinned him up against the wall?

"You've got a funny look on your face." Nate glanced at her as he separated eggs, cupping the yolk in his palm and letting the white run through his fingers. God help her, even that she found sexy.

"Just thinking." She shrugged around the question.

Everybody thought of her as sweet, a good girl. To be fair, it was a part she'd played since birth. She didn't like thinking of herself as a people-pleaser, but if the Mary Jane fit . . .

Nate put a bowl of pasta in front of her and took the seat opposite. "Those are some big thoughts you got going on there."

Thoughts aside, she was hungry, and the pasta smelled delicious. She dug her fork in. "It's the sweet thing."

"You are sweet." Nate twirled spaghetti like an expert. "Even when I dunked your hair in paint, you were sweet about it."

"I wasn't thinking sweet thoughts." The incredible thing going on in her mouth demanded attention. "And, damn, this is good."

"You should have kicked me, or punched me. At the least pinched me."

"Nah." Because from that moment on, he'd soared as boy god in her eyes. "I didn't want to get you into trouble."

"See." He stabbed his fork at her. "Sweet."

He tucked into his dinner with relish. Watching him love on food ranked right up there as one of her most sensual experiences. Didn't that make her some kind of sad? "Can I ask you something?"

"Sure."

"It's kind of a weird question."

He smiled. "Those are often the best kind."

Here went nothing. "If I hadn't been sweet, would you . . . ? I mean . . . would we . . ." She couldn't do this, not with him shifting in his seat and looking like he'd gone off his dinner. "Forget it."

"Shit." He breathed through his nose. "When you said weird, you really meant awkward as hell."

"Don't answer that." She waved her hand and stuffed her mouth full of pasta. That way she couldn't open it and make even more of an idiot of herself.

Narrowed eyes on her the entire time, he ate three bites of pasta. Then he put his fork and spoon down. "Actually, I want to answer that."

"I really don't want you to anymore." Because his silence screamed louder than anything else.

"I'm a guy, so I'm always looking." He shrugged. "Anyone who tells you different is lying. Did I notice your hot little body? Sure. Did I like your big, beautiful smile? You betcha." He picked up his utensils again. "But the thing is this: some girls you put in your not-fuckable category and keep them there."

Never ask a question you don't want to hear the answer to. *Hi, my name is Bella and I'm not fuckable.* There had to be a support group for that somewhere. People Pleasers Anonymous, we'll be over here having a meeting if nobody else minds.

"But they don't always stay there," he said. "Sometimes, no matter how hard you try, the girl keeps crossing out of the box and then you're in big shit."

She didn't want this conversation. It depressed the crap out of her. Leaping up, she took her bowl to the washer.

"Sweetheart." He grabbed her hand. "We gotta talk about what's going on."

"No, we really don't." She tried for arch. "I'm in the not-fuckable category."

"You should be." When she tried to free her wrist, he held on. "You for damn sure should be, but you're not. And that kiss didn't help."

"It was just a kiss." And the *Titanic* was just a ship that hit a minor snag in the ocean.

Giving her hand a tug, Nate grinned. "Is that so?"

Cocksure son of a bitch actually got a smile out of her, which, given how her day had gone so far, constituted a miracle. "Maybe I'm downplaying it a bit."

"Yeah, maybe." He turned and pulled her between his splayed thighs. "I want to kiss you again, Bella. Put my hands all over you." His voice deepened. "Taste you. Fuck you."

Should she be slapping his face 'round about now? Instead, she melted. Her breathing came a little faster and her skin grew sensitive. "Er . . ."

"But here's the thing." He swept his thumbs in slow circles over the backs of her hands. "I'm not a forever kind of guy. I won't stay, Bella. We might have some laughs, hang out a bit, but at the end of the day, I will go."

"Why are you telling me this?" A war erupted inside her. Her girl parts yelled for her to get on board with him, her heart vacillated, and her head issued a firm, Nana-sounding warning.

He looped her arms around his neck and stood. He brushed against her on the way up and stood there connecting all the right parts. "We're attracted to each other. We're both adults. Want me to draw you a picture?"

"I'm good." More than good, in fact. Her girl parts surged into the lead.

He stepped away from her, taking all that lovely heat with him. "I like you, Bella. And I'm attracted to you as well, and I'd like to do something about that, but only if you understand the way it is."

Her lust fog faded. "So, you're saying we do this your way or not at all?"

He grimaced. "It sounds even more dickish when you put it like that, but yeah. I really don't want to hurt you."

"I think you should go." Before she did something stupid.

Whether that would be cry or throw herself at him remained uncertain.

Face inscrutable, he stared at her for a long time. Then he nodded and grabbed his jacket. "See you around, Bella." He tugged up his jacket zipper. "We would have had fun, sweetheart. No doubt about it."

She locked the door behind him and trailed back into the kitchen. Picking up Nate's beer, she finished it. She should clean up the kitchen after dinner, but Nate hadn't even made that much of a mess. What a truly crazy day. So far, her Prince Charming options amounted to a stalker or a player. Way to go, Bella. Way to live the dream.

Chapter Sixteen

Most days Nate felt okay with the man he saw in the mirror. Sure, he'd messed up big as a kid, but he'd gotten his life together, made good on his promise to old Sheriff Wheeler. This morning, as he shaved, he saw a self-involved prick.

Since he first hit puberty he'd been laying down that line with women, and it had never occurred to him how screwed up it really was. Ergo how screwed up he was. The take-it-or-leave-it, sex-with-no-strings, love-'em-and-leave-'em kind of messed up. In his defense, he'd started laying it all out in an attempt to stop the women in his life from getting hurt by his inability to commit. Seeing a woman you'd cared about hurting and knowing you were the cause really sucked, and if she knew going in that you weren't the hanging-around type, she could make the choice to leave or stay. But while he was having a moment of ruthless introspection here, he might as well confess that he had also started with his patter as a built-in escape clause, a way of leaving the back door open for when he was ready to make his escape.

Which was why he had always stayed away from Bella. He was no good for her. Bella needed a different sort of man, one who hung around, and he'd never be that.

So why couldn't he get Bella out of his mind? Not just his X-rated version of her, but her eyes. Every thought she had went through those eyes like a ticker tape. It had always disconcerted him, the way she looked at him. As if she saw some better version of him, and it scared the shit out of him. He washed shaving foam off his face and stared at his reflection. What exactly did Bella see in him? It sure as hell wasn't the same man he saw.

This introspection crap sucked. He flipped the shower knobs until he got the temperature right. He should have done what he'd been doing since first grade. He should have walked away. He still should walk away.

Too pissed at himself to want to spend more time in his own company, he got his workday started.

Already halfway through her cup of coffee, Gabby beat him to it again. The woman must get up in the middle of the night and hit the office.

She nodded to him as he walked into the small Ghost Falls satellite office. "Morning, Sheriff."

"Isn't it your day off?"

"Yeah." Gabby picked up her cup and walked over to the machine. "But Jeff's wife is having a hard time with the new baby, so I said I'd take his shift."

"You take the day off tomorrow." He snagged a mug and poured. "I can't have tired, stressed-out officers on my hands."

"Stressed out?" Strolling back to her desk, Gabby sniffed. "Please, Sheriff, nothing ever happens in this town."

Gabby had a past; he would bet every dime the county didn't pay him on it. He knew that look. Hell, he wore that look often enough. But she'd come highly recommended from a former colleague in Salt Lake City, her record had impressed him, and his options around Ghost Falls came down to Jeff . . . and Jeff. Jeff already had the job, so Gabby had been hired.

"I want you to run a background check for me."

She raised her brows. "Adam Smith?"

"You got it in one." Like she said, not much happened around here. "Not really liking our chances of that being a real name."

"Me neither." Fingers flying across the keys, she went back to staring at her screen.

Despite her attitude, Gabby was pretty. Dark hair, tawny skin, startling green eyes that tipped up like a cat's. Fortunately, she'd never done it for him, or him for her, which made working together a lot easier. She'd also give him the unvarnished truth, and he was having enough of a navel-gazing day to want to hear it.

Hiding his face behind pouring another coffee, he waded in. "What do you see when you look at me?"

Gabby's keyboard-tapping stopped. "What?"

He'd started this crap, may as well finish it. "How would you describe me?"

Glancing at him askance, she frowned and then said, "White male, six three, early thirties, dark hair, light eyes." She shrugged. "Actually, your eyes are kind of weird; I'd have to say yellow."

"And . . . ?"

"And what else?" She shrugged.

Despite feeling stupider by the minute, the need to know drove him forward. "I meant, when you look at me, what sort of guy do you see."

"A cop?"

Shit, she sucked at this game. He'd ask Pippa, although

he suspected he knew what her answer would be. He stalked toward his office.

With his hand on the door handle, Gabby's voice stopped him. "You mean like do I see a nice guy or a jerk? That sort of thing?"

"Yeah." Now she was getting this.

From top to bottom and back again, she studied him. "A player," she said. "Basically a nice guy, but mostly a player."

Exactly what Pippa would have said and did say often enough. Good thing he loved the hell out of his sister-in-law. "What makes you say that? Specifically, I mean."

Gabby rolled her eyes and snatched a pile of notes off her desk. "Let's see here. Mrs. Kranz would like you to go around to check her panic button. Old Lady Myers can't find her cat again, and she didn't use the word *cat*." Raising her eyebrows, she consulted her notes. "Blythe, Carly, Pippa, Maggie, Anna, and Rachel all want you to call them."

"Pippa's my sister-in-law, so she doesn't count."

"She said you weren't answering your cell." She squinted at her pile and tapped the top one. "Actually, Rachel here got quite pissy with me when I wouldn't give her your cell number."

"They call me." It looked bad, but things often looked bad out of context.

"I know that." Gabby shrugged. "Because you're basically a nice guy but still a player."

Which meant what exactly? "Why would they call me if I'm a player?"

"You're saying you're not a player?" She snorted.

"I never said that." It would be stretching the truth too far. "But if I'm a player, why would they call me? Knowing that about me?"

Gabby smirked. "Because of the nice-guy thing."

"Explain."

"When women look at you, they see crack on legs. A

man who shows the potential for being reformed." She went back to her keyboard. "Are we done with this whole Oprah thing or would you like to talk about your childhood?"

Nate slammed his office door on her smug expression. Is that what Bella saw when she looked at him? The player thing didn't bother him too much. All right, it did, but he'd done enough to earn it, so there didn't seem much point in getting his shorts in a wad about it. The other thing stuck like a splinter under his nail. Did Bella want to reform him? Did she look at him and see a work in progress?

He checked on the dog he'd put in the pound yesterday. The pound manager agreed with him; the dog just needed some obedience training and he'd be fine. He put in a call to the boy's parents and delivered the ultimatum: take the dog to training or say good-bye. He really hoped they went with the former.

Midmorning, he got called out to referee the long-standing battle between two crusty old plot owners on the outskirts of town. They'd been at each other's throats for so long, he was convinced they'd be lost without each other.

When he got back to the office, Gabby pounced.

"So, I got the information on your Adam Smith," she said, handing him a bunch of printer pages. "Seems Adam Smith really is his name, at least as far back as I went."

"Which was how far?"

"Five years." She tapped the top sheet. "But it was hard enough finding that. Our boy likes to move around. He makes big money, works in computers, but he never sticks at one job too long. No record, no outstanding arrests, one parking ticket about a year ago. Mr. Average Joe."

He caught her tone and glanced up. "But . . . ?"

"I don't know." Gabby frowned. "He's like a ghost. He moves in and out of people's lives and once he's gone, it's like he's never even been there. Nothing of him on social media at all. No tweets, no Facebook friends. He's not even on LinkedIn."

"I'm not on those things either."

"Yes, you are." She motioned him over to her computer and clicked away with her mouse. "Maybe you don't have an account. But see, here on Pippa's page, there you are."

True enough—and standing next to Bella. In the picture, she gazed up at him, wearing that look that made him itchy. Damn, she looked pretty in her green dress.

"I ran facial recognition software on him and got no hits," Gabby said.

"We have that?" Nate glared at the computer.

Gabby rolled her eyes. "Of course we have that. But our Mr. Smith doesn't leave any traces of himself behind." She shrugged. "That's weird, right? I mean, everybody leaves some kind of trail behind them."

"Yes, they do." Gut tingling in a way that had nothing to do with Gabby's tricked-out software and more to do with instinct, he said, "Dig deeper. Go back farther. Everyone leaves a trail; we have to find his."

At lunchtime, he went out to get a sandwich, which happened to mean going past Bella's store, which also meant, being a responsible cop, he should check on her.

He was so full of crap and Ghost Falls didn't warrant this much of his time. That still didn't stop him from taking a moment before opening the door and watching her for a minute.

Bella was unpacking a large carton at her feet. Her face lit up with her big, gorgeous smile that came from her toes as she looked at something blue in her hands.

As he pushed open the door, she glanced his way and her smile wavered.

Damn! Had he done that to her? Bella had the sort of

smile that made you want to be part of it for as long as it lasted.

"What you got?" He jerked his chin at the box.

Immediately, he got his sunshine back as she smiled at her box. "Some stuff I ordered just came in. It's new stuff, from a small designer who lives upstate." Diving into the box, she hauled a bunch of material out. "And it's beautiful. It goes perfectly with what I have in mind for the store."

He wanted to hold on to his happy for a while longer. "How's that?"

"Well . . ." She blew a strand of hair out of her face. "Firstly, I want to cater to a different sort of clientele. At the moment, we sell to the blue-rinse brigade and they're all twinsets and sensible shoes."

He didn't have a clue what a twinset or a blue rinse was and he didn't care. "And you want to cater to a different crowd?"

"Yes." She shook something out and spread it over her body. The something was a dress. "See, this will appeal to a more stylish woman. Someone who wants to stay on trend and age appropriate at the same time."

"It's a nice dress," he said.

She wrinkled her nose at him—fucking adorably—and laughed. "You have no idea what I'm talking about, do you?"

"Not a clue."

"It means change." She beamed at him. "My vision for the store is coming true."

Going on pure instinct, Nate hooked his hand behind her nape and tugged her mouth to his.

She came willingly, bringing all that was Bella and good with her. Her mouth opened on a soft *O* of surprise and Nate went for the prize, the sweetness inside that was

100 percent Bella. The taste of her rocked through him, making him crave more.

He pressed her closer, wanting to feel the fullness of her breasts against his chest, needing it at an elemental level that shattered his control. A kiss had never gotten him so hard so fast before. He discovered her soft curves with his hand, the delicious dip of her waist that swelled into her hips.

She moaned and writhed under his hand.

No stick insect, Bella was made for his touch. He ground his erection closer to her core. They stood in the middle of her store, fair game for anyone walking past, and Nate didn't give a shit. All he wanted was more Bella.

He backed her into the counter behind her. A pencil holder clattered onto the floor. Her hands dug into his hair, holding him in place as if she wanted him to never let her go. If he could separate from her enough, he would tell her not to bother; he sure as hell wasn't going anywhere.

He stroked his tongue into her mouth.

Her nipples pressed into his chest, hard and demanding his attention.

Cupping the full weight of her breast, he stroked his thumb over her nipple.

Bella arched into his touch, her hands tightening in his hair.

He could lift her onto the counter and drive into her. He bet she was wet under that prim skirt, wet and ready for him. His dick throbbed at the idea. It took him a second to register she was pushing him away.

Bella ripped her mouth away from his. "We have to stop."

He knew she was right, but he stood still a moment, fighting his urges back down to normal. "You need to make a decision." His breath rasped. "Or this heat between us is going to make it for you."

Bella dug her fingers into the counter to keep herself from running after him, dragging him into the back and demanding he finish what he'd started. Every time she saw Nate, he left her more confused and so in lust she was about ready to explode.

She'd broken new ground here, wandering into unfamiliar territory. Wandered, her sainted butt; she'd gone running and leaping where angels feared to tread. She needed some expert advice.

Liz agreed to meet her for drinks after work. She insisted they go out and not prop up Bella's kitchen table again. "We still need to stick to our list of ten," Liz insisted.

Which was how Bella ended up at Ed's later that evening, threading her way through people she'd gone to high school with. She stopped several times to say hello as she made her way over to Liz. A depressing number of former classmates were married, most of those with children.

Liz caught sight of her and pulled a face.

Yeah, her friend looked as out of place as she felt. Ed's catered to a far more relaxed set than Liz in her tight blue cocktail dress.

"Now I remember why I never come here." Liz stood and kissed her cheek. "Is it me or did you go to school with everyone in here?"

"Just about." Bella levered herself up onto the barstool. Damn things weren't made for pencil skirts. "All except the old-timers, and you went to school with them."

"You're a bitch," Liz said and sipped her martini.

"That must be the first time someone's called me a bitch." Bella motioned to Jo. Did she tend every bar in Ghost Falls? "Most people insist I'm supersweet."

Liz grinned at her. "Are we getting to the good stuff right away?"

"May as well."

Smiling, Jo appeared across the bar from them. "We don't see you in here much."

"You seem to be working hard." Talking about Jo's brother with her behind the bar might get awkward.

"No." Jo tucked her hands into her back pockets. "Some of the time I study."

"I never understood the nautical theme in here." Liz peered around her with her lip curled. "I mean, we're not even close to a mud puddle, let alone the ocean."

"I'd tell you, but then I'd have to kill you." Jo wiped the bar counter. "Now, are you girls drinking or just polishing the barstools?"

"Oh, we're drinking." Liz tapped the side of her glass. "You better get me another one of these, and something for Bella that a good girl very definitely wouldn't drink."

"I smell girl talk coming on." Jo grabbed a bottle of vodka from the shelves behind her. "I think a dirty martini should do the trick." She winked at Bella. "But don't tell Nate. He told me not to let you get hammered."

"Seriously?" Bella's blood pressure spiked and she dropped her forehead onto the bar. "That man is hounding me."

"Hounding?" Jo stopped shaking for a second before resuming.

"We're here to dissect your brother," Liz told her.

Jo put two martini glasses on the counter. "Then I'm staying because I've got more stories about my brothers than anyone." She put olives in each glass and pushed them across the bar. "Are you going to sit up, Bella, or should I get you a straw?"

"She's overwrought." Smacking her lips, Liz sipped her martini.

"Now there's a word you don't hear every day." With a

clatter, Jo emptied the shaker's leftovers into a sink below the bar. "And Nate is the reason she's overwrought, I'm guessing."

"Smart *and* beautiful," Liz said.

Jo snorted. "Isn't Nate the reason most women in Ghost Falls are overwrought?"

There! Bella sat up. That there was exactly the issue. "Yes."

Liz and Jo stared at her.

Bella took a fortifying slug of martini. It tasted like formaldehyde, or what she imagined formaldehyde tasted like. "Ugh! That's horrible. How do you drink these things?"

"You don't want to be sweet, you've got to drink like a bitch." Liz savored her next sip.

Jo slid her glass away. "Why don't I get you something else?"

"Put a frilly umbrella in it," Liz called after her. "Now, let's have the dirt."

"Did you have to tell Jo we were talking about him?" Bella squirmed on her stool. The Evans brood were a tight-knit bunch.

"Yes, I did." Liz grinned back at her. "I believe in transparency."

"You've got a big mouth."

"That too."

Bella waited for Jo to return with a glass of white wine. Straight out of the box and still flavored with cardboard, but better than the martini. For a girl who never drank, she certainly seemed to be doing a lot of it lately. She could lay the blame for that at Nate's feet too. "It happened again."

Liz blinked at her.

"He kissed me again." Not wanting anyone to hear her,

Bella leaned far forward. Everyone in this bar had gone to school with Nate as well.

"Was it good?"

"Amazing." Bella hauled her head out of the past. "So not the point. I don't know what to do."

Liz reared back. "I'm not teaching you how to kiss."

"Liz." Bella fixed her with a glare. She was having a hard enough time as it was without wisecracking.

"Okay, okay, sorry." Liz waved her hands in front of her. "Why do you have to do something?"

She regretted not calling Pippa now. Even though Nate was her brother-in-law and Matt always tagged along. "Of course I have to do something. I have to decide do I want to have . . ." She checked for any flapping ears. "I have to decide if I want to have sex with him or not. But on his terms."

Liz's eyes lit with amusement. "Can you say sex without being scared someone might hear you?"

"No, I can't." A humbling realization, but there you had it.

"If you can't even say sex, how the hell are you going to have it?" Liz motioned to Jo for another martini. "You're driving, by the way."

"Why am I friends with you again?" Right now, she had a hard time remembering.

"Screwed if I know." Liz shrugged. "You must have incredibly shitty taste."

"So, either I have sex with Nate on his terms or I walk away and stop all the kissing him." A thought that depressed her even further.

Liz turned to face her. "Now, I suck at advice generally, but I'm about to lay some good stuff on you. So listen up."

Bella nodded obediently and sipped her wine.

"First off, if you think you can stop kissing Nate, you're in la-la land. You've had it hot for that man since before you knew what your vajayjay was, and now it looks like he's got a hard-on for you. Do you honestly think you're going to be able to tell him no next time he lays a hot, wet one on you?"

She had trouble not wincing through Liz's speech, but she managed. "I'm not some kind of mindless sex maniac."

"Well done; you said sex without checking," Liz said. "And it's not being a sex maniac, it's a natural response to something you've always wanted. Suddenly, someone is saying you can have this thing you crave." She shrugged and thanked Jo for her new drink. "You're going to grab it with both hands, regardless of what we discuss here tonight."

"I might not." She didn't fool Liz any more than she fooled herself. Grabbing Nate sounded like a better and better idea. "I'm in so much trouble."

"Yeah, you are." Liz nodded. "Because take it from me, the only thing you ever change on a man is his diaper. Nate isn't going to suddenly see the light and settle down and raise kids with you. He's going to leave you crying but hopefully rock your world before he does it."

"Is there any good news in your advice?" Bella could really do with some right now. As much as she wanted to tell Liz how wrong she was, honesty wouldn't allow her to. It sucked being a good girl. You didn't even get the luxury of lying to yourself.

"You're human. He's human. For whatever reason, the fates have aligned, Mars is rising in Venus." Liz pulled a face. "Or who knows what else, but you two are on a runaway train straight to O land."

Liz had a way with words. Not a good way, but a way. "That's enough to kill the spark."

"You might fumble around a bit and tell yourselves you're not gonna go there, but you will. Someday you'll find yourselves alone." Liz widened her eyes and pressed her hand to her chest. "However did you get there? Hormones." She snorted. "Mating heat. Call it what you will, but you're gonna do it."

Bella didn't buy all this. It seemed a horribly jaded way of looking at people and love. "What if we resisted? If we both decided it was a bad idea and walked away?"

"Bam!" Liz smacked her palms together. "You'll only make it more intriguing. What person in the history of the world resisted?"

Not at all what Bella wanted to hear. "Maybe that's because they don't write stories about them."

"No, they don't." Liz nodded. "Because who wants to read a story about some stick-up-the-ass self-righteous dingbat who had a chance for a taste of something good and settled for water."

"Ever heard of a little thing called free will?"

"Buck up, sweet cheeks." Liz gave her an evil grin. "The good news is that you're going to get laid."

She'd been abstaining for too long not to get a little cheered by that. "You're saying this thing is beyond my control?"

"Nope." Liz puffed up her cheeks. "I'm saying you're human and you won't control it. You'll make up some justification for why it's okay. But here's what you can control."

"I'm all ears." Bella had trouble keeping the snark out of her voice.

"You're not going into this blind." Liz upended her empty glass on the bar and motioned Jo for another. "You know what he is and who he is. You've known him your whole life. Don't go in there expecting turtledoves and rings and you won't be disappointed. Go in there knowing that you're gonna take what you can when you can and pick up the pieces later."

Chapter Seventeen

*N*ate checked out the run-down apartment complex Daniel had texted him the address for. He grabbed the six-pack of soda from the passenger seat and climbed out of his car. Sitting here like a pussy wasn't going to bring him any answers.

Daniel had invited him to watch the Broncos game. Something they always used to do but in a different time, when he was a different man. Daniel claimed he'd changed, and it seemed like he'd changed. It surprised Nate that a part of him still believed in miracles enough to believe it could happen.

He stepped over an upturned garbage bin that had hurled its contents all over the sidewalk in front of the apartment block. Four days' past collection day and nobody had made any effort to pick it up. Over the token patch of grass beside the entrance, a woman walked a scraggly mongrel. Catching his eye, she nodded and glanced behind her.

In a place like this, the sheriff showing up wouldn't go over well. The front door hung ajar and he let himself in. Not trusting the battered elevator, he walked the three flights up to Daniel's apartment. The hallway stank of cigarettes, stale beer, and piss.

Daniel's door opened before he got there. "Hey. I expected you to change your mind."

"You live in this dump?" Nate sidestepped a threadbare stroller.

With a grin, Daniel shrugged one shoulder. "Where I just came from, they don't let you out with a trust fund."

A woman yelled at someone called Reese from the closed doorway across the hall.

The smell stopped inside Daniel's apartment. An old, sixties-style kitchen opened onto a living room. The generic brown furniture looked clean but bashed up.

"I see you took care of priorities." Nate nodded at the big-screen dominating one side of the room.

"Yeah." Daniel rubbed the back of his neck. "I couldn't resist. They didn't make them that size when I went away." He nodded at the soda. "You could have brought beer; it doesn't bother me."

"Nah." Nate put the soda on the counter. "I'm half on duty anyway. Jeff's got a sick baby at home and he might need to take off."

Daniel nodded. "Okay, then. Shall we watch the game? You can tell me what I missed."

Leaving the big recliner for Daniel, Nate took a seat on the sofa.

On the small table in front of the TV, Daniel had laid out a bowl of chips and some salsa.

Daniel laughed and rubbed his hands on his thighs. "I was never much of a cook; that much hasn't changed."

"It's all good."

They sat in silence for a while, watching the Broncos' defense annihilate the Seahawks.

Daniel waited for the ad break to storm the heavy silence. "So, how long have you been sheriff?"

"Not long." Fetching a soda, Nate handed one to Daniel. "I was working up in Salt Lake City when I got the call the town wanted me to run."

Eyebrows raised, Daniel stopped with his soda halfway to his mouth. "They asked you to run? This town?"

"Yeah." Nate had to laugh. Could have blown him over at the time as well. He'd have thought they had the pitchforks at the ready for him. "After Sheriff Wheeler died, they brought in someone from Bitter River, but Ghost Falls didn't take to him. The diva suggested me as a replacement and somehow managed to convince the rest of the town and the county to get on board with her."

"She still alive?"

"Oh yes." It would take a force of nature to kill Diva Philomene St. Amor. "Alive and as much the diva as ever."

"Huh." Daniel watched Siemian take the field. Incomplete. "She wrote to me when I was inside."

"She did?" It didn't much surprise him. The diva had her own way of doing things, and she never allowed anyone else to form her opinions for her.

"Once a month, like clockwork."

He turned to keep Daniel's face in view. If Phi had written to him, Daniel would have known everything she knew, which meant pretty much everything that went on in Ghost Falls. "So, you already knew how long I'd been sheriff."

"Yeah." Daniel pulled a face. "But I was sitting here hunting for a topic of conversation and that seemed like a good one."

It never used to be like this. Back in the day, he and Daniel almost never ran out of shit to say. Even better, they'd had that rare kind of friendship that often meant not needing to talk.

"And you wanted the job?"

"I did." Another incomplete ended the drive and Nate hissed his frustration. Damn Broncos' offense left all the work to defense. "I was working a tough detail up in Salt Lake City. Special Victims Task Force. It got to me." It had taken him a long time to come to his next realization. "And I missed it here. Missed the people. Mainly my brothers and Jo, but I wanted to come home."

"And Matt married Pippa Turner?" Chuckling, Daniel shook his head.

True. Nate hadn't seen that one coming either. Still didn't get what the glamorous Pippa saw in his hick of a brother. Still . . . "Matt's a good guy. He deserves some happy."

Daniel nodded, and they watched the Broncos' defense come out again and put more hurt on the Seahawks.

Nate let the ads start again before he asked one of the burning questions. "What's the plan now that you're out?"

"Not sure." Daniel threw him a look that said how much he knew Nate wanted to hear his answer. "Not what I was doing before I went in."

"Glad to hear it."

"I'm sure." Daniel leaned forward and grabbed a handful of chips. "I finished high school while I was inside. Even did some courses through an online college."

Daniel and studying weren't two things Nate ever thought he would hear in the same sentence. "Studying what?"

"Social work. Counseling." Daniel went a bit pink. "I know it's a cliché and all, but we had this counselor who used to run a weekly group. He got me thinking about how someone like me is well positioned to do that sort of thing."

Daniel might not have liked school, but he never lacked for smarts. If they'd ever needed a plan, back in the day, Daniel had been their go-to guy. "So you're going to get your degree?"

"Um." Daniel stuffed his mouth full of chips. "Already got it."

"You're kidding me." Nate didn't bother to hide his surprise.

"I had nothing but time on my hands." He cleared his throat. "So, Siemian, huh?"

"Yeah." Looking at Daniel was weird. Like seeing two people cohabit the same body. His cynical side clung to his old image of Daniel, but the new Daniel kept busting through regardless. "What are you going to do with your degree?"

"Work with at-risk teens." The passion in Daniel's voice was straight-up truth and no bullshit. "Try to make sure kids don't pull the same dumb shit we did." Elbows on knees, he leaned forward. "I don't know if it would have made any difference, but when I was inside, I kept wondering if I'd had someone to talk to. Someone who'd been there, walked that road, and come to a dead end, maybe I would have made different choices."

"Do you think we would have listened?" And it was a *we*, because regardless of where they'd ended up, he and Daniel had started at the same point.

Daniel laughed. "I don't know. We were pretty stubborn little shits."

"That we were." Here they sat, two kids who'd made the mistakes and paid for them. Daniel more so than him, but only because Nate had wised up a bit sooner. But then, he'd had Matt who, despite being young, had kept the ship sailing for them. And Eric had picked up some slack for Matt when he could. Nate could never prove it, but he had the feeling Eric had spoken to old Sheriff Wheeler about him. "You make contact with your family?"

"Nah." Sadness flashed over Daniel's face and disappeared again. "I tried, when I first got out, but they only want enough money from me to drink themselves to death." He shook his head. "Do you ever speak to Blake?" Daniel named the third musketeer in their group.

"He left town." Nate shook his head. "Last I heard, he was working in Vegas."

"Counting cards?"

Nate had to laugh. "Maybe, but for the right side this time."

They sat through another defensive annihilation.

Somehow, they'd all made it. God knows how, and they probably didn't deserve it, but they had. "Here's to us." Nate raised his soda can. "And getting our shit together."

Daniel raised his can and grinned. "To getting our shit together."

Jeff's baby developed a high fever and Nate got called into the station. Things would be quiet until the Broncos game ended and then there'd be a spate of alcohol-fueled celebration or mourning antics going on.

"Do you even have a life?" He greeted Gabby, perched at her desk and tapping away at her keyboard.

"Not like yours." She smirked. "Player."

He should fire her ass or toss her in front of a disciplinary committee or something. But he kind of liked her anyway. "I was with a friend. A male friend."

Up went her eyebrows as she raised her hand. "Hey, Boss! I don't judge."

He settled for a glare, because it was probably the closest they'd come to a meaningful exchange in the eighteen months she'd worked there. "What are you doing anyway?"

"Chasing a little rabbit called Adam Smith," she said.

"You find anything more?" Nate peered over her shoulder. She tapped a couple of keys. "You could say that. Seems like Adam Smith doesn't have a record, or much of anything, but Aaron Sykes has been a very busy boy."

"Okay, I'll bite. I'm guessing Aaron and Adam are one and the same."

"You got it." Gabby beamed at him.

It struck him dumb for a moment. She was goddamned gorgeous when she smiled. "Tell me."

"So Adam Smith first makes an appearance about eight years go," she said. "When I tried to go back farther, nothing."

"Fake Social Security?"

"Nope." She glanced at him. "You wanna hear this?"

"Tell me about Aaron."

"When Adam came up as a squeaky-clean nothing, I started looking for similarities in MO. Stalkers who appear in a town, the flowers, even ran Bella's physical description through the database. About nine years ago, an Aaron Sykes is charged with beating the crap out of his wife. According to the police report, it wasn't the first time Mrs. Sykes had ended up in the emergency room. But this time Aaron took it too far and Mrs. Sykes wanted out."

Nate's nape prickled. This was going nowhere good.

"Aaron didn't take so kindly to his wife leaving him. She filed a restraining order against him." Gabby pulled up a new screen. "It all goes quiet until Mrs. Sykes gets a new boyfriend. Seems she has a thing for bad boys and this time bags herself a scumbag called Tony White, aka Tony the Tiger, aka Terrible Tony, aka Torture Tony."

"These are his nicknames?" Nate subtracted originality points from Tony.

"Tony runs a prostitution ring that doesn't care too much about the age of his girls."

"Shit." Nate perched on the edge of her desk. Shit like this was what made him not miss his old job. "And this relates to our boy how?"

"So, Aaron breaks into Tony and Mrs. Sykes's love cottage one night. He's there to get himself a helping of revenge but stumbles on a whole lot more than Mrs. Sykes."

Nate had heard enough. "So, Aaron shares his findings, DA cuts a deal, and Adam Smith crawls out from his sewer."

Her face carefully blank, Gabby shrugged. "That's the gist of it. But there's one more thing."

"What?" He knew he was going to hate what she said next.

"Mrs. Sykes turns up in an emergency room again about three months later. Cops would have looked at Tony for it, but he's locked up tight. Nothing points to our boy at all, and Mrs. Sykes is saying nothing more than yes to Jell-O, but I spoke to the detective who worked the case and his gut told him Aaron Sykes was the perp."

"Damn!" He sprang to his feet. Was he fucking psychic or what? Cops and their hunches were worth listening to. Adam Smith had made his gut chatter since that night he'd first seen him cozying up to Bella. Alarm spiked through his veins and congealed into rage and he kicked a dustbin across the office. "I gotta go."

Gabby leaned back in her chair. "Thought you might."

Chapter Eighteen

*A*s Nate left the station for Bella's, his mom summoned him. He didn't have time for this today, not when he'd been on his way to see Bella. But if he ignored his mother, she'd keep on at Gabby and his cell until he responded.

Nate pulled up outside his mother's ranch-style home and took a moment before he went inside. He'd grown up in this house and it still looked the same as the day his dad died. Mom kept everything like a shrine to their father.

Not even Matt had been able to make her change the paint color or fix the sagging porch.

He climbed out of his car. Knowing you were walking into the lion's den didn't make it any easier to get your ass in there. Mom had been trying to get him to come around since the party the other night. Best guess was that she needed an ally in her one-woman battle against Pippa. It didn't matter how many times he refused to take sides or told her the battle was already lost. Mom kept right on fighting.

The entire thing made his teeth ache. Matt loved Pippa and they were good to each other and for each other. Mom only saw the loss of her influence over Matt. Nate had no doubt anyone who married into the Evans clan would be met with the same reception as Pippa. Pippa just had the misfortune to be the first.

As he opened the back door, Mom sat at the kitchen table waiting.

She went through the usual inquiries about his job, the people he worked with, a couple of acquaintances. And then she got down to business.

"So you're going to be an uncle." She tittered as she bustled around making coffee. "Quite the change for you."

"I think it's great." The sooner he got this over with, the sooner he could go.

"Isn't it?" Mom beamed, gave a little sigh, and turned her back. "I was beginning to wonder if I'd ever be a grandparent."

"Now you are." Nate added sugar to his coffee.

"Of course, it would have been nice to know beforehand." And here it came. "Not to find out with everyone else."

"It's great news, Mom." He didn't know why he still bothered. Hoping against hope that reason would one day prevail.

"Hmm." Mom took the seat opposite him and sipped her coffee. "I hope Pippa isn't going to be one of those women who tries to raise a baby and hold down a career."

His head throbbed. It was like Mom wanted to hold on to her anger and her heartbreak. She clung to them tenaciously, kept the wound fresh. Damn, and people wondered why he'd never married. This, right here, could drive a man out of his mind.

Nate missed his dad. He wished like hell Dad was still alive. Dad wouldn't have wanted any of them to be stuck in some kind of grief loop.

"Lots of women have children and careers," he said.

"And the children suffer." Mom's eyes flashed fire. "Nobody thinks about the children."

With Matt married, Eric shuttling between here, Denver, and Salt Lake, Isaac still MIA, and Mom and Jo never able to have a reasonable conversation, it left him as Mom's go-to child.

He couldn't do it today or any day. But especially not with the news he'd gotten from Gabby. "Look, Mom, I gotta go."

She looked up, her face folded into injured lines. "Do you have plans? I thought you might stay for dinner."

It still got to him, that sense that he let her down all the time. Even though she never knew the worst of it because Matt had protected her from it. "I can't, Ma. I need to go past Bella's to see that she's all right."

"Bella?" Mom's eyes narrowed. "What's wrong with Bella?"

"Official business. I can't say." His job was good for some things. He bent and kissed her on the cheek. He loved his mother, but he couldn't be her bitching board today. "I'll call you and maybe we can have dinner during the week."

"Okay."

She slumped at the kitchen table, a sad, lonely figure. She did it to herself. He knew that, and Eric hammered the point home whenever he was in town. It still didn't alleviate the guilt. Her thing with Pippa had nothing to do with Pippa, which made it doubly frustrating. If Mom could let go of her resentment long enough, she'd find an ally and friend in Pippa. With the new baby on the way, Pippa would need help.

He stopped with his hand on the door. "Call Pippa, Mom. Tell her how happy you are and offer to help her."

"She doesn't want my help."

"How do you know that?" He dug his fingers into the wood to keep his tone civil. "You never ask. You're always getting angry at her about one thing or another."

Mom jerked her spine straight. "I am not the one who gets angry, Nathaniel."

God help him. "I'll call you."

The new information on Adam festered as he drove to Bella's. The situation had escalated and he needed to get Bella to understand without panicking. It might help if he could keep his own nagging worry down to a simmer. He wanted to tuck her someplace safe until this was over.

He scanned Bella's street as he turned into it. No sign of a silver Lexus, and he breathed a small sigh of relief. He counted all the vehicles as he passed them, made sure he knew who they belonged to.

Maybe Adam aka Aaron had gotten the message and moved on. It happened. Sometimes.

Bella sent a text to Liz before starting her Wii. Not being much of a dancer, she'd never take her moves out in public, but with *Just Dance* pounding away in her living room, she could let her inner wild woman free. If anyone asked, she always said she did it for exercise, but she really liked letting it all hang out until her muscles burned and her lungs demanded she take a load off.

She'd hesitated before inviting Liz, but then done it anyway. Liz had no filters, true, but she also didn't judge people, and Liz certainly had an inner wild woman. And an outer wild woman too.

First, though, she checked to make sure her doors and windows were all locked. Although she hadn't had a message from Adam in days, in part courtesy of her new cell-phone number. She really didn't look forward to explaining all this to her family. The easiest, and most cowardly way, would be to send them an email to explain why she had changed all her coordinates.

Unfortunately, the picture forming in her mind wasn't pretty. Nana would have a shit fit and then lecture her about men and bars. In the next breath, she would go on and on about her settling down. How the hell she could find a nice guy at the same church social dating pool she'd fished dry years ago, Nana couldn't say. A Christmas alone had seemed like such a great break from routine. A chance to do something different. Be someone different.

She selected her favorite song and hit Play.

Mom would cry and Dad would exhaust himself trying to appease her, Nana, and Mom, and make everything okay in their world again.

This was the other reason she liked to let fly with her *Just Dance*. You couldn't very well think and follow the dance routines at the same time. With Bella, one definitely messed with the other. So she stopped the thinking, punched up the volume, and found her groove.

It took her a while to register the pounding on the door. Pausing in midsong, she ran and whipped the door open. "You changed your mind."

"Shit, Bella, the music is so loud—" Nate's hot gaze swept her from head to toe. "What the hell are you wearing?"

Bella tried to use the door as a shield because finding your groove demanded the right sort of outfit. In her case, booty shorts and a crop top. "I thought you were Liz."

"Nope." He pushed the door wider. His voice dropped deeper. "And you really should check before you answer the door."

"I locked it." The look in his eyes dragged what little breath she had left right out of her.

"Good." He stepped into her entrance hall. His gaze

made it back to hers, and her mouth dried. She'd seen that look on his face before, just not directed at her. Nate Evans on the prowl.

She crossed her arms in front of her. They didn't cover up much, but it made her feel a little less exposed. She shivered.

Nate shut the door with a soft snick and locked it behind him. "I gotta say, babe. I'm struggling for words here."

"I was dancing."

"Uh-huh."

"Is there something you wanted?" Damn, shit, bugger! That sounded exactly like a come-on.

Nate thought so too, because his eyes smoldered. "I actually came here to talk to you." He shook his head. "But that's not gonna happen with you prancing around all covered in sweat and nearly naked."

"Talk to me about what?"

His jaw tightened. "Babe."

Her belly dropped in a whoosh of heat. Words formed but darted away before she could say them. Some women would have something sexy to say in return, a sassy comeback to bring him to his knees. But she stood there, like he'd planted her in the quicksand of her own longing. "I should get dressed."

Really? *Really!* Dr. Childers threw up her hands and left Bella's head, slamming the door behind her.

"Your call." Nate's stillness prickled along her skin. "I'm really partial to what you're almost wearing right now."

Nate stepped closer.

Bella held her ground.

He traced the line of her shoulder with his fingertips. "I came here to talk."

"You did?" Her eyelids grew heavy as she watched his

thick, blunt fingertip trail the edge of her top to the curve of her breast.

"Bella, this shit is getting out of hand." His fingers moved across the swell of her breasts.

Bella's nipples tightened in response.

His other hand slid behind her nape. "I can't seem to stop thinking about you."

Some garbled response that sounded vaguely like an agreement came out of her mouth.

"Tell me to get the hell outta here, babe." His fingers pressed into her nape, urging her closer.

"I can't." The truth of that resonated through her. She'd wanted this man for far too long. Craved the hunger she read on his face. She stepped into him.

He sucked in a deep breath. "I want you."

Bella slid her hands up and over his shoulders. His coat whispered to the ground. Her heart thundered in her ears. "Stay."

"Last chance." His head dipped.

Bella fastened her hands in his silky hair and tugged. "Duly noted."

On a groan, he fastened his mouth on hers. Sweeping his tongue between her parted lips possessively, his mouth took hers.

Bella surrendered to the inevitable. She stopped second-guessing, questioning, and tiptoeing through her life. She wanted Nate, and by some miracle, he wanted her. Only a stupid idiot walked away from this much hot in her life. Satisfaction blazed through her as she returned his kiss, pushing her breasts against his hard chest.

He freed his mouth from hers. "Be sure, Bella."

She wasn't sure of anything right then, other than that she wanted to feel the kind of alive he offered.

His mouth seared the skin beside her ear. He licked and nibbled along her neck, sparking her nerve endings.

Against her stomach, his erection pressed hard and insistent.

Her breathing came in pants. His shirt buttons irritated her, standing between her touch and all that beautiful skin of his. Her fingers fumbled and she tugged impatiently.

Nate hooked his hands under her thighs.

She wrapped her arms around his neck and dragged his mouth back to hers.

"Bedroom?" He managed to growl against her mouth.

Bella whimpered at the heat of his stomach against hers. "Too far."

He moved with her into the living room. Tossing her onto the couch, he ripped his shirt off and came down on top of her. His thighs pressed between hers.

Bella opened to him, clamping her thighs around his hips. His cock pressed where she ached and Bella tilted her hips up to increase the friction.

Rearing up, he whipped her top over her head. Then he stilled. Hungry gaze locked on her breasts, he ran his hands, slowly, almost reverently up her rib cage to cup their fullness. "You're beautiful."

His mouth on her nipples seared Bella. She arched into his mouth, her hands on his head pressing him closer.

He sucked her deep into the heat of his mouth, first one breast and then the other.

The ache between her legs grew urgent and soft pleading noises came from her throat.

His hand slid beneath her ass, palming it, squeezing and pressing her closer to his cock.

"More." Bella writhed beneath him.

His fingers slid beneath her shorts, seeking the wetness between her legs.

"So wet," he murmured against her mouth. "Wet and ready for me."

"Yes." To all of it. Everything he had to offer. She dug her nails into the smooth skin of his back, hanging on to him as everything spun around her.

He raised his hips to slide her shorts off her legs, taking her panties with him.

She grabbed his belt and tugged it open. Her fingers shook on his zipper as she lowered it. Underneath his boxers, his cock strained against the fabric. Bella fastened her hand around him and stroked.

Nate dropped his head back and growled. "Shit. So good."

Between her thighs, she throbbed in response. Knowing how hard he was for her cranked her up another notch. She shoved his pants off his hips, desperate to feel all that hot and hard inside her.

Nate stood and shucked his pants. He bent to untie his boots and toe them off.

He was so much more beautiful than she'd imagined. And she'd spent a lot of time imagining him like this. Sculpted muscle bunched beneath his smooth skin. A happy trail snaked between his perfect abs to his cock. Nate dropped to his knees at the side of the couch. Fastening his hands around her thighs, he tugged her around and to the edge. He bent forward and licked between her folds.

Bella jacked up on a low moan.

His head lowered between her thighs and his tongue and lips were right there.

She dug her fingers into his hair and he worked her over with that clever mouth. Sucking on her clit just right, circling with his tongue, driving her closer to coming with each touch.

"Nate." It came out as a garbled whimper. "I'm going to—"

"Come for me, Bella." He brought his fingers into play, sliding first one and then another inside her, as he continued to feast on her.

Her orgasm built hard and fast and she came on a low keen. It roared through her body, tightening her muscles, and she clamped her thighs over his ears to keep him there.

He pressed her thighs away with a soft chuckle. "I would ask if that was good, but my ears are ringing."

"Shut up," she whispered, her boneless body at one with the soft cushions beneath her.

He grabbed a condom from his wallet. "Let's see if we can build another one."

The head of his cock pressed against her entrance. Broad and blunt, he eased inside her, filling her. Tugging her up, he pulled her off the couch and onto him.

Bella slid farther down him, her knees bracketing his thighs.

"Okay?" His voice had grown hoarse.

Bella nodded. She had no words to describe how good he felt inside her. Beyond good. Perfect.

Tendons strained along his neck and he bent to kiss her. Hard hands gripped her hips as he surged up into her, pulling her down on him at the same time. His thrust ricocheted through her.

Angling his hips, he thrust again, hitting a sweet spot that made her cry out.

"That's it, baby." He thrust harder, his breath coming in muted grunts. "Let it go, Bella. I want to feel you come around me."

If his cock and that angle didn't do it, his filthy mouth would for certain. He whispered to her between hard thrusts, telling her all he could feel, driving her deeper and deeper into his dark world of lust.

"Yes, baby, I can feel you tightening around me." He thrust harder and faster. "Let it go. Milk me dry."

Bella grabbed onto his shoulders and came in a slow, building wave that went on and on.

Beneath her, he kept pounding until his hands gripped her hips almost painfully, and with one last thrust he joined her.

He dropped his forehead onto her shoulder and rode the wave with her.

His hands slid around her waist. Sweat slicked their bodies together.

Nate pressed soft kisses on her shoulder. "Babe," he murmured. He lifted his head and met her gaze.

His expression was gentle, unguarded, and it cut straight through Bella.

She needed to lighten the mood before she did something crazy like start crying. "Now I really need a shower."

Chapter Nineteen

$\mathscr{B}$ella woke alone the next morning, and she was good with it.

Nate had left sometime in the very early hours. Tucking the covers under her chin, he'd given her a sweet kiss as he left.

She lay in bed and giggled at the memory of his failed tattoo. Somewhere between the bouts of the most incredible sex, ever, they'd found time to chat. She'd asked him about the large tattoo covering his ribs and learned it covered up an older mistake. Under duress, he'd told her about his credo gone wrong.

Live hard, die young, and leave a good-lurking corpse.

She'd laughed so hard he'd had to shut her up in the most effective manner he knew.

Bella stretched, her body twinging in all sorts of places. What a night! She put off getting out of bed for as long as possible. Her sheets still smelled like Nate, but she stripped them anyway. Only indulging in one last breath of him before shoving them into the washing machine.

Nate had come over and they'd had mind-blowing sex,

more than once. And now he'd gone. Life would go back to normal.

She amazed herself at how okay she felt about that. If she'd known she'd be this okay, she'd have jumped his bones years ago. Shower turned on, she brushed her teeth as she waited for the water to heat. Here she'd been building this up into some great tragedy. Nate would break her heart, *blah blah blah*.

She stepped into the shower and, tilting her head, let the warm water run all over her.

Finally, she'd had the sort of sex Liz went on about. The sort that rocked your world and left you craving more. Except there wouldn't be more. She and Nate had been friends for years and they would go right back to that.

And she was . . . fine with that?

Oh God! She wasn't fine with that. Not at all. Not even a tiny bit. The wave of sadness grew from her toes and hit every major organ on the way up.

Nate had moved the earth for her and then taken that away. Every fiber of her rejected the notion. Her tears mingled with the water.

She'd made a horrible miscalculation. Dreaming and knowing weren't the same thing. In the past, Nate had been some kind of phantom desire, always floating outside her grasp. Last night that phantom had become flesh and joined with her flesh, grafting itself onto her, sinking into her with sharp, hooked claws. Her gut had warned her all along how it would go. Too late to listen to it now because she'd just eviscerated herself.

"Stop it." She hauled out her Nana voice for the occasion. "You slept with him, it was great, now it's done. Get over it."

Pressing her hands into them, she willed her eyes to stop leaking. Worse things happened in the world than getting your heart broken. People got their hearts broken every day and they survived. She would too.

Nate had made her no promises; quite the opposite, in fact. He'd told her straight up the way it would be and she'd taken her gamble. Win some, lose some. She never wanted him to regret last night.

Over the years, she'd seen the girls come and go in Nate's life. Most of the time through the green haze of jealousy. The only thing they had in common was that they eventually all went. Some went with tears and pleading, others got a little clingy before he scraped them off, and a few had even walked away with their heads held high. She didn't have a time machine to go back to change last night, and even if she did, she wouldn't do it.

Foolishly, she'd wished with all her heart for one taste and she'd gotten it.

Time to buck up and be one of the girls with dignity. Fake it till you make it and all that.

Pushing the heaviness in her middle down as far as she could, Bella dressed and drove to the store. Life went on, and she intended to ride along with it. She stopped for her usual coffee.

"Bella, right?" a tall man with brown hair greeted her.

There was something very familiar about him, but she couldn't place him. "Hi . . . er . . . hi."

"Daniel." He grinned and took the lid off his coffee. "We went to school together."

"I remember." Bella forced a smile and placed her order for a caramel latte. Faces cycled through her brain as she tried to place him. "How are you?"

"Good." Daniel took a careful sip from his cup. "You don't remember me, do you?"

"Of course I do." Bella prayed her face wasn't going red because she did remember him. Sort of.

In an attractive flash of white teeth, he laughed. "Bella, we went to school together from first grade."

"Are you sure?" She would have remembered.

"Not that I was there much." Daniel shrugged and gave her another smile. Good-looking in a rugged way, his face softened when he smiled. He really did have a great smile. "And I was a year older."

Bella did a scan through her memory banks. Something vague flickered in her memory. "You were Nate's friend?"

"There ya go." He nodded and handed her drink to her. "Of course, in those days you pretty much didn't see past Nate."

Not much change there. Except maybe even more so now. "Well, you know." Bella had no idea what she would say if he didn't know. Fortunately, he nodded and fell into step with her.

Bella paused at the door to the coffee shop. Things with Adam had gotten started like this. "Well, see you around."

Daniel jerked his chin. "Later."

She increased her pace toward her store. Talk about paranoid, but Adam wasn't an experience she wanted to repeat.

Daniel walked behind her.

Bella tried a secret glance over her shoulder.

"I swear I'm not following you," Daniel called from behind her. "We just happen to be walking in the same direction. I'm on . . . what the fuck!"

Bella swung her gaze to Daniel.

He stared at something over her shoulder.

Bella turned. Her cup slid from her dead fingers and hit the ground, splashing hot coffee over her ankles. The pain barely registered.

Scrawled across her storefront in big red letters: *Fucking slut*.

"What . . . who?" Her vision grew hazy around the edges.

Daniel gripped her elbow. "Are you going to faint?"

"No," she said, but she couldn't be entirely sure. She wanted to puke and her head buzzed.

"Here, sit down." Daniel guided her to the sidewalk and plonked her butt down. "Sit there and get your breath back." He slid a phone out of his back pocket.

Bella couldn't take her eyes from her storefront. Taunting her, the words danced around in front of her.

Adam.

"Hey, Nate." Daniel spoke somewhere near her. "Yeah. I'm at Bella's . . . the store . . . yup. You better get down here."

Nate hit the siren, pulled a doughnut in the middle of Eighth Avenue, and gunned his cruiser over to Main Street. His sweaty palms slid on the steering wheel. Damn things had been sweating since Daniel had uttered Bella's name.

Actually, he'd been doing an internal meltdown all morning. Last night might have been the biggest mistake of his thirty-four years. This thing with Bella kept growing bigger. No woman had pushed him off his axis before, and considering his long list of conquests that was saying something.

Yeah, the sex had been mind-blowing, but the sweet had been worse. Sugar-sweet, honey, and spice Bella had hacked through the carefully constructed protective barrier he'd built. And he didn't like it.

A small crowd milled outside the store. Heads turned as he approached.

Bella's pale face jumped out from the others around her.

It punched a hole through his chest. Something had shaken her up badly. His inner barbarian threw back his head and bellowed. The urge to smash raged through him.

He took a moment, calling the scene in to Gabby. So shaken he even managed radio protocol.

Arm over her shoulder, Daniel stood beside Bella.

Nate wanted to twist that arm off and shove it up Daniel's ass.

"Are you okay?" He brushed through the curious on-lookers. Only when he had his hands on her shoulders did he take his first deep breath.

"I think it might be Adam," she whispered.

Fuck procedure! Nate needed to hold her. He tugged her closer, fitting her under his chin and breathing in Bella.

A couple of voices murmured behind him. This would be all over town by noon, but he didn't give a shit. When he had his arms around her, he knew she was safe. Nate dropped his head lower, closed his eyes, and let the feel of her, well and safe, seep into him.

Daniel cleared his throat. "I took some pictures."

Nate nodded. He took one more moment and then stepped away from Bella. Adam had dared to put the fear in her beautiful, big blue eyes and he would pay for that.

He stepped back and assessed the situation. He had a goddamned job to do here.

"I've got something that will clean that right off." Hank Baker shook his head. "What the hell is this world coming to? Nice girl like Bella with this filth on her store."

"Appreciate it, Hank." Before he strangled something, Nate shoved his hands in his pockets. "I just want to check it out first." He turned back to Bella. "Do you have the keys?"

Nodding, she fumbled them out of her purse. Her hands shook as she held them out to him.

"Did you change the locks?" His voice came out a whole lot rougher than he intended.

Her eyes widened. "Not yet. I was going to speak to Hank today."

"Do it." He turned the lock, almost throwing the door open. He looked at the small crowd around them. "You can all move along now. This is a crime scene."

Anger sat like a devil on his shoulder as he went through the store. This kind of thing could get a cop hurt. Anger clouded judgment and he forced himself to breathe slow and deep.

The front of the store was clear; so was the stockroom behind.

When he got back to the street, Gabby had arrived and was taking statements. Thank God someone was thinking straight. He gave her a nod.

Gabby moved closer to him. "Doesn't look like anyone saw anything." She shrugged. "And, of course, no security cameras or anything like that."

"I think we have a fair idea who did this." Anger simmered beneath his skin.

Gabby gave him a hard stare. "That may be, but we still have to prove it. That's generally how this works."

Nate bunched his hands into fists before he punched something. "I know my job."

"Huh." Gabby adjusted her utility belt. "Does that include handing out hugs to crime victims now?"

"Don't." He couldn't deal with her bitchiness right now.

"Nate?" Daniel interrupted their stare-down. "I'm going to take Bella to get a cup of coffee."

He opened his mouth to protest, but there was Gabby with her sharp gaze on him. "Fine."

"I've got her statement already," Gabby said.

Not sure he could watch Daniel walk away with his Bella, Nate turned back to the storefront. *Whoa!* He stopped in midstep and Gabby swore behind him as she sidestepped quickly. *His* Bella. She wasn't his, and someone like him had no business having that notion.

"Got what you need here?" He got his voice under control again.

Gabby nodded and headed for her cruiser.

"Deputy," he called after her. Gabby turned around. "Find him."

Bella had heard Nate had a bigger, fancier county head-quarters. One with detectives and jails and lots more deputies. The Ghost Falls sheriff's office hadn't changed much since Sheriff Wheeler had died. The battered old filing cabinet with its Broncos stickers down the side. Two desks behind the counter. One clearly Jeff's because of the liberal scattering of baby pictures. The other as neat as if nobody ever used it and the one Bella presently sat at.

Through the open door to Nate's office, the deep rumble of his voice on the phone distracted her. He'd been terse and professional since she'd arrived at the station to lay a charge. Pacing, his tall body crossed the open doorway. He nodded and rubbed at the back of his neck as he spoke. Everything girl inside her ached.

She edged her shoulder around slightly, putting him out of her sight line.

Gabby pecked away at her keyboard. What a crying shame to drag that gloriously thick, curly hair into a pony-tail. She'd bet Gabby looked like some kind of pagan god-dess with her hair down. Good God, you couldn't buy skin like that at any price. Beneath her butt-ugly uniform, there was no denying that Deputy Gabby rocked a hot bod. She must introduce her to Pippa. She'd lay good money on

Pippa getting the same itch to make her over. "How long have you lived here now?"

Gabby looked up at her, her mouth dropping open slightly. "About two years."

Two years in a town the size of Ghost Falls and Bella had never seen her out and about anywhere. "Do you like it?"

"It's okay." Gabby shrugged.

Uh-oh. A very definite negative, or did they say negatory in police stations? She might be losing her mind here. Still, her inane mental meanderings beat the hell out of obsessing about some psycho out there with her name on his hit list. "Where did you live before here?"

Gabby narrowed her eyes. "A few places."

"Ah." Even to her, it sounded like someone had strangled the sound out of Gabby. "A woman of mystery."

"Not really." Gabby glared at her computer screen. "Just a private one."

Hand slap. A very definite hand slap there. "Sorry."

"Appreciate that." Nate's voice floated into the uncomfortable silence. "I'll make sure you get something today. Yup . . . BOLO . . . aha."

"Would you like a cup of coffee?" Gabby's cheeks went a dusky pink color.

Bella shook her head. Any more coffee and her back teeth would float. "Actually, I need a bathroom."

"Oh, right." Gabby rose. She had that sort of unconscious grace some women did. No doubt about it, pathologically private Deputy Gabby was a knockout. "There's one back here."

"Thank you." Thank God her legs had stopped shaking; she walked mostly straight to the bathroom.

"It's not you," Gabby called after her. Shrugging, she stuffed her hands in her pockets. "It's just . . . I'm out of practice. With people."

"That's a pity." Bella had the insane urge, one that would no doubt get her face smacked in, to give Gabby a huge hug. "If you ever want to get back in practice . . ."

Gabby nodded. "I'll bear that in mind."

"Okay, good." She hesitated to push her luck, but what the hell? "Liz and I have this thing going for people who spend Christmas alone. If you don't have anything . . ." Gabby's face hardened. "No, sorry, stupid idea, you probably have family here and stuff. Pretend I never said anything. Put it down to shock."

She finished up in the bathroom, taking the time to do something about her mascara-raccoon eyes.

When she got back, Gabby sat with her hips propped on her desk. "If you're ready, Sheriff asked me to make sure you got home."

"He's gone?" She tried to keep the disappointment out of her voice. By the quick flash of sympathy Gabby gave her, she'd failed.

They walked in silence to Gabby's cruiser.

"When can I get back into the store?" Christmas was still one of her busiest seasons.

"Tomorrow." Gabby blipped the locks. "We'll be all done by then. Sheriff Evans already spoke to Hank. They're changing your locks this afternoon."

Some women got rings and romance, others got their locks changed. She had the insane urge to giggle.

"What thing?" Gabby started the car and backed out.

"Huh?"

"The thing with Christmas you mentioned."

"Oh." With Gabby, you couldn't really gauge her thoughts. "It's this list I found on the internet. Ten things to do if you're spending Christmas alone."

Gabby nodded.

Bella took that as encouragement to continue. "One was decorating, and we did that. Well, I did. Liz says if she wants to see where Christmas vomited she can always come over to my place." She leaned a bit closer to Gabby. "Secretly, I think she loves it."

Gabby chuckled. Sweet, a little bit raspy, and totally adorable.

"Two was to get out and do things you wouldn't normally do."

"Like what?"

"Anything. Liz and I went to singles' night up at Whispering Pines." Which was where she'd met Adam. "Actually, that didn't turn out so well."

Gabby gave her a sympathetic grimace. Or at least she thought it was a sympathetic grimace. It could also be a how-stupid-are-you grimace. "What's three? On the list. What's the third thing?"

"Volunteer." Which reminded her that she needed to speak to Liz. "We need to find something for us to do together."

Gabby drove down Main, turned into Eighth, her attention on the road. She flicked her forefinger in response to a driver passing with a wave. They drove through the residential streets, quiet at this time of day with the kids in school.

They pulled up outside Bella's house.

"Sheriff already checked it out." Gabby nodded at her house. "Said it was safe for you to go in."

"Oh." Bella hadn't thought that far ahead. "Thanks. And thanks for the ride."

Liz popped onto her porch and hustled over. Clearly, the Ghost Falls gossip lines had been humming.

"I can volunteer." Gabby poked her head out the car

window. "When you do your volunteer thing, I could tag along. I mean, if I'm not busy."

"Oh my God." Liz picked her way over on her high heels. "I heard it from everyone. Are you okay? Did Nate find that fucker and pop a cap in his ass?"

She enveloped Bella in a perfume-soaked hug. So skinny, Bella didn't want to hug too hard. "I'm fine and no, they haven't found him yet. Maybe it's not even Adam." Even as she said it, she knew it wasn't likely.

Liz made a raspberry. "It's him all right." She glanced around her. "Is it too early to drink wine?"

"Maybe a little." Still . . . "Nah, it's four o'clock somewhere in the world."

Nate tracked Daniel down at his apartment. Hammering on the door helped keep his anger down to a manageable level.

He had every set of eyes he could call on looking for Adam. The guy couldn't have gone far. But he'd already checked out of his room at the resort and nobody had seen him. Sooner or later, though, he would have to come up for air, and Nate would be waiting for him when he did.

"What the hell?" Daniel wrenched open the door. His frown dropped when he saw Nate. "How's Bella?"

"She's fine." He pushed into the apartment. What he had to say didn't need to be yelled out in the hallway for everyone to hear. "My deputy took her home."

"Good." Gaze steady but wary, Daniel cocked his head. "You wanna tell me what's going on?"

"No." Nate shut the door behind him. "And I want you to stay away from Bella."

Daniel gaped at him and then gave a small, short laugh. "What?"

"Bella." Nate ground the words out through his clenched jaw. His hold on his temper had gotten more tenuous as the day wore on. "Stay away from her. She doesn't need any more shit right now."

"I took her for coffee, Nate." Daniel folded his arms. "I did what anybody else would do."

"Seriously?" Temper spiking dangerously, Nate stepped closer. Did Daniel think he could fool him? Shit, they'd grown up together, gotten into enough shit together for Nate to know what the other man thought. Daniel might have changed, but that gleam in his eyes hadn't. "I saw you today. And I'm telling you, stay away from Bella."

As Nate had known he would, Daniel stood his ground. Triumph surged through him. He'd stopped by his house and changed out of his uniform before he went looking for Daniel. His official persona went with the uniform. It was him and Daniel now, and the rage burning a hole right through his brain.

"Just what is Bella to you anyway?" Daniel folded his arms.

If Daniel wanted to go there, Nate was more than ready, and he grabbed Daniel by the shirtfront. "That doesn't matter. What matters is that she's nothing to you. Nothing."

"What the hell." Daniel wrenched free of his hold. His shirt tore. "I'm not going to fight you, Nate."

"Stay away from her." Some part of his brain tried to grab control and tell him he was behaving like a complete dick. But the anger was louder.

"Is she yours?" Daniel stepped back, putting the tattered sofa between them.

Yes! The word pounded through his brain. He clamped his jaw shut before it spilled out.

"You need to chill the fuck out." Daniel's gaze hardened, but he kept his voice calm. "You came here looking for a fight. What happened? You couldn't find that Adam guy?"

Nate balled his fists. The rational whisper grew louder. If he'd found Adam, he might not be quite so angry right now. Or at least he'd be venting his anger on the right person. Except what did he plan to do when he found Adam? Pound the hell out of him? Yeah, that would be police brutality.

"I'm not gonna fight you," Daniel said again. "I'm on parole and I'm not going to screw that up for anyone."

Nate's shoulders slumped and he dragged in a deep breath. All day he'd been charging around like a crazed man.

Daniel moved closer. "Come on; you need a drink and I'll keep you company while you have it."

"Yeah." Nate nodded. The anger burned away and left him feeling like a prick. He'd come here determined to pick a fight with a man who couldn't afford to fight back. Driven by some caveman shit to stake a claim on a woman who wasn't even his.

He shoved the idea of Bella to the back of his mind. Daniel had asked what she was to him and he didn't have an answer. Not a clue. Scrubbing his hands over his face, he wished he could yank the crap out of his brain and make sense of it.

Following Daniel out of his apartment, he tried to get his head together. Today, the thing with Bella's store had hit a nerve. A nerve he'd been covering up for so long, he'd almost forgotten it was still there.

"My last job. In Salt Lake." Talking never came easy to

him, but he owed Daniel this much. "Victim was a woman. It was bad."

Daniel nodded. "And Bella?"

No way in hell was he going there. "Drop it."

Daniel smirked. "Sure, I can drop it, but I think the real question is, can you?"

Chapter Twenty

*B*ella opened the door later that night to a pale Pippa clutching a huge bar of chocolate.

"I've never seen you eat chocolate." Bella swung the door wide.

"Don't start with me." Pippa charged in and dropped her coat. Beneath it she wore a pair of beautifully tailored charcoal pants with a cashmere sweater. Pippa always looked great. "The chocolate is for you." She put her hands on her hips. "And oh my God, Bella. What the hell? Why didn't you call me?"

"You heard about the store?" She didn't know why she hadn't called Pippa. Maybe because the connection to Nate felt a little too close for comfort and Pippa was also married, expecting a baby, and hosted the biggest makeover show on television. It made Bella's problems seem very small town and insignificant.

"Yes, I heard about the store." Pippa trailed her into the kitchen. "From Matt. Who heard it from Nate. Are you okay?"

"Yeah; a little shaken but fine." She put the chocolate on the table and grabbed two glasses. She filled both with milk.

Staring at her over the rim, Pippa drank her milk. "Good, because I'm about to be really pissed at you and I don't want to yell at someone in crisis."

"Then I'm most definitely in crisis."

"Too late." Pippa clanked her glass down on the table. "You've been avoiding me."

"I have not." Had she?

"Yes, you have." Pippa stuck her chin out at a fighting angle. "I know I'm not around as much as I could be, and Liz is, but we're friends, Bella. At least I thought we were. I shouldn't have heard about today from Matt."

Clutching her glass for fortitude, Bella sat. "I haven't been deliberately avoiding you, if that helps."

Pippa narrowed her eyes. "Nope. Doesn't help at all. What's going on, Bella?"

"You might want to sit down." Pippa made her nervous standing there looking like a Valkyrie. "You remember that date I made with Liz to go up to Whispering Pines?" She took a slug of her milk. "Well, I met this guy called Adam."

Pippa listened as Bella told her all about Adam, the possessiveness and the increasingly erratic behavior. Mad as she was, Pippa didn't interrupt, and then she said, "That really, really sucks."

"Yes, it does." Bella topped up her glass. "But Nate has been a huge help."

Pippa grabbed her hands and gave them a squeeze. "Tell me you're being careful?"

"I'm being careful. All the locks here and at the store have been changed. Phone numbers, all that sort of thing."

"Good," Pippa said. "Because I might be mad at you for

keeping me in the dark, but I love you, and this is all very scary."

Bella had been putting that thought off all day. Circling around it by keeping busy after Liz left. Still, she found herself peering out the window all the time, double checking her locks, picking up the phone to make sure she could still hear a dial tone. "I keep asking myself what I could have done differently," she said.

"Nothing," Pippa said. "You know this isn't your fault, right, Bella?"

Bella avoided her stare by making circles on the table with her glass. "I suppose, but I just keep going over and over it in my head. There was something, the first time I met him, that felt . . . weird. Not off, but not right either. I told myself I was never going to have a normal dating life if I didn't at least give him a chance."

"And that's right." Pippa rapped her knuckles on the table. "Look at me." She waited until Bella complied before she continued. "That's how normal dating works. Men are like dresses. You have to try them on for size. Some look great on the hanger but don't look great on you. Others are fine but don't really do much for you, and others are killer." She clapped her hands over her mouth. "Bad choice of word there, but I think you get what I mean."

"I do." Along with avoiding thinking about how shaken she was, Bella had been avoiding thinking about her stupidity. "But when he first sent me all those texts . . . I mean, that's not right. And then the flowers. Nobody sends flowers like that. I even thought that, and still I went on a date with him."

Pippa fetched herself some more milk and broke off another piece of chocolate. She popped it into her mouth. "I stayed with a man for about two years more than I should have. We hadn't had sex for nearly eight months and still it shocked the life out of me when I found out he was cheating."

"Maybe he was really good at hiding it?" Bella took the piece of chocolate Pippa offered. This was a chocolate kind of conversation. "Even with my long dry spell, eight months with no sex while you were in a relationship had to ring all sorts of bells."

"You would think." Pippa grimaced. "I think I didn't see it because I wasn't looking for it. For whatever reason. Maybe I didn't want to face the truth. Maybe it suited me to stay in a relationship, however toxic." She took another piece of chocolate. "My point is this: Hindsight is twenty-twenty. It's easy to look back and see what you should have done and could have done. But this Adam is sick, Bella, and I doubt anything you would have done differently would have made any difference. He's fixated on you, and that's because he's got things all twisted in his head." Pippa tapped the side of her head. "His head is twisted. Not yours."

"Fixated." Bella shivered as she said the word. She didn't want any of this, but that wasn't going to change it or make it go away.

"Listen to what Nate tells you," Pippa said. "He used to work in a unit that dealt with sex crimes in Salt Lake City. Be careful, and know that we're all here for you. What did your family say?"

And her night for confessions rolled forward. "I haven't told them."

"Why?"

"I don't want them to freak out and have them come running back here." Which sounded good but was only half the truth. "And I don't want the interrogation about how I let this happen."

Pippa knew Nana and made a face. "Your nana gets

things twisted in her head as well." Leaning forward on her elbows, Pippa pinned her with a stare. "And I gotta warn you, Phi's in a state about this."

"You told her?"

"Nope." Pippa handed her more chocolate. "This is Ghost Falls and she found out. She's talking bodyguards."

That was all she needed. "Talk her out of it."

"I have." Pippa shrugged. "For now. But you know Phi. When she makes up her mind about something, it takes an act of God to change it." She settled back in her chair with another piece of chocolate. "Now tell me about Nate."

Her face heated and Bella cursed herself.

"Hah!" Pippa slapped her palms on the table. "I knew there was something going on. Both of you get all squinty-eyed when you talk about each other."

"Squinty-eyed?" Bella tried to check her reflection in her glass, but all she could see were a pair of grossly exaggerated hamster cheeks.

"Shifty." Pippa nodded. "Like you're keeping secrets. I'm not leaving here until you spill."

"There's not that much I can tell you." Too tired to make up any more lies, Bella went with the truth. "I'm not really sure what's going on with me and Nate."

"But there is a something?" Pippa got that look on her face that meant she would keep after this like a ferret.

"We had sex." Bella got it out in a rush. "And it was incredible, amazing. But that's all it was. Nate is Nate."

"Are you okay with that?"

"Yes," Bella said.

Pippa raised a brow.

"No, actually, I'm not. I thought I would be, but I'm not." Her head felt too heavy and she propped it on her palm. "I'm making all sorts of super decisions about men at the moment."

"He's another one who's got things all twisted in his head," Pippa said.

"But I knew that." Nate had never made any secret of his allergy to commitment. "I knew that and I thought I could handle it."

"Well." Pippa sighed. "I think the best thing to do is order pizza and watch a movie."

"But no chick flicks," Bella said. "They might be part of why I'm in this mess in the first place."

They ended up watching an action movie, finishing all the pizza, and going through half a large bag—okay, the whole bag—of M&M's.

Matt picked up Pippa but came in first to check all her locks for her.

They left after making her promise to call if she needed them.

Locking her door behind them, silence oozed around her, and Bella did another window and door check. She drew all her blinds and drapes and sat down at the detailed plan for her store Matt had left behind.

A dog barked down the street and she tensed. Carefully, she teased out each sound until she could identify it. And the street made a lot of sounds in the night. Liz's water pipes creaked a bit. The kids three doors over slammed the doors as they let their dog in and out.

She got up, wiped her kitchen counters again, then tidied the detergents and cleaners under her sink. Turning on the TV, she kept it low enough to hear but loud enough to distract.

Tomorrow, she would call her parents and explain why her phone numbers had changed. Or she might make up a plausible lie. She sat down and watched half a reality show without having any idea what it was about.

Her phone lit up and Bella nearly leaped out of her skin.

She stared at it, too scared to check. It vibrated on the coffee table with an incoming message. But it was her new phone, with the new number Adam didn't have.

Nate texted: How you doing?

Fine, she typed back and then deleted it. Okay.

Did you lock the front door?

She had to smile at that. About twenty times.

The phone stayed blank for a little while and then: Are you freaked?

A little.

By little, you mean a lot?????

Yup.

I have a car driving by every hour or so.

That made her feel a little better.

And my phone will be on all night. Even the smallest thing, call me.

Okay.

Good night.

Nite nite. She resisted the urge to add a smiley face. Liz would bitch-slap her if she did.

The phone lit up again.

Would you like me to come over?

With every functioning nerve ending she had. Bella stared at the words on the screen. She needed to be smart. Goddamn, but she didn't want to be smart. Nate could come over and rock her world again. Take her to that place where there was no creepy Adam doing creepy things.

Except, in the morning, Nate would leave again. And Adam was still out there somewhere.

She picked up the phone and put it down again. After a slug of wine straight from the bottle, she picked it up again and typed: No, thanks.

Chapter Twenty-One

Tired and nervous, Bella arrived at her store the next morning. Somebody had done their best to wash off the words. The windows were now clear, but a bright square of new paint around them stood as a reminder.

Almost setting off the new alarm system as she opened the door, she managed to punch in the code, but not before she'd spilled hot coffee all over her hand and onto the carpet.

Never mind the carpet. She stepped over the small spot. If all went according to plan, Matt would be ripping it up as soon as her Christmas season finished.

The phone rang.

Bella's heart skipped a beat. She needed to change the number, but that meant changing all her business cards, flyers, website information . . . Her hand shook a bit as she picked it up.

"Bella." Nana's strident tones burned down the line. "You're not answering your cell."

Relief that it wasn't Adam was quickly replaced by a new sort of nerves. "Hi, Nana. How's the weather?"

"Hot." Nana sniffed. "What sort of numbers are you doing?"

They talked sales figures for a few minutes. Nana grudgingly conceded that Bella had done very well this year so far.

"What's wrong with your cell?" Nana ended Bella's reprieve. "When we call it, this message says that number is not in service. Did you lose it or something?"

"No." Bella took a deep breath for courage. "I've had some trouble and I needed to change the number."

"What sort of trouble?" Nana's tone sharpened.

There really wasn't an easy way to say this. "I have a stalker."

"A what?"

"A stalker." It got easier saying it the second time. "Someone who won't leave me alone. Follows me around."

Silence.

"What did you do?" Nana's voice rose.

Even expecting it, it still took a chunk out of her. "I didn't do anything," she said. "I met a man. We dated a couple of times and I ended it. He decided not to accept that."

"Oh." Nana laughed. "Is that all? You young girls today. Always with the naming things and the getting hysterical. In my day, we would call him persistent and be flattered."

Bella didn't know exactly where the line between persistent and creepy lay, but she knew painting insults on her storefront was definitely over it. "He painted some ugly words on the storefront."

Nana sucked in a breath. "On my store?"

"Actually, it's my store." Bella often let that reference go, but she didn't feel like it this morning. "And yes. We got it off, but I had to shut the store yesterday."

"But you're open today?"

"Yes, the store is open today." Bella wanted to hang up. She felt drained already. "Are Mom or Dad around?"

"No, they've gone out to lunch," Nana said.

"Oh." No hope of getting all the difficult conversations over in one. "I'll give you my new cell number and perhaps you can get Dad to call me."

"Hmm." Nana's standard response when she didn't want to come out with a straight no. Bella would be calling her parents later. "I think you should keep this business to yourself."

Her anger almost got away from her. It came on so fast and strong, she had to grip the counter to stop herself from yelling. "You mean about me being stalked?"

"This is their first vacation in years." Nana's tone got huffy. "They're enjoying it, and it's not like you're in any real danger."

The only crazy part about this conversation was that she had expected something different. Her parents might have reacted differently, but with Nana telling them the story, they'd only get the truth as Nana saw it. "I think they should know." She surprised herself with her balls. "I'm their daughter and I know they would want to know."

"Of course I'll tell them," Nana said. "Just not now. I'm going to ask you to be considerate and not go behind my back." Steel in a cement glove, that was Nana.

Bella channeled her inner Dr. Childers. "I'm afraid I can't agree with you. I'll call Dad later and let him and Mom know."

Nana gasped. "Bella! It's not like you to be so selfish."

"It's also not like me to be stalked by a psychotic whack job." That felt so good. "Also, I'll be making some changes to the store while you're away. I'll send you a copy of the plans once they're finalized."

"What changes? I didn't approve any changes." You could always rely on store talk to veer Nana off course.

"No, you didn't."

The bell chimed over the door and a middle-aged woman walked in.

"I have to go now. Customers." She hung up on Nana firing questions, slapped a smile on her face, and approached the woman.

Adam's graffiti turned out to be a backward favor. Bella had more than the usual number of customers. Some of them came out of curiosity, others to express their concern, but quite a few ended up browsing and buying. She was so busy she could almost tell herself she hadn't ducked Nate's call.

But she had. She'd sent him a text to say she was fine. He hadn't called or texted back, so a good result all around. Sort of.

About an hour before closing time, Daniel walked into the store. He looked horribly out of place in among all the pink in his jeans and battered leather jacket. Not pretty, but he had the sort of rugged attractiveness that screamed male.

"Hey." He took off his sunglasses. Despite frigid temperatures, the sun outside bounced off the white snow.

She returned his smile. "Hey yourself."

"So, I could pretend I was passing by." He gave her a charmingly boyish smile. "But I really am a crap liar. So why don't I just tell you straight up that I'm checking up on you?"

"That sort of honesty deserves an honest response." Bella thought about it and then gave him her best answer. "I think I'm okay. A bit freaked out, definitely nervous, and mad as hell at my nana."

"Huh." He unzipped his jacket and shrugged out of it. His long-sleeved T-shirt clung to an upper body she'd bet her last dime was ripped. "I get freaked and nervous." He grimaced. "That nana thing, though? Clueless."

"It's a long story." And not one she wanted to get into right then.

Daniel dug in his back pocket and pulled out a card. "I imagine you're not handing out your number much, so here's mine. You can call it anytime you want. For any reason." He took a step closer. "Even if that reason happens to be a cup of coffee. Dinner, even?"

Bella stared at the card in her hand without taking in the information on it. "Dinner?"

Daniel shoved his hands into his pockets and shrugged. "I'm kinda out of practice on this whole asking-a-girl-out thing." He held up a hand. "And I know the timing is terrible and all. What with the Adam thing, and you and Nate being an item. Just keep the card. Maybe you'll feel like giving it a call anyway. At worst, you'll get a friend."

"Nate and I aren't an item." Saying it out loud shouldn't hurt because she knew it by now. But it came out with claws on it.

Daniel raised his eyebrows. "Okay," he said but didn't sound convinced. "Whatever. But I like you, Bella, and not in a creepy, spray-paint-your-store-window way. I'd like to get to know you better."

Bella ran her thumb over the card edge and tried to think of something to say. A month ago, she'd been all alone with no prospects in sight. Suddenly, she seemed to have all sorts of men coming out of the woodwork, and not all of them in a good way. "How about I take your card as a friend?"

Daniel flashed her a wicked smile. "That works too."

A customer walked in and Bella greeted her before turning back to Daniel. "I need to . . ."

"Yeah." He put his sunglasses back on. "Just remember,

I won't be eating or sleeping until you call. No pressure."
He grinned over his shoulder. "Just kidding."

"Wow." Her customer turned and watched Daniel's ass
leave the store.

It was a nice ass. She might be off dating, but she hadn't
gone blind.

Her customer fanned her face and grinned. "I'd definitely call that."

Bella got another call from Nate that night.

She couldn't not reply, not with the situation with Adam
and all Nate had done to help her with it. But being the total
wuss she was, she texted again.

Liz popped in, on her way out on a date with Noel.

"Tomorrow night," she said. "We're doing our charity
thing. Be ready at about four and wear comfortable shoes."

Then Liz was gone in a waft of heady perfume and a
glitter of sequins.

Bella fired off a quick text to Gabby, asking her if she
wanted to join them.

Unfortunately, Gabby was busy, but she asked Bella to
keep her in mind for another outing.

As she packed the dishwasher after a solitary dinner, her
dad called. She told him everything. He wanted to rush
back from Florida, but Bella persuaded him to stay. She
spoke to her mother and reassured her.

Nate texted: All locked up for the night?

Yes. She included a smiley face because what Liz didn't
know wouldn't hurt her. Good nite.

She still checked the locks three times and all the windows
before going to bed. But she slept better and woke the next
morning feeling more cheerful. Snow had fallen in the
night and a crisp, sparkly, white wonderland stretched outside her window.

Getting dressed, she hummed along to "It's Beginning

to Look a Lot Like Christmas." It really was, in a way. She had a new friendship with Liz. Both of them single and both of them keen to embrace life.

Dr. Childers's last sessions had lulled her to sleep last night. The exhortation to get out there and be the best her still rang in her ears. She had survived her Nate crush for all these years and she would recover from this as well. Her best Bella didn't include any reenactments of Miss Havisham or any other pining sort of woman.

She even had the option to date again if she wanted. Not that she wanted to, but it cheered her to have options.

Adam. Her good mood dipped. He lurked around somewhere out there, and she might not have heard the last of him. She mentally pulled up her big-girl panties. Right now, Adam wasn't a factor, and until he made himself one again, she wasn't going to worry about it. Or she'd try not to at least.

Her new notoriety meant another busy day in the store.

Matt brought around her final plans around midday, along with a quote and a schedule. Customers kept her too busy to look at it. So it sat beneath her counter whispering temptation through her day. She closed early enough to run home to get changed and get ready for Liz at four.

Checking her phone, she saw she had two missed calls from Nate and three texts.

"Where are we going?" She jumped into the passenger seat beside Liz. She quickly fired off a text: Sorry I missed you today. Busy at store. On my way out with Liz. Am fine.

She would listen to his messages and read his texts later.

Liz wore a super-toned-down version of herself tonight, her makeup minimal and her nails a subdued nude. Sure, she still had sparkles, but they were limited to the back pocket of her jeans. "We're going to serve dinner at a homeless shelter," Liz said as she pulled into the light traffic down Main Street.

That sounded perfect, and Bella told her so.

Liz drove to a rougher part of town and parked in front of St. Peter's, an imposing stone church that, like an aging prom queen, still clung to traces of her former glory.

Peering through the windshield, Liz huffed. "I sure hope that list of yours knows what it's doing."

A ragged man shambled down the sidewalk and disappeared down an outside staircase. The sign on the railing read: "Come to me, all who labor and are heavy laden, and I will give you rest."

Bella had lived her entire life in Ghost Falls and had never visited this part of town. Nana always warned her against it.

"Come on." She opened her door and stepped out. With the sun sinking below the horizon, a frigid wind chased a paper bag down the street.

Liz clung to her as they made their way down the metal staircase to an outside door at basement level. The door opened onto a small entryway. Another door opened onto a long, drab corridor. The strong smell of antiseptic made Bella's nose itch as they followed the gentle murmur of voices down the corridor.

The room they entered was as large as a high-school gym and filled with folding tables. Bright red plastic chairs stood out against the institutional beige of the rest of the place. Someone had attempted to cheer it up with inspirational posters on the walls.

A tall blond man with lumberjack shoulders and matching scruff along his square jaw approached them. "Elizabeth?"

"Yes." Liz kept staring around the room. Otherwise, she wouldn't have missed the hot man mountain smiling down at her. He had those sexy laugh lines around his eyes and mouth that made a girl want to make him smile some more.

"And you must be her friend." He held his hand out to Bella. He gave her hand a reassuring warm and firm grip. "I'm Reverend Bradford, but please call me Michael; everyone else does. We're always happy to have a fresh set of volunteers."

Wow! Clearly Anglicans had a different recruitment policy for their priests. One Bella approved of, and then immediately felt like the scum of the earth. There must be a special level of hell for women who lusted after the clergy. Then again, Anglican priests married . . .

Most of the tables were occupied by people like the man who'd entered before them. A collection of men and women, some of them painfully young, dressed in discarded and ragged coats and scarves. She found the silence unnerving. As interested as she was in the occupants, they barely looked up from their tables.

Michael led them to a large serving station at one end of the room. The only thing remotely priestlike about Michael was his clerical collar. He wore it beneath a long-sleeved shirt, the tails of which hung over the waistband of a pair of well-loved and battered jeans. His well-used hiking boots were laced with hot pink.

"As you two are new, we'll break you in slowly," Michael said with his huge smile. "We'll put you on the serving station. Only when you show real skill there will we allow you anywhere near the kitchen." He winked at Bella.

She nearly tripped over her sensible sneakers and gave herself a stern warning to pay attention.

Through a large open hatch, a group of people manned the kitchen. The smell of baking bread and chicken soup drifted into the dining area.

Michael handed them each an apron that read, "As each

has received a gift, use it to serve one another, as good stewards of God's varied grace."

And suddenly she stopped feeling so sorry for herself. Yes, her Christmas was taking a few unexpected twists, but here in this room the despair was palpable. Good people like the smoking-hot Reverend Michael had put aside whatever they had going on in their lives to hold out a helping hand.

"I think I feel it." She squeezed Liz's arm as they stood behind a huge stainless-steel cauldron. "The Christmas magic."

Chapter Twenty-Two

*B*ella tied her apron strings and put a smile on her face. She got why this was on the list.

Liz smiled back, her eyes growing a bit damp. "Yeah." She stiffened. "What the hell?"

"I'm not sure you should swear." Bella glanced around to see if anyone had heard.

Reverend Michael winked at her. "Watch out for the lightning bolt."

Noel threaded his way through the tables, stripping his jacket off as he came. He smiled at Bella and stopped close to Liz, his shoulders squared and his chin at a determined angle. "Babe."

"I'm not your babe." Liz fiddled with her apron. "And what are you doing here?"

"I heard you organizing this. You won't come out to dinner with me, so I thought I'd join you here," Noel said, then accepted an apron from a smirking Reverend Michael.

"Desperate men." Reverend Michael leaned close enough for only Bella to hear. "They make my best converts."

Liking this priest more and more, Bella giggled.

"Daniel, my brother," Reverend Michael sang out in a beautiful baritone. "Get over here and help my new victims out."

As Daniel Carver walked in and exchanged shoulder thumps with Reverend Michael, Bella's gut twinged.

He stopped when he saw her, eyes widening for a moment, and then he smiled. "Bella?" He trotted over to her. "This is a nice surprise."

"Are you stalking her too?" Brandishing a ladle, Liz appeared at her side. "We don't need any more creeps."

"What?" Daniel paled and took a step back. "Shit—sorry, Michael—but I had no idea she would be here." He held up his hands. "I come every Tuesday to do this."

"He does." Reverend Michael handed Daniel an apron. "I recruited him when he was here for another meeting."

"He means my AA meeting," Daniel said. "That's every Monday and Thursday."

"AA?"

Daniel nodded. "As in Alcoholics Anonymous. Although I kind of blew the anonymous part just then."

Reverend Michael clapped his hands and silence fell.

"I'd like to welcome everyone here tonight. And say a special thank you to our volunteers. I'd like to ask you to bow your heads while we thank the Lord for this meal."

After they'd said Grace, the people at the tables stood and formed an orderly line. Liz doled out chicken noodle soup and sass. Noel worked cheerfully beside her, not seeming to mind her outrageous flirting. Bella handled the bread rolls and Daniel seemed to be a sort of on-the-fly guy. He changed the tureens when they emptied, brought more bread rolls, took fresh cups to the coffee station. He stopped a few times to talk to the diners. They seemed to know him here.

After dinner, they stayed and helped with the cleanup.

Daniel joined Bella wiping tables. "So, I haven't checked my phone for at least fifteen minutes. Did you call?"

He was such an easy guy to like. The problem being she didn't like-like him. "Daniel . . ."

"Nope." He took a clean cloth and moved to the next table. "You're about to friend zone me. I get it."

He didn't look upset about it, which relieved her and gave her ego a little cut at the same time.

Reverend Michael sat at a table in the far corner and talked to a few stragglers.

Noel and Liz appeared to be arguing in the kitchen. Well, Liz argued. Noel merely nodded and listened and kept washing pots.

When they left, the night had turned bitterly cold. A sharp, ice-edged wind whipped between the buildings and snatched Bella's breath away. She and Liz hustled to the car.

"What's next on our list?" Liz glanced up from clipping her seat belt.

"I enjoyed that," Bella said.

"Me too." Liz winked. "And don't tell anyone or rumor might get out that I've discovered a human emotion."

Bella squeezed her forearm. She might have been one of those people before she got to know Liz.

Daniel left the church basement, hands shoved deep in his pocket. Noel called to him and he turned. They both got into Noel's pimped-up truck. He didn't seem to have much, Daniel, but still he volunteered.

"Administration," Bella said. "Next on the list is catching up on life admin."

"Ugh." Liz eased into the quiet street. "I say we skip that one and move onto the next."

"All right." Admin didn't blow Bella's skirt up either. "Then we should move on to exploring new culinary experiences."

"In Ghost Falls?" Liz snorted. "Where we have the choice of burgers, pizza, and the hella-expensive restaurants on the hill."

"Hmm?" That could present a problem. "Or we could host our own dinner party." Bella floated the idea out there, not sure how she felt about it.

"Bella." Liz chuckled. "I love you, girl, but let's not forget the pink-marshmallows-in-everything factor."

Bella giggled; cooking lay outside her skill set. "Then I think we should move on to attending a Christmas party."

"Got any leads on that?" Liz pulled into the deserted street.

"Phi." And did she ever have a lead on a Christmas party. "Phi holds a Christmas party every year for Christmas waifs and strays."

"That's us." Liz grinned at her.

They drove the rest of the way home in a contented silence.

Nate's cruiser sat outside her house.

Peering through her windshield, Liz whistled. "Looks like the sheriff is making house calls."

Her headlights illuminated Nate sitting in the driver seat.

"And he doesn't look happy about it." Liz parked in her drive. "Want me to come in with you, or maybe make a dash for my house and lock yourself in?"

Nate climbed out of the cruiser and leaned his hips against the door. Arms folded, he watched them. Wind ruffled his hair, but other than that he didn't seem bothered by the cold.

Bella could feel the eye burn. Her strategy of avoidance had come to an end.

Nate straightened and stalked in their direction. With his face set in lines of granite, he looked pissed.

"If you're gonna make a run for it, you need to do it now." Liz kept her eyes on Nate.

"I'm going to talk to him." Bella opened her door. The wind nearly ripped it out of her hand. "Thanks for driving. Let's talk about going back next week."

"You got it." Liz's eyes widened. "Hey, Nate."

"Liz." Nate stood in the path of Bella's open door. His tone put the wind to shame for chill factor. "Are you getting out?"

Feeling like a naughty toddler, Bella climbed out.

He stood way too close and her nose nearly touched his chest. Too much of a coward to look up, she spoke to his throat. "Hi, Nate. What are you doing here?"

"House," he said. "Now."

See, this was the part where any sassy chick-flick heroine would be tossing her curls back and giving him lip. But then, they weren't facing six-three of muscular, badass, pissed-off male. "Okay."

Bella scurried for her house. Aware of Nate right on her heels, she fumbled the key into the lock trying to get the door open.

Nate leaned over, engulfing her in body heat and spicy man smell. He got the door open on the first try.

In the hall, Bella unbuttoned her coat.

"Phone." Nate shrugged out of his coat and hung it over the newel post.

She didn't get it. "Sorry?"

"Give me your phone." He thrust out his hand.

That seemed to be taking bossy badass too far. "What do you want with my phone?"

"I want you to give it to me." He barely moved a muscle, his hand staying right where it was.

"Fine." Bella dug it out of her purse and slapped it into his hand.

Nate scrolled, grunted, and then scowled. He held the phone up in front of her. "Let's see here, shall we? Six missed calls from Nate. Do you want me to count text messages as well?"

"Um . . . no." First off, she could have told him the number because she'd counted. Eight. "I texted you, so you know I'm fine." She grabbed her phone back.

"What the fuck, Bella?" He balled his fists and shoved them into his pockets.

She got the feeling he wanted to shake her or something. "I've been avoiding you."

"No shit." Tight enough to break teeth, his jaw clenched. "Why?"

She knew he'd ask that, hence the avoidance. "I need a drink," she said and headed for the kitchen. "You can come and have one with me or stand there and glower."

Nate stalked into the kitchen after her and loomed too close as she got a beer out of the fridge and handed it to him. Not wanting the fuss of opening wine, she grabbed one for herself and popped the cap. She downed half the bottle before she felt able to reply. "Self-preservation."

Nate thunked his beer down on the table. Foam spilled over the side. "What?"

"Self-preservation." Bella got it under control enough to meet his gaze. He looked angry, yes, but also hurt. "Turns out I'm not so good at this friends-with-benefits thing."

"Fuck." He spun around and stared out of the window. Fabric strained across his shoulders as he pressed his hands into the countertop. "So this is about us hooking up."

"Partly." It was easier talking to his back. "Turns out I

can't shut off my feelings and have sex with you. It's too confusing."

"So you thought you'd cut off all contact instead." He turned, tension eking out of every muscle. And that meant a lot of tension.

It had seemed the most logical thing to do. Not so much with him standing in her kitchen, those lion eyes demanding some sort of explanation. "I don't want sex to make things weird between us."

"We had this discussion before." Nate's knuckles whitened as he gripped the counter. "You knew the score."

"I did." He certainly hadn't lied to her. "I thought I could handle it." She tried for a light shrug, but inside felt scraped raw. "I was wrong."

"So you decided it would be better to cut off contact with me altogether." He thumped his fist into the countertop. "You've got some whack job chasing you and you decided it would be a good idea to stop talking to me?"

That was stupid, and she hadn't thought of it in those terms. She didn't want to fight with him, ever, and not now, when she felt like an open nerve ending. "I'm sorry."

Nate dropped his head. "You could have talked to me before you decided to ignore me."

"And say what?" Bella almost laughed. "What would you have said? That you don't do relationships. I know that, Nate. You made it perfectly clear."

"Hell." He ran a hand through his hair. "I don't know what I would have said, but I would have liked to have been given the chance."

"You're right." Some stupid-girl part of her wanted to ease his frustration. "I'm sorry about not taking your calls and ignoring you. I honestly thought it would be better."

He looked up. "So where does this leave us now?"

"Friends." She nearly crumpled under the impact of that word. "It leaves us as friends. Like we were before."

"What if I want more?"

Her heart leaped into her throat. "Do you?"

He blew out a harsh breath. "I don't know." And there, in a nutshell, lay the problem. "But I don't like being cut off from you. I know that much."

Her hurting heart took a little comfort from that. "I'll stop avoiding you."

"And I know that the idea of some dickhead making your life hell makes me mad enough to do something stupid," he said.

It hurt and it soothed all at once. Nate the protector, and hidden beneath that allergy to relationships was a good guy. Sure, he sucked at commitment, but he had so many qualities she loved.

And yes, she did love them.

"Okay." He shoved his hands into his pockets. "But you have to know the other night was incredible."

"For me too." Maybe if it hadn't been that way, and maybe if she hadn't felt like every one of her dreams had come true, they might not be having this conversation. But she did and they were, and facts were facts. "But I can't do it again and come away unscathed."

He closed the gap between them and cupped her face. "Damn, Bella. I wish you had answered differently." He lowered his mouth to hers and kissed her. Hot and demanding and leaving a scorch mark all the way through her. He owned her mouth as if he wanted to leave his brand on her. Too late. He was already embedded deep in her heart.

Nate broke off the kiss. "See you around, Bella."

Chapter Twenty-Three

$\mathcal{B}$ella went through her nighttime routine. She checked the front and back doors. Then the dining room, checking the windows were closed.

Self-pity had her by the hand and walked through the house with her.

In her make-believe world, Nate told her he had no idea how he'd gone through his entire adult life without realizing she was right there all the time. That the past few days, and especially the other night, had given him a massive wake-up call.

Except Nate wasn't the one who needed the wake-up call. She did. Rattling each of the living room windows, she made sure they were still locked tight.

One more circuit and she went to bed. Sleep took its own sweet time, but with the help of some late-night television and a couple of chapters in her book, Bella settled down for the night.

Heart pounding, she jerked wide awake.

The dark shape beside the window was her dresser. Dim

light reflected in the mirror. On the bedside table, moonlight limned her lamp. Her cell clock read three-seventeen.

Everything normal. Still, she held her breath, waiting and listening. For what?

There. A sound like a footfall. Then nothing.

Bella strained her ears.

Nothing.

There, again! But closer this time. Someone was in the house.

Bella shot out of bed. She shut her bedroom door. No freaking lock. Snatching up her phone, she sprinted into the bathroom. Not wanting to make any noise, she eased the bathroom door closed and rammed the lock home.

Fingers shaking, she misdialed, then finally hit Nate's number.

He answered almost immediately. "Bella?"

"Nate." Her whisper screamed around the silent bathroom. "I'm not sure, but I think somebody is in the house with me."

"Shit." The phone crackled as he moved. "I'm on my way."

"Nate, I'm scared."

"I know, babe." So calm and certain, his voice kept her from losing it. "Where are you?"

"In the bathroom. I locked myself in." It could be nothing. She might be stupidly nervous because of Adam. At this stage, however, she wasn't taking any chances.

"Good girl."

Her bedroom door creaked.

"He's in the bedroom," she whispered.

"Fuck." The phone thumped as if he'd dropped it, and then Nate was back again. "Stay locked in. Don't move."

The footsteps padded closer to the bathroom door.

"Nate." Bella's voice came out in a squeak. "He's right outside."

"Don't hang up, Bella. Leave me on the line."

Bella scrabbled as far from the door as she could get. The bathtub pressed into her spine and she climbed inside.

"What's happening, Bella?" Nate's voice, calm and grim, but there.

"Nothing."

Sounds from her bedroom, drawers opening and closing. Her intruder was going through her stuff.

Nate's voice. "You still with me, babe?"

"He's opening my drawers." Part of her wanted to march out there and defend her stuff, but it was a very small part, hiding behind the need for self-preservation.

The bathroom door handle turned.

"He's trying the door." Bella couldn't drag her gaze away from it. Her phone slipped in her sweaty hand.

"Stay very quiet, baby." A car started over the phone line. "I'm on my way."

Someone pushed the door. The lock held.

"Bella?" Adam! "I know you're in there."

"Stay with me, baby," Nate said.

Bella nodded. Her voice froze in her windpipe.

"Open the door, Bella." Adam sounded annoyed. He tried the lock again, rattling the door in its frame. "I just want to talk to you. Please open the door."

"Do not fucking open that door," Nate said. "Are you still there?"

"Yes," she whispered.

"Bella!" Adam pounded on the door. "Open this door. I want to talk to you. Come on, Bella, you know me. Now open the door."

"Say nothing," Nate said. "Do not engage him. I'm nearly there."

The faint wail of a siren cut through the night.

Bella strained to hear and there it was again. A siren, getting louder.

"Damn." Adam thumped the door. "This is not over, Bella. You can't treat me like this. I love you."

"I'm on your street," Nate said.

"I can hear you," Bella whispered.

Footsteps across her bedroom floor, and then the door opening again.

"He's not in my room anymore. I don't know where he is." She didn't want Nate walking into whatever nasty surprise Adam had planned.

"Stay where you are," Nate said.

A car door slammed outside and then boots pounded up her walk.

Nate couldn't get in. The front door was locked, just like he'd told her. "The door's locked," she said into the phone.

"Don't worry about it," Nate said. "And don't come out to try to open it."

Half-standing, Bella crouched back in the bath again.

She could make out the sounds of movement through her house. She had no idea what was happening on the other side of that door. Time actually seemed to move backward as she waited.

A knock on the bathroom door.

Bella froze.

"Bella, it's Nate. Open up, baby."

Bella must have seen one too many movies because her response came almost automatically. "How do I know it's you?"

"It's Nate. I know you're scared, but you can open the door now."

It sounded like Nate. "Tell me something only Nate would know."

"Shit, Bella." Silence. "Okay, when we were in fourth grade, you came to school sick and barfed all over Miss Feinburger."

Bella nearly tripped over the bath lip as she shot for the

door. She unlocked it, wrenched it open, and threw herself at Nate.

His big arms came around her immediately. "Hey, I've got you."

"Don't let me go." She buried her nose in his neck, relishing the Nate-ness of him.

"Not a chance." He ran his big hands down her spine and kissed the top of her head. "I'm here now."

"Is he gone?" She dared not look up from Nate's neck. She felt safe here, cocooned in the smell and feel of him.

"He's gone." Nate's voice held a grim note, like maybe he'd been hoping for something else. "I checked the house before I let you out."

Bella edged an inch away from Nate. "Are you sure?"

"I'm sure." Nate tightened his arms around her. "I've got you now."

The shudders kept growing. Adam had broken into her home, her sanctuary. He'd stood right where she and Nate stood now and tried to get to her. She couldn't ignore this anymore. Much as she wanted to pretend Adam would go away, he wasn't going to. "What do I do?"

"You can't stay here." Nate's voice rumbled through his chest.

No way in hell would she spend the night here. Not now. Damn Adam and this bullshit. He'd made her home feel like a danger zone. "I could go to my parents' house."

"Alone?" Nate pressed her away from him. His beautiful face was so serious. "No."

"Okay." She didn't even bother with a token protest. She really, really didn't want to be alone. Maybe she could stay with Liz.

"What the fuck." As if Bella had summoned her, Liz rounded the bend in the hall at a run. She'd thrown a jacket and UGGs on, but the black silk of her negligee peeped out. "Are you okay? What happened?"

"Adam broke in." Saying the words brought the damn tears. She hadn't even known she was close to crying until Liz gave her that sympathetic face and rubbed her back. As if bawling her eyes out had been waiting in the wings for its cue, Bella couldn't seem to stop.

Nate rocked her in his arms, murmuring something.

Liz stroked her back with different murmurs.

"She can stay with me," Liz said.

Bella sobbed harder. Liz was so kind and so giving all the time. She couldn't believe she hadn't given her friendship a chance before now.

"No." Nate's arms got like a vice, but she welcomed them. "She's staying with me."

Liz quirked a brow. "Bella?"

The part of her that really wanted to be feisty and fiercely independent whispered that she should turn the offer down with a flounce and a few choice words. But she was tired and scared out of her tiny mind and next to Nate was the only place she wanted to be. "I'll be okay with Nate."

"Well, if that changes . . ." Noel appeared behind Liz. "You only have to call and Liz and I will come get you."

Liz turned on him. "Don't say *Liz and I* like we're a couple. You lost that right. Actually, you pretty much fucked your way out of that right."

"I understand." Noel nodded and stepped around a vibrating Liz. He pressed a business card into Bella's palm. "You can call me, or you can call Liz, anytime."

"Thank you." Bella had the horrible feeling she might start bawling again.

"Pack a bag, honey." Nate stroked her spine. "Take a few things for the next couple of days. This is now an active crime scene. If Adam left behind any DNA, we're gonna find it."

Red and blue lights flashed around the corner and a second cruiser drew up. Gabby climbed out, hitched up her utility belt, and strode toward them. "Sheriff." She nodded at Nate. "What happened?"

"I'll walk you through it." Nate pressed Bella away from him. "Pack that bag. I don't want anyone else inside until we've processed the scene."

Now her house, which she had been so proud to buy and spent hours decorating, making it into the sort of place where she felt safe and happy, was a crime scene. Bella dragged herself to her bedroom.

Nate's instincts howled not to let her out of his sight, but they had one shot at Adam and Nate aimed to make sure he had enough evidence gathered to make it a slam dunk. He had Bella's testimony, but some physical evidence linking the bastard to the scene would certainly help.

Gabby trailed him into the kitchen.

"Far as I can see, he broke in through the kitchen." He motioned her around some broken glass. "Make sure you check for footprints outside in the morning. We might get lucky. Then—"

"Sheriff." Gabby crouched down near the glass. "I got this. This isn't my first crime scene."

Maybe not, but it was her first crime scene where Bella was the victim. Make that second crime scene. He should have found Adam before it got to this, but after the incident at the store, Adam had pulled a vanishing act. Nate aimed to make sure they got the twisted shithead before there was a third incident. Adam was escalating, and that scared Nate more than he cared to admit.

Fuck! Adam had gotten too close. One flimsy door had stood between him and Bella. His hands shook and he shoved them into his pockets.

"You okay there, Sheriff?" Gabby kept on examining the back door. It was like she had ESP or some such shit.

"Yeah." Because what else could he say? That he was freaked way the fuck out and he didn't like it one little bit? He knew enough about shock to get that his reaction was setting in now. Now that Bella was safe, his mind was playing *what if* with him and he hated the direction it was headed. Working with living victims was always harrowing, and faces from his SLC days lined up and jeered at him. All the ones he hadn't gotten to in time. All the women and kids left to piece their lives together again after some shithead had torn them apart.

Not his Bella. He wasn't going to add her face to that lineup.

"I'm taking Bella home with me," he said. Fuck what Gabby made of that.

She nodded. "Sounds like the best plan."

Nate left her to it. Who the hell was he kidding? It was the only plan he could get his head around. Gut deep, he needed to be close to her, to have his eyes on her at all times, and he couldn't make that go away.

On her fridge, she had her plan for Christmas pinned with a fridge magnet that read: "Live Now." Beside it hung a birthday calendar for the year. He checked August 10, just for shits, and sure enough, there he was in Bella's neat handwriting. In middle school, she used to dot her *i*'s with little hearts and flowers.

She'd jammed a little slip of paper under the same magnet. The number looked familiar. He pulled out his cell and checked.

Daniel Carver. Motherfucker!

Chapter Twenty-Four

*N*ate lived at the opposite end of town, where the buildings thinned into the national park. Bella had always known where his house was, but this was her first visit. She sat quietly beside him as he drove through the pitch-black night and parked in front of a neat stone house. A porch wrapped around most of the house and took advantage of the views. Not that she could see much in the dark.

From here, he must be able to look out on the park from three sides of the house.

"You okay?" With his hand on the door, he turned to her.

"Not really." His face had settled into grim lines and she wanted to alleviate them. "But I will be."

"We'll get him, Bella." Nate opened his car door on what sounded like a promise.

He was at her side before she could fully open her door. Taking her bag from her, he shouldered it and wrapped his larger hand around hers. Security lights blinked on as they got closer to the front door. Of course Nate locked his door, and he dropped her hand as he worked the key in the lock.

Inside, honey-colored wood floors gleamed under the

overhead light. Town gossip had shared with her that he'd bought the house for a good deal a few years back and was busy renovating it. "Did you do the floors?"

"Yeah." Nate dropped her bag beside the door. "Matt helped me with the supplies, but I'm doing the work myself."

The hall opened onto a living room with large windows facing the park. The absence of any sort of ambient town light made the dark outside absolute.

Nate turned left past a staircase with a truly ugly yellow and orange floral runner. The top half of the glass banister had been replaced with wood and wrought iron. She sure hoped he got to that runner as well.

"I started in here," Nate said and led her into the kitchen.

Cherry cabinets cast a warm amber glow. Granite counter-tops ran across all the surfaces. A central island with barstools held the stovetop.

Nate led her over to the stools and she perched on one.

Stainless-steel appliances shone like he might polish them every day. It was warm, welcoming, and if that range was anything to go by, a place in which someone actually knew how to cook.

"Are you hungry?" Nate opened the fridge.

"Not really."

He glanced at her. "How about I make you something anyway?"

"Want me to cook?" The devil made her ask. That and some need to break the seriousness.

Nate stiffened. "No. I'll cook."

She smiled at him to let him off the hook. "I'm not really hungry."

"Good thing." His answering smile warmed her. "Because I don't have any pink marshmallows."

"Maybe I could just take a shower and go to bed." She didn't feel sleepy, but they both had to be up and at it in the morning.

Nate grinned. "I think I can do one better than that. Come."

He led her up the stairs onto a wide landing. The carpet of yellow and orange flowers had been given free rein up here. *Dear God.*

"Yeah." Nate grimaced. "I haven't gotten around to doing these floors yet."

A new-looking set of double doors opened onto the master suite. Here the floors had been changed to the same hardwood she'd seen downstairs. A huge bed dominated the room, flanked by a pair of mismatched side tables.

Nate walked through another door and into a bathroom. Bella stopped inside the door and stared. Cream and wood blended together in a haven that made her want to stay there all day.

Bent over a massive tub, which looked out onto the night, Nate opened the faucets. Oval and deep, it was the sort of tub a girl would want to lounge in for hours and soak her problems away.

"I don't have any of that bubble stuff." Nate shrugged and shoved his hands in his pockets.

"That's okay." Bella wanted to hug him. "I don't really like bubbles."

"You don't?" He raised his brow.

He knew her too well. "Okay, I do, but the bath will be great."

"I'll get your bag." He left the bathroom.

Bella ran her fingers over the cool marble counters. Wow; Nate had spared no expense in this bathroom, which seemed a bit weird. He wasn't the type to luxuriate; she was pretty sure about that. Yet he'd made a place for someone who liked to spend time in the tub, or take her time on her makeup. He'd built a bathroom with a woman in mind.

Her chest throbbed. Not her, apparently. Or any woman

she knew. Perhaps in some distant future, a Mrs. Nate would crawl out of the woodwork. Please God, Bella hoped to have moved on with her life by that time.

Nate's footsteps rapped on the wood and then he was back again. Bag in one hand, a glass of wine in the other. "I can't do bubbles, but wine I've got."

Lucky, lucky Mrs. Future Nate. Beneath all the bristle and attitude lurked the soft heart of a man who lived to make his woman happy.

"Hey." His expression gentled and he put the wineglass beside the tub. "You okay?"

"I'm okay." Bella tried her best not to lean into his warmth, but his hands on her waist weakened her resolve and she went with it, burrowing deep into the smell of laundry detergent and Nate.

"It's gonna be okay, babe." He kissed the top of her head. "I'm gonna make it that way."

Bella nodded and, after another squeeze, let him go and stepped back. "I'll have my bath."

"You do that." He stood there, hands back in his pockets. "You need any help?"

The sort of help that involved Nate's big, rough hands stripping off her clothes, running over her skin. Nate cupping her breasts, sliding his hand down her stomach and into her pajama pants. The sort of help that had her wet and aching. Her voice sounded a mite too bright and chipper. "No, thanks."

Nate thought so too because he raised his brow. His lids drooped heavily over the heat of his eyes. "I'll just . . ." His walk to the door seemed stiff, without the usual Nate grace.

The door closed behind him.

This getting-over-Nate wasn't getting any easier.

He'd made a stupid mistake bringing her here, but damned

if he knew what else to do. That primal hunk of Cro-Magnon left inside him wouldn't have it any other way.

And here he was, sporting wood, as he tried not to think about Bella glistening naked and pink in his bathroom. What the hell was the matter with him? He wasn't this guy. He had a horrible track record with women in so far as sticking around went. Sure, he never made promises, and if a woman wasn't down with how he needed things to play out, he walked away, but women still got hurt, and nice girls like Bella always wanted what he couldn't give them.

Where did that leave him? Sweaty and hard. He could kid himself and say all he wanted from her was sex, but he didn't have enough bullshit inside for that. This need for Bella ran deeper, a need to mark her as his, to celebrate her escape from harm in the most elemental way. Nate adjusted himself and took up a position in front of his TV. There had to be something on here to get his mind off Bella.

A naked Bella sliding soapy hands all over those lush curves.

He flipped through the channels and found some hockey. Big guys pounding the shit out of each other would work as a distraction.

The thing with Bella was that he'd always known this on some gut-deep, self-preservation level. She spelled trouble for him, blinked out in Morse code from those big blue eyes that looked at him as if he embodied the love child of Santa Claus and Captain America.

Horrible thought.

On the TV, Barrie slammed Giroux into the boards, hard enough to have the Philly crowd braying for blood and pounding on the glass.

She was his Mary Jane Watson, the woman he wanted to be a better man for. For her, he wanted to strip away the mask and show her who he really was.

But beneath the badge he was what he'd always been—a POS punk with no sense of loyalty or integrity. A punk who had put his family through all kinds of hell and left a string of broken hearts behind him. Bella deserved better than that, better than him.

But Daniel Carver sure as hell wasn't it. He didn't care that Daniel seemed to have turned his life around. The man wasn't good enough for Bella. Nobody was. He dug in his pocket and pulled out the slip of paper with Daniel's phone number on it. With relish, he balled it into a wad and stuffed it down the couch cushions.

Okay, not his best move. Taking the scrap of paper in the first place crossed some sort of line. He really didn't want to think about that or he might have to dig the paper out and return it to Bella. Screw it. He wasn't perfect; never pretended to be either.

Bella's soft footfalls padded across the wood. She appeared beside the couch and stood there looking uncertain. Long hair still wet and hanging in a thick braid down her back, her pretty face flushed and scrubbed. Her glance flickered to him and then the TV. "What are we watching?"

So goddamn sweet. Pure sugar all the way to the bone.

He moved the remote so she could sit beside him.

With her soft smile, she curled up beside him in a waft of honey and the soap he always used.

The siren blared as the Avalanche evened the score.

A man could see every thought she had in those huge eyes. Her lashes spiked dark and thick against her creamy skin. He'd always liked her nose. A little button turned up at the end that she wrinkled as she thought, making twin lines across the bridge. Her mouth was sin. In a full, pouty curve that almost seemed too big for her delicate face. Matt had nicknamed her Tinker Bell because she looked a lot like the Disney fairy. Peter Pan needed to have his head examined for turning her down.

A tentative smile quivering, Bella blinked at him.

"You like hockey?" He had to clear his throat.

Damn if she didn't wrinkle her nose. "Maybe." She laid her head against his shoulder, her damp hair cool on his cheek. "Thank you, Nate."

The need to hold her freight-trained through him. He had to keep it cool, controllable. "It's my job."

She stiffened. Her breath caught. "Okay."

He was such a dick. He slid his arm around her shoulders and tucked her closer to him. "I didn't mean it like that."

She resisted.

Nate increased the pressure until she gave and sank against his side. "You mean more than that, Bella. You have to know that."

"Yeah." She nodded, nudging his chin with the top of her head. "I just don't know where that leaves me."

Neither did he.

Bella closed her eyes and breathed in undiluted Nate. His warmth beneath her cheek, the solidity of him pressed against her side. She'd had what could only be called a really shitty couple of days. Right now, she clung to the life raft that was Nate.

Tension radiated from him and she should move away, give him space, but she couldn't make herself do it.

"Bella." He wove their fingers together. Hers looked tiny and slim between his, but their hands fit palm to palm, like they'd been designed that way. She couldn't afford to think like that. Not when he didn't share those feelings.

"It's fine, Nate." She squeezed his fingers. "It wasn't a question. More like a statement."

"Babe." He pressed his cheek to her head. "You should get some sleep."

Hell no! "I don't want to be alone."

"You're safe here. With me."

"I know."

Questions hurtled around and around in her mind. What would have happened if Adam had gotten through that door? Would he keep going until he got to her?

Cold stroked down her spine and she shivered.

Nate rubbed her arm. "Are you freaking out on me?"

"A little."

He shifted, lifting her onto his lap. Their eyes were on the same level. His glowed that weirdly beautiful gold-green. "It's going to be okay, babe."

"I know." Because she did. Nate would fix this, make it right. She threaded her fingers through the silky hair at his nape, needing the connection.

His gaze flickered to her mouth. "Babe."

Beneath her palm, his heartbeat kicked up, his skin warmed.

The two inches of air between their faces thickened until it dragged hot with promise into Bella's lungs. "Kiss me."

His lids hooded over the scorching heat in his eyes. "You know where that leads, Bella."

"Yes, I do." She spread her fingers wide over his chest and slid two of them between his buttons to find the skin beneath. "And I want that."

"Fuck." His breath hit her mouth. "You say that and I get hard, but you're in shock."

"Maybe." She pressed their foreheads together. Their breath mingled. "But right now I need this. I need you."

Gripping her hips, he groaned her name against her mouth, "Don't let me be the asshole who takes advantage of you."

"I'm the one taking advantage." Bella straddled him.

Against her, his erection pressed hard and ready, and Bella ground down.

Nate moved, jogging her. He stood with her in his arms. "If we're going to do this, we do it right."

Bella tightened her legs around his hips.

He moved them up the stairs, barely even breathing hard as they reached the top.

In his bedroom, he put her down gently on the bed, coming down between her thighs. His broad hands framed her face as he stared down at her. "You sure?"

Never more sure of anything in her life, Bella tugged his mouth to hers.

Nate slowed the kiss, exploring her mouth with deep, drugging thoroughness.

Bella writhed beneath him. She wanted to get lost in the heady rush of him.

Refusing to be hurried, Nate moved down to her neck. "So soft," he murmured. "And so damn sweet."

Bella tugged his shirt out of his pants and finally got her hands on his back. Muscle flexed beneath her palms. She dug her nails into it.

Nate hissed in a breath. He straightened his arms and loomed above her. "You got a little wild in you tonight, honey?"

"I want to forget," Bella said. His lion eyes stripped her to the raw.

"Trust me." He shifted his weight and slid his hand beneath her sweatshirt. "Let me take this slow and easy."

"Maybe I don't want that."

His hand slid over her ribs to cup her breast. "Why don't we give it a try?"

With her nipples being gently tugged, she would agree to just about anything. "Okay."

Chuckling, he sat back and whipped her sweatshirt over her head.

Bella hadn't put a bra on after her bath.

"I still see these when I think of you." Almost reverently, he put his hands on her breasts, weighing them in his palms. "You're such a tiny thing and yet you have such incredible curves."

Enough with the chatting. Bella arched into his hands.

He lowered his head to her breast and sucked. Hard.

Heat shot through her and Bella pushed into the pressure of his mouth. She wanted his imprint on her skin, to have him sink soul deep into her and keep him there. Threading her fingers through his hair, she tugged his head closer.

Gently grasping her wrists, he pulled her hands down, pressing them into the mattress. "Bella, baby." He kissed her. "You need to slow the hell down."

"Why?" She whimpered.

"Because I want everything from you." His lips skimmed her ribs, found her belly, and lingered in the hollow of her navel.

Okay, then. Bella sucked in her breath against the wet heat of his mouth. She shifted her thighs together, trying to alleviate the building pressure.

Releasing her wrists, he hooked his thumbs in her waistband and tugged her yoga pants down her legs. Her panties followed.

Nate stood and stared. "Look at you, baby." He parted her knees and slid his palms up the inside of her legs.

With a tug, his shirt came over his head and sailed across the room.

Never mind *look at her*. Look at him. Damn, he was beautifully put together. Muscle bunched across his shoulders and chest. His pecs stood proud over a hand-on-her-heart eight-pack he had going on. Bella's mouth watered. She rolled toward him and crawled forward, desperate to get her mouth on that.

His skin tasted slightly salty on her tongue. She skimmed her teeth across his muscle.

Nate dropped his head back and groaned. Beneath her mouth, his abs contracted into a sharp ladder.

Bella grabbed his belt and unbuckled it. She tugged his pants open and slid her hands inside.

Yes, Nate was going commando again. She wrapped her hand around his cock. It jumped in her hand, silky smooth and hard and so hot it tingled against her palm.

Impatiently, she pushed his pants down.

"What are you doing, baby?"

She thought that was rather obvious. Bella took him in her mouth and sucked him deep.

Nate gripped her head, fingers pressing into her scalp.

She flattened her tongue along the underside of his cock and dragged it all the way to the tip.

His eyes bored into her, hot enough to incinerate.

He tasted salty on the top. Gripping the base of his shaft, she slid him back into her mouth. Dear God, she enjoyed doing this to him.

The inarticulate sounds coming from Nate encouraged her further. He wanted her to slow down, and she did. Working him in and out of her mouth, cupping his heavy balls, sucking him deep. She even added the slightest graze of her teeth.

Nate tugged her head back. "Enough." He pushed her back. "My turn."

His lips hit her core with no preliminaries, sending Bella arching off the bed. He ate her as if he couldn't get enough of her. She was primed and ready to go. So horny already that she could barely stand it.

Nate worked his fingers inside her. His mouth found her clit and sucked.

Bella's orgasm slammed into her. It seemed to go on and on.

He crawled up, laying heavy on her. "Do you even know what slow means?"

"Maybe." Bella couldn't help it; she felt so damn good that she laughed.

Nate kissed the corners of her smile. He nibbled her lips with his.

Against her thigh, his cock pressed hot and hard. It reminded her that they weren't finished here. Nate had more to give her and she wanted to collect.

He slid his tongue into her mouth, sharing the taste of her.

Bella sank into the kiss, letting it take her with it on a lazy swirl of sensation that settled between her thighs. She reveled in the heat and strength of his body on hers. Opening her thighs, she let his slim hips slide between. She gripped his ass and pressed him against her.

Damn, he was so hard. It was a turn-on all by itself.

His chest rubbed her sensitive nipples. It felt even better when she undulated against him. Now she felt content to play. To relish in how good he felt on her, sink her teeth into the swell of his deltoid, dig her fingers into his ass.

Nate snatched a condom from the bedside table and separated from her to put it on.

Then he was at her entrance, pushing his cock's blunt head into her, stretching her around him. He went slow, letting her feel every part of him until he was fully sheathed in her.

Bella wrapped her thighs around his hips. She wanted to pull him as close to her as she could get him.

He moved in slow, sure, deep thrusts that drove her into the bed. Rising up on his elbows, he watched her. Their eyes met and locked.

Bella held on to his forearms as he drove them forward.

The gentle slap of skin hitting skin filled the room. She felt him driving inside her. He held her with a loaded intensity in his gaze.

It was almost too much at once. All her senses latched on to him. Only him and her in the vortex they created together.

Their skin grew slick. Their breath came in short rasps, soft moans.

Nate's orgasm built in the tightening of his jaw, the blaze of his eyes. For once his face was an open book, allowing her deep inside him, to that secret place she had sensed but never seen. His thrusts deepened, filling her completely.

Bella felt the finish begin in her core, spread hot through her belly in a slow, steady wave until she vibrated with it.

She watched Nate drop over the edge with her. Their eyes never lost their connection. In that moment she was his and he was hers.

Tears prickled beneath her lids and forced Bella to close her eyes. The intensity shook her. It was as if she had caught an agonizing glimpse of his soul.

He pressed his forehead to hers, giving her his full weight. Her name came out of him in a gentle sigh. "Bella."

She wrapped her legs and arms around him and held on.

Cooling as fast as the sweat covering their bodies, already the moment was slipping away. Bella wanted it back, so desperately it left a gaping hole right in the middle of her.

She almost cried when he rolled to her side.

He kissed her forehead and tucked her head onto his shoulder.

Beneath her palm, his belly rose and fell as his breathing returned to normal.

He tightened his arms around her. "Bella."

Chapter Twenty-Five

$\mathscr{N}$ate lay beside her as the sun rose on Bella's sleeping face. Her thick, dark lashes and pouty mouth were pure Disney. She slept curled into herself like a tiny bundle of candy.

The need to make sure she stayed safe and peaceful ached through his chest. Even now, he wanted to tuck her against him, keep himself between her and anything that might harm her. Shit! He uncurled and sat on the edge of the bed.

What the hell did he think he was doing?

He couldn't offer any woman any of those things. Strong, protective, reliable—that wasn't him; he was the family screwup. After his dad died and the family needed someone to step up, Matt had done it, and even Eric to a lesser extent. Him? The black sheep might have changed his outer ways, but he'd stayed rotten and broken to his core. He'd caused more trouble. Made things infinitely worse and nearly landed his ass in juvie. What he wouldn't give to go back and not stress Matt to the breaking point, drive his mom to an overdose. But there was no going back, only forward, and try like hell not to screw up anymore. Best to stick to his kind. Women who didn't want things he couldn't give them.

Bella was white lace and forever, picket fences and preschool, with a man she could count on by her side. People didn't count on Nate Evans.

If he had turned his life around to the point where the county trusted him, why couldn't he be the man Bella needed? He froze and let that bit of crazy percolate through his spinning brain.

"Nate?" Bella touched his back.

This shit was getting so mixed up in his head, he leaped to his feet. "I'll put some coffee on. Feel free to shower or whatever. There's an extra toothbrush under the sink."

He hotfooted it into the kitchen and got the coffee on. Down the hallway, heaven lay in his bed. Or the nearest a man like him could ever come to it. Wanting to take a layer of skin off, he scrubbed his hands over his face.

His history with women had never included anything like last night. Mostly, he tried not to think too much about his history with women. Before he'd learned—hook up and get the hell out before it got messy—he'd left plenty of broken hearts behind him. The idea of Bella hurting because of him soured his gut. For years he'd been patting himself on the back for his honesty. In the light of the pure thing Bella offered, it made him seem less like a hero and more like a coward, because as much as he tried to stamp on it, this *what if* flickered into life and blinked on and off like a faulty electrical circuit. What if he could be the man Bella deserved? And what if he broke her so bad he took the sweet out of her?

Filling in time, he got out some eggs and bacon and made her breakfast.

The pipes moaned as Bella turned the shower on. The sooner she realized he had nothing to offer, the better off she would be, which would leave him alone. But alone suddenly seemed like a bad place to be.

He was putting breakfast on the table when she pattered into the kitchen. "Hey."

"Hey." He managed to crank out a noncommittal smile.

Until he looked at her, and then his head scrambled again. Scrubbed clean, hair braided and wet, she looked like she had last night. Vulnerable, pure, and so beautiful it hit him like a rib punch.

She looked at the table. "You made breakfast?"

"Yeah." He had to get away, clear his head and find clarity before he did something stupid. "Coffee's over there. I need to get ready for work."

"Nate." Her voice stopped him at the kitchen door. "It's all right, you know. I don't expect anything from you."

Why that made him feel like shit, he couldn't say. "I know."

Under Nate's watchful eye, Bella opened the store three hours later than usual.

She'd barely managed to choke down enough of her breakfast to make his effort worthwhile. She didn't need Dr. Childers to recognize a man in full retreat. Bitched the entire time about her opening the store but drove her over anyway. He'd even fetched her favorite coffee for her. All in the brooding silence that made her relieved when his cruiser finally backed into Main Street and drove off.

She leaned against the door and let the hurt roll through her. The problem with expectations was they hurt like hell when they weren't met. Nate was Nate. He hadn't changed much since first grade. Ten years from now, Nate would still be—surprise, surprise—Nate.

Yet, somehow, being with him put all those self-preservation thoughts into hibernation. Until the next morning. Even if she didn't love the stupid man, watching your lover go into chew-his-arm-off retreat the next morning stung.

She called Pippa and told her about what had happened—the Adam part, not the Nate part. The Nate part still scraped raw inside her.

Pippa said enough of the right things to help Bella feel sort of all right. She had it firmly in place as Liz's flashy red SUV pulled up outside the store.

Bella did a double take as Liz climbed out. Hair scraped back into a ponytail and sweatpants poking out from beneath an old parka.

She scurried into the store, slamming the door behind her. "Babe! I must be the best motherfucking friend on the planet to come out like this to see you."

Yes, she was, and Bella grabbed her into a hug.

"Hey." Liz hugged her back. "What's with the PDA?"

She really couldn't talk about it. She had to sniff a little as she pulled back. "What brings you out in sweatpants? I didn't even know you owned any."

"I'll deny it if you tell anyone." Liz strolled into the store. She flipped through a rack of dresses. "So, last night?"

Bella knew a clever deflection when she saw one. "How about you tell me what's going on with you?"

"I'm not going to talk about me after what happened to you last night." Liz stopped clacking hangers together. "How're you doing?"

"Okay." Bella chased dust bunnies out from beneath the racks. "Trying not to think about it." She fixed Liz with a stare. "A good friend would take my mind off it by telling me what's going on with her."

"This is the problem with having friends." Liz threw herself onto the chaise. "People get to know you."

"Uh-huh." Bella turned on her register and grabbed up her duster. "They also know when you're stalling."

Laughing, Liz tucked her legs up beneath her. "It's Noel. He's driving me batcrap crazy. After what happened to you last night, I swear the man thinks he's going to be my knight in shining armor or something."

"In what way?" Keeping to her dusting, because Liz would be more comfortable that way.

Liz dropped her face into her hands and growled. "He's so . . . determined."

"To get you back?"

"Uh-huh." Liz propped her chin on her palm and looked so much like a tween, Bella had to smile. "And I was so sure I wasn't going to go there with him. Even for the sex. And girl"—Liz raised a brow—"the sex was awesome. That man is hung—"

"You told me."

"Well." Liz huffed. "It bears repeating. Donkey!"

"Somehow I sense that's not the problem."

"Well, look at you." Liz sat back. "All sassy and mouthy. A couple of trips around our hot sheriff's bedroom and you're a new woman."

Her chest ached and she swallowed. "We're not talking about me."

"Now." Liz pointed a royal-blue talon. "We're not talking about you now. But once we're done with me . . ."

"Okay." Because fighting with Liz was like holding back the tide with one hand tied behind your back. "Noel is driving you crazy."

"He's there all the time. I get home and he's waiting for me." Liz jerked straight. "Not like your psycho . . . shit . . . I mean, Adam."

"I know that."

"He wants to spend time with me. He wants to be with me and he's making it impossible to say no."

Bella took a seat beside her. "So what's stopping you from saying yes?"

Liz gaped at her. "Are you kidding me right now? That man hurt me. He slept with a friend of mine while I was going through chemotherapy."

Yeah; Bella couldn't put a positive spin on that. "What does he say about that?"

"This is the shitty part." Liz sighed. "He makes no excuses. He tells me he's sorry. Apparently, it scared him when I got sick and he did a stupid thing. He swears nothing like that will ever happen again. That he loves me."

"And you?" Bella said slowly. Liz seemed so fragile.

"I've never stopped loving him." Liz's shoulders slumped and she looked beaten. "I dealt with the cancer. The feeling sick all the time with the treatment. But Noel . . ." Her voice wobbled. "He broke me, Bella."

Screw Liz and her boundaries. Bella wrapped her arms around her. "No, he didn't, because here you are. Still standing and telling the story."

"Just barely." Liz sniffed. "I really don't know if I can go there again."

"You don't have to. This is your choice." Look at her with all the great advice she didn't use herself.

Liz growled again. "I know what the smart thing to do is. Yet there's this other side of me that's still pining away for the dickhead." She wiped her eyes on her sleeve. "And I so don't want to be that girl. The one who's always whining about her shitty man but goes right back to him time and time again."

"I'm pretty sure you're not that girl."

"But I'm doing a damn fine impersonation." Liz snorted. "Sometimes I want to bitch-slap everyone with ovaries. Myself included."

"Let's blame it on the ovaries." Bella propped her feet on the coffee table. "Want me to do something about the sweatpants aesthetic?"

Liz straightened and scowled around the store. "What are you offering?"

"Sackcloth and ashes?"

The bell over the door jangled and Phi swept in, looking like Big Bird reloaded, as she trailed scarlet feathers behind her. "Darling girl!" She paused in the doorway, then swept Bella into a patchouli-scented hug. "What a terrible, terrible time you've been having. I rushed straight over the moment Pippa told me."

Bella stood still as Phi scrutinized her. No choice really; Phi would only let her go when she was good and ready.

A tall black man stood behind Phi, shoulders so wide they blocked out Bella's view of the street. Hands crossed in front of him, he wore a white button-down and a precisely pressed pair of khakis. He made it look like a three-piece suit.

Never slow to notice any hovering hotness, Liz unfolded from the divan. "Well, hello there."

The man looked at Liz's outstretched hand for a beat before giving it a shake.

Phi gave a gusty sigh. "Isn't he lovely?" She nudged Bella. "All tall, dark, and deadly."

"Hi." Bella waved from Phi's clutch around her shoulders.

The man nodded. His gaze swept the store, and she got the feeling it took him no more than that to assess every item in it.

"Pippa is worried sick about you." Phi let go of Bella long enough to flap her hands. "Poor thing. She is quite overwrought."

"Is she okay?" Bella hated the idea of pregnant Pippa doing anything but concentrating on that new baby.

"You know Pippa." Phi swept over to the rack of dresses. "She soldiers on, and dear Lord, is this not the most heavenly color?" She held up a cobalt-blue wrap dress about six sizes short of the diva's impressive bosom. "This color would be heavenly with my sapphires, don't you think?"

Bella searched her mind for a good answer and came up short.

Tall, dark, and deadly almost smiled.

"You know it." Liz grinned at Phi.

"Anyway," Phi racked the dress, "I've been tossing and turning about you, Bella, *ma fée*. And of course about my poor, dear *enceinte* Pippa." One hand to her bosom, the other on the rack, she trilled. "And then it came to me."

Liz gaped at Phi.

Bella didn't blame her. Those pipes had brought royalty to its knees in Phi's time. She knew the diva well enough, however, for her skin to itch. "What came to you, Phi?"

"My darling Simeon," Phi said, as if she'd pulled an SUV out of a hat. "Simeon, meet the beleaguered Bella."

"Simon," he said. "It's nice to meet you. Phi's told me a lot about you." Bella just bet Phi had, and was that a Bronx accent?

Phi floated over to a jewelry display and snatched up a sparkly choker. "Is this not too divine?"

"Yeah." Ready to enjoy the show, Liz settled back on the divan with a grin.

"Of course I didn't think of Simeon first." Phi preened in front of the mirror with the choker held to her neck. "First I thought of his most delicious father." She paused, eyes cast up. "I still have dreams about that man."

Simon flinched. So tiny a movement, Bella almost missed it.

"Tell us about the dreams." Liz tucked her legs beneath her.

"The dreams." Phi shivered. "Such vivid details. There

is the one that begins on a beach with a magnificent white stallion pounding through the surf."

"Phi knew my dad," Simon said.

"On his back is my darling Timothy. Naked."

"Naked is good." Liz propped her chin on her fists.

Simon took a deep breath.

Bella took pity on him. "So, you're new in town?"

He nodded.

"By all the saints!" Phi wheeled about. "I almost forgot the point of my being here."

That happened a lot. Bella shared a look with Simon that told her he knew that too.

"Simeon and I have long been acquainted. Almost from the moment of his birth. Not his actual birth." Phi gesticulated. "But his rebirth as a modern-day warrior."

"Phi helped me get into a college and then Quantico," Simon said.

Liz bounced liked a three-year-old on sugar. "A Fed."

"Not anymore." Shutters slammed down around Simon.

"Do you see, Bella?" Phi wafted over and put her arm about Bella and Simon. She looked at Bella eagerly.

Bella didn't see.

"I have hired you a champion, a paladin."

Simon almost smiled again. "I'm your protection detail."

"Protection detail?" Bella felt all kinds of stupid as she stared up at Simon.

Liz exploded from the couch. "A bodyguard! Bella, you've got a bodyguard."

"No, I don't."

"It's the perfect solution." Phi whipped her head around before bustling away. "Lord preserve us! Are those the gowns over there?"

Bella stared at Simon.

He stared at her. "I understand you're having some trouble with a stalker."

Bella knew what roadkill felt like. Phi had flattened her. "Yes. No. I mean, I do have a stalker, but the sheriff is handling it."

"That's not all the sheriff is handling." Liz spread her arms over the divan back.

Bella's face went radioactive.

Nothing from Simon.

A throaty chuckle from Phi. "You bad girl." She waggled a finger at Liz. "Simeon! I simply must introduce you to darling Elizabeth. Does she not have the most divine breasts?"

"Pleased to meet you." Simon nodded at Liz.

"Hi." Liz gave him an evil grin. "They're not real, you know. Want to get a closer look?"

Phi snickered.

"Pippa briefed me." Simon glanced at Phi. "He broke into your house?"

"Yesterday."

Simon frowned. "Phi called me at about 5 a.m. Asked me to get here ASAP."

"Phi shouldn't have." Phi really, really shouldn't have. Bella tried to find the words to tell her so, but the diva meant so well. Everything she did came from that huge heart of hers. "I really don't need a bodyguard. I don't think I can afford one."

"I come prepaid." Simon nodded. "Phi asked and here I am."

"This is silly." Bella wanted to squirm.

"Maybe. But while I'm here, why don't I have a look around?" He smiled. "I may as well; have you ever known anyone to successfully say no to the diva?"

Chapter Twenty-Six

*N*ate's shitty start to his day spiraled straight into the toilet.

Bella collected men like lint. Adam, Daniel, and now some hotshot glory boy with his flashy credentials and his permit to carry concealed. Guy had checked in about five minutes after Nate arrived at the office.

It didn't help that Gabby had actually taken the stick out of her ass long enough to offer hotshot a cup of coffee. She'd never offered him coffee, not once.

He pulled into the circular driveway outside his brother's place and hopped out. He needed to go right to the source of the problem: Pippa.

Damn it! He knew they meant well, but taking care of Bella was his job. The last thing he needed was some vigilante-type shit in his town.

Actually, the source of the problem was Diva Philomene, but he didn't have the balls for that. The diva didn't hold back on the trips down handcuff memory lane.

With a brief knock, he opened the kitchen door and stepped inside.

"Nate." Pippa greeted him with her million-dollar smile. Matt looked up from his laptop. "Hey."

"Coffee?" Pippa opened the cupboard where they kept the mugs.

"Who the hell is Simon Walker?"

Matt's chair scraped on the floor. "You got a bug up your ass?"

"Yeah, I do." The same bug he'd had up his ass for what seemed like months. "Did you know Philomene hired a bodyguard for Bella?"

Matt grinned. "Sounds like something she would do."

"That's all you've got to say about this?" Nate wanted to punch the smile off Matt's face.

Pippa put a full mug on the table, with the sugar and cream beside it. "You seem upset."

"I'm not upset, I'm fucking mad!"

"Watch yourself." Matt squared off.

Nate forced a deep breath and then another. Matt always played big brother. It was part of who he was, and getting into a pissing contest with him wasn't going to get Nate anywhere. "This situation is bad enough without adding another complication."

"Sit, Nate." Pippa pressed him into a chair. "You know Phi. Once she got the idea into her head, there was no stopping her." She pushed his coffee closer to him. "Simon's very good at what he does. He's not going to complicate your life."

"I had this under control." Needing it, Nate added an extra spoon of sugar to his normal three.

Pippa took the seat beside him. "I didn't think this would make you angry."

"It did." He sipped his coffee and found a moment of calm. Pippa made great coffee. Not like the sludge Gabby made. She should know better than to go offering that shit around.

"What's up?" Matt resumed his seat and closed his laptop.

His normal *nothing* came up, but he shoved it away. First off, Matt wouldn't buy it for half a second, or Pippa either. Secondly, maybe he could get some perspective here. "I'm so screwed."

"We're talking figuratively, right?" Pippa grinned at him.

He smiled back. You couldn't help it when Pippa gave you that smile. It started in her grass-green eyes, crinkled around her cheeks, and then curled her mouth up. No wonder she was one of TV's most-loved celebs.

Matt tugged his wife and her chair close enough to kiss. "Is this about Bella?"

His big brother knew him better than most. "Yeah."

"More than her situation?"

"Yeah."

Matt stiffened. "What the hell did you do?"

What did a girl do with a bodyguard? Bella tried not to watch Simon, but she couldn't help it. Other than the serious hot factor, the man slid around her store like a ghost, nowhere and everywhere all at once.

"Would you like a cup of coffee?" Bella needed some caffeine. Phi had blown out like a storm, taking Liz in her wake.

The idea of Simon made Bella want to squirm. Who the hell needed a bodyguard? Like she was some kind of celebrity or something.

He flashed her his quick smile. "I'm good, thanks."

"Tea?" Like her mouth got stuck in a rut, it kept going. "Water? Juice? Beer?" Dear Lord, not beer. "Sorry. I bet you don't drink while you're on duty. Not that you're on duty or anything, just taking a look around."

"Bella." He materialized right in front of her. "Breathe."

She breathed, and breathed again, taking in a spiced citrus fragrance that ought to be illegal. Maybe he had secret squirrel aftershave designed to render women weak and susceptible. Okay, time to take another breath.

Simon's dark gaze twinkled. "You got it under control yet?"

Did she? Nope. Bella held up her hand. "Give me a little bit."

"Take your time."

Strangely enough, embarrassment aside, she did feel better having him there. "I've never had a bodyguard before."

"I would never have known." Simon winked.

Bella's giggle shot out of her nose on a snort. Which only made her laugh harder and blush even more.

The door jangled.

Gaze locked on the door, Simon tensed. "Someone you know?"

Daniel stopped with the door in his hand and stared at Simon.

"It's Daniel," Bella cut in quickly, before Simon did any guarding of her body. "He's a friend of mine. He's fine."

"Bella?" Daniel gave Simon the top-to-toe. "I came to check on you."

There seemed to be a lot of that going around this morning. "Daniel, this is Simon."

"Daniel Carver." Daniel approached, hand out.

Simon shook. "Simon Walker."

Daniel threw her a quizzical glance, but Bella couldn't bring herself to introduce Simon as her bodyguard, so she smiled back. "I'm fine. A little shaken up but fine."

"What the hell happened?" Daniel shoved his hands in his pockets. "I heard Adam broke into your place."

Of course he'd heard. Ghost Falls hadn't had gossip this

juicy since Pippa's fall from grace on national television. Bella went through the story as quickly as she could.

Simon drifted over to the far side of the store.

"Who is he?" Daniel whispered.

Bella opened her mouth, then changed her mind. "You wouldn't believe it if I told you. Can we call him sort of a gift from the diva and leave it at that?"

With a grin, Daniel nodded. "That's probably for the best."

Daniel didn't stay long. His exit opened the floodgates, and person after person found their way into her store. Not to buy something but to hear the story from her mouth. Toward closing time, Pippa and Matt paid her a visit.

Pippa glowed with her pregnancy and Matt walked beside her as if he was the first man on earth to sire a child. Their happiness beamed from them. It made Bella a little jealous.

"Shit, Bella." Pippa swept her into a huge hug. "This is getting crazy."

"Yeah, it sucks." With Pippa, Bella didn't have to pretend to be brave and she relaxed into the hug.

"You must be Simon." Matt held out his hand. "My brother met you earlier."

"The sheriff?" Simon nodded. "I make it a point to check in with the local law. Makes things go easier down the road."

Pippa laughed. "Not with our sheriff getting all territorial it won't."

"Thought that might be the case." Shoving his hands in his pockets, Simon nodded.

"What does that mean?" Bella glared at Pippa, willing her to give a straight answer. "What's wrong with Nate?"

Matt lifted a brow at her. "Really?"

"It's not like that." A flush climbed her cheeks.

Pippa cocked her head. "Oh no? How is it, then?"

If they'd been alone, she might have said more. In fact,

talking to Pippa would have been a great idea, but not with Matt and Simon looking as if they were collecting each word in a bucket.

"Uh-oh." Pippa leaned closer. "Do I sense the need for girl talk?"

"Maybe." As in definitely and soon.

Right." Pippa clapped. "Matt, why don't you buy Simon a cup of coffee?"

"I don't—"

"It wasn't a suggestion." Matt clapped Simon on the shoulder. "Coffee shop is two doors down and we can stand outside. You can keep an eye on Bella from there."

Not wasting any time, Pippa patted the divan next to her. "Let's hear what's going on with Nate."

Bella waited until they'd shut the door behind them before she turned to Pippa. "A bodyguard. Phi gave me a bodyguard."

Pippa winced. "I warned you. I thought I had her headed off, but you know what she's like."

"Yeah." Bella nodded. You'd have more luck holding back an avalanche with a bucket and a spade. "What do I do with him?"

"Nothing." Pippa shrugged. "You let him do his job and you go about your life."

Simon and Matt hugged the wall outside Mugged.

"He must be costing a fortune," Bella said. She didn't want to spend Phi's money.

"Probably." Pippa peered at the two men. "But why don't you let Phi worry about that and tell me what's going on with Nate?"

"It might have been easier when I only crushed on him from a distance." Too restless to sit, Bella paced over to the window and stared out. "It certainly hurt a lot less than this does."

"Ah, Bella." Pippa came up behind her. "You so don't need this on top of everything else you're going through."

"It's weird." Bella took her time putting this into words. "I started this whole self-improvement thing because my life had drifted into a rut. I was thirty-three and stuck in a rut. Isn't that pathetic?"

"Pathetic? No." Pippa put an arm around her shoulders. "Sad, yes. You have too much to offer to get caught in a rut."

"I keep thinking if I hadn't started self-improving, none of this would have happened."

"Whoa!" Pippa turned her face to her. "Please tell me you're not taking the blame for any of this."

Bella couldn't maintain eye contact. Because yes, there was this little voice in her head—one that sounded exactly like Nana—that kept insisting if she had left things alone . . . "I wanted something different. More."

"You're entitled to more." Pippa gave her a little shake. "We're all entitled to have life in abundance. All of us, including you. We just need to be brave sometimes and reach for it."

"That doesn't seem to be working so well for me." Bella glared at her pink store. The eighties' decor closed around her like a trap. "Nothing has really changed. Except I have some psycho asshat trying to break into my bedroom and I think my heart may be well and truly broken. And I still have this fucking pink store."

"Bella!" Pippa stood back. "That's the first time I've ever heard you swear."

Heat climbed her cheeks. "Well, I often think bad words."

"Say it again." Pippa's smile was pure evil. "I dare you."

"Fuck," she whispered it, because now Bella had started to feel a bit silly. Silly but strangely liberated. Hadn't that giddy sense of liberation gotten her into enough trouble?

"Matt's going to fix this pink nightmare." Pippa hugged her quickly. "And look what else you got."

"Great outside Christmas lights?"

"That," Pippa said. "And you made new friends. Liz. Daniel. Would you change things and not have them in your life?"

"No." For sure not. Liz had been a great addition to her social life. Daniel had stopped asking her out and they'd drifted into a budding friendship she hoped would grow. "And I really enjoyed the volunteering at the church."

"There you go." Pippa sounded like her cheering section. "You've done a good thing, Bella. You didn't like the way your life was going and you changed that. That's more than I managed. If Ray hadn't pulled that shit on me, I might still be caught in my rut."

Bella doubted that. From her classy-as-hell clothes to her high-powered career, and now her gorgeous husband, Pippa defined the term kick-ass. When Pippa wanted something, she stormed out there and got it. "You weren't in a trap."

"Yes, I was." Pippa laughed. "I convinced myself I had everything I wanted and ignored that little voice in my head that said it was a lie. Ray forced me to get real. I had my head jammed so far up my ass, I almost let Matt get away from me."

Okay, that did make her feel a little better.

Pippa peered out the window. "Damn, how does my grandmother do it?" She pointed to where Simon and Matt stood. "My entire life, Phi has managed to find the hottest men."

"I can't believe Nate got territorial." The burn of that suddenly made itself known. The man couldn't shove her out of his house fast enough and yet still felt it was okay to pee all over her to mark his territory.

"Head-up-assitis." Pippa nodded. "There's a lot of that going around. And just because Nate doesn't know whether to fish or cut bait doesn't mean you have to wait around for him to decide."

No, she didn't, but with Adam still lurking around somewhere, she wasn't exactly ready to fling herself back into the dating scene.

Dr. Childers chimed away in her head: *Own the life you want to have.*

Oh, shut the fuck up!

Chapter Twenty-Seven

*N*ate tapped his foot as Gabby pecked away at her keyboard.

"Tell me we have something." His unease prickled beneath his skin. Adam had disappeared like smoke, and as long as the bastard couldn't be found, Bella remained in danger.

Gabby huffed. "Nothing." She rubbed her eyes. "He was last seen at a gas station about twenty miles from here. I got a grainy image from the station's surveillance cameras."

Nate wanted to punch something. He paced instead. "You can't move in this town without someone asking where you're going. But this bastard manages to slip through our fingers."

"Sheriff," Gabby stood and eased her back, "he's been doing this for years. The reason he's still walking around is because he's seriously good at it."

Nate knew that. Some part of his brain remained objective enough to see that. Adam had to be holed up somewhere. No sign of that fancy car of his either. Clever enough to know they would have all the motels and hotels covered, Adam had to have found a hideout. But where?

It was driving Nate crazy. His department covered a huge area, a lot of nothing but forest and wilderness, and that was just where that little shit had to be hiding. There wasn't enough manpower, even if he pulled everyone from throughout the county, to launch the kind of search he needed. The mountains around Ghost Falls left way, way too many places for someone to hide.

"What are the chances he's given up?" Gabby stirred sugar into her coffee.

"None."

Gabby nodded. "So we keep looking." She blew into the hot cup. "At least you know Bella's got that rent-a-cop following her around."

Which was the other bug up his ass. He wanted to be the one protecting Bella, standing between her and this shitstorm. His brain reminded him that the rent-a-cop gave him the space to do his job, but his gut didn't give a crap.

Matt had reamed him out that morning. Much as he'd like to have fought back, his brother was right. Bella had enough to deal with without Nate making it worse. Going near her tonight wasn't an option. The only thing he could do was his job.

He threw himself into his day's work because the rest of the county wasn't going to sit still while he went through his personal crisis.

As he followed her home from the store, Bella kept Simon's rental car in sight.

Her street looked the same as it always did. The two Simpson children chased each other with snowballs. Mr. Powell patrolled his front yard, checking for snow-damaged plant limbs. He raised a hand to her as she drove past.

Simon pulled into her driveway behind her.

Opening her door, his gaze scanned the quiet neighborhood as if they were standing in the middle of Kabul. "Stay put," he said. "I'm going to check the house first."

"Bella." Mr. Powell trotted over. "Mrs. Powell is worried sick about what happened last night."

"Tell her I'm fine."

"Good. Glad you weren't hurt." Mr. Powell rubbed his palms on his thighs. "The thing is, though, how can we be sure he won't be back?"

"That's what Simon is here for."

Mr. Powell stared at her house. "For you. You have a Simon. Mrs. Powell doesn't feel safe in her own house anymore."

"Tell her she's fine." Every man for himself, and suddenly, she didn't want to have this conversation with Mr. Powell anymore. "Adam isn't here for anyone else but me."

Mr. Powell frowned. "Are you sure?"

"I'm sure." The fear she'd pressed down all day came back in a wave.

"Well, good." Mr. Powell beamed. "Mrs. Powell will be so relieved."

So much for good neighbors.

Simon came up beside her. "All clear. We can go in now."

"What happens now?" Someone had put new locks on her door.

Locks that Simon engaged. "You mean tonight?"

"Yup." She had another strange man in her house. What was she supposed to do with him?

"Phi says you have a spare room I can use." Simon didn't seem at all uncomfortable as he strode down the hall to her kitchen. "She also strongly recommended I do the cooking."

After dinner, Simon checked the house again before they settled down for the night.

She got a text from Nate, checking to see if she was all

right, and she replied that she was. That set the pattern for the next week. Bella went to work, came home, volunteered with Liz. Simon merged into her life as if he'd been there all along. He even helped her pick out a couple of Christmas gifts.

One week dribbled into two and Bella relaxed a bit more. Her parents called from Florida to find out her plans for Christmas. She and Liz had been invited to the Folly to spend it with however many other stragglers Phi had unearthed before they spent Christmas alone.

Meanwhile, Matt set a start date on the store renovation for early January and, as if the fates aligned to approve her plans, she had a record-breaking Christmas and her internet orders continued to grow. All in all, scary Adam aside, she had a lot of be grateful for this year.

She did her best not to think of Nate and very nearly succeeded for a couple of hours a day. He texted every night to check on her, but there was no other contact. It was better this way. Liz, Pippa, Daniel, even Simon, when pressed for his opinion, said it was better this way. Which would be fine, if she felt it. Yes, she knew she should be feeling it. How many times did she have to sink before she tried to swim?

"I'm not really much help." Liz looked up from painting her nails pond-scum green.

Snowy weather provided the perfect excuse for a *Buffy* marathon on Netflix.

Noel had kept up his campaign. The man had the patience of a saint. Although Liz stayed firm, Bella found herself softening to him. He seemed to genuinely regret what he'd done, and the romantic in her wanted to give him a second chance. A trait, Liz quickly pointed out, that worked against her in the Nate situation.

"I think you should give him a chance." Simon spoke from the sofa. "And what the hell are you putting on your nails?"

"It's festive." Liz held up her hand.

"Red is festive," Simon said.

"So is green."

Simon snorted. "It makes your fingers look like they're gangrenous."

Liz pointed at him. "You're working your way out of the girls' club, my friend."

"You need me." Simon folded his arms. "To give you the male perspective."

Liz frowned and painted her other hand. "Okay, so give me the male perspective on Noel."

Simon muted *Buffy*, which demonstrated he wasn't really in the girls' club because he couldn't chat and watch *Buffy* at the same time. "First off, Noel got luckier than he ever thought he would when he landed a woman like you."

"Aww." Liz blew him a kiss.

"It's true." Simon shrugged. "You're way out of his league."

"Do we still have leagues?" It didn't sound very Dr. Childers to Bella.

"Of course we have leagues." Simon gave her his *duh* look. He did it very well. "Men like Noel don't expect to end up with women like Lizzie over there. They're okay with that. But occasionally, the fates align and someone like Liz gives a man like our Noel a chance. If he wins the lottery, she sticks around because she likes what he gives."

"His dick." Liz nodded.

Simon didn't even blink and neither did Bella, which still surprised her on occasion.

"Dick's nothing if you don't know what to do with it." Simon smirked.

Liz chuckled. "So says every man with a small one."

"Lizzie." Simon raised a brow. "You know what they say? Dicks come in small, medium, large, extra-large, and Simon."

Liz and Simon snickered for a couple of minutes.

"Anyway . . ." Apparently, Bella hadn't totally lost the ability to blush. "What's your point about Noel?"

"My point is that when a man is faced with losing something so precious to him, he panics. Suddenly, he sees everything disappearing and he loses his shit."

"That's what Noel says." Liz pulled off her wooly socks and examined her toenails. "Should I paint them green as well?"

"No." Simon grimaced.

"I think you should do what you want." Bella held up the girls' side. "They're your toenails."

"Your boy Noel lost his shit more than most. But think about this"—Simon held up his hand—"he's back. He's owning what he did and he's clever enough to know how much he lost. By my book, that means he'll do anything to get that precious back."

Liz examined her toes. "Do you think I can trust him again?"

"I do. But it doesn't matter what I think." Simon turned *Buffy*'s volume back up. "You're the one who has to trust him."

Nate had officially crossed the line into pathetic. Determined not to screw Bella over anymore, he had stayed away. Stayed away and done everything he could to track Adam down.

Nothing moved on that front until that morning, when a message came through the main office that tagged Adam in Chicago. An attached picture confirmed his identity. It didn't make a helluva lot of sense to Nate. Certainly went against pattern for all the predators he'd encountered. Still, Adam in Chicago meant breathing room.

So where did his screwed-up head go? Straight to Bella

and maybe running by to give her the news. She'd be relieved, grateful even. Maybe they could celebrate life in the most basic way possible.

God, he was a dick. A pathetic dick.

So beyond help, in fact, that here he sat with Daniel, trying to work Bella's name into the conversation so he could find out how she really was. He knew Daniel saw her every now and again, which burned, but apparently, Bella had friend-zoned Daniel, so that made it bearable.

The Avalanche was getting an ass-kicking courtesy of Minnesota and he couldn't watch anymore.

"So . . ." Sharing the news on Adam wasn't really bringing Bella into this. "I got a verified report this afternoon that Adam has been seen in Chicago."

"Really?" Daniel stopped with a fistful of chips halfway to his mouth. "That's good news, right?"

"It's good in that he's all the way over there." Nate took the recliner next to Daniel. They'd moved their game watching to Nate's house. No boiled cabbage and ratchet neighbor smell here. "But it bugs me as well."

Munching his chips, Daniel raised a brow. Nate always put a bowl of them next to him. When the need for beer rose, Daniel liked his chips close at hand. "Why's that?"

"He gave up." Nate let the Avs take the power play before he finished his thought. "Guys like him don't give up and move on just like that."

"You think he'll be back?" Daniel double-fisted chips.

Nate felt his pain. They'd all been jumpy over Adam's missing act. "I know he'll be back. After all he went through, he sees her as his. He's not going to let Bella go."

"Have you told Bella?" Daniel gave him that look that said Nate wasn't kidding anyone.

"Not yet." Someone scored; screwed if he knew who. He'd catch it on the replay anyway. "I thought I might have a word with that rent-a-cop."

"Simon." Daniel grinned at him, and not in a nice way. In a gloating way that made Nate want to punch him. In the old days, they'd be rolling on the floor throwing punches by now. Sometimes he missed the old days. "His name is Simon, but you know that. And he's a really good guy, but you know that too."

Nate did know that, but no way in hell was he admitting it. He grunted and tried to get into the game.

"She's good," Daniel said. "In case you were wondering. Bella is doing great."

He shrugged, but the news both relieved and pissed him off. Of course he was glad Bella was doing okay. Except the dickwad in him wasn't so sure she should be okay without him around.

"You're doing the right thing," Daniel said.

Nate wished he could take some kind of comfort from that, but he missed her. Missed her big blue eyes. Missed the way she crinkled her nose at him. Missed the way she seemed to be surrounded in a cloud of happy, sparkly fairy dust. He nodded.

"Bella is a forever girl," Daniel said. "She deserves a guy who'll go the distance for her."

"Like you?" It was a low blow and Nate wasn't proud of himself, but it had gotten away from him.

"Dude," Daniel shook his head, "she doesn't want me. If she did, though, I'd be there for the whole thing. Unless you can say the same, you need to stay away and let that girl find someone who will."

Chapter Twenty-Eight

*B*ella's Christmas Day began with a call to her parents and Nana. Nana had a lot to say, as per usual, about the store. Mom cried because they weren't spending Christmas together and Dad wanted to know all about Adam. Outside her window, the weather did its best to help her throw off the gloom. Bright sunlight bounced off a sparkling white layer of fresh snow.

With Adam and Nate disturbing what Dr. Childers called *the calm center of your power*, Bella's Christmas spirit was dented. Flipping on her Binger Christmas carols, she made a decision: enough of this. She loved Christmas and she refused to be depressed.

From the kitchen came the sounds of Simon up and about. You had to love a man who got the coffee going before you even hit the shower.

She slopped into the kitchen in her robe and bunny slippers. He also made the best coffee. Ever.

"Morning." Simon smiled at her over his mug. "Merry Christmas."

"Merry Christmas." Bella wished she could better appreciate

the view of a shirtless Simon. The man put the *fine* in defined abs. "What? No little Santa hat?"

"I'm saving that for Phi." He poured her a mug, added cream as she liked it, and handed it to her. "We're due there in a couple of hours, so you best start gathering that mountain of presents you've got under your tree."

She pulled a face at him. Simon didn't get the Christmas spirit. It didn't bother him in the least to be spending Christmas without his family. You learned a lot about a person when you lived with him. Except if that person was Simon Walker, and then you were left with a whole lot more questions than answers.

"Noel's at it early this morning." Simon stared out the window at the street. "Damn, and he's loaded up."

Bella joined Simon at the window.

Noel came over every day to see Liz. Whether she'd agree to see him was a crapshoot. Still, undeterred, he would be back the next day.

He staggered up Liz's walkway, arms loaded with gifts.

Apparently, Liz was either moved by the Christmas spirit or curious as hell to know what was in all those brightly wrapped packages because the door opened and Noel gained admittance.

"Do you think she'll take him back?" Bella sipped her coffee. Sometimes the door opened again and Noel got kicked out. The door stayed shut this morning.

"Not sure." Simon shrugged. "But even the best of men do bad things sometimes. Nobody's perfect."

The echo of old pain in his words stopped Bella for a moment.

"Go and get dressed." Simon glanced at her. "I hate being late."

Bella topped up her coffee. "You know I'll get your secrets out of you eventually. All of them."

"Nah." Simon gave her a sad smile. "You don't want my crap in your brain."

Phi loved celebrations and Christmas was her second favorite holiday. Valentine's Day took the number one slot and buried Phi's Folly under acres of red ribbons and hearts. For Christmas, the weird house drifted straight into a Victorian Christmas card.

Bella and Simon parked outside in what Phi called the kitchen yard. A ratty dog trotted past wearing a red-and-green bow that dwarfed his head.

"Ho! Ho! Ho!" Phi appeared in the kitchen door, resplendent in gold and green like the Ghost of Christmas Past.

"Who you calling ho?" Simon grinned at her.

"Oh you." Phi swept Simon into a hug. "So like your gorgeous father."

Bella came next for a patchouli-engulfing hug.

"We're going to have so much fun." Phi chuckled and capered back into the house.

Simon sucked in a breath as they entered Christmas on crack. Every available surface had been decorated with bows, bells, angels, and sparkles.

June, Phi's longtime housekeeper, scowled her hello from the oven.

Something smelled incredible and Bella took a big breath. She loved her family, but Christmas Day with Nana's burned turkey and dishwater gravy wasn't something she missed.

The sitting-room fire ate its way through most of a tree. A massive real Christmas tree sparkled and shimmered under the weight of decorations.

Bella added her gifts to the pile beneath it. They'd agreed on a Secret Santa type of thing. From the pile of presents, it looked like Phi had broken her own rule. No surprise there.

Pippa and Matt sat curled together on the sofa and rose when Bella entered.

Pippa's sister, Laura, and her husband were there with their two kids as well.

Flawless as ever, Pippa's mother, Emily, sat in an armchair beside the tree and kept the children at bay.

"Fabulous dress." Pippa gave her a hug, looking even more fabulous in an understated wraparound dress that screamed designer.

Matt drew her into a hug. "Merry Christmas."

As the people kept coming, so did the Christmas hugs and kisses.

Noel and Liz arrived, followed by Eric Evans, flying solo again. Another hot Evans brother, and this one also determinedly single. Jo and Cressy arrived together, the tension already leaking off them.

Deputy Gabby slunk in, still in uniform because she could only drop by briefly before she had to go back on duty.

Of course Phi had unearthed Daniel and insisted he join them. He headed for Bella with a big smile. "Hey, sweet thing."

He had taken to calling her that and she rather liked it. He also seemed to have embraced that they were going to be friends.

Accepting a glass of wine from Simon, she drifted around the room and did her best not to tense every time someone new walked in. Back to the door, she examined the ornaments on the tree.

Still, Bella knew the moment Nate entered the room. It was like the air in the room suddenly vibrated with him, then rushed over to her and sent tingles all over her skin.

As if sending her positive thoughts, Daniel caught her eye and winked.

Simon moved to flank her.

Feeling safer, Bella turned.

Shit! Three weeks hadn't in any way diminished the Nate-to-the-knees factor. His gaze came straight to her and stuck. Those strange and beautiful lion eyes stopped her world in its tracks.

He walked toward her.

Her vision tunneled until he stood right in front of her.

"Bella." His voice stroked her name. "Merry Christmas."

"Merry Christmas."

He leaned into her, his lips hot on her cheek, his hand a brand on her hip. "You look beautiful."

You are beautiful. Always. "Thank you."

"Nate." Daniel gave him a hearty clap on the back.

Nate looked away.

Bella sucked air into her starving lungs.

Simon glanced at her with a wink. "You're fine."

Was she? Not so much.

Nate walked away to greet his family and she wanted to fling herself at his broad back and hang on for dear life. "I'm an idiot."

"We're all idiots from time to time." Simon toasted with his wineglass. "To idiots."

"To getting your secrets," Bella said.

"Good luck." Simon winked, then jerked his head to the other side of the room. "And what's up with that?"

Daniel and Jo stood next to each other, bristling and throwing off screw-you vibes like a pair of lightning rods.

"I'm not sure." Bella tried to think whether Pippa had ever mentioned anything about Jo and Daniel. Nope.

Phi barreled in with a tray of hors d'oeuvres, which she managed to foist on Pippa, and headed straight for the bar. Matt clearly knew the drill and had a Manhattan all ready for her.

"Darlings," Phi tapped her glass, "I wish you all a wonderful Christmas. We are so thrilled to have you here with us. Especially this year, with my first great-grandchild on the way." She sipped her Manhattan. "Of course I will be naming the little one."

"No," Matt said.

"Not happening, Phi." Pippa spoke at almost the same time.

Phi patted her hair. "We shall see. In the meantime, I thought I might sing for my supper. Pay attention, darlings; this only happens once a year."

With anyone else, this might have seemed the most incredible moment of egomania, but this was Phi. She'd sung for kings, queens, and heads of state and performed at every great opera house in the world.

Phi launched into "Pie Jesu."

Over seventy, and still Phi's voice soared above the room as if lifted by angels. Pure, powerful, and clear as the bells decorating her Christmas tree.

Pippa had tears in her eyes as she watched her grandmother. Even restrained Emily looked moved.

Phi was a star. She may live a quiet existence—as much as Phi could ever be quiet—here in Ghost Falls, but this woman had once commanded thousands of people to silence with her voice.

Phi held her final note, let it linger and touch everyone in the room, and fell silent. Pure magic.

Bella stomped her feet and cheered with the rest of the room.

"Now," Phi lifted her chin, "Let's eat."

Some inborn sense of self-preservation made Bella choose a seat well away from Nate's. Unfortunately, she now had an excellent view of him. Years of secret crushing had honed her peeking skills and old habits died hard.

Except she now knew what his face looked like moments before he kissed her. How passion spread a flush to his high cheekbones. The way his eyes would turn liquid gold when he was buried inside her. The gentle smile he wore when he framed her face with his hands and tried to look deep into her soul.

"What?" Liz nudged her.

"What-what?" Bella nudged her back.

"You sighed," Liz said. "Loudly."

Bella flushed and returned her gaze to her plate. June had done an excellent job on dinner and it seemed a crying shame to push it around her plate. Bella made more of an effort to eat, laugh, interact. This was why she'd launched the epoch of the new Bella anyway, to change old habits, and the habit of waiting around for Nate no longer served her well. Only Dr. Childers never said how breaking some habits felt akin to ripping out your heart and lungs and stomping on them.

Merry Christmas, Bella.

Nate could feel her eyes on him, softer than the caress of her hands on his skin but no less tangible. As she had scurried to the far end of the table, he'd had a brief, bloody skirmish with his better self. Better self had emerged the victor and let her put distance between them. What choice did he really have? He liked Bella too much to let her waste time on a man who had nothing better to offer.

Phi kept him entertained throughout dinner with an endless and agonizing stream of stories involving the diva and handcuffs.

After dinner, he tracked down the rent-a-cop.

Simon nursed a glass of orange juice, his dark gaze

always tracking Bella. As much as it bit Nate's ass to admit it, Simon knew his job and did it well. According to Gabby's internet search, Phi had hired the best for Bella. Not really a surprise. Phi, for all her drama, had the biggest heart of any human being.

"Hey." Simon greeted him. "Any sign?"

"Not a whisper." Nate allowed his gaze to find Bella. Perfectly legitimate, given that they were talking about her. "It's making me edgy."

Bella laughed at something Liz said. Through her smile, though, he could see the underlying tension in the line of her jaw and the way she held herself stiff. *This has to be hell on her and yet a stranger looking at Bella would have no idea what was going on behind her incredible smile.*

"I hear you." Simon nodded. "Anything since spotting him in Chicago?"

Nate's irritation spiked. "I would have let you know, but I don't think we've heard the last of him."

"I'd bet everything I have on him reappearing." Simon cleared his throat. "So, I've been thinking."

"Did it hurt?"

Simon laughed, too cool a customer to be dragged into an infantile argument. "He's not gonna come within a breath of her as long as I'm with her."

Nate's skin prickled. He hated where this was heading. "Don't even suggest it."

"Ordinarily I wouldn't." Simon sipped his juice. "But my read on him is that he's a patient man."

"Yeah." Nate knew Simon was right. Still, the idea of Bella being exposed to Adam again dripped acid into his gut and made it churn. "Let's hear what you're thinking."

"I'm thinking he's beat a strategic retreat." Simon propped his shoulder against the wall. Only a fool would read the posture as relaxed. "If I back off far enough to give him his gap, he'll take it. It's gotta be driving him crazy that he can't get near her."

"So you want to use Bella as bait."

Leaning over her shoulder, Daniel said something to Bella that made her flush and smile. Even in heels she didn't reach Daniel's chin and Simon wanted to dangle her as bait. Like the tiny glass figurines on Phi's tree, she would break so easily under Adam's heel.

Nate clenched his fists and shoved them into his pockets. "Not gonna happen."

"I don't think that's your decision." Simon put down his glass. "This is Bella's life and she deserves to have it back."

"By exposing her to unnecessary risk?" Every instinct of Nate's roared its protest. He needed to keep her safe. "If your sources know everything we do about him, then you also know how dangerous he is."

"I know." Simon nodded. "And he's not gonna give up until he gets to her."

"Forget it."

Bella glanced up and froze. She looked from him to Simon and frowned. Yeah, she knew they were talking about her. Sunlight danced off her blond hair and bathed her in a pool of golden light. So tiny and so fragile, it made his gut hurt. "If I ask you not to do this, would you leave it?"

Simon sighed. "I get it, man, I really do. You don't want her in danger. Neither do I. But we both know she's never going to get her life back until we catch this douche."

Nate fucking hated how much sense Simon made. "What kind of guarantees can you offer?"

"You'll be there every step of the way." Simon met his stare. "Nothing's going to touch her while we're watching."

Nate still hated it. "Let me talk to her about it. I need to know she's on board."

Nate's presence washed over Bella before she heard him speak.

"Bella," he said, "if you've got a moment . . ."

Liz stared at her, telling her silently that if she didn't want to give him a moment, Liz had her back.

Bella appreciated the support, but she and Nate lived in the same town, had done all their lives, and sooner or later she was going to have to find that moment for him. She turned and forced an easy smile. "Sure."

Nate led her out of the sitting room and into Phi's library. The room was cold after the people press in the other room and Bella shivered.

Nate shut the door behind them. "Simon and I have been talking."

She nodded, not liking how grim he looked.

"Simon came up with this." Nate laid it out for her.

Funny thing; with Adam going so quiet, she'd almost convinced herself that he was gone for good. Reality came screaming back at her. "I thought he might stay away."

"Bella . . ." Nate's expression softened. "Babe, I wish I could tell you that was true." He shrugged. "And maybe it is, but not in my experience."

It still seemed incredible to her that this all had happened. One night, she'd met a man in a bar. Done what most people did and gone on a date. Liked him enough to go on another.

"Don't." Nate cupped her face and turned her to look at him. "Don't go thinking what you could have done differently. Because there's nothing. Nothing."

"It's been easy to pretend over the last couple of weeks," she said.

Nate nodded. "Simon brought you some peace of mind. But this can't go on forever. You deserve more."

The irony of that statement lanced through her. "You say that to me a lot."

"Yeah, I do." His smile dripped regret. "And that's because it's true."

So easy for him to say and only one degree removed from *it's not you, it's me.*

"Yeah." Her laugh sounded bitter. "And yet here I am."

"Don't." Face achingly solemn, he brushed her tear away. "You're breaking my heart here."

Funny, she thought that was her line.

He pressed his forehead to hers. "I wish I could be that man for you, Bella. You've gotta know how much I wish that."

"Really?" She jerked out of his hold. "Those are just words, Nate. And they don't mean a whole helluva lot unless you back them with some action."

He straightened and wiped any expression off his face.

She knew she'd scored a hit, but she was so damn tired of being the only person hurting here. So damn tired of the men in her life letting her down. This had to end. All of it. "I'll tell Simon I'll do it."

"Bella." He grabbed her arm. His eyes held a wealth of stuff she didn't have the energy to decipher.

"Nate." She met his stare. He stared back silently.

Her bravado took her back into the lounge.

Simon looked up as she walked in. Eyebrow raised, he glanced at Nate and back at her.

Bella nodded. She would do this.

Simon strolled over and touched her cheek. "You okay?"

People asked her that all the time. Most of the time, she went with *fine*. "No," she said, "but I will be."

"What the hell did you say?" Simon glared over her head at Nate.

Nate bristled. "That's between Bella and me."

"Leave it." Bella touched Simon's arm when he kept his scowl going in Nate's direction. "It doesn't matter."

Simon looked at her. "You have to know I'm gonna take care of you, Bella girl. He's not getting anywhere near you."

His sincerity twisted through her and made her want to cry. She was scared. Weak-kneed, belly-churning, toss-your-cookies scared, but most of all she needed this to be over. This place she found herself in hurt and confused her. Heart aching for one man, scared shitless of the other, and her feelings jammed in the middle with no safe place to go. It had to end.

Chapter Twenty-Nine

Simon moved out of her house two days later.

As he loaded his bag into the back of his sleek black SUV, Bella swallowed the lump in her throat. She'd gotten used to having him around. Simon made the very best kind of housemate: he gave her plenty of space, cleaned up after himself, and made coffee without being asked. Bella swore her bathroom had never been as clean as it was after Simon used it.

Liz stood behind her and sniffled. "I'm going to miss that hunk of burning man love."

"Yeah." The fact that they were being silly didn't stop Bella from feeling like she was losing a friend.

"Nobody mixes my Manhattans like he does." Liz blew her nose.

"Not even Noel?" Bella had seen more and more of him in the last couple of days. He arrived at Liz's house in the evening and stayed all night.

Liz blushed. "Not even Noel."

"So . . ." Simon stood in front of them. "It's been fun, Bella girl." He held his large hand out to her.

Screw that! Bella tugged him into a big hug.

Arms like steel bands came around her.

Then Liz threw herself into the hug and turned it into a three-way.

"Hey, now." Simon disentangled himself. "You girls are getting me all wrinkled. I'll only be one town over, you know."

"But it won't be the same." Liz scrubbed at her eyes with her palms. "We won't be doing girls' nights anymore."

Simon winced. "Liz, I hate to break it to you, but I'm not a girl."

"That's what made them so special," Liz wailed.

Simon laughed. "Get it together, woman. I'll come to see you soon. And I'll bring the movie. I'm all chick-flicked out."

As Simon drove away, Liz sighed and leaned against Bella. "Are you sure you're not a little bit in love with Simon?"

"No." Bella wished she could answer differently. "He's going to make some girl so lucky one day."

"True." Liz sighed again. "He even has that broody, man-of-secrets thing going on."

"I tried that." Bella turned them back into her house. She felt bad about not letting Liz into their plan. Simon had discouraged her, saying they needed everyone around Bella to behave much as they would if Simon really had left. "Next time I fall in love," she said as Liz followed her into the kitchen, "it's going to be with a nice guy. One with no dark past or skeletons."

Liz snorted. "Good luck with that. Noel was one of those."

Bella refused to be depressed. "There are nice, normal

men out there who are looking for the right girl to share their life with."

"Name one," Liz said. "Name one we know who isn't already taken."

Keeping it positive, Bella said, "Maybe we should get a dog?"

Bella joined Daniel chopping vegetables at a large stainless-steel kitchen counter while Liz went off to set up tables because she said she hated chopping. Bella remained convinced she only did the setting up to get a look at Michael's ass and back as he hauled furniture around in preparation for the soup kitchen. Michael had a spectacular rear view. The front didn't suck either.

"Where's your shadow?" Daniel handed her an apron.

"He went home." Bella ducked her head and tied her apron. If Daniel saw her face, he'd know she was lying. "We think Adam is gone."

Daniel frowned and put down his paring knife. "Did Nate confirm that?"

"Yup." Damn, her voice sounded too chipper. She grabbed a handful of carrots. "What are we doing with these?"

"Peel and grate." Daniel tilted his head and studied her. "Nate said this Adam guy was nothing to worry about anymore?"

"No." She stuck as close to the truth as she dared. "But Adam was seen in Chicago just before Christmas, so he thinks the threat to me is over."

"Bella." Daniel caught her hand in midpeel. "You're lying and you totally suck at it."

"Yes, I am." Bella gave up. "But could you leave it at that for me? Could you do that?"

Daniel stilled. Then he nodded. "Okay, Bella." He grated three carrots and then slammed his grater down on the table. "Fuck! No, I can't leave it there. Tell me you're going to be safe?"

She didn't want him worried about her. Bella covered Daniel's hand with hers. "I'm going to be perfectly safe."

"Huh." Daniel scowled. He picked up his grater and went back to work.

Bella let out the breath she'd been holding. A new subject was called for. She pointed to a handmade poster pinned to the wall. In multicolored marker, it announced the St. Peter's New Year's Bash. Then somebody had drawn a bunch of sombreros and maracas, which she took to indicate a Mexican theme. "You going to that on New Year's Eve?"

Daniel glanced at the poster. "I hadn't really thought it out. Why? You asking me out on a date, finally, Bella?"

"No." Her face heated. Daniel's teasing had lost some of its edge. "But Liz and I haven't made plans yet. I don't feel like one of those swank places up on the hill. And staying home is sad. So, if you're going and I'm going, we could meet there."

"I'm going." Daniel grinned at her. "Ex-cons don't exactly have a full social calendar."

"But not as my date." She needed to know he got this.

His gaze held hers. "I get it, Bella."

Bella read the uneven writing along the bottom of the sign. "It says its potluck. What should I bring?"

"Whatever Liz makes." Daniel threw her a wicked look.

Bella could get huffy, but what was the point? She couldn't cook for crap and everyone knew it.

Nate couldn't say the hammering on his door came as a surprise. Tonight was Bella's night to volunteer at the church with Daniel. He also knew firsthand how badly Bella lied.

He opened the door to a fuming Daniel.

"What the fuck?" Daniel stomped into his entrance hall, scattering loose snow. "Bella is all on her own?"

"Take your boots off." Nate had finished those floors himself. "And hang up your coat."

Daniel did as he was told and followed Nate into the kitchen. He'd lost none of his steam as he glared at Nate. "Don't even think of feeding me that bullshit about how fuckwit has given up and disappeared."

"How's Bella tonight?" Nate got Daniel the soda he liked from the fridge and dropped it onto the counter in front of him.

"Bella is gorgeous." Daniel popped the cap. "And you could have all that gorgeous if you got your head out of your ass long enough to do something about it."

Nate stared at him. This from Daniel? "You're always telling me I'm no good for her."

"You aren't." Daniel sipped his soda. "But she seems to care for you, and any man who has a Bella wanting to be with him is a lucky one."

"What the hell?"

Daniel shrugged and fiddled with the tab on his soda can. "I've been thinking about what I said to you last time."

"And . . . ?" Nate fetched a beer. He had the feeling he was going to need it for this conversation.

"The way I spoke to you. That wasn't right. I came back here expecting you to give me a second chance. And you did." Daniel chugged his soda. "I didn't do the same for you. You turned your life around and became a man I'm proud to call my friend. You're not the same punk kid who screwed up. Just like I'm not that kid anymore."

"Still doesn't mean I'm the right kind of guy for Bella." Nate savored the sharp bite of hops, wishing he could wash away the sour taste in his mouth with it.

Daniel studied him. "Dude! You're the only one who can decide that. Now tell me what's really going on with Bella."

Nate hesitated. Daniel wasn't on his need-to-know list, but he might be useful. Daniel still had some of his old contacts, in places Nate as sheriff wasn't welcome. He outlined Simon's plan, such as it was.

"Shit," Daniel said.

Pretty much what Nate kept thinking. Simon had checked in with him as soon as he left Bella's place. Since then, the man had gone ghost. Not a sign of him, and Nate had looked carefully. Only the occasional message from a burner phone let Nate know Simon was still around.

"You trust this Simon?" Daniel parked it on a stool and rested his elbows on the counter. "You trust he can get to Bella before Adam does?"

"Yeah." Nate had to laugh at them all. "I trust that he's another member of the Bella Fan Club."

Daniel stared and then laughed. "Damn. We're a truly sorry bunch of assholes. I bet you wish you'd tied that up when she was still following you around school."

Nate shook his head and got another beer.

Lately, he'd been thinking a lot about him and Bella. He missed her, bone deep missed the hell out of her, and it was getting harder and harder to remember why he was no good for her. People did change, if they really wanted to. Matt had gotten his head out of his ass and gone for Pippa. Daniel had turned his addiction and his jail time into something good. Nate had taken a huge step in the right direction when he'd entered the police academy and then served first in SLC and now here. Was it really impossible for him to make another leap forward? Especially when he knew what, or who, waited for him to take the jump.

Chapter Thirty

The renovations meant closing the store for January. Nana would lose her mind, but it had stopped mattering so much what Nana thought.

January had always been one of Bella's quietest months. After the December spending spree, people took stock and opened their credit card bills. Yeah, January pretty much sucked.

Her online business would carry on through the renovations and Bella cleared out a space in her house for popular stock. A lot of the stuff she could leave in the store's storerooms. But that meant moving everything from the storefront into the back.

Liz and Noel jumped in to help, and the three of them now stood knee-deep in fabric and coat hangers.

"Fucking hell." Liz held up a sateen dress Nana had ordered in the eighties. "What is this?"

Bella had to laugh. If Liz of the butt-bedazzled velveteen sweatpants wouldn't touch the dress, it was truly hopeless. One of the advantages to this renovation would be finally getting rid of the stuff that made her shudder. The store needed a different direction and the few anchors still hanging around kept it and its tired décor in the eighties.

In the past, even clearing out old, outdated stock had ended in a nasty battle with Nana. Bella had developed a way of pushing that stuff to the edges of the racks or burying them in sales racks at the back of the store.

"Put it in the box for the Salvation Army." Bella pointed to a growing number of boxes in the front of the store. Years of hiding fashion atrocities had gathered quite a haul.

Liz eyed the dress, poking her finger at a large, floppy neck bow. "Do you think they'll want it?"

Bella couldn't be sure anyone would want that dress. Judging by how many sizes of that particular one remained, so far there'd been no takers. Nana also didn't believe in working on consignment.

Noel talked a whole lot less than Liz and therefore got a number of boxes sealed against the dust and neatly labeled and stacked in the storeroom.

Pippa rapped on the glass door, holding up a carry tray of coffees.

Bella let her in

"I bring sustenance," she said, putting the coffees on the checkout counter. "Matt has forbidden me from picking up heavy things, but I can bring coffee, and pack boxes." From her large bag, she hauled out a paper bag. "And what would coffee be without a sweet friend?"

Pippa wandered across the store. "You're making good progress here." She picked up the recently maligned dress, shuddered, and dropped it back. "My honey is going to make your store look fabulous."

Bella found her coffee and joined Pippa in the center of the store. "This is a whole new era for Bella's."

"And a whole new era for Bella." Pippa slung her arm over Bella's shoulder. "I'm hella proud of you, sweet Bella."

The compliment rushed straight through Bella on a warm, fuzzy cloud of aw-shucks. "It was time."

"Past time." Pippa took a huge sniff of Bella's coffee. "God, I miss coffee."

"How are you feeling?"

In her wool dress pants and cashmere sweater, Pippa looked as slim and elegant as ever. "I feel great." She grimaced. "But between Matt and Phi, it's hard to do anything. They watch me like hawks."

Bella got a little misty-eyed. Matt Evans had waited too long for his happily ever after. She could imagine how protective he would be of Pippa and their unborn child.

"Speaking of Phi . . ." Pippa chuckled. "She's offered her help if you want some guidance in the matter of the store's color scheme."

"Thanks?" Bella had found the pink too much. Let loose in her store, Phi could do just about anything.

Pippa eyed Liz and winced. "Really, Liz? Didn't we have a conversation about bedazzled sweatpants?"

Liz snorted. "I'm working here, give a girl a break."

"Just so you know, I'm accepting the excuse this once because you're helping our Bella." Pippa tucked into a chocolate muffin. "Also, chocolate mellows me out."

"I like 'em," Noel said.

All female eyes swung his way.

Noel flushed and tried to hide behind the counter. "I mean, I like Liz's pants. They work for her."

"Thank you, honey." Liz gave him a tender smile.

Progress? Who knew with those two.

Pippa sniffled. "Damn hormones, but that was really, really sweet."

"Not really." Noel blew on his coffee. "Liz always looks beautiful."

"Stop already." Pippa wiped her eyes.

Noel sipped. "She always did."

"Always?" Liz jammed her hands on her hips, but her tough-guy act wore paper thin, underscored by the vulnerability on her face.

"Always." Noel nodded. "Thought so the first time I saw you. Still think so."

"Then why?" Liz tossed up her hands. "Why?"

The rawness in her voice hung like jagged tears between her and Noel.

Pippa nudged her. "Perhaps we should—"

"No." Liz marched over to Noel. "I need to understand this."

"I wish I had a good answer for you." Noel dropped his gaze. "I wish I could give you a reason, because if I could do that, I could show you that it will never happen again."

Bella really didn't feel right witnessing this. "Liz, we're going to leave you two alone."

"No, Bella." Liz thumped the counter. "This can't go on. I need to understand this and perhaps you can help me do it."

Outside the silent store, a car drove down Main Street. A man stepped out of the hardware store and climbed into a dusty pickup.

Noel's stricken expression grabbed hold of Bella and dug its claws in.

"I don't think you do." Bella stepped closer to Liz and moved the cups out of striking range. "I think you do understand. I think you know the why, maybe even better than Noel does. What you have to do is decide what you're going to do about it."

"Just like that?" Liz snapped her fingers.

"No, not just like that, but you can't spend your life being afraid." Bella touched Liz's hand, wanting to make the connection between them and to ease some of the hurt radiating out of her. "And I do know a little something about spending your life afraid."

Liz turned to her, her face stretched taut. "What do I do?"

"What do you want to do?"

"I want to be loved. Wholly. Completely. Passionately."

Noel stepped around from behind the counter. "I can do that, Liz. I already do."

"Shit." Liz pressed her hands into her eyes. "Shit, shit, shit."

"Your move, babe." Noel took her hands from her eyes. "I won't keep coming around if it's making you unhappy. I won't do that anymore. I'll do anything for another chance with you, but if it makes you unhappy, it's not worth it. I love you, Liz, and I want to show you how much. Even if that means letting you go." He gathered up his keys and wallet from the counter and left.

Liz's shoulders slumped. "I hate crying."

Bella put her arm around her. "Ask yourself if he never came back how you would feel."

"He hurt me." Liz pulled free.

"It happens." Bella shrugged. "None of us are perfect. Nobody can love perfectly. In the end, it's always going to be a leap of faith."

Liz stared out the window.

Noel bleeped the locks to his truck. He stopped and looked back at the store.

Bella had never seen a man look more broken.

"Fuck this." Liz ran. She hit the door with her palm. The bell jangled loudly. She stopped on the sidewalk, tense as a cat.

Noel's smile brought tears to Bella's eyes when he opened his arms.

Liz went into them and clung.

Pippa sniveled and dug a Kleenex out of her purse. "Damn, Bella, when did you get so insightful?"

Liz climbed in the passenger side of Noel's truck and waved.

Bella waved back. "I hope they make it."

"They will if they both want to." Pippa dabbed at her creeping mascara.

Pippa hung up her coat and got to work beside Bella. Mindful of Matt's orders, Bella lifted the boxes when they were filled.

Matt brought a truck to the back of the store and loaded up the stuff to go to the Salvation Army. He would drop it off before he went home. A tired and dusty Pippa hopped up beside him.

Bella turned back into the store and locked the storeroom. She hoped Liz would be busy for the rest of the night. For her, it looked like a hot bath, a pizza, and a good movie.

She wasn't quite sure what she'd occupy herself with while the store was closed. She'd spent nearly every afternoon after school here at Bella's, helping out first her grandmother and then her mother. Some kids might have resented the expectation that they would one day take over the store, but not her. She wandered through the front of the store and locked the street door. She turned the "Closed" sign to face the street. Dust motes hung in the air. Empty, the store seemed twice as big. Faded squares on the paint showed where she'd taken down old posters and pictures. Stains and worn patches on the carpet looked more obvious without the furniture and clothes racks. She toed the indentations where the sofa and table set had rested.

Pippa had called it right. Bella's stood on the edge of a brand-new start.

How many times had she dusted the yellowed sweater shelves? She pushed a drawer closed and picked up an old price tag from the floor. Working in Bella's, she had built her dreams for it over the years. Countless thoughts about what she would change, how she would make it hers.

Winter had brought down the early dark and she flipped off the lights to the scrolled window sign. Come Monday it would join everything else in the large Dumpster Matt had had delivered to the store back.

Streetlights made yellow pools on the sleet-slicked road.

In four weeks, her new sign would face the street, announcing to everyone who saw it that things had really changed at Bella's.

For the last time, she pulled her purse from beneath the cash register. Time to go home.

Footsteps sounded from the storeroom. A tall, blond man stepped into the light. Adam smiled. "Hello, Bella."

Chapter Thirty-One

Bella woke with her stomach knotted tight. Weaving through the nausea was the constant thump of a sense of dread.

Adam.

She opened her gritty eyes. A flocked, yellowing ceiling hovered above her. Muscles screaming, she moved her neck. She couldn't seem to move her arms and legs.

Because they were tied down. She was tied down. Oh God! Tied to a sort of table in a dingy room that she didn't recognize.

She needed to keep it together. She needed to think. The panic shoved and howled against the pane of her conscious mind, demanding she let it in. Bella took a deep breath. Simon had told her panic was the biggest enemy. If she could keep her head, she might find her way out of this.

How had she got here?

Her brain felt fuzzy, as if she was staring through rain-splattered glass. She'd been in her store. That's right. The last thing she remembered was switching off the light in her store. Then, he'd come through the back.

Adam.

She'd run. He'd caught her. A sharp prick in her neck and now she lay here.

Simon must have seen something. She clung to the knowledge that Simon had waited in the shadows for Adam to appear. He was probably on his way right now. Might even be here.

But what if he wasn't coming? The worry wormed its way into her head.

She couldn't afford to think like that. *Get information. Process. Plan.*

He could be anywhere. Thick boards covered the windows. It smelled damp and musty, and it was cold. A darkened doorway stood open to a dim passage beyond.

Someone had tagged the wall opposite her in garish, unreadable script. An abandoned building would be her best guess.

She worked her fingers to get the circulation going. Cold cramp sparked and skittered along her arms. He'd strapped her down with brightly colored bungee cords. The vivid red and yellow cut into the skin of her wrist. Craning her neck, she saw the same cords around her ankles.

Her mouth tasted like medicine. She worked her tongue against the roof to create some saliva.

Footsteps approached.

Still hoping despite the certainty it was Adam that she might be mistaken, Bella turned her head.

"Bella." Adam smiled at her. "You've been asleep for such a long time."

"Where—?"

"No." He raised a hand. "We aren't going to do this like a movie script. I'm not going to tell you where you are or launch into a soliloquy about what you're doing here and my reasons."

Bella didn't dare ask what he did have planned.

Adam leaned over the table and studied her, his gaze making a careful inventory of her. "What we're going to do, Bella, is talk about you."

He looked so calm and reasonable, icy fear punched her in the belly.

"I've been watching you," Adam said. "But then, you know that already." He frowned and returned his gaze to her face. "I really don't understand."

"What don't you understand?" Surely Simon had gotten here by now and waited outside the room to rescue her. Or Nate. He always checked in by text to see if she was okay.

"You dumped me." Adam grimaced. "Me. You dumped me. At first I thought it was because of that sheriff. But you had him. Then you had the other one. The one who dresses like the homeless he serves dinner to. And now the big one has moved into your house. How many men do you need, Bella?"

"I—"

"Don't answer that. I really don't want to know." Adam turned and walked across the room. "I think we should discuss Greek."

"Sorry?"

"Did you know the word *hysterical* is from the Greek *hystera*, meaning womb?"

Bella's tongue sat thick and clumsy in her parched mouth and she shook her head.

"Well, it is," Adam said. "Early definitions of hysteria had it as a female disease caused by a dysfunction in the womb."

She had no idea why he was telling her this. Right now, she might be having an attack of the uterus.

"Oh yes." Adam nodded. He had a scalpel in his hand. "Would you call your behavior hysterical?"

Dim light gleamed off the blade.

"You wouldn't even speak to me." Adam tested his thumb against the edge. "I sent you gifts and you gave them all away. I wasn't good enough for you. Everyone else was, though."

"Adam." Maybe she could get him to see reason. Her thinking grew muddled. All she could focus on was that scalpel heading her way. "I'm not seeing any of those men. They're only friends."

"Friends?" Adam glanced up. "I'm not sure I believe you. Men don't make friends with a woman like you. They all want what you've got." He leered at her legs.

Bella jerked against the restraints, instinct making her try to pull away from him. "That's not true. I—"

"Let's be real here." Adam huffed. "You're tied to a table and I'm holding a scalpel. Why would I believe anything you said? You'd lie to save yourself. Not that I'd blame you." He shrugged and loomed over her. "I'd do the same thing if I were in your position."

"Adam." It came out as a whimper. His gaze crawled over her skin. The desire to run thundered through her.

"I don't like this skirt," Adam said. He grabbed the side seam and tugged. Fabric ripped and cold air touched the tops of her thighs.

She wanted to hide herself from his view. Put her hands over the small triangle of satin that hid her from him. The cords scraped her wrists. She tried pressing her thighs together, jerking at the ankle restraints.

Adam cut through the waistband of her skirt.

"This is much easier." He unbuttoned her shirt. His fingers pressed foreign and loathsome against her chest, brushed her breasts and then her belly.

Bella heaved. Simon might not get here in time.

"Don't want to dull the blade." He smiled at her. "This is going to hurt enough as it is."

The scalpel brushed her skin. Harsh breathing, like raw pants. Dear God, it was coming from her.

"Now, back to the *hystera* thing." Adam smiled, his teeth white in the shadowed darkness of his face. His aftershave a bright splash of citrus that turned her stomach. "If the old medical texts are to be believed, the root of a woman's irrational behavior is her womb."

The scalpel scraped her belly. One thrust and it would part her skin like butter. The last time she'd seen Nate, they'd fought. Funny how right now, her anger and hurt didn't matter. Did he understand she loved him? She'd never said the words.

"So, by extrapolation, we can deduce that if one removes the root, the problem goes away." The blade moved lower, touching the edge of her panties.

"Adam, please." A board creaked, deafening in the dank silence.

"I'll make it quick, Bella."

Bella screamed.

A deafening crack.

Then another and another.

Adam jerked. Red bloomed on his chest, his stomach, his shoulder.

There. Hanging over her. Nate's face. Frowning. Taut. "Bella?" He cupped her cheeks, forcing her gaze to his. "Baby. It's me. It's Nate."

"Is she okay?" Simon's voice came from where Adam had dropped.

"She's in shock." Nate pulled out a utility knife.

And Bella screamed. She screamed as he dropped it

beside the table. Her mouth wouldn't close and stop that horrible noise coming out of her.

Simon appeared.

Then she was free and Nate scooped her up and held her close. "Baby, you're okay. We're here. You're okay. I've got you."

The screaming stopped.

Nate never wanted to live the last two hours again. From the time Simon had called and said he didn't have eyes on Bella anymore until now all blurred into one horrible nightmare. The chilling disconnect he forced himself into unraveled as he held her against him.

His palms confirmed what his brain desperately needed to know. She was safe. He had her. She was whole.

Simon draped a blanket over her shoulders and Nate tucked it around her. After the screaming had stopped, Bella cried. Silent sobs shook her tiny frame and wet the front of Nate's shirt. He gloried in the wet fabric. Proof of life.

"Ambulance is here," Simon said. "We need to get her checked out, bud."

His brain confirmed it, but he couldn't let her go. Blue, red, blue, red, lights flickered across her beautiful face. Bodies and voices moved around them. Nate couldn't unfasten his arms to let someone else touch her. Since he and Simon had started their hunt, all he'd known was that if he ever got to hold her again, there was no fucking way he was letting her go.

Jesus. So much time he'd wasted, bitching and whining about his inability to commit. What did it all amount to?

That bastard had been within an inch of taking his sweet away. Nate wasn't sure if Simon's or his bullet had hit

Adam first. Right now, though, he was tempted to spend the rest of his clip in the fucker just to make sure.

Already, the scene swarmed with people. Gabby had correctly interpreted his garbled message and thrown every resource they had at this. She could be pissy with him for the rest of his life.

He owed Gabby. She had found Adam, moments before Simon had called and uttered those gut-chilling words: "I lost her, man."

"Nate." Simon touched his shoulder.

"Yeah." Faces stared at him. Gabby, the EMTs, Jeff, Simon . . . other faces he couldn't put names to.

An EMT reached for Bella and Nate snarled at him. "I've got her."

He carried her through the staring mass to an ambulance outside. Climbing up, he settled himself inside, Bella still tucked tight to him. Her heartbeat a steady pounding against his.

"Nate?"

"Shh, baby. We're going to take you to the hospital and have you checked out." He scowled at the EMT hovering around the open ambulance doors. "Fucking move!"

He'd apologize later. Grovel if he had to, because some part of his brain did recognize he was being a dick.

"Bella?" An annoying tapping on her cheek chased sleep away. "She's coming around."

"I'm not passed out." Bella pushed the hand away and glared at the culprit. "I was sleeping."

"Sweetheart." Mom's face appeared beside Nana's. "Do you need anything? A glass of water? Juice?"

Nana? What the hell were her grandmother and parents doing there?

"Sheriff Evans called us." Nana touched Bella's forehead. "She's warm. Too warm. She's running a fever. Are you sure that doctor knew what she was talking about? She looked very young to me."

Everyone looked young to Nana.

Three shocked faces turned to her. Oops, seems she'd said that out loud. Must be the drugs talking.

The hospital had made an effort to cheer up the institutional beige with bright floral drapes and pictures of places most people lying in this bed would much rather be than here.

Dad shouldered his way past Mom. "We came as soon as Nate called us. Caught the next flight out."

"You should have told us." Nana scowled.

"Really?" Bella met her grandmother's angry blue eyes. So much like her own, only meaner. "You're going to get on my case about why I didn't call you?"

"Yes, Mother." Dad straightened his shoulders. "Now is hardly the time. We'll talk about this another time."

No, they wouldn't.

More shocked gazes on her. There went that brain-mouth-filter failure again.

"Darling girls!" Phi's voice ricocheted off the hospital walls. "How I have missed my ministering angels. Tyler, darling, come and give me a hug. And you, Bethany."

"Dear Lord." Nana rolled her eyes. "What is she doing here?"

As if she'd heard her, Phi answered the question from outside. "I'm here to check on another of my darlings. My dear, sweet little Bella fairy. I'm sure you girls are taking such good care of her." She appeared in the doorway in blue spangles and a rush of patchouli. "Bella."

"Good evening, Philomene." Nana bristled, never happy to have to share the limelight and even unhappier when so clearly overshadowed. "What can we do for you?"

"I came to see *ma petite fée.*" Phi bustled into the room. "Simeon is beside himself." She clasped her hands to her bosom. "Be. Side. Himself. For allowing that evil monster near you." She glanced over her shoulder. "Are you up to seeing him?"

Simon. He had burst in right after Nate and been a quiet, calm presence at her side all through the hospital examination. When Nate proved to be overprotective, Simon had firmly put him outside the room and taken his place.

"Of course she isn't." Nana sniffed. "What sort of bodyguard allows a woman to be abducted and then mutilated?"

They couldn't give her strong enough drugs to deal with Nana right now. She pressed her palm to the small, stitched incision low on her abdomen. The cut had been clean and the repair easy. The doctor didn't expect it to scar.

"The worst kind." Simon entered behind a massive bunch of daisies. "Hey!"

When you lived with a man, you got to read some of his expressions, and Simon was mad. Bella would bet that anger had turned on himself. "It wasn't your fault."

"Damn straight it was." Simon put the flowers on the end of the bed. "How are you feeling?"

"Okay." Because she wasn't really sure how she was feeling. Physically okay, and they would discharge her tomorrow. But inside, the invisible incision Adam had made still bled. She felt shaky, uncertain, the knot of dread in her gut a constant.

"Nate's caught up in paperwork." Simon nodded to her parents and Nana. "He said to tell you he'll be by later." Simon peered into her eyes. "Tell me you'll see someone and talk this through."

Shoulder-checking the six-three Simon on her way past, Nana bustled over. "We don't need any of those counselors. Bella will be fine. She has her family around her."

"Simon says." Simon raised his eyebrow.

From somewhere, he teased out a small smile in her. "Well, if Simon says . . ."

"This crap can stay with you," he said.

"I will if you will." Bella caught his hand.

Simon pressed her hand to his lips. "Deal."

"I don't understand." Mom dug up her cardigan sleeve for her ever-present Kleenex. "Why didn't we know anything about this until that animal attacked her?"

"Bella didn't want to worry you." Phi flanked her on the other side.

Nana snorted. "She should have told her parents."

"She did tell us." Dad squeezed her foot through the blankets. "We weren't listening."

"Oh dear." Mom dabbed at her streaming eyes.

Phi handed her a packet of Kleenex. "There you are, dear. This is all very distressing. We all underestimated the man's determination."

"I told you not to see that man anymore." Nana folded her arms.

Pure rage flashed through Bella. She remembered almost every word of her conversation with Nana and she was done pretending. "Just don't."

"You need to be sensible with men, Bella. You have such—"

"I suggest you not finish that sentence." Phi swelled beside her. "Because you're about to say something so unforgivable you'll regret it for the rest of your life. None of the blame for this rests with Bella. Not one iota."

Nana bristled. "Well, in my day—"

"You mean in our day." Phi's voice rose, and given how famous those pipes were, her voice soared through the room. "In our day, men did awful things to women in the name of being manly. There is no excuse for what he did. None. Bella did not encourage him. She did not ask for this and she did not deserve it. Anyone who suggests otherwise is purely wicked."

Nana opened and shut her mouth. Huffed and dropped her gaze. "I wasn't going to suggest any such thing."

"Good." Phi was hardened steel, but when she turned back to Bella she had it buried beneath a gentle smile. "Now, darling, I wanted to offer my home to you. I don't know where you plan to go once you're discharged, but know that you are always welcome under my roof."

"Of course." Mom sidled closer. "I'm so stupid not to think of that. You might not want to be alone. You know you can always come home. Your old bedroom is just waiting for you."

"You should be with your family." Nana hefted her purse onto her shoulder. "You need your family at a time like this."

Over Nana's head, Simon's face said he didn't think she needed that at all. Bella was inclined to agree.

Nurse Tyler came in and kicked everyone out so they could feed her dinner. Bella pushed around her food. The quiet room pressed on her. Outside, the sounds of the hospital surrounded her. The medication cart going past. A bell pinging the nurse. The garbled announcements for doctor this or doctor that.

"Hey." Nate's voice made her jump. He appeared in her doorway, still in his uniform and looking tired and rumpled. "The nurses let me in. As long as I promised not to stay too long."

"You look tired," she said, not really knowing what else to say. The Adam thing stretched between them like quicksand.

"Paperwork." He grimaced. "Suddenly, everyone wants to know what the hell happened and they want to hear it from me." He dragged the one chair over to her bed and sat. "Simon tells me your family were here earlier."

"Yup." She wanted to smooth his tousled hair. "Nana is . . . Nana."

He pulled a face. "Simon also said you agreed to get some help. Just to talk this thing through."

"Simon has been saying a lot."

They both laughed, but not because either of them found that particularly funny.

He took her hand and kissed it. "I'm glad you're okay." He dropped his gaze and cleared his throat. "Worst fucking moment of my life."

"Mine too." She bet if both of them closed their eyes, they would see the same thing from different angles.

Kissing her hand again, he looked up. "I'll be by to get you in the morning. Have you thought about where you want to go?"

"Yes." She braced for a fight. "I want to go home. To my house."

"On your own?" He frowned.

"Yes. It's mine, Nate. I made it my safe place and that's where I want to be."

"You could always stay with me. Indefinitely." His topaz eyes held a depth of stuff she was suddenly too scared to question. The future lurked, gray and scary beyond this room, and Bella couldn't face it, didn't want to even acknowledge it.

"You don't want that, Nate. Not really. Besides, I want to go home."

He watched his fingers play with hers. "There are a lot of things I want and don't want, Bella. I need to talk to you about them. But now isn't the time."

Bella didn't want to talk. Ever. She'd spent so much of her life talking about Nate and her, it seemed like too much of an effort right now. That Bella had been left behind when Adam kidnapped her. Funny, she'd spent all those months finding a new Bella and, in the end, it had found her.

Chapter Thirty-Two

Someone had taken down her Christmas lights. Snow had melted and dull patches of earth and dead grass had reclaimed her garden from its blanket of white. The holidays were officially over. Going up the front walk seemed both familiar and strange.

Nate opened her door and disabled the alarm. "Let me have a look around first."

Too late, Bella wanted to shout. *The bogeyman already got me.*

Adam was dead. Her logical brain knew that, but the fear inside had nothing to do with logic and kept rehashing every B-grade horror plot it had ever absorbed.

Nate reappeared in the hallway. "It's all clear," he said. "Get settled and I'll make us some dinner."

"You don't need to do that." Bella didn't think she'd eat much anyway.

Nate gave her a hard look. "I know I don't need to, but I'd like to. Why don't you have a shower and I'll have dinner ready when you're done?"

A shower to get the hospital stink off her skin sounded

great. How is it that, in theory, the cleanest, most sanitary place had an undeniable smell of sickness? Her bathroom looked exactly as she'd left it. Had it really been only three days ago? The jeans she hadn't put in the hamper still lay on the floor where she'd dropped them. Her toothbrush lay on the counter next to the toothpaste tube. She hadn't put the cap on.

Bella flipped on the water. She turned her back to the mirror and stripped off her clothes. Staving off the horrible vulnerability of her nakedness, she slipped into the shower. She didn't want to see her body. See what Adam had seen. She hurried through her shower and dressed in some old sweats that covered nearly all her skin.

She followed the incredible smell into the kitchen.

Nate had set the table and glanced up as she walked in. His smile threatened to take her back to a place she didn't want to go. A place of intimacy and warmth between them. She needed to keep the ice inside her intact. The ice was safe, pain free.

"Something smells good," she said.

"I worked with what you had in the fridge." He shrugged and brought a casserole dish to the table.

Bella couldn't honestly say what they ate, but it had bits of bacon, cubes of chicken, and vegetables. She barely tasted the food but ate more to keep Nate from insisting than anything else.

Nate leaned back in his chair, hooking one elbow over the back. "I could stay. Tonight."

"No." The ice mustn't crack. Loving Nate threatened the ice. "No, thank you. I'll be fine."

He frowned. "Bella?"

"It's fine. I'm fine." She got up and cleared her plate. Standing by the sink, she stared into the night-darkened garden. In that abandoned house something had gone missing. She'd left some element of herself on that awful table.

Inside, she was cold and empty. She had nothing more to give.

"Babe." Nate's hand was on the small of her back. "Can we talk?"

"No." He threatened her fragile control. Heartsore and hanging on by a thread, her composure still remained hers.

Nate rubbed circles over her spine. "Okay." He took a breath. "How about I talk and you listen?"

"I can't." His strong body provided a barrier between her and her thoughts. Bella leaned into him and pressed her face into his chest.

"No talking." He rested his cheek on her head. "Let's get you to bed." He led her down the corridor to her bedroom. "Are you going to sleep in that?"

Bella nodded. She didn't want to see her body. She didn't want eyes on her body at all.

Nate pulled back the duvet and she climbed into bed.

The night pressed around her, quiet and dark, and despite what she'd said in the kitchen, it suddenly seemed full of unseen threats. "Nate?"

He looked at her.

"Could you . . . stay? As a friend, I mean."

He grimaced, then nodded. "I'll get ready for bed. I can sleep in the living room." He looked around. "Or maybe on the floor in here."

Now they'd gone beyond ridiculous. Bella patted the other side of her bed. "Here is fine."

By the time he'd showered and finished in the bathroom, Bella was asleep.

Knees curled into her chest, she lay on her side.

So tiny and fragile and still pale from her ordeal, his heart hurt looking at her. Try as he might, he couldn't keep the reel of horror out of his head, of what might have happened if he and Simon hadn't gotten there in time. As he went through the details in reports, again and again, the images haunted him.

Moving carefully, he slid into bed beside her.

Murmuring, she sought his heat.

Nate folded himself around her from behind. Soap and the honey smell of her shampoo surrounded him. Needing skin contact, he slipped his hand beneath her sweatshirt and onto the warmth of her belly, just above the adhesive dressing.

He'd lived his whole life never expecting to fall in love and, certainly, never believing someone could love him back. Happily ever after belonged to guys who sacked up, did the right thing. Guys like his brother Matt. Him? Not so much.

Seeing Adam with that scalpel on Bella's skin, knowing he stood inches away from losing her had a way of slapping a guy into wise-up time. He loved her. Probably had loved her for some time. How long? He couldn't say, and it didn't seem to matter anymore. Sitting by her bed in the hospital had brought more unwelcome realizations. She had offered her love to him and he'd thrown it back at her. He winced, thinking of all the bullshit things he'd said to her. All in a desperate effort to keep her in the safe zone. Safe for him, because Bella had never played it safe. She wore her heart on her sleeve. Hell, she waved it around like a banner for the world to see.

He didn't deserve her, but he was through pretending he didn't want to try. Maybe she would realize what a bad deal she'd made and walk away from him somewhere down the line. But never taking the chance, never knowing for sure, that would be worse. He'd nearly lost her while he dicked around.

He whispered the words into her hair. "I love you."

* * *

Morning brought a lazy fall of thick, heavy snow. Fat flakes meandered down to join the growing accumulation.

Nate rubbed his gritty eyes. He hadn't gotten a lot of sleep.

Bella stirred against him and opened her eyes. "Hi."

"Hi yourself." As he propped himself up to get a better look at her, his tiredness dissipated.

She looked well rested this morning. Even sported a little color in her face.

"Breakfast." He hauled ass out of bed. "You stay there and I'll bring you some coffee."

Bella gaped at him.

Yeah, he'd earned that look. Now he needed to earn it right off her face again.

He hauled on his pants.

"Nate?" Bella's voice stopped him at the door. "Why are you doing all this?"

Tell her! screamed his brain. His chickenshit heart yelled it back down again. The girl had just gotten out of the hospital yesterday. He needed to go slowly. "Eggs okay?"

He made tracks to the kitchen.

Bella followed him. "Nate?"

He disappeared into the fridge. Cool air hit his hot face. He could spend all day in here. What a dick! He turned and faced her. He needed to finesse this, say the right thing. You didn't come right out and blurt shit like this. "I love you."

She blinked at him. "You what?"

Damn! "I love you, Bella."

"No, you don't." Bella laughed, but it had a bitter edge. "Okay, you love me like someone you've known for most of your life. But you don't love-love me."

So. Not the way he'd seen this going. "Yes, I do."

"Ah, Nate." She slumped, like someone had let all the air out of her. "You only think you do."

"I'm pretty sure I know it." She might be hurting his feelings here. The experience was new to him, so he couldn't be entirely sure. But it certainly sucked. "What the hell, Bella? I tell you I love you and you react like this."

"Nate." She twisted her hands together. "You got a fright when you saw me with . . . like that. It scared you. It made you rethink things."

Okay, she'd pretty much nailed him there.

"This is a reaction." She shrugged. "How many times have you told me you're not the commitment sort?"

"Maybe I've changed."

"Overnight?" She shook her head. "The only thing that changed is what happened to me."

For all of fifteen seconds Nate thought it over and knew she was wrong. This change hadn't happened overnight. In fact, it had begun as he sat in her kitchen after hanging the Christmas lights. The only thing that had happened overnight was him waking the hell up. "No."

"I can't do this right now." Rubbing her hand over her eyes, she looked worn out and beaten down. "I've waited for most of my life to hear you say that." She slid into a chair as if her legs refused to hold her up. "I would have given anything to hear you say those words, but not like this. The thing is, Nate, when you've waited for someone all your life, you want everything from them. Not some fear-based reaction that won't last."

His timing sucked. True, he could go on about the slow-leak epiphany that had gone on for weeks now, but he needed to be patient. Keeping himself busy, he got the coffee started and made the eggs.

Seeing Bella with Adam had shocked the sense into him, but he wasn't the one still in shock. Adam had taken something from Bella. Working up in SLC, he'd seen it in all the victims, the delayed reaction that set in. An attack like the one Bella had suffered took the illusion of security from its victims. The world suddenly became a much scarier, less reliable place. In the aftermath, victims confronted their own vulnerability. The screwed-up part of this was that the victims had to claw their lives back. It wasn't fair and it wasn't right, but if they wanted their lives back, they needed to find their way past this. Otherwise they spent their lives trapped in the fear.

He hoped like hell the killing bullet had been his and not Simon's.

Bella glanced up as he slid the eggs in front of her. "Thank you."

Her beautiful blue eyes, always sparkling with life and joy, had dimmed. The smile that used to knock him on his ass had been turned way down low.

Nate wanted nothing more than to get those things back for her.

Chapter Thirty-Three

Ignoring her protests, Liz drove Bella to her store. "Four weeks." Liz parked the car and turned and stared at her. "It's time."

Even her therapist had hinted it was time, but Bella wished they'd all leave her alone. "I'm here, aren't I?" Before this, her twice-weekly therapy sessions were the only things that had taken her out of the house and she liked it that way.

January had stayed surprisingly mild. The clear, bright day held no hint of threat, but her legs still shook as she climbed out of the car.

Liz took her hand and gave it a squeeze.

Signs of construction littered the sidewalk outside the store. Piles of lumber neatly stacked against the front window. A team unloaded sheets of drywall.

Stopping at the door, Bella couldn't make her legs move.

Liz stood beside her. "We can do this. Just go in there, look around, and we can leave again."

Bella took a deep breath. If it would get Liz off her back, she'd do it.

"This is your business," Liz said. "You've put your heart and soul into it. Don't let him take that from you."

Bella's heart thundered in her ears and she felt dizzy.

"Bella?" Matt appeared in the doorway. He wore plaster dust in his hair and a face mask balanced on his forehead like a horn. "You came."

Matt still got down and dirty with his crews. He said the work soothed him and helped him think.

"Hey, Matt." She put one foot in front of the other.

The last time she'd stood in her store, Adam had attacked her. It almost seemed like that girl had splintered off from the original Bella. When she could step back and be splinter Bella, it became easier to think about what had happened. Her therapist, however, wasn't a big fan of splinter Bella. She never said anything, but nothing got the woman scribbling in her jaunty notebook faster. "I came to see how you were getting on."

Matt glanced at Liz. "Good. We're doing good."

"Can I come in?"

With a grimace, Matt stepped aside.

Bella walked into her store and stopped. Matt had transformed the place. Standing braced for an onslaught of unpleasant memories, she suddenly wanted to laugh. The relief was sharp-edged. Nothing looked the same. The dreadful pink had all disappeared, along with the awful carpet. Even the smell of the store had changed.

"We've finished all the framing." Matt kept pace with her. "Electrics are all in. We just need to finish the drywall, plaster, and paint."

Under her feet, thick paper crackled. "Are the floors done?"

"Yup." Matt smiled at her. "And you were right: The darker wood looks great."

His smile reminded her so much of Nate that it hurt.

Nate had been a constant feature in her life over the last four weeks. He popped in and out a couple of times a day. Often, he stayed long enough to cook her dinner and then watched TV with her until she got tired enough to sleep. Some nights he slept over, but always he waited for her to ask, and other than cuddling, he didn't lay a finger on her. Fortunately, he seemed to have recovered from the whole love thing. She was glad; she really was. Sure, she thought about those three words a lot, and how it had felt hearing them from him. But the words never penetrated past the surface fog that filled her these days. The thing was, she liked the gray. The gray surrounded her in a comfortable cloud. If light penetrated the mist, it came with a sharp pain she ducked from.

Bella ran her hand over the smooth pale oak shelves Matt had installed. Simple, classic, and deep enough to allow her to create piles of color. If she ever got around to ordering new stock. Her suppliers were waiting for her to move forward with her orders. She'd been sitting on placing those orders since the attack. Every time she fired up her computer, she ended up on social media sites. Hours of trolling Facebook, crying at some posts and railing at others. Just idly flipping through the details of other people's lives.

Without being asked, Liz had taken over the internet business. She was really good at it, and Bella was considering taking her on part-time, but as soon as the thought formed, she allowed it to drift away again.

Some small part of her brain understood she was stuck, but she rather liked it there. Her therapist had been prodding her about taking action during the last couple of visits.

And she would. But every time she came close to doing something—anything—she retreated again.

When Liz had come around this morning and bullied her into the car, it had almost been a relief, doing something without having to be the one to initiate the act.

Sliding open a new drawer, Bella brushed away wood shavings. She'd been so excited about filling these drawers with naughty lingerie. Stuff she kept for special customers. The sort of lingerie that would make a woman glow just knowing she wore it.

So many plans. Good plans she'd spent hours formulating, and around her, they faced off with her and demanded she finish what she had started. The construction in the store challenged her to get moving again. Bella's chest tightened and breathing became harder. "We can go now," she said to Liz.

"Have you seen these rails?" Liz put as much enthusiasm as she could into the question.

Bella loved her for the effort. Dutifully, she walked over and admired the hanging spaces. "Very nice. Matt does excellent work."

"This is all you, Bella." Matt ran his large hand over the finish on the sides. "This was your vision, I'm just the jock with a hammer who made it happen."

Her vision. Her plans. Her excitement. She could see them as a part of her life that stretched out in the past but didn't seem part of her reality anymore. She smiled because he seemed to be waiting for some reaction. "It looks great, Matt."

The outer door to Nate's office slammed open and Matt charged in.

"Nate here?" Matt hadn't seen him yet and he'd asked the question of Gabby.

She pointed to where Nate stood getting himself some coffee.

Matt turned, steam coming out of his ears. Matt didn't get mad often, but when he did, it paid to give it some time and attention.

"Got a minute?"

It wasn't really a request, and Nate nodded and motioned him into his office.

Heat rolling off him in waves, Matt dogged his heels.

Nate shut the door.

"What the fuck?" Matt pounded Nate's desk so hard an empty paper cup jumped off. "What the fuck!"

Nate waited.

Matt pushed his hands through his dusty hair. "Bella came by the store."

"Ah." Nate's chest throbbed in that special place that was all Bella. Day after day, he watched her walk through her life as if she wasn't really a part of it. Her detachment cut deep into him each time he faced it, but he kept coming back around. Firstly, because that dispassionate ghost was his Bella, and secondly, wherever or whoever she chose to be, right beside her was the only place he wanted to stand.

Matt shook his head, clearly struggling to find the right words. "Is she always like this?"

"Pretty much." Nate shrugged, as if it didn't carve a trench through him. "She needs time to deal with what happened to her."

"But . . . Bella." Matt threw himself into a chair. The legs screeched on the linoleum floor. "Bella is . . . was . . . Bella."

Nate almost laughed. How to put Bella into words? That stupid kid's saying about sugar and spice and all things nice, that was Bella. Or that had been Bella. The woman walking around in a daze bore an uncanny resemblance to that soap bubble of pure light that used to drift around Ghost Falls.

"Isn't there anything we can do?" Matt leaned his elbows on his knees. "It's like she's there but she's not there."

"I don't think she is." Nate moved closer to Matt, needing the connection with another person who saw what he did. "I think our Bella is locked down tight inside that shell. She's scared to come out."

"We have to get her back." Matt glanced up at him. "I liked the old Bella just fine."

"I loved the old Bella." No point in pretending anymore. "I love this one too."

Matt stared at him, frowning. "This is new."

"Not really." Matt was one of the few people he would bother explaining himself to. "I think some part of me always did. I've been running shit scared from that part for most of my life. At least since first grade."

Matt gave a rueful laugh. "Now you see it."

"I was never the brain in the family."

"That's bullshit, Nate." Matt stood and clapped a hand on his shoulder. "Almost as big a pile of crap as that chip you carry on your shoulder. You weren't the black sheep either."

"Ah, come on." Matt must be suffering from early onset senility. "How many nights did you have to drag my sorry ass out of trouble?"

"I remember." Matt's grip tightened on his shoulder. "But you know what I saw?"

"Hit me." May as well air all the family dirty laundry.

"I saw a kid who was hurting. The same thing old Sheriff Wheeler saw. A good kid with so much pent-up hurt he didn't know where to go with it."

He couldn't quite buy that. "We all lost Dad. I was the only one who played up."

"Really?" Matt snorted. "You have a selective memory. Were you the one who locked himself in the house for the first six months?"

Nope, that had been Mom.

"Or the one who tried to drop out of college and then, when I wouldn't let him, failed a semester just to prove a point."

"Eric did that?"

"Yeah, Eric did that." Matt laughed. "Jo dropped out of life altogether and Isaac is still MIA. So next time you cast yourself in the role of family screwup, you might want to consider the competition. And then there's me."

"You?" Matt, who had turned down a full-ride scholarship to take care of the family after their father died and their mother turned mourning into a profession?

"Yeah, me." Matt punched his shoulder. The old guy still had some power going there. "I more or less hid out behind Dad's company until it was almost too late. If Pippa hadn't come into town and forced me out of hibernation, I might still be in there."

Nate had never really considered things from that angle.

Matt shoved his hands in his pockets. "I'm proud of you, Nate. If anyone knows how to pick yourself up and start over, it's you."

Goddamn. If Matt kept this up, they might both start bawling. "Shut up."

"Good idea."

"Bella will be okay." Nate cleared the lump that seemed to have lodged in his throat. "She'll be okay because I'm never giving up on her."

Bella stuffed the invitation under a pile of paperwork sitting on her desk. It didn't diminish the effect.

When Phi issued an invitation, she did it the old-fashioned way, through the mail and on her own stationery. A royal summons to Bella's own store from the Ghost Falls royalty.

Matt had finished in the store three days ago, and still she hadn't managed to go around and see the final outcome. People thought she avoided the store because of frightening memories, and Bella wished she could say they had it right. The real reason was much more embarrassing. She was hiding out from her life. She'd even deleted all her Dr. Childers downloads because she didn't want to hear all that take-charge crap.

Her last visit to the store had almost broken through the gray nothing and she couldn't risk that. Each day it got harder to stay numb.

Liz had eventually placed the orders for stock on her behalf and unloaded them into the storerooms. Bella didn't even know if the right garments had arrived.

She wandered through to the kitchen and put some coffee on. Not that she wanted any coffee, but she needed something to do while she worked on her excuse for Phi. Unlike other people, Phi didn't take no lightly. If you tried an excuse Phi didn't think held water, the diva straight-up told you and then insisted you came anyway.

Phi clearly thought the time had come to open the store again because the invitation was to the grand opening of Bella's.

Bella slammed her cupboard door closed. It kind of pissed her off that Phi had taken the initiative and decided to open her store for her. She detected the sly hand of Pippa in this. Why couldn't Pippa mind her own business?

The smell of coffee reminded her how much she really didn't want a cup.

Of course, if she got all irritated with Pippa, she'd have to start taking on a whole bunch of other people. Ghost

Falls seemed to have decided as a town that Bella needed to buck up.

Outside, Noel shoveled Liz's walk. When he was done, he would come over and do hers. Not because Bella had asked but because Noel had taken it on all by himself.

People didn't get it. They all thought she should get on with her life and cheer the hell up. Cheer up! Bella made a retching noise.

She checked the time on the kitchen clock. Nate would be around soon to make sure she ate. Who knew all you had to do was get kidnapped by a psycho to get a man to pay attention to you? No matter what she said, what she tried to text him, Nate showed up at her door.

Like right now. His cruiser drew up outside her house and Nate climbed out. He took a moment to chat with Noel.

So ridiculously hot with the shadow of the day's growth darkening the clean-cut lines of his face. Wind ruffled his dark hair with loving fingers. If she didn't have this dead place in the middle of her, she might be getting all giddy with excitement around about now.

Nate spotted her at the window and waved.

A little something twanged through her chest. Could be indigestion for all she knew.

She opened the door for him and Nate trotted up the walkway.

"Hey, babe." He bent and kissed her cheek. His frozen cheek pressed against hers as if they were a couple. "Have a good day?"

"Yup." Because if she said anything else, he'd want to hear all about it. "And you?"

He pulled a face, shrugging out of his coat. "Spent most of it driving around the backcountry. Damn roads haven't been plowed yet. Had to make sure some of the senior citizens made it through for their hospital appointments."

She got him a beer and poured herself a glass of wine.

Nate cooked while she sat at the kitchen table. The conversation drifted from one subject to another. Small talk about his day, her day, things going on in town. This she could handle, even admit it was kind of nice. Not that she had much of a choice; any attempt to put Nate off failed dismally. He'd arrive anyway and barge his way into her house.

"I got an invitation today." Bella watched his face to see if there was any reaction.

"Phi, I'm guessing." He grinned and took a sip of his beer.

It was like a damn conspiracy. "Did you put her up to this?"

"I might have had a part in it." He turned back to his cooking onions.

"Why?" She had a bunch of other questions, but she'd start with that one.

"Babe." Nate glanced at her. "The store is done. It's time."

She wanted to throw her wine at him, but it was wine, and she wanted to drink it more. "Because you decided it's time."

"Maybe." His tone got wary. "You have to open the store, Bella."

"I don't have to do anything." She knew she was being childish, but this assumption that she could just pick up her life where Adam had ripped it up really got under her skin.

Nate flipped off the burner. "Bella . . ." He crossed his arms and gave her the sheriff face. "That renovation cost you money, and every day the store stands there is costing you money."

"So this is about saving me money?" Hell, if he wanted to go there, she would so go there.

"No." Now he gave her that tone that said he was exercising all his patience. "This is about a lot of things. One of those things is money."

"Does it occur to you that I don't need your help?"

"No." He snagged the bottle and refilled her wine. Then went right back to cooking. "And I think we've been through this before."

Bella scowled at his back. They had been through this before and she'd lost every single one of those times too.

"Isn't it against the law to force yourself into someone's house?"

Nate stirred something that smelled great. "Not if you're cooking them dinner."

His glibness made her want to smack him. Like everyone else, Nate thought she could pick up her life where Adam had torn it apart, sew together the tattered ends, and be back to the way she was before. None of them understood. "Why do you care?"

Nate turned and looked at her. Really looked at her, and she dropped her head to dodge the way he saw so much. "You know why." The toes of his boots moved into her line of vision. "But just in case you've forgotten, I'll tell you again." Nate crouched at her feet. His lion gaze held her captive. "I. Love. You."

Like arrows, the words pierced the comfortable gray, and Bella came back swinging. "No, you don't. You just think you do." She had to get away. His eyes, his face, the sincerity demanded stuff from her. Made her feel. Bella stood. Why did they all insist she start feeling again?

Nate pressed her back into her chair. "I love you." He caught her hands and held them firmly. "When I saw Adam standing over you with the scalpel, it all crystalized for me, but I loved you before then."

"No." She needed to hold on to being numb. Everything hurt less that way. But light forced its way into the gray and a sob caught in the back of her throat.

"Yes." Nate kissed first one palm and then the other. "I might even have loved you when I used to stomp on the things you made in the elementary-school sandbox."

"They were sand cakes."

He slid his hands to her hips and held her still. "I might even have loved you when I nearly asked you to prom."

"You did?" He must be making this up.

"I did." Nate winced. "I changed my mind at the last minute because I was scared of your nana, and she was there the day I came around to ask." He wiped a tear from her cheek.

When had the tears started? All she knew was that the cold inside her was retreating, tickling, prickling, and hurting, like when you walked into the warm after the cold. "You can't have."

"Maybe it was better this way, because I wasn't any good for you then. I wasn't even any good for you when you dropped your dress in my hands and strutted your hot ass away from me. Only I quit fighting it then."

"I didn't strut."

"Babe!" He chuckled. "You worked it. And it slayed me. All this time I've been pushing you away, telling both of us I'm not the right man for you, when all along it turns out I was only being a coward."

She so wanted to believe him, but she held back. Doubting. Not trusting herself to know what was good for her. Bella shook her head. He needed to stop saying this stuff to her.

Nate cupped her cheeks in his rough palms and she had

no choice but to look at him. "Yes, Bella. I was scared and uncertain and running away from you. I hurt you in the process and I'll spend the rest of my life making it up to you for that. But when I saw you in that room, it all became clear. I didn't realize I loved you at that moment; I just realized I'd been dicking around for so long, it had almost cost me you."

"I can't." Couldn't so many things.

Nate nodded slowly, his beautiful eyes sad. "I understand. I pushed you away for so long, and then Adam. You're not ready."

"I may never be ready."

"I'll take that chance." He kissed her, softly and undemandingly. "Because if there's even a possibility you'll change your mind and trust me with you, it's worth it."

"Darling!" Bella held the phone away from her ear as Phi bellowed down the line.

"Hey, Phi." All day she'd been hiding in her house, but that hadn't prevented Nate's words from last night following her from room to room. Try as she might, the detachment kept evading her. She felt sad and mad and scared and hopeless—and then hopeful, and then it started all over again. She'd even caught herself with a smile on her face as she read a text from Nate.

"Now listen, darling," Phi yelled. "Pippa and I are engaged in a brouhaha."

"Oh yes." Bella braced for where Phi went next. The word *brouhaha* brought that smile creeping back.

"Pippa is being stubborn," Phi said. "Not there, Mathieu. How will I get the fur rug underneath that? Sorry, Bella." Phi took a deep breath. "Mathieu has no sense of style."

"Where are you?"

"At your wonderful little shop, of course, darling." Phi chuckled. "Tomorrow night is your grand opening after all, and we have so much to do."

Excitement tried to wriggle through, but she stamped on it. "Listen, Phi, about that—"

"That's why I'm calling," Phi said. "Pippa keeps trying to interfere with my decorating scheme. I need you to tell her that the purple will be divine."

Bella went a bit light-headed. "Purple?"

"Yes, purple with gold accents because one color is so blah. Darling, it's sublime." Phi sighed. "The shop is so dreary with all this cream. The purple is just the thing to make it pop."

Facing the annihilation of her elegant, understated décor she'd chosen to showcase the clothing, Bella had to sit down. Surely Pippa wouldn't let Phi do it. "Why must it pop?"

"Because, darling, we need some more drama in here. Just a moment," Phi yelled on her end. "Drape the gold lamé in great swaths, Mathieu. Swaths! I'm back," Phi said. "I know you're going to love it. Anyway, see you tomorrow, darling. Make sure you wear something purple to match the decorations."

Bella stared at the dead phone in her hand. She should leave them to do what they wanted. She hadn't sent any invitations, set the date, nothing. They could just carry on.

Purple? Purple!

Dear God.

Bella snatched up her keys. Damn it, she didn't want to do this. But, even more, she didn't want Phi turning her store into a purple hell.

Annoyed at herself, she drove too fast to the store. Part of her hoped Nate would pull her over for speeding and she could vent some of her ire on him.

Foiled when she arrived uncontested, she marched into the store with her pissed-off flag flying high.

"Oh, hello, darling." Phi waggled her nails at her. "Nice . . . um . . . sweatpants."

Okay, she could have changed the sweatpants and food-stained T-shirt, especially with everyone staring at her. But, holy crap, the store looked amazing and there wasn't a trace of purple anywhere. Wood floors, crystal chandeliers, taupe silk curtains for the fitting rooms, walls painted a warm off-white. Garments in jewel-bright splendor framed by the discreet elegance all around them.

"Well?" Pippa strolled over to her and flung an arm about her shoulder. "What do you think?"

"It looks amazing."

"I know." Pippa jostled her. "My honey did good by you."

Her store. Bella ran her fingertips over the smooth finish of the wooden service desk. "He sure did."

This was her store. Not the candy-pink nightmare she'd babied along for years now. Her dream had come to life. Something trickled through her that felt a lot like anticipation, with a touch of pride. She'd done this. Along with a lot of help.

Matt stood beside Pippa, his gaze keen on her.

"It's perfect," she said. She didn't have any other words, only a hard knot of emotion stuck in her throat. While she'd been recovering, her friends had completed her vision for her. "It's exactly as I imagined it."

"So . . ." Nana stomped into the store. "Are you happy now?"

Happy? Seemed like an odd concept, but standing in her store with her friends all beaming at her, she came perilously close, so she nodded.

"How much did this cost us?" Nana fingered the silk drapery.

"Me," Bella said. "It's costing me. Not us."

"Huh!" Nana drifted over to a rack of dresses and flipped through them. "These aren't bad."

"Not bad?" Pippa snorted. "You're looking at dress magic right there."

"Did I get it right?" Liz appeared in the doorway to the storeroom. She indicated her sprayed-on skinny jeans and bedazzled sweater. "Because I'm not exactly the best person to be ordering for you."

Bella flipped through the hangers. Liz had done great. More than great. "You nailed it."

Liz grinned and fanned her face. "Whew! Because it scared the shit out of me to do those orders. Mainly, I ordered stuff I thought would make me look old."

Noel arrived clutching two champagne bottles. He looked at Liz first. "Did she like it?"

"She liked it." Liz winked at Bella.

"Good." Noel gave his shy smile. "Then let's all have a drink to celebrate."

Chapter Thirty-Four

*P*utting on makeup and wearing heels again felt alien. For her store opening, Bella wore a discreet pencil skirt and a blouse. After so many weeks in sweats, it was like putting on another person.

Her therapist had come as close to cheering as a therapist did when Bella had called and told her she was attending the store opening. "I know this is frightening," she'd said in her no-nonsense voice, which beat the crap out of all Dr. Childers's crooning. "But you're doing this because you're ready."

"Hey." Nate's reflection appeared beside hers in the bathroom mirror. "You look beautiful."

"You were supposed to wait outside until I was dressed."

"You are dressed." He held her shoulders. "And I got tired of waiting."

Through her thin blouse, Nate's body heat tempted her to lean back. For a split second, she almost gave in to the temptation. "You know you don't have to come with me."

"Of course I do." He frowned and kissed her temple. "There's nowhere else I'd rather be."

"What if I don't want you here?" She had no idea why she said it, but the more he pushed at the walls around her, the more she knee-jerked and fought back. In truth, she didn't think she could do this without him.

His gaze met hers in the mirror. "Do you want me here?"

"Yes." He didn't deserve her bitchiness, not after all he'd done since Adam. "I'm sorry."

"It's okay."

This nice-guy thing pressed against her like she owed him something. "It's not okay." Bella fiddled with her mascara. "Because you're doing everything right and I . . ." The words weren't there. "Can't," she said.

Nate took the mascara out of her hand and placed it on the counter. "Can't what?"

"Do this." Bella indicated the two of them. The tangle inside wouldn't coalesce into words that made sense. "You and me. The store. Pippa. Liz. I can't do any of it."

"I don't understand."

That was the understatement of the year. Nobody did. "I'm dead inside." Bella scooped her makeup into a drawer. "There's nothing left. Adam ripped it out of me and it's gone forever."

His expression thoughtful, Nate studied her in the mirror. "Can you do this opening tonight?"

"Yes." Because everyone had gone to so much trouble and she couldn't let them down.

"Okay, then." He nodded. "Let's go and attend to your hordes."

Not quite hordes, but the store was filled later that evening. Phi had cast her net wide. Over glasses of wine and canapés, people flipped through hangers, held up clothes to see what they liked, and strolled about.

Liz manned the cash register, leaving Bella to move around her guests.

When the store was up and running again, maybe she would do this more often. Host an event once or twice a year. Even Nana seemed to be having a good time with a small cluster of her cronies. When one of those cronies bought a cardigan, Bella nearly crowed.

Nate stayed by her side the entire time, giving her a front-row seat to the Nate hotness factor. Even standing with his arm about her, he was a chick magnet. Women cooed, fluttered, batted lashes, and blushed when he was in their vicinity. Case in point, a peer of Phi's and seventy if she was a day, stroked Nate's arm and winked at him before sashaying away.

You would think after a lifetime of watching this, she'd be immune.

"You're frowning." Nate kissed her cheek.

Even knowing he couldn't help being this hot and he certainly hadn't encouraged any of them, it still pissed her off. "What is it with you and women? They all love you. It doesn't matter what age."

"Not all of them." He tucked her against his warm, hard body. "One of them seems determined to resist my charms."

"Well," Bella couldn't help feeling a little smug, "she has good reason."

"Maybe." His enigmatic smile tossed down the gauntlet. And damn, but she wanted to snap it up. "Or maybe I need to work harder."

Bella snapped her mouth shut. Then she blurted the first thing to come into her mind. "Did you not hear what I said earlier, at my house?"

"I heard." He handed her a flute of champagne.

"And . . . ?"

Nate took a sip of her champagne and grimaced. "I hate this stuff. But I love you, and I have more faith in you than you do in yourself right now. You're still here, Bella, and

I'm going to stay right by your side until you're ready to come back to me."

Nate tucked his special bundle in his office and shut the door behind him.

"Everything okay?" Gabby looked up from her computer terminal. Who knew Gabby had a soft, gooey center? But his little bundle had Gabby melting so much she'd damn near smiled.

"Perfect." Nate grinned back at her. Bella didn't stand a chance. For weeks, her detachment had baffled and frustrated him. He'd hung in there, waiting for a sign, something to clue him in. Then, the night of the opening, she'd given him the insight he needed. Telling everyone you were dead inside, pushing everyone who loved you away, even believing you didn't give a fuck about anyone or anything—this was stuff he knew a lot about, and he also knew what lay beneath all that. Because he'd been pulling all that crap until a big, grizzled, gruff old sheriff had laid it down for him—jail or the police academy—and then told teen Nate that he hoped he chose the latter because he was worth it.

Too long had passed since Nate had caught a glimpse of his Bella. The way her big blues would widen and she'd go pink-cheeked when he said something shocking. The way she looked at him as if he'd single-handedly brought the world to her feet. When Bella looked at him that way, it reminded him of the man he could be. The man he intended to spend the rest of his life trying to be.

"Anything doing?" He picked up the stack of papers from Gabby's desk.

Like he knew she would, Gabby scowled and snatched

them back. She hated when he messed with her shit. "Nothing that I need to bother you about."

"You know you're never a bother, Gabby." He propped a hip on her desk and gave her one of his Nate-on-the-hunt smiles. Now that he was permanently off the market, he liked to mess with Gabby a bit. Because it got under her skin even more than him messing with her shit.

"What the hell are you so cheerful about?" Gabby glared at him. "You're taking a huge chance that your little . . . surprise is going to work."

She had a point, but he felt so positive this morning, he couldn't stop the bubble of happy sitting in his middle. He was a man with a plan. "First off, it worked on you, so Bella is a no-brainer."

Gabby snorted.

Nate raised his brow.

"Whatever." Gabby rolled her eyes, but they both knew he'd called her bullshit.

"And if it doesn't," he snagged one of her crackers and popped it in his mouth, "I'll have to find something else."

"There's always the cells." Gabby slapped his hand. "Nothing says *I love you* like being arrested."

"Aw, Gabby." He winked at her. "Look at you getting all romantic."

"Get to work," she said, but not fast enough to completely disguise the tiny smile she tried so hard to hide.

"You're right. Keep your eye on the package." He stood and adjusted his utility belt. "Wish me luck, Gabby. I'm off to scour the trees of Ghost Falls for a needy cat. Small-town police work at its finest."

He closed the door on the rasp of her laughter.

Bright winter sunlight bounced off the crisp white snow. Above him stretched an endless arc of winter blue. He loved a good plan.

* * *

The momentum from the opening kept her store busy. Also, with Valentine's Day around the corner, women from town and on the hill were all on the hunt for *that perfect little number*.

"What do you think?" Liz stepped out of the dressing room. She had a big date coming up with Noel.

Pippa sat on the new sand linen sofa and ate grapes. Last week it had been cherries, which, considering the season, had presented Matt with a dilemma because if Pippa wanted them, Matt got them for her. The grapes were a vast improvement.

Pippa tilted her head. "Depends." She popped a grape into her mouth. "What are we trying to say with this?"

Liz shoved her hands on her hips. "Take me now."

"To the entire football team?" Pippa raised a brow.

Liz scowled, stomped over to the mirror, and glared at her reflection. She had insisted on trying on a new short and sparkly dress Bella had ordered with the prom girls from the high school in mind. Liz, being Liz, saw no reason not to give it a try.

"What's wrong with it?" Liz tugged at the hem in a way that clearly stated she saw exactly what was wrong.

Pippa laughed and raised an eyebrow. She held up her dress choice for Liz.

"Fine." Liz snatched the dress from her.

Pippa smirked and went back to her grapes. "I don't know why she still argues with me."

"You'd be disappointed if she didn't," Bella said.

"Too true." Pippa popped another grape in her mouth. Pippa and Liz had settled into a weird sort of relationship.

Liz yanked open the curtains to the dressing room. "Okay, so I've got it on."

"Oh, Liz." Pippa blinked at her. She rummaged in her purse for a Kleenex. Along with the near-constant eating, Pippa's pregnancy brought a lot of mood swings. "You look . . . perfect."

Liz did look as close to perfect as anyone Bella had ever seen.

The shimmering black dress ended at the knee but hugged Liz's curves all the way down. A modest neckline gave no hint of the sheer plunging back that would probably give Noel heart failure.

"Good God, she's crying again." Liz rolled her eyes. She preened in front of the mirror. "But I do look pretty damn perfect."

"What about you, Bella?" Pippa stood and grabbed a pair of red stilettos and handed them to Liz. "Got any plans for Valentine's Day?"

"No." The question struck her as strange. Everyone knew she wasn't dating at the moment.

"Nobody offering to rock your world?" Pippa shook the heels at Liz. "Don't make me sit on you and put these on your feet."

"Those are old lady shoes." Liz grimaced.

"If by that you mean they don't come with their own stainless-steel pole, you'd be quite correct. Now put them on," Pippa said. "Ooh, and speaking of rocking Bella's world . . ."

They were? Bella shook her head at Pippa. Hormone brain was having its way with Pippa.

The bell over the door jingled.

"Nate." Pippa beamed at him.

Liz smoothed her hands down her hips. "Hey, Sheriff. Want to frisk me for concealed weapons?"

"Sweetheart." Nate kissed Pippa's cheek, then grinned at Liz. "I'm not trained for that."

"Damn straight you're not." Liz slid into the shoes and turned back to the mirror.

Bella ignored the spark that lit inside her the minute Nate walked through the door. He still made his nightly visits but didn't often come around the store.

The look in his eyes made Bella want to squirm. She should be used to it by now, but it always left her feeling a bit breathless. "Liz has a hot date for Valentine's."

"Looking like that, it's going to be a very hot date." Nate slid his arm around Bella's waist.

Bella left it there because she didn't totally hate it.

"Have you got another dress like that?" He jerked his chin at Liz. "Something that would fit you?"

Bella glared at Pippa. She could have warned a girl instead of that half-assed attempt earlier. Was Nate going to ask her on a date? Not that she intended to date. Ever. Again.

"Not really." Bella tried to slip away from Nate's grip on her waist.

He tugged her against his side. "In this whole store, not one dress that would make a man want to sit up and beg?"

"Sure she has." Liz the betrayer trotted over to a rack and started flipping hangers. She stopped and held one out. "This would look killer on Bella."

"Liz . . ." Pippa pressed a hand to her chest. "As much as it pains me to admit it, you're absolutely right."

"What do you say, Bella?" Nate smiled down at her. "Want to wear that sparkly dress and let me take you out for Valentine's Day?"

They'd all lost their minds. This time Bella managed to get free. She marched over to Liz and snatched the dress from her hands. She hung it back in its spot on the rack. "I'm not dating. Anyone."

Nate shoved his hands in his pockets. "Hmm." He shook his head. "That's a pity. But if you won't go out with me, maybe you could do me another favor."

"That would depend on what it was." Bella gave him a repressive glare. He didn't look in the least bothered by the fact that she wouldn't go out with him.

"Shit, is that the time?" Liz disappeared into the fitting room.

Pippa grabbed her purse. "I have to go and do something pregnant."

Less than two minutes later, Bella and Nate were alone in the store. She smelled a rat. People did a lot of this sort of thing with her these days. She glared at the architect of her current setup. "What's the favor?"

"Wait here." Nate went out to his cruiser and came back with something tucked into the crook of his arm.

A puppy!

"This is Sugar." Nate held the fluffy, tawny ball in one of his big hands. "She's the last of her litter and she needs a home."

He'd lost his grip on reality. What the hell was she going to do with a puppy?

Sugar yawned with one of those puppy squeaks.

"I don't want a dog." Sugar needn't think that blinking at her in that sleepy way was going to work either. She didn't have space in her life for anyone right now. Particularly not a bundle of fur that needed her.

"I'm not giving her to you," Nate said. "But I'm asking you to look after her for me."

"She's your dog?" Bella searched his face for signs of

the lie, but Nate had perfected the poker face somewhere around fifth grade.

"I thought it was about time I made my house a home." Nate shrugged. "But I need someone to watch her for the day."

"What are you doing?"

He looked taken aback. "I'm working. I can't take her with me. You know I spend a lot of time moving between the various county outposts."

"Leave her at the station."

"Gabby's out on calls all day."

Sugar squirmed in Nate's arms.

"What am I supposed to do with a puppy in a clothing store?"

"You'll think of something." Nate pressed Sugar into her arms. "I'll be back to pick her up later." He stared at her. "I need your help, Bella."

Damn. Shit. Crap. That way he had of looking at her still worked her over as well as it had in school.

Sugar wriggled in her arms and tried to lick her.

Nate had been so kind to her since the attack. How could she say no to him? Especially after she'd turned him down flat about the date. "You'll pick her up later?"

"Promise." Nate crossed his heart. His kiss came and went before Bella had a chance to pucker up or evade. "I'll see you later."

Sugar spent large portions of the day sleeping. In between she trundled around the store in Bella's wake. Bella found her a plastic container for water, but Sugar preferred to upend it and chase the empty container around the store. She really was a good puppy. Only one accident the entire day and Bella took her out to the loading area behind the store for the rest.

Closing time came. Outside, night had fallen and Bella went about locking up the store. With Sugar trotting along in her wake, she managed to press back the unease that always came around this time. Not that the fur ball could do anything, but her presence seemed to keep the monsters at bay.

She'd texted Nate about the puppy and gotten no reply. She called the office and got Gabby.

"Sorry, Bella, he's been out for most of the afternoon. I don't expect him back."

"But he left his dog here." Sugar chased a price tag across the wood floor, slipping and sliding all the way.

"Why don't you take her home with you?"

She knew it. Bella had smelled the setup all along. "Or I could bring it by there and you could watch it?"

"Sure," Gabby said. "But I'd have to lock her in a cell."

Sugar yawned and dropped onto her puppy butt, back legs splayed.

Damn, Gabby was good. Picturing Sugar alone in a cell made Bella shudder. "You tell Nate I'm on to him," she said.

Gabby chuckled. "Will do."

Her suspicions were confirmed by the fluffy pink dog bed, the bowls, and the puppy food on her porch. Nate had saddled her with a dog. She picked up the envelope left in the dog bed.

Sugar, it seemed, was a golden retriever and she was ten weeks old.

Bella carried her into her kitchen and fed her.

The puppy's face disappeared into her bowl as she devoured the food Bella had carefully weighed out.

By ten that night, Bella was forced to admit Nate wasn't coming around. She heated up some lasagna he'd left in her fridge and ate it with Sugar curled up next to her on the couch. For the first time since the attack, she checked her house without Nate by her side. She hated admitting it, but she missed the way he seemed to fill the house. She picked up Sugar and tucked her close. The puppy blinked at her, little pink tongue going all the time.

Bella buried her face into the hair at Sugar's scruff and took a deep breath of the sweet-milk puppy smell. It helped a little, but she still missed Nate.

She had no idea where he was. He could be doing anything. Maybe he was on a call and in danger? She refused to contemplate the idea of him out on a date. But sooner or later, Nate would get tired of chasing her and move on. What would she do then?

A horrible idea struck her. Had he given her Sugar because he needed to distance himself from her? Bella dragged the dog bed into her bedroom and got ready for bed.

Sugar whined from her dog bed.

"No." Bella tried to fix the puppy with a strong look. "You sleep there. This is a human bed."

Sugar didn't think much of that and put her fat little paws up on the side of the bed. She lowered her ears and gave Bella a blast of those big brown eyes.

"Only because you're a baby." Bella lifted the puppy onto the bed. "But as soon as you get big enough, you'll sleep in your bed."

By Valentine's Day, Bella wasn't even fooling herself anymore. Sugar had nestled into her life. Also, Sugar was unlikely to ever spend a night on the floor. Not when they got so comfortable watching *Game of Thrones* together.

Nate stayed away. Oh, he sent her the occasional text, but other than that, he remained MIA.

Another thing she couldn't keep lying to herself about. She missed the hell out of him. His cooking, for one, because she was running out of leftovers, but more his company over dinner. The way they would chat and share their days. So many times, Sugar did something cute and she wanted to tell Nate. Once or twice she even looked up to speak to him before she realized he wasn't there.

She didn't have the guts to ask Liz if she'd heard if Nate had found a date for Valentine's. Twice this week she'd made sure to drive past his office on her way to and from the store. Just to see if he was there. Once the cruiser had been parked outside. The other time, his usual parking space stood empty.

How could he be so much a part of her life and then up and disappear on her? And leave her with a dog. Except she really did love Sugar.

Even her therapist was dumping her, gently suggesting they didn't need to see each other quite so often anymore.

She took Sugar outside to do her thing. Another half hour and she could shut up the store. Yay! Another evening of watching the sidewalk to see if Nate would come by.

"Bella!" Nate yelled from inside the store.

"I'm out here," she yelled back. Her heart sped up and she forced herself to wait for Sugar to finish. "I'll be in soon."

"Hey." Nate appeared at the door. Still in his uniform, with wind-ruffled hair and the day's scruff darkening his chin, he looked incredible. Not so long ago, she would have been hard-pressed not to fling herself at him. "Sorry I've been MIA."

"It's fine."

"I had a . . . situation I needed to handle." He cleared his throat. "Police business."

Bella shrugged. If she told him how much she'd missed

him, it would only encourage him to keep hanging around. "What can I do for you?"

A muscle jumped in his jaw. "I came to get my dog."

"What?" Bella must have missed something because it sounded like he'd said he was here to get his dog. "Your dog?"

"Sugar." He scooped a squirming, happy Sugar into his arms and held her against his big chest. "Thanks for looking after her for me."

"But you gave her to me." Bella wished Sugar would quit looking so comfortable in Nate's arms. "She's my dog."

"No." Nate shook his head. "I asked you to look after her for me."

"You disappeared for eight days."

"You noticed?"

What the hell was he on about now? He had her dog in his arms. As she struggled to formulate words, Nate turned and strode back into the store. With her dog. "You can't just take my dog."

"My dog." He flung the words over his shoulder and kept walking away from her.

Bella had to run to keep up. "She's mine."

"No, she's not." Nate opened the street door. Frigid air rushed inside.

"But . . ." With no words, she flung her arms up. Nate was stealing her dog and she wanted Sugar back.

Sugar shivered in the cold air and gave a tiny whine.

Screw it! That was her dog and she was getting cold. Bella marched over and slammed the door shut. "Give her back to me."

"No."

"Give her." Bella tugged at Nate's arm, the one holding Sugar. "She's mine. I don't care what you say. You left her with me for more than a week and that makes her mine."

"No, it really doesn't." Nate stared at her like she was a bug. "What do you care anyway?"

What did she care? *What did she care?* "She's my dog. I love her."

"Really?" Nate raised a brow and peered down his nose at her. "I thought you didn't have anything left in you to give."

The tricky shit. Bella suppressed the urge to smack him. "I didn't mean it like that and you know it. Now give her to me."

"No, Bella. She's mine." Nate tucked her into his jacket and unzipped it enough that Sugar's little head poked out. "I'm not leaving her with someone who has nothing to give."

He was using her words against her and making her want to kick him. "That's not what I meant."

"What did you mean, then?"

"I meant . . ." What *had* she meant when she said that? Not that he could take her dog, that was for sure. Not that he could come into her store and take the only thing she loved. Hadn't she suffered enough? Hadn't he taken enough from her? "I don't have anything to give you."

"Me?" He tilted his head. "Why?"

"Why?" God! Was he kidding right now? "Haven't I given you enough?"

"Like what?"

He stood there, staring at her with this look of mild disinterest on his face, like they were discussing the weather, and like he didn't give a crap. How dare he? How. Dare. He. How dare any of them. "Twenty-fucking-seven years," Bella yelled. "Since I was six, I've chased you, pined for you, cried for you, loved you. And not once did you turn around and see me waiting for you."

Nate flipped the lock on the door and put Sugar on the floor. "I'm here now."

"Great." As if that didn't beat all. He was here now and she should be happy about it. "Nate Evans suddenly looks down from his throne and sees pathetic Bella Erikson gazing up at him. After most of her life, he decides to give her a chance and love her."

"You were never pathetic to me." Nate stepped closer to her.

"Yes, I was." If he touched her now, she didn't know what she'd do. "Everyone knew about me and you and they all thought it was so funny. Poor, deluded, pathetic Bella."

"Bella . . ."

Her vision clouded and she swiped at her eyes. Her fingers came away wet. Could she get any more pitiful? Now she was fucking crying. She sucked in a deep breath and tried to get it under control. "I thought I'd show them. I'd change, and then they would stop laughing at me. And what happened?"

"Bella—"

"Some whack job tried to give me a hysterectomy." Nate stood there like he didn't get any of this and Bella shoved him. "While I was still awake. And that's not even the worst part."

He reached for her.

Bella evaded his hand. "Wanna hear the worst part?"

Nate nodded. Emotionless. Impenetrable.

Bella shoved him.

He didn't move.

She shoved harder. "He made me scared." Her voice bounced around the store. "He made me scared to go home. He made me scared to breathe. He made me scared to live." But it wasn't Adam who truly terrified her. "But that's nothing compared to what you did." She wanted him to hurt like she did and Bella punched him.

Nate grunted.

Bella punched harder. Shock waves shot up her hand and it hurt like hell. Cradling her hand, she glared at him. "Whatever Adam did or did not do to me, you hurt me more."

Nate flinched. "Babe . . ."

"You did." The fight evaporated and left her aching. A sob caught in her throat and then another behind it. This was what she'd tried to avoid. The hurt, and she hurt so much. "After loving you for so long, you made me hope."

Stepping closer, he cradled her sore hand. "I know."

"And then you took it away again." Her words came out in a jumbled mess of sobs.

"I know." His mouth warm against her fingers, Nate kissed her aching hand. "And now you're terrified to trust me again."

He did get it. Bella stared at him. "And I can't."

"Yes, you can." Nate crowded her. "You can because there's so much sweet in you, it humbles me. You can because you're so much stronger and braver than I am."

"I don't want to love you."

"You shouldn't." He wrapped his arms about her and drew her closer. "Because I really don't deserve your love. But I want it anyway."

"Nate . . ." She didn't have it in her anymore.

"I gave you Sugar to prove to you that all the sweet and love is still inside you." He tightened his arms as if he could physically absorb her into him. "I know it's still there and I'm praying like hell you still have enough left for me."

"I'm mad at you."

"I know."

"No, you don't." How could he know what she'd only this moment discovered? Bella freed herself enough that she could see his face. "I'm so, so angry with you."

Nate nodded. "I know and I deserve your anger."

"Wait a minute." He looked a touch smug. "You gave me Sugar to make me love her." Oh, tricky bastard didn't even cover this. "And then you took her away to make me mad."

Nate looked a bit sheepish. "It was part of my plan."

"Plan to do what?" Bella needed to put some distance between them before she hit him again. Given his dickhead plan, maybe he deserved hitting.

"Get you back." Nate held on to her. "You've been angry for a long time, Bella, but the anger is a mask. When Adam attacked you, you retreated into your hurt and your fear and snarled at the world." He grimaced. "I know all about putting on an angry mask. I did it when my dad died. I told the world to go to hell so they wouldn't see how scared and hurt I was inside when my dad left us."

Yeah, he really did know about angry. She had watched him with her heart breaking for him. "When did you stop being angry?"

"It took a long time." Nate shrugged. "And I'm not even sure when it stopped, but it did. Yours will too." He pressed his forehead to hers. "But not if you keep it all locked inside of you. You're Bella Erikson, the sweetest girl in Ghost Falls, and sweet girls don't let themselves get angry."

"So you gave me a reason to get angry?" She didn't know how she felt about that. Resentful for sure, but also strangely cleansed. There was definitely something to be said for getting some of the stuff simmering inside of you out there. "What now?"

"That's up to you."

"I want my dog."

"She's yours." He dropped his arms and stepped away.

It left her feeling all alone and exposed and she wanted his arms back again. Which she shouldn't because they weren't safe arms. Only they were, and he'd been going out of his way to show her that much. Since the attack, she'd wanted someone to hurt like she did, and Nate had hurt her enough over the years. Except Nate wasn't hurting her anymore; he stood in her store with his heart in his eyes. "I'm scared."

He shoved his hands in his pockets. "Me too, but I'm not willing to let that stop me from taking a chance on us."

The silence between them resounded with words and feelings, none of which Bella could pin down and name. "I need to hear you say it again."

"Which part?"

"The good stuff. All of it." Bella stood close enough to feel the heat radiating from him.

His gentle smile started in his eyes, reached down, and blew on the smoldering embers inside her. "I love you, Bella." He shoved his hands in his pockets. "I can't tell you exactly when it happened, but it wasn't when Adam attacked you."

Bella put her palm against the sharp rise and fall of his chest. Beneath her palm, his heart pounded. "And what else?"

"What else is there?" He pressed his hand over hers. "I'm not the first man not to realize how good what he had was until he's lost it." He scoffed. "And I for damn sure won't be the last. Like every sad jerk before me, I'm hoping like hell you'll overlook my dumb-assery and give me another chance."

"And if I can't?"

Nate sucked in a breath. "I really don't know, Bella, but I don't see myself giving up any time soon."

"Tell me again." His chest scorched her palm as she traced the line of muscle beneath his shirt.

"Which part?"

"The important part. I need to hear you say it."

He cleared his throat. "I love you, Bella."

Damn; her knees gave way.

He caught her hips and held her against him. "Your turn."

Oh, that was a good one. "After all this time, you really need me to say it?"

"Uh-huh." He nodded. "I really, really need you to say it."

"I love you, Nate." She pressed her face into the crook of his shoulder and breathed deep.

"Thank God. I'll do better, Bella. If you give me you one more time, I'll make sure you're never sorry."

"Oh, Nate." With the anger cleared, at least for now, she could see what she'd been trying so desperately to deny. "I never stopped loving you. Not once in all these years."

"I'll make that up to you."

"No more tricks." Later they would have words about today's stunt.

"No more tricks." His beautiful smile took her breath away because here, finally, was what she'd been waiting for. Nate loved her.

"Only the truth between us," she said.

"Only the truth." He pressed her closer to him. "When you're mad at me, you don't push me away."

"You didn't go far." Heat blossomed between them. It had been too long since she'd allowed herself to feel anything.

"I'll never go far." His lips feathered hers.

"Promise?"

"Promise."

"I love you, Nate." It was the one thing that was undeniable. They would have some hurdles to get over, and in light of tonight, she may very well need a couple more trips to her therapist. "Since the day you dipped my braid in purple paint in the first grade."

He tensed. "Um . . . Bella?"

Her heart dropped. When she anticipated hurdles, she wasn't thinking right this second. "What?"

"Don't hit me again." Hard hands at her hips held her still. "But I have a confession to make."

Before she agreed to no hitting, she needed to hear this confession. "What?"

"It wasn't me who dipped your braid in purple paint."

Connect with Us

Visit us online at
KensingtonBooks.com
to read more from your favorite authors, see books
by series, view reading group guides, and more.

Join us on social media

for sneak peeks, chances to win books and prize packs,
and to share your thoughts with other readers.

facebook.com/kensingtonpublishing
twitter.com/kensingtonbooks

Tell us what you think!

To share your thoughts, submit a review,
or sign up for our eNewsletters, please visit:
KensingtonBooks.com/TellUs.

Books by Bestselling Author
Fern Michaels

___**The Jury**	0-8217-7878-1	$6.99US/$9.99CAN
___**Sweet Revenge**	0-8217-7879-X	$6.99US/$9.99CAN
___**Lethal Justice**	0-8217-7880-3	$6.99US/$9.99CAN
___**Free Fall**	0-8217-7881-1	$6.99US/$9.99CAN
___**Fool Me Once**	0-8217-8071-9	$7.99US/$10.99CAN
___**Vegas Rich**	0-8217-8112-X	$7.99US/$10.99CAN
___**Hide and Seek**	1-4201-0184-6	$6.99US/$9.99CAN
___**Hokus Pokus**	1-4201-0185-4	$6.99US/$9.99CAN
___**Fast Track**	1-4201-0186-2	$6.99US/$9.99CAN
___**Collateral Damage**	1-4201-0187-0	$6.99US/$9.99CAN
___**Final Justice**	1-4201-0188-9	$6.99US/$9.99CAN
___**Up Close and Personal**	0-8217-7956-7	$7.99US/$9.99CAN
___**Under the Radar**	1-4201-0683-X	$6.99US/$9.99CAN
___**Razor Sharp**	1-4201-0684-8	$7.99US/$10.99CAN
___**Yesterday**	1-4201-1494-8	$5.99US/$6.99CAN
___**Vanishing Act**	1-4201-0685-6	$7.99US/$10.99CAN
___**Sara's Song**	1-4201-1493-X	$5.99US/$6.99CAN
___**Deadly Deals**	1-4201-0686-4	$7.99US/$10.99CAN
___**Game Over**	1-4201-0687-2	$7.99US/$10.99CAN
___**Sins of Omission**	1-4201-1153-1	$7.99US/$10.99CAN
___**Sins of the Flesh**	1-4201-1154-X	$7.99US/$10.99CAN
___**Cross Roads**	1-4201-1192-2	$7.99US/$10.99CAN

Available Wherever Books Are Sold!
Check out our website at **www.kensingtonbooks.com**